Salon
Fantastique

Other Anthologies
by Ellen Datlow and Terri Windling

THE ADULT FAIRY TALE SERIES
Snow White, Blood Red
Black Thorn, White Rose
Ruby Slippers, Golden Tears
Black Swan, White Raven
Silver Birch, Blood Moon
Black Heart, Ivory Bones

The Green Man: Tales from the Mythic Forest
The Faery Reel: Tales from the Twilight Realm
The Coyote Road: Trickster Tales (forthcoming)
A Wolf at the Door
Swan Sister

Sirens

The Year's Best Fantasy and Horror, Volumes 1 through 16

Salon
Fantastique

Fifteen Original Tales of Fantasy

Edited and with an Introduction by
Ellen Datlow and Terri Windling

Thunder's Mouth Press
New York

Salon Fantastique
Fifteen Original Tales of Fantasy

Published by
Thunder's Mouth Press
An imprint of Avalon Publishing Group, Inc.
245 West 17th Street, 11th floor
New York, NY 10011

www.thundersmouth.com

AVALON
publishing group incorporated

First printing, October 2006

Compilation and introduction copyright © 2006
by Ellen Datlow and Terri Windling

Page v serves as an extension of this copyright page

Library of Congress Cataloging-in-Publication Data is available.

ISBN: 1-56025-833-0
ISBN-13: 978-1-56025-833-9

9 8 7 6 5 4 3 2 1

Book design by Pauline Neuwirth, Neuwirth & Associates, Inc.

Printed in the United States of America
Distributed by Publishers Group West

Permissions

‿❧‿

Contents

Introduction

Ellen Datlow and Terri Windling

THE "LITERARY SALON," as we know it today, origi-
nated in seventeenth-century France, where writers,
artists, philosophers, and political figures gathered together
in private living rooms (*salons*), finding creative stimulation
in an atmosphere removed from the strict protocols of the
French court. In the salons, men and women could mingle
more freely, progressive (even radical) ideas could be aired,
and rigid lines of class, rank, and wealth could be crossed
in the service of art. Intelligence, conversational skills, and
creative achievement were all highly prized, elevating the
status of writers and artists and allowing them to converse as
equals with influential members of the aristocracy. Literary
salons played an important part in the flowering of French
arts and letters from the seventeenth-century onward, just as
political salons were instrumental in fomenting the movement that became the French Revolution.

Madame de Rambouillet established the first important salon at the Hôtel de Rambouillet, where she presided over regular gatherings of writers and other intellectuals in her famous *chambre bleue*. The vast majority of French salons were run by influential women with an unusual degree of social independence. Legendary *salonnières* include Mademoiselle De Scudéry, Madame de Sévigné, Madame De La Fayette, Madame de Lambert, Madame De Tencin, and Madame Geoffrin, all of whom presided over gatherings renowned beyond the borders of France. The salons provided receptive audiences for new novels, new poems, new polemics, new ideas, new ways of thinking about art and society, and they allowed promising young writers to interact with older, established figures. Stories and plays-in-progress were read, new musical compositions debuted, and theoretical positions argued with a freedom unthinkable at court—or even at the French Academy (which still barred women from its ranks).

In the history of fantasy literature, the French salons also play a distinctive role, for it was in these same salons at the very end of the seventeenth century that Madame D'Aulnoy, Charles Perrault, and others created a vogue for magical stories rooted in the folk tradition, coining the name we still use for this genre today: fairy tales (*contes des fées*). These literary fairy tales proved so popular with French writers and readers that the art form flourished well into the middle of the eighteenth century, when the stories were collected in a forty-one volume edition called the *Cabinet des fées*.

Although the salons of the eighteenth century were often decried as frivolous or lacking in prestige compared with the great salons of the prior century,[1] nonetheless new salons continued to pop up across western Europe and far beyond, providing a useful forum for artistic camaraderie and the lively exchange of ideas. In the nineteenth century, "Bohemian" salons brought painters, writers, and slumming aristocrats together with a colorful variety of underclass figures (prostitutes, circus performers, gypsies, etc.) to escape the restraints of Victorian society (with the help of absinthe, hashish, and opium). In the middle of the nineteenth century, a group of women intellectuals in Berlin (many of them from the German Romantic movement) created the Kaffeterkreis, a conversation salon modeled after the fairy-tale salons of Paris. They met weekly for a number of years, producing a great deal of fantasy and drama during the period. Famous salons of the twentieth century include those of the Dada group in Paris, the Bloomsbury circle in London, and the Algonquin Round Table group in Manhattan, as well as A'Lelia Walker's "Dark Tower" events in New York during the Harlem Renaissance and gatherings of the Beat writers at Six Gallery in San Francisco.

History will have to judge whether any of the literary circles and salons in existence today will prove to be as lastingly influential as these well-known circles, but certainly artistic salons of various kinds can still be found the world over, including "virtual salons" created through the new technology of the Internet.

---

[1] In the eighteenth century, Madame de Lambert wrote wistfully about the decreasing number of salons run by women, where both sexes could gather on a somewhat more equal footing: "There were, in an earlier time, houses where women were allowed to talk and think, where muses joined the society of the graces. The Hôtel de Rambouillet, greatly honored in the past century, has become the ridicule of ours."

In putting together this anthology of stories, our aim was to evoke the liberating, creative spirit of a literary salon by inviting a number of writers to gather together in these pages exchanging tales and ideas in literary form. As editors, we've spent quite a few years now creating "theme" anthologies for adults and younger readers: volumes of fiction based on fairy tales or on mythic and folkloric topics. For this anthology, however, we decided not to restrict ourselves or our contributing authors to a central theme. Instead, we simply invited the writers of this volume into a *salon fantastique*, asking them to create and share new tales that show the fantasy form at its best. Together, these stories form a conversation between established writers and emerging writers, between historical and contemporary fiction, between the timelessness of folklore themes and the immediacy of modern politics, between gravity and whimsy, between traditional linear narratives and other means of storytelling.

Welcome to the *salon fantastique*. We hope you enjoy the conversation.

Salon
Fantastique

La Fée Verte

~⦁~

Delia Sherman

W HEN VICTORINE WAS a young whore in the house
of Mme Boulard, her most intimate friend was a girl
called La Fée Verte.

Victorine was sixteen when she came to Mme Boulard's,
and La Fée Verte some five years older. Men who admired
the poetry of Baudelaire and Verlaine adored La Fée Verte,
for she was exquisitely thin, with the bones showing at her
wrist and her dark eyes huge and bruised in her narrow face.
But her chief beauty was her pale, fine skin, white almost
to opalescence. Embracing her was like embracing absinthe
made flesh.

Every evening, Victorine and La Fée Verte would sit in
Mme Boulard's elegant parlor with Madame, her little pug

dog, and the other girls of the establishment, waiting. In the early part of the evening, while the clients were at dinner, there was plenty of time for card-playing, for gossip and a little apéritif, for reading aloud and lounging on a sofa with your head in your friend's lap, talking about clothes and clients and, perhaps, falling in love.

Among the other girls, La Fée Verte had the reputation of holding herself aloof, of considering herself too good for her company. She spoke to no one save her clients, and possibly Mme Boulard. Certainly no one spoke to her. The life of the brothel simply flowed around her, like water around a rock. Victorine was therefore astonished when La Fée Verte approached her one winter's evening, sat beside her on the red velvet sofa, and began to talk. Her green kimono fell open over her bony frame and her voice was low-pitched and a little rough—pleasant to hear, but subtly disturbing.

Her first words were more disturbing still.

"You were thirteen, a student at the convent when you grandmother died. She was your step-father's mother, no blood kin of yours, but she stood between you and your step-father's anger, and so you loved her—the more dearly for your mother's having died when you were a child. You rode to her funeral in a closed carriage with her youngest son, your step-uncle."

Victorine gaped at her, moving, with each phrase, from incredulity to fury to wonder. It was true, every word. But how could she know? Victorine had not told the story to anyone.

La Fée Verte went on: "I smell old straw and damp, tobacco and spirits. I see your uncle's eyes—very dark and set deep as wells in a broad, bearded face. He is sweating as he looks at you, and fiddling in his lap. When you look away for shame, he put his hands upon you."

Victorine was half-poised to fly, but somehow not flying, half-inclined to object, but listening all the same, waiting to hear what La Fée Verte would say next.

"He takes your virginity hastily, as the carriage judders along the rutted lanes. He is done by the time it enters the cemetery. I see it stopping near your grandmother's grave, the coachman climbing down from his perch, opening the door. Your uncle, flushed with his exertions, straightens his frock coat and descends. He turns and offers you his hand. It is gloved in black—perfectly correct in every way, save for the glistening stains upon the tips of the fingers. I can see it at this moment, that stained glove, that careless hand."

As La Fée Verte spoke, Victorine watched her, mesmerized as her hands sketched pictures in the air and her eyes glowed like lamps. She looked like a magician conjuring up a vision of time past, unbearably sad and yet somehow unbearably beautiful. When she paused in the tale, Victorine saw that her great dark eyes were luminous with tears. Her own eyes filled in sympathy—for her own young self, certainly, but also for the wonder of hearing her story so transformed.

"You will not go to him," La Fée Verte went on. "Your uncle, impatient or ashamed, turns away, and you slip from the carriage and flee, stumbling in your thin slippers on the cemetery's stony paths, away from your grandmother's grave, from your uncle, from the convent and all you have known."

When the tale was done, La Fée Verte allowed her tears to overflow and trickle, crystalline, down her narrow cheeks. Enchanted, Victorine wiped them away and licked their bitter salt from her fingers. She was inebriated, she was enchanted. She was in love.

That night, after the last client had been waved on his way, after the gas had been extinguished and the front door locked, she lay in La Fée Verte's bed, the pair of them nested like exotic birds in down and white linen. La Fée Verte's dark head lay on Victorine's shoulder and La Fée Verte's dusky voice spun enchantment into Victorine's ear. That night, and many nights thereafter, Victorine fell asleep to the sound of her lover's stories. Sometimes La Fée Verte spoke of Victorine's childhood, sometimes of her own first lover in Paris: a poet with white skin and a dirty shirt. He had poured absinthe on her thighs and licked them clean, then sent her, perfumed with sex and anise, to sell herself in cafés for the price of a ream of paper.

These stories, even more than the caresses that accompanied them, simultaneously excited Victorine and laid a balm to her bruised soul. The sordid details of her past and present receded before La Fée Verte's romantic revisions. Little by little, Victorine came to depend on them, as a drunkard depends on his spirits, to mediate between her and her life. Night after night, Victorine drank power from her lover's mouth and caressed tales of luxury from between her thighs. Her waking hours passed as if in a dream, and she submitted to her clients with a disdainful air, as if they'd paid to please her. Intrigued, they dubbed her la Reine, proud queen of whores, and courted her with silk handkerchiefs, kidskin gloves, and rare perfumes. For the first time since she fled her uncle's carriage Victorine was happy.

Spring 1869

That April, a new client came to Mme Boulard's, a writer of novels in the vein of M. Jules Verne. He was a handsome man with a chestnut moustache and fine, wavy hair that fell over a wide, pale brow. Bohemian though he was, he bought La Fée Verte's services—which did not come cheap—two or three evenings a week.

At first, Victorine was indifferent. This writer of novels was a client like other clients, no more threat to her dream-world than the morning sun. Then he began to occupy La Fée Verte for entire evenings, not leaving until the brothel closed at four in the morning and La Fée Verte was too exhausted to speak. Without her accustomed anodyne, Victorine grew restless, spiteful, capricious.

Her clients complained. Mme Boulard fined her a night's takings. La Fée Verte turned impatiently from her questions and then from her caresses. At last, wild with jealousy, Victorine stole to the peephole with which every room was furnished to see for herself what the novelist and La Fée Verte meant to each other.

Late as it was, the lamp beside the bed was lit. La Fée Verte was propped against the pillows with a shawl around her shoulders and a glass of opalescent liquid in her hand. The novelist lay beside her, his head dark on the pillow. An innocent enough scene. But Victorine could hear her lover's husky voice rising and falling in a familiar, seductive cadence.

"The moon is harsh and barren," La Fée Verte told the novelist, "cold rock and dust. A man walks there, armed and helmed from head to foot against its barrenness. He plants a flag in the dust, scarlet and blue and white, marching in rows of stripes and little stars. How like a man, to erect a flag, and call the moon his. I would go just to gaze upon the earth filling half the sky and the stars bright and steady—there is no air on the moon to make them twinkle—and then I'd come away and tell no-one."

The novelist murmured something, sleepily, and La Fée Verte laughed, low and amused. "I am no witch, to walk where there is no air to breathe and the heat of the sun dissipates into an infinite chill. Nevertheless I have seen it, and the vehicle that might carry a man so high. It is shaped like a spider, with delicate legs."

The novelist gave a shout of pleasure, leapt from the bed, fetched his notebook and his pen and began to scribble. Victorine returned to her cold bed and wept. Such a state of affairs, given Victorine's nature and the spring's unseasonable warmth, could not last forever. One May night, Victorine left the salon pretending a call of nature, stole a carving knife from the kitchen, and burst into the room where La Fée Verte and her bourgeois bohemian were reaching a more conventional climax. It was a most exciting scene: the novelist heaving and grunting, La Fée Verte moaning, Victorine weeping and waving the knife, the other whores crowded at the door, shrieking bloody murder. The novelist suffered a small scratch on his buttock, La Fée Verte a slightly deeper one on the outside of her hip. In the morning she was gone, leaving bloodstained sheets and her green silk kimono with a piece of paper pinned to it bearing Victorine's name and nothing more.

SUMMER 1869–WINTER 1870

RESPECTABLE WOMEN DISAPPOINTED in love went into a decline or took poison, or at the very least wept day and night until the pain of their betrayal had been washed from their hearts. Victorine ripped the green kimono from neck to hem, broke a chamber pot and an erotic Sèvres grouping, screamed and ranted, and then, to all appearances, recovered. She did not forget her lost love or cease to yearn for her, but she was a practical woman. Pining would bring her nothing but ridicule, likely a beating, certainly a heavy fine, and she already owed Mme Boulard more than she could easily repay.

At the turn of the year, Victorine's luck changed. A young banker of solid means and stolid disposition fell under the spell of Victorine's beauty and vivacity. Charmed by his generosity, she smiled on him, and the affair prospered. By late spring, he had grown sufficiently fond to pay off Victorine's debt to Mme Boulard and install her as his mistress in a charming apartment in a building he owned on the fashionable rue Chaptal.

After the conventual life of a brothel, Victorine found freedom very sweet. Victorine's banker, who paid nothing for the apartment, could afford to be generous with clothes and furs and jewels—sapphires and emeralds, mostly to set off her blue eyes and red hair. She attended the Opera and the theatre on his arm and ate at the Café Anglais on the Boulevard des Italiens. They walked in the Tuileries and drove in the Bois de Boulogne. Victorine lived like a lady that spring, and counted herself happy.

JUNE 1870

NEMESIS IS AS soft-footed as a cat stalking a bird, as inexorable, as unexpected. Victorine had buried all thoughts of La Fée Verte as deep in new pleasures and gowns and jewels as her banker's purse would allow. It was not so deep a grave that Victorine did not dream of her at night, or find her heart hammering at the sight of a black-haired woman with a thin, pale face. Nor could she bear to part with the torn green kimono, which she kept at the bottom of her wardrobe. But the pain was bearable, and every day Victorine told herself that it was growing less.

This fond illusion was shattered by the banker himself, who, as a treat, brought her a book, newly published, which claimed to be a true account of the appearance of the Moon's surface and man's first steps upon it, to be taken far in an unspecified future. Victorine's banker read a chapter of it aloud to her after dinner, laughing over the rank absurdity of the descriptions and the extreme aridity of the subject and style. The next morning, when he'd left, Victorine gave it to her maid with instructions to burn it.

Victorine was not altogether astonished, when she was promenading down the Boulevard des Italiens some two or three weeks later, to see La Fée Verte seated in a café. It seemed inevitable, somehow: first the book, then the woman to fall into her path. All Paris was out in the cafés and bistros, taking what little air could be found in the stifling heat, drinking coffee and absinthe and cheap red wine. Why not La Fée Verte?

She had grown, if anything, more wraithlike since quitting Mme Boulard's, her skin white as salt under her smart hat, her narrow body sheathed in a tight green walking dress and her wild black hair confined in a snood. She was alone, and on the table in front of her was all the paraphernalia of absinthe: tall glass of jade green liquor, carafe of water, dish of sugar cubes, pierced silver spoon.

Victorine passed the café without pausing, but stopped at the jeweler's shop beside it and pretended an interest in the baubles displayed in the window. Her heart beat so she was almost sick with it. Having seen La Fée Verte, she must speak to her. But what would she say? Would she scold her for her faithlessness? Inquire after her lover? Admire her gown? No. It was impossible.

Having sensibly decided to let sleeping dogs lie, Victorine turned from the sparkling display and swept back to the café. While she had been hesitating, La Fée Verte had tempered her absinthe with water and sugar, and was lifting the resulting opaline liquid to her lips. There was a glass of champagne on the table, too, its surface foaming as if it had just that moment been poured.

Victorine gestured at the wine. "You are expecting someone."

"I am expecting you. Please, sit down."

Victorine sat. She could not have continued standing with that rough, sweet voice drawing ice along her nerves.

"You are sleek as a cat fed on cream," La Fée Verte said. "Your lover adores you, but you are not in love with him."

"I have been in love," Victorine said. "I found it very painful."

La Fée Verte smiled, very like the cat she'd described. "It is much better to be loved," she agreed. "Which you are, which you will always be. You are made to be loved. It is your destiny."

Victorine's temper, never very biddable, slipped from her control. "Are you setting up for a fortune-teller now?" she sneered. "It's a pity the future, as outlined in your lover's novel, appears so dull and unconvincing. I hope he still loves you, now that you've made him the laughingstock of Paris. Your stories used to be much more artistic."

La Fée Verte made a little movement with her gloved hand, as of brushing aside an insect. "Those stories are of the past," she said. "Me, I have no past. My present is a series of photographs, stiff and without color. My future stares at me with tiger's eyes." She held Victorine's gaze until Victorine dropped her eyes, and then she said, "Go back to your banker. Forget you have seen me."

Victorine picked up her champagne and sipped it. She would have liked to throw the wine at La Fée Verte's head, or herself at La Fée Verte's narrow feet. But the past months had taught her something of self-control. She took money from her purse and laid it on the table and rose and said, "My destiny and my heart are mine to dispose of as I please. I will not forget you simply because you tell me to."

La Fée Verte smiled. "Au revoir, then. I fear we will meet again."

JULY–AUGUST 1870

LA FÉE VERTE'S prophecy did not immediately come to pass, possibly because Victorine avoided the neighborhood of the café where she'd seen La Fée Verte in case she might be living nearby. It was time, Victorine told herself, to concentrate on distracting her banker, who was much occupied with business as the General Assembly of France herded the weak-willed Emperor Napoleon III toward a war with Prussia. Kaiser Wilhelm was getting above himself, the reasoning ran, annexing here and meddling there, putting forward his own nephew as a candidate for the vacant Spanish throne.

"How stupid does he think we are?" the banker raged, pacing Victorine's charming salon and scattering cigar ashes on the Aubusson. "If Leopold becomes king of Spain, France will be surrounded by Hohenzollerns on every side and it will only be a matter of time before you'll be hearing German spoken on the Champs-Élysées."

"I hear it now," Victorine pointed out. "And Italian and a great deal of English. I prefer Italian—it is much more pleasing to the ear. Which reminds me: *La Bohème* is being sung at the opera tonight. If you'll wait a moment while I dress, we should be in time for the third act."

Victorine was not a woman who concerned herself with politics. It was her fixed opinion that each politician was duller than the next, and none of them, save perhaps the Empress, who set the fashion, had anything to do with her. She did her best to ignore the Emperor's declaration of war on July 16 and the bellicose frenzy that followed it. When her banker spoke to her of generals and battles, she answered him with courtesans and opera-singers. When he wanted to go to the Hôtel de Ville to hear the orators, she made him go to the Eldorado to hear the divine Thérèsa singing of love. When he called her a barbarian, she laughed at him and began to think of finding herself a more amusing protector. Men admired her; several of the banker's friends had made her half-joking offers she'd half-jokingly turned aside. Any one of them would be hers for a smile and a nod. But none of them appealed to her, and the banker continued to be generous, so she put off choosing. She had plenty of time.

One Sunday in late August, Victorine's banker proposed a drive. Victorine put on a high-crowned hat with a cock-ade of feathers and they drove down the Champs-Élysées with the rest of fashionable Paris, headed toward the Bois de Boulogne, where the sky was clearer than within the city walls and the air was scented with leaves and grass.

As they entered the park, Victorine heard an unpleasant noise as of a building being torn down over the clopping of the horses' hooves. The noise grew louder, and before long the carriage drew even with a group of men wearing scarlet trousers and military kepis. They were chopping down trees.

The banker required his driver to stop. Victorine gaped at the men, sweating amid clouds of dust, and at the shambles of trampled grass, tree trunks, and stumps they left in their wake. "Who are these men?" she demanded. "What are they doing?"

"They are volunteers for the new Mobile Guard, and they are clearing the Bois." He turned to her. "Victorine, the time has come for you to look about yourself. The Prus-sians are marching west. If Strasbourg falls, they will be at Paris within a month. Soon there will be soldiers quartered here, and herds of oxen and sheep. Soon every green thing you see will be taken within the walls to feed or warm Paris. If the Prussians besiege us, we will know hunger and fear, perhaps death."

Victorine raised her eyes to her lover's pink, stern face. "I cannot stop any of these things; what have they to do with me?"

He made an impatient noise. "Victorine, you are impossible. There's a time of hardship coming, a time of sacrifice. Pleasure will be forced to bow to duty, and I must say I think that France will be the better for it."

She had always known his mouth to be too small, but as he delivered this speech, it struck her for the first time as ridiculous, all pursed up like a sucking infant's under his inadequate moustache.

"I see," she said. "What do you intend to do?"

"My duty."

For all her vanity, Victorine was not a stupid woman. She had no need of La Fée Verte to foresee what was coming next. "I understand completely," she said. "And what of my apartment?"

He blinked as one awakened from a dream. "You may stay until you find a new one."

"And my furniture?"

The question, or perhaps her attitude, displeased him. "The furniture," he said tightly, "is mine."

"My clothes? My jewels? Are they yours also?"

He shrugged. "Those, you may keep. As a souvenir of happier times."

"Of happier times. Of course." Really, she could not look at his mouth any longer. Beyond him, she saw a tall chestnut tree sway and topple to the ground. It fell with a resounding crack, like thunder. The banker started; Victorine did not. "Well, that's clear enough." She put out her hand to him. "Good-bye."

He frowned. "I hadn't intended . . . I'd thought a farewell dinner, one last night together."

"With duty calling you? Surely not," Victorine said. He had not taken her hand; she patted his sweating cheek. "Adieu, my friend. Do not trouble yourself to call. I will be occupied with moving. And duty is a jealous mistress."

She climbed down from the carriage and walked briskly back along the path. She was not afraid. She was young, she was beautiful, and she had La Fée Verte's word that it was her destiny to be loved.

SEPTEMBER 1870

VICTORINE'S NEW APARTMENT was a little way from the grand boulevards, on the rue de la Tour, near the Montmartre *abattoir*. It was small—three rooms only—but still charming. When it came to the point, none of the admiring gentlemen had been willing to offer her the lease on a furnished house of her own, not with times so troubled. She had sent them all about their business, renting and furnishing the place herself on the proceeds from an emerald necklace and a sapphire brooch. She moved on September 3. When evening came, she looked about her at the chaos of half-unpacked trunks and boxes, put on her hat, and went out in search of something to eat, leaving her maid to deal with the mess alone.

Although it was dinnertime, everyone seemed to be out in the streets—grim-faced men, for the most part, too intent on their business to see her, much less make way for her. Passing a newspaper kiosk, she was jostled unmercifully, stepped upon, pushed almost into the gutter. A waving hand knocked her hat awry. Gruff voices battered at her ears.

"Have you heard? The Emperor is dead!"

"Not dead, idiot. Captured. It's bad enough."

"I heard dead, and he's the idiot, not me."

"Good riddance to him."

"The Prussians have defeated MacMahon. Strasbourg has fallen."

"Long live Trochu."

The devil take Trochu, Victorine thought, clutching purse and muff. A thick shoe came down heavily on her foot. She squealed with pain and was ignored. When she finally found a suitable restaurant, her hat was over her ear and she was limping.

The Veau d'Or was small, twelve tables perhaps, with lace curtains at the windows and one rather elderly waiter. What made it different from a thousand other such establishments was its clientèle, which seemed to consist largely of women dressed in colors a little brighter and hats a little more daring than was quite respectable. They gossiped from table to table in an easy camaraderie that reminded Victorine at once of Mme Boulard's salon.

The conversations dropped at Victorine's entrance, and the elderly waiter moved forward, shaking his head.

"We are complete, Madame," he said.

Presented with an opportunity to vent her ill-temper, Victorine seized it with relief. "You should be grateful, Monsieur, that I am sufficiently exhausted to honor your establishment with my custom." She sent a disdainful glance around the room. "Me, I am accustomed to the company of a better class of tarts."

This speech elicited some indignant exclamations, some laughter, and an invitation from a dumpling-like blonde in electric blue to share her corner table.

"You certainly have an opinion of yourself," she said, as Victorine sat down, "for a woman wearing such a hat as that. What happened to it?"

Victorine removed the hat and examined it. The feather was broken and the ribbons crushed. "Men," she said, making the word a curse. "Beasts."

The blonde sighed agreement. "A decent woman isn't safe in the streets these days. What do you think of the news?"

Victorine looked up from the ruin of her hat. "News? Oh, the Emperor."

"The Emperor, the Prussians, the war. All of it."

"I think it is terrible," Victorine said, "if it means cutting down the Bois de Boulogne and stepping on helpless women. My foot is broken—I'm sure of it."

"One does not walk on a broken foot," the blonde said reasonably. "Don't spit at me, you little cat—I'm trying to be friends. Everyone needs friends. There's hard times ahead."

"Hard times be damned," Victorine said airily. "I don't expect they will make a difference, not to us. Men desire pleasure in hard times, too."

The blonde laughed. "Possibly; possibly not. We'll find out soon enough which of us is right." She poured some wine into Victorine's glass. "If you're not too proud for a word of advice from a common tart, I suggest you take the veal. It's the specialty of the house, and if it comes to a siege, we won't be able to get it any more."

"Already I am bored by this siege," Victorine said.

"Agreed," said the blonde. "We will talk of men, instead."

THAT NIGHT, VICTORINE drank a glass of absinthe on her way home. It wasn't a vice she usually indulged in, finding the bitterness of the wormwood too intense and the resulting lightheadedness too unsettling. Tonight, she drank it down like medicine. When she got home, she dug the green kimono out of her wardrobe and fell into bed with it clasped in her arms, her head floating in an opalescent mist.

Her sleep was restless, her dreams both vivid and strange. Her banker appeared, his baby mouth obscene in a goat's long face, and disappeared, bloodily, into a tiger's maw. A monkey wore grey gloves, except it was not a monkey at all, but a pig, beyond whose trotters the fingers of the gloves flapped like fringe. It bowed, grinning piggily, to the dream-presence that was Victorine, who curtsied deeply in return. When she rose, the tiger blinked golden eyes at her. She laid her hand upon his striped head; he purred like the rolling of distant thunder and kneaded his great paws against her thighs. She felt only pleasure from his touch, but when she looked at her skirts, they hung in bloody rags. Then it seemed she rode the tiger through the streets of Paris, or perhaps it was an open carriage she rode, or perhaps she was gliding bodily above the pavement, trailing draperies like the swirling opalescence of water suspended in a glass of absinthe.

She slept heavily at last, and was finally awakened at noon by a group of drunks singing the "Marseillaise" at full voice on the street under her window. She struggled out of bed and pulled back the curtains, prepared to empty her chamber pot over them. Seeing her, they cried out "Vive la République," and saluted, clearly as drunk on patriotic sentiment as on wine. Victorine was not entirely without feeling for her country, so she stayed her hand.

France was a Republic again.

Victorine considered this fact as her maid dressed her and pinned up her hair. If the drunkards were anything to judge by, the change of government had not changed a man's natural reaction to the sight of a shapely woman in a nightgown. She would walk to the Tuileries, buy an ice cream, and find someone to help her celebrate the new Republic.

It was a warm day, grey and soft as mouse fur. Victorine bought a patriotic red carnation from a flower-seller on the steps of Notre Dame de Lorette, and pinned it to her bosom. The streets were full of workers in smocks and gentlemen in top hats, waving greenery and tricolor flags with democratic zeal. Spontaneous choruses of Vive la République! exploded around Victorine at intervals. As she drew nearer the Tuileries, her heart beat harder, her cheeks heated; she felt the press of strange bodies around her as the most intense of pleasures. Soon she was laughing aloud and shouting with the rest: Vive la République!

At last, she reached the gate of the Tuileries. A man thrust a branch in her face as she passed through. "This is it!" he cried blissfully. "Down with the Emperor! Vive la République!"

He was a soldier, young, passably good-looking in his little round kepi and gold-braided epaulets. Victorine turned the full force of her smile at him. "Vive la République," she answered, and brushed his fingers with hers as she took the branch.

He didn't seem to notice.

For the blink of an eye, Victorine was filled with a rage as absolute as it was unexpected. And then it was gone, taking her patriotic fervor with it. Suddenly, the pressure of the crowd seemed intolerable to her, the shouting an assault. She clung to the iron railings of the high fence and fanned herself with her handkerchief while she caught her breath.

All of the wide promenade between railings and palace overflowed with a seething mass of humanity. Victorine's view was obstructed by top hats and cloth caps, smart hats and shabby bonnets and checked shawls. By standing on tiptoe, she could just see a stream of people swarming up the steps like revelers eager to see the latest opera. La République had moved quickly. She noticed that the "Ns" and imperial wreaths had been pried from the façade or shrouded with newspapers or scarlet sheets, which gave the palace a blotched and raddled look. And above the gaping door, someone had chalked the words UNDER THE PROTECTION OF THE CITIZENS on the black marble.

The open door of the palace beckoned to Victorine, promising wonders. She put away her handkerchief, took a firm hold on her bag, and launched herself into the current that flowed, erratically but inevitably, toward the forbidden palace where the Emperor and his foreign wife had lived so long in imperial splendor.

The current bore Victorine up a flight of shallow steps, the press around her growing, if possible, even denser as the door compacted the flow. She stepped over the threshold, passing a young infantryman who held out his shako and cried out with the raucous monotony of a street vendor: "For the French wounded! For the French wounded!" Impulsively, Victorine fished a coin from her bag, dropped it into his shako, and smiled up into his sweating face. He nodded once, gravely, and then she was in the foyer of the Imperial Palace of the Tuileries.

It was every bit as magnificent as she'd imagined. Victorine, who had a taste for excess, worshipped every splendid inch of it, from the goddesses painted on the ceiling, to the scintillating lustres on the chandeliers, the mirrors and gold leaf everywhere, and the great, sweeping staircase, designed to be seen on.

There must have been a hundred people on that staircase, mounting and descending, gawking over the rail. But Victorine saw only one woman, standing still as a rock in the waterfall of sightseers. The woman's hair was dark under her green hat, and her profile, when she turned her head, was angular. Victorine's blood recognized La Fée Verte before her mind did, racing to her face and away again, so that she swayed as she stood.

A hand, beautifully gloved in grey leather, touched her arm. Victorine became aware of a gentleman in a top hat and a beautifully tailored coat, carrying a gold-headed cane. "Mademoiselle is faint?" he inquired.

Victorine shook her head and sprang up the steps so heedlessly that she caught her toe on the riser. The solicitous gentleman, who had not moved from her side, caught her as she stumbled.

"If you will permit?" he asked rhetorically. Then he slipped one arm around her waist, shouting for everyone to make way, and piloted her firmly out of the palace without paying the slightest heed to her protestations that she was very well, that she'd left a friend on the stair and wished to be reunited with her.

⌐

THE SOLICITOUS GENTLEMAN was plumper than Victorine

liked, and his hair, when he removed his tall glossy hat, was woefully sparse. But he bore her off to the Georges V for coffee and pastries and then he bought her a diamond aigrette and a little carnelian cat with emerald eyes and agreed that it was a great pity that an exquisite creature like herself should be in exile on the rue de la Tour. What could Victorine do? She took the luck that fate had sent her and gave the gentleman to understand that his gifts were an acceptable prelude to a more serious arrangement. A week later, she and her maid were installed in an apartment off the Champs-Élysées, with her name on the lease and furniture that was hers to keep or sell as it pleased her.

It was not a bad bargain. The solicitous gentleman wasn't as good-looking as the banker and his lovemaking was uninspired. But, besides being very rich, he was as devoted to amusement as even Victorine could wish.

"Why should I worry about the Prussians?" he said. "I have my days to fill. Let everyone else worry about the Prussians if it amuses them. It is of more concern to me whether M. Gaultier beats me to that charming bronze we saw yesterday."

Still, the Prussians, or rather the threat of the Prussians, was increasingly hard to ignore. Victorine and her solicitous gentleman made their way to the antiquaries and the rare bookshops through platoons of National Guardsmen marching purposefully from one place to another and ranks of newly inducted Mobile Guards learning to turn right in unison. She could not set foot outside the door without being enthusiastically admired by the soldiers camped along the Champs, and the horses stabled there made pleasure drives to the Bois de Boulogne (or what was left of it) all but impossible. Even the theatre wasn't what it had been, houses closing left and right as the timid fled the anticipated discomforts of a siege. The Comédie Française and the Opéra remained open, though, and the public balls and the cafés-concerts were frequented by those without the means to fly. However tenuously, Paris remained Paris, even in the face of war.

One night, Victorine and her solicitous gentleman went strolling along the boulevard de Clichy. Among the faded notices of past performances that fluttered like bats' wings in the wind, crisp, new posters announced the coming night's pleasures.

"Look, ma belle," the gentleman exclaimed, stopping in front of a kiosk. "A mentalist! How original! And such a provocative name. We really must go see her."

Victorine looked at the poster he indicated. It was painted red and black, impossible to ignore:

> The Salon du Diable presents
> La Fée Verte!
> The mists of time part for her.
> The secrets of the future are unveiled.
> Séance at nine and midnight.
> La Fée Verte!

Tears sprang, stinging, to Victorine's eyes. Through their sparkling veil, she saw a white bed and a room lit only by dying embers and her palm tingled as if cupped over the small, soft mound of La Fée Verte's breast. She drew a quick breath. "It sounds very silly," she said weakly. "Besides, who has ever heard of the Salon du Diable?"

"All the more reason to go. It can be an adventure, and well worth it, if this Fée Verte is any good. If she's terrible, it will make a good story."

Victorine shrugged and acquiesced. It was clearly fate that had placed that poster where her protector would notice it, and fate that he had found it appealing, just as it was fate that Victorine would once more suffer the torment of seeing La Fée Verte without being able to speak to her. Just as well, really, after the fiasco on the Champs-Élysées. At least this time, Victorine would hear her voice.

⌒

THE SALON DU Diable was nearly as hot as the abode of its putative owner, crowded with thirsty sinners, its only illumination a half-a-dozen gaslights, turned down low. A waiter dressed as a devil in jacket and horns of red felt showed them to a table near the curtained platform that served as a stage. Victorine, as was her habit, asked for champagne. In honor of the entertainer, her protector ordered absinthe. When it came, she watched him balance the sugar cube on the pierced spoon and slowly pour a measure of water over it into the virulent green liquor. The sugared water swirled into the absinthe, disturbing its depths, transforming it, drop by drop, into smoky, shifting opal.

The solicitous gentleman lifted the tall glass. "La Fée Verte!" he proposed.

"La Fée Verte," Victorine echoed obediently, and as if at her call, a stout man in a red cape and horns like the waiter's appeared before the worn plush curtain and began his introduction.

La Fée Verte, he informed the audience, was the grand-daughter of one of the last known fairies in France, who had fallen in love with a mortal and given birth to a son, the father of the woman they were about to see. By virtue of her fairy blood, La Fée Verte was able to see through the impenetrable curtains of time and space as though they were clear glass. La Fée Verte was a visionary, and the stories she told—whether of past, present, or future—were as true as death.

There was an eager murmur from the audience. The devil of ceremonies stepped aside, pulling the faded plush curtain with him, and revealed a woman sitting alone on the stage. She was veiled from head to toe all in pale, gauzy green, but Victorine knew her at once.

Thin white hands emerged from the veil and cast it up and back like a green mist. Dark eyes shone upon the audience like stars at the back of a cave. Her mouth was painted scarlet and her unbound hair was black smoke around her head and shoulders.

Silence stretched to the breaking point as La Fée Verte stared at the audience and the audience stared at her. And then, just as Victorine's strained attention was on the point of shattering, the thin red lips opened and La Fée Verte began to speak.

"I will not speak of war, or victory or defeat, suffering or glory. Visions, however ardently desired, do not come for the asking. Instead, I will speak of building.

"There's a lot of building going on in Paris these days—enough work for everyone, thanks to le bon Baron and his pretty plans. Not all Germans are bad, eh? The pay's pretty good, too, if it can buy a beer at the Salon du Diable. There's a builder in the audience now, a mason. There are, in fact, two masons, twice that number of carpenters, a layer of roof-slates, and a handful of floor-finishers."

The audience murmured, puzzled at the tack she'd taken. The men at the next table exchanged startled glances—the carpenters, Victorine guessed, or the floor-finishers.

"My vision, though, is for the mason. He's got stone-dust in his blood, this mason. His very bones are granite. His father was a mason, and his father's father and his father's father's father, and so on, as far back as I can see. Stand up, M. le Maçon. Don't be shy. You know I'm talking about you."

The audience peered around the room, looking to see if anyone would rise. In one corner, there was a hubbub of encouraging voices, and finally, a man stood up, his flat cap over one eye and a blue kerchief around his throat. "I am a mason, Mademoiselle" he said. "You're right enough about my pa. Don't know about his pa, though. He could have been a train conductor, for all I know. He's not talked about in the family."

"That," said La Fée Verte, "was your grandmother's grief, poor woman, and your grandfather's shame."

The mason scowled. "Easy enough for you to say, Mademoiselle, not knowing a damn thing about me."

"Tell me," La Fée Verte inquired sweetly. "How are things on the rue Mouffetard? Don't worry: your little blonde's cough is not tuberculosis. She'll be better soon." The mason threw up his hands in a clear gesture of surrender and sat down. A laugh swept the audience. They were impressed. Victorine smiled to herself.

La Fée Verte folded her hands demurely in her green silk lap. "Your grandfather," she said gently, "was indeed a mason, a layer of stones like you, Monsieur. Men of your family have shaped steps and grilles, window frames and decorations in every building in Paris. Why, men of your blood worked on Nôtre Dame, father and son growing old each in his turn in the service of Maurice de Sully."

The voice was even rougher than Victorine remembered it, the language as simple and undecorated as the story she told. La Fée Verte did not posture and gesture and lift her eyes to heaven, and yet Victorine was convinced that, were she to close her eyes, she'd see Nôtre Dame as it once was, half-built and swarming with the men who labored to complete it. But she preferred to watch La Fée Verte's thin, sensuous lips telling about it.

La Fée Verte dropped her voice to a sibylline murmur that somehow could be heard in every corner of the room. "I see a man with shoulders like a bull, dressed in long stockings and a tunic and a leather apron. The tunic might have been red once and the stockings ochre, but they're faded now with washing and stone-dust. He takes up his chisel and his hammer in his broad, hard hands flecked with scars, and he begins his daily prayer. *Tap*-tap, *tap*-tap. *Pa*-ter *Nos*-ter. *A*-ve *Ma*-ri-*a*. Each blow of his hammer, each chip of stone, is a bead in the rosary he tells, every hour of every working day. His prayers, unlike yours and mine, are still visible. They decorate the towers of Nôtre Dame, almost as eternal as the God they praise.

"That was your ancestor, M. le Maçon," La Fée Verte said, returning to a conversational tone. "Shall I tell you of your son?"

The mason, enchanted, nodded.

"It's not so far from now, as the march of time goes. Long enough for you to marry your blonde, and to father children and watch them grow and take up professions. Thirty years, I make it, or a little less: 1887. The president of France will decree a great Exposition to take place in 1889—like the Exposition of 1867, but far grander. 1889 is the threshold of a new century, after all, and what can be grander than that? As an entrance arch, he will commission a monument like none seen before anywhere in the world. And your son, Monsieur, your son will build it.

"I see him, Monsieur, blond and slight, taking after his mother's family, with a leather harness around his waist. He climbs to his work, high above the street—higher than the towers of Nôtre Dame, higher than you can imagine. His tools are not yours: red-hot iron rivets, tin buckets, tongs, iron-headed mallets. His faith is in the engineer whose vision he executes, in the maker of his tools, his scaffolds and screens and guard-rails: in man's ingenuity, not God's mercy."

She fell silent, and it seemed to Victorine that she had finished. The mason thought so, too, and was unsatisfied. "My son, he won't be a mason, then?"

"Your son will work in iron," La Fée Verte answered. "And yet your line will not falter, nor the stone-dust leach from your blood as it flows through the ages."

Her voice rang with prophecy as she spoke, not so much loud as sonorous, like a church bell tolling. When the last echo had died away, she smiled, a sweet curve of her scarlet lips, and said, shy as a girl, "That is all I see, Monsieur. Are you answered?"

The mason wiped his hands over his eyes and, rising,

bowed to her, whereupon the audience roared its approval of La Fée Verte's vision and the mason's response, indeed of the whole performance and of the Salon du Diable for having provided it. Victorine clapped until her palms stung through her tight kid gloves.

The solicitous gentleman drained his absinthe and called for another. "To La Fée Verte," he said, raising the opal liquid high. "The most accomplished fraud in Paris. She must be half-mad to invent all that guff, but damn me if I've ever heard anything like her voice."

Victorine's overwrought nerves exploded in a surge of anger. She rose to her feet, snatched the glass from the gentleman's hand, and poured the contents over his glossy head. While he gasped and groped for his handkerchief, she gathered up her bag and her wrap and swept out of Le Salon du Diable in a tempest of silks, dropping a coin into the bowl by the door as she went.

The next day, the gentleman was at Victorine's door with flowers and a blue velvet jewel case and a note demanding that she receive him at once. The concierge sent up the note and the gifts, and Victorine sent them back again, retaining only the jewel case as a parting souvenir. She did not send a note of her own, since there was nothing to say except that she could no longer bear the sight of him. She listened to him curse her from the foot of the stairs, and watched him storm down the street when the concierge complained of the noise. Her only regret was not having broken with him before he took her to the Salon du Diable.

IN LATE SEPTEMBER, the hard times foretold by the blonde in the Veau d'Or came to Paris.

A city under the threat of siege is not, Victorine discovered, a good place to find a protector. Top-hatted gentlemen still strolled the grand boulevards, but they remained stubbornly blind to Victorine's saucy hats, graceful form, and flashing eyes. They huddled on street corners and in cafés, talking of the impossibility of continued Prussian victory, of the threat of starvation that transformed the buying of humble canned meat into a patriotic act. Her cheeks aching from unregarded smiles, Victorine began to hate the very sound of the words "siege," "Prussian," "Republic." She began to feel that Bismarck and the displaced Emperor, along with the quarrelsome Generals Gambetta and Trochu, were personally conspiring to keep her from her livelihood. Really, among them, they were turning Paris into a dull place, where nobody had time or taste for pleasure.

A less determined woman might have retired for the duration, but not Victorine. Every day, she put on her finest toilettes and walked, head held high under the daring hats, through the military camp that Paris was fast becoming. Not only the Champs-Élysées, but all the public gardens, squares, and boulevards were transformed into military camps or stables or sections of the vast open market that had sprung up to cater to the soldiers' needs. Along streets where once only the most expensive trinkets were sold, Victorine passed makeshift stalls selling kepis and epaulets and gold braid, ramrods and powder-pouches and water bottles, sword-canes and bayonet-proof leather chest-protectors. And everywhere were soldiers, throwing dice and playing cards among clusters of little grey tents, who called out as she passed, "Eh, sweetheart! How about a little tumble for a guy about to die for his country?"

It was very discouraging.

One day at the end of September, Victorine directed her steps toward the heights of the Trocadéro, where idle Parisians and resident foreigners had taken to airing themselves on fine days. They would train their spyglasses on the horizon and examine errant puffs of smoke and fleeing peasants like ancient Roman priests examining the entrails of a sacrifice, after which they gossiped and flirted as usual. A few days earlier, Victorine had encountered an English gentleman with a blond moustache of whom she had great hopes. As she climbed the hill above the Champs de Mars, she heard the drums measuring the drills of the Mobile Guards.

At the summit of the hill, fashionable civilians promenaded to and fro. Not seeing her English gentleman, Victorine joined the crowd surrounding the enterprising bourgeois who sold peeps through his long brass telescope at a franc a look. A clutch of English ladies exclaimed incomprehensibly as she pushed past them; a fat gentleman in a round hat moved aside gallantly to give her room. She cast him a distracted smile, handed the enterprising bourgeois a coin, and stooped to look through the eyepiece. The distant prospect of misty landscape snapped closer, bringing into clear focus a cloud of dark smoke roiling over a stand of trees.

"That used to be a village," the enterprising bourgeois informed her. "The Prussians fired it this morning—or maybe we did, to deny the Prussians the pleasure." The telescope jerked away from the smoke. "If you're lucky, you should be able to see the refugees on their way to Paris."

A cart, piled high with furniture, a woman with her hair tied up in a kerchief struggling along beside it, lugging a bulging basket in each hand and a third strapped to her back. A couple of goats and a black dog and a child riding in a handcart pushed by a young boy. "Time's up," the enterprising bourgeois said.

Victorine clung to the telescope, her heart pounding. The smoke, the cart, the woman with her bundles, the children, the dog, were fleeing a real danger. Suddenly, Victorine was afraid, deathly afraid of being caught in Paris when the Prussians came. She must get out while there was still time, sell her jewels, buy a horse and carriage, travel south to Nice or Marseilles. She'd find La Fée Verte, and they could leave at once. Surely, if she went to the Place Clichy, she'd see her there, waiting for Victorine to rescue her. But she'd have to hurry.

As quickly as Victorine had thrust to the front of the crowd, so quickly did she thrust out again, discommoding the English ladies, who looked down their long noses at her. No doubt they thought her drunk or mad. She only thought them in the way. In her hurry, she stepped on a stone, twisted her ankle, and fell gracelessly to the ground.

The English ladies twittered. The gentleman in the round hat asked her, in vile French, how she went, and offered her his hand. She allowed him to pull her to her feet, only to collapse with a cry of pain. The ladies twittered again, on a more sympathetic note. Then the crowd fell back a little, and a masculine voice inquired courteously whether Mademoiselle were ill.

Victorine lifted her eyes to the newcomer, who was hunkered down beside her, his broad, open brow furrowed with polite concern. The gold braid on his sleeves proclaimed him an officer, and the gold ring on his finger suggested wealth.

"It is very silly," she said breathlessly, "but I have twisted my ankle and cannot stand."

"If Mademoiselle will allow?" He folded her skirt away from her foot, took the scarlet boot into his hand, and bent it gently back and forth. Victorine hissed through her teeth.

"Not broken, I think," he said. "Still, I'm no doctor." Without asking permission, he put one arm around her back, the other under her knees, and lifted her from the ground with a little jerk of effort. As he carried her downhill to the surgeon's tent, she studied him. Under a chestnut-brown moustache, his mouth was firm and well shaped, and his nose was high-bridged and aristocratic. She could do worse.

He glanced down, caught her staring. Victorine smiled into his eyes (they, too, were chestnut-brown) and was gratified to see him blush. And then they were in the surgeon's tent and her scarlet boot was being cut away. It hurt terribly. The surgeon anointed her foot with arnica and bound it tightly, making silly jokes as he worked about gangrene and amputation. She bore it all with such a gallant gaiety that the officer insisted on seeing her home and carrying her to her bed, where she soon demonstrated that a sprained ankle need not prevent a woman from showing her gratitude to a man who had richly deserved it.

OCTOBER 1870

IT WAS A strange affair, at once casual and absorbing, conducted in the interstices of siege and civil unrest. The officer was a colonel in the National Guard, a man of wealth and some influence. His great passion was military history.

His natural posture—in politics, in love—was moderation. He viewed the Monarchists on the Right and the Communards on the Left with an impartial contempt. He did not pretend that his liaison with Victorine was a grand passion, but cheerfully paid the rent on her apartment and bought her a new pair of scarlet boots and a case of canned meat, with promises of jewels and gowns after the Prussians were defeated. He explained about Trochu and Bismarck, and expected her to be interested. He told her all the military gossip and took her to ride on the peripheral railway and to see the cannons installed on the hills of Paris.

The weather was extraordinarily bright. "God loves the Prussians," the officer said, rather sourly, and it certainly seemed to be true. With the sky soft and blue as June, no rain slowed the Prussian advance or clogged the wheels of their caissons or the hooves of their horses with mud. They marched until they were just out of the range of the Parisian cannons, and there they sat, enjoying the wine from the cellars of captured country houses and fighting skirmishes in the deserted streets of burned-out villages. By October 15, they had the city completely surrounded. The Siege of Paris had begun.

The generals sent out their troops in cautious sallies, testing the Prussians but never seriously challenging them. Victorine's colonel, wild with impatience at the shilly-shallying of his superiors, had a thousand plans for sorties and full-scale counterattacks. He detailed them to Victorine after they'd made love, all among the bedclothes, with the sheets heaped into fortifications, a pillow representing the butte of Montmartre, and a handful of hazelnuts for soldiers.

"Paris will never stand a long siege," he explained to her. "Oh, we've food enough, but there is no organized plan to distribute it. There is nothing really organized at all. None of those blustering ninnies in charge can see beyond the end of his nose. It's all very well to speak of the honor of France and the nobility of the French, but abstractions do not win wars. Soldiers in the field, deployed by generals who are not afraid to make decisions, that's what wins wars."

He was very beautiful when he said these things—his frank, handsome face ablaze with earnestness. Watching him, Victorine very nearly loved him. At other times, she liked him very well. He was a man who knew how to live. To fight the general gloom, he gave dinner parties to which he invited military men and men of business for an evening of food, wine, and female companionship. Wives were not invited.

There was something dreamlike about those dinners, eaten as the autumn wind sharpened and the citizens of Paris tightened their belts. In a patriotic gesture, the room was lit not by gas, but by branches of candles, whose golden light called gleams from the porcelain dishes, the heavy silver cutlery, the thin crystal glasses filled with citrine or ruby liquid. The gentlemen laughed and talked, their elbows on the napery, their cigars glowing red as tigers' eyes. Perched among them like exotic birds, the women, gowned in their bare-shouldered best, encouraged the gentlemen to talk with smiles and nods. On the table, a half-eaten tart, a basket of fruit. On the sideboard, the remains of two roast chickens—two!—a dish of beans with almonds, another of potatoes. Such a scene belonged more properly to last month, last year, two years ago, when the Empire was strong and elegant pleasures as common as the rich men to buy them. Sitting at the table, slightly drunk, Victorine felt herself lost in one of La Fée Verte's visions, where past, present, and future exist as one.

Outside the colonel's private dining room, however, life was a waking nightmare. The garbage carts had nowhere to go, so that Victorine must pick her way around stinking hills of ordure on every street corner. Cholera and smallpox flourished among the poor. The plump blonde of the Veau d'Or died in the epidemic, as did the elderly waiter and a good proportion of the regulars. Food grew scarce. Worm-eaten cabbages went for three francs apiece. Rat pie appeared on the menu at Maxim's, and lapdogs went in fear of their lives. And then there were the French wounded, sitting and lying in rattling carriages and carts, muddy men held together with bloody bandages, their shocked eyes turned inward, their pale lips closed on their pain, being carted to cobbled-together hospitals to heal or die. Victorine turned her eyes from them, glad she'd given a coin to the young infantryman that day she saw La Fée Verte in the Tuileries.

And through and over it all, the cannons roared.

French cannon, Prussian cannon, shelling St. Denis, shelling Boulogne, shelling empty fields and ravaged woodlands. As they were the nearest, the French cannon were naturally the loudest. Victorine's colonel prided himself on knowing each cannon by the timbre and resonance of its voice as it fired, its snoring or strident or dull or ear-shattering *BOOM*. In a flight of whimsy one stolen afternoon, lying in his arms in a rented room near the Port St. Cloud, Victorine gave them names and made up characters for them: Gigi of the light, flirtatious bark on Mortemain, Philippe of the angry bellow at the Trocadéro.

October wore on, and the siege with it. A population accustomed to a steady diet of news from the outside world and fresh food from the provinces began to understand what it was like to live without either. The lack of food was bad enough, but everyone had expected that—this was war, after all, one must expect to go hungry. But the lack of news was hard to bear. Conflicting rumors ran through the streets like warring plagues, carried by the skinny street rats who hawked newspapers on the boulevards. In the absence of news, gossip, prejudice, and flummery filled their pages. Victorine collected the most outrageous for her colonel's amusement: the generals planned to release the poxed whores of the Hôpital St. Lazare to serve the Prussian army; the Prussian lines had been stormed by a herd of a thousand patriotic oxen.

The colonel began to speak of love. Victorine was becoming as necessary to him, he said, as food and drink. Victorine, to whom he was indeed food and drink, held his chestnut head to her white breast and allowed him to understand that she loved him in return.

Searching for a misplaced corset, her maid turned up the ripped green kimono and inquired what Mademoiselle would like done with it.

"Burn it," said Victorine. "No, don't. Mend it, if you can, and pack it away somewhere. This is not a time to waste good silk."

That evening, Victorine and her colonel strolled along the

Seine together, comfortably arm in arm. The cannon had fallen to a distant Prussian rumbling, easily ignored. Waiters hurried to and fro with trays on which the glasses of absinthe glowed like emeralds. The light was failing. Victorine looked out over the water, expecting to see the blue veil of dusk drifting down over Nôtre Dame.

The veil was stained with blood.

For a moment, Victorine thought her eyes were at fault. She blinked and rubbed them with a gloved hand, but when she looked again, the evening sky was still a dirty scarlet—nothing like a sunset, nothing like anything natural Victorine had ever seen. The very air shimmered red. All along the quai came cries of awe and fear.

"The Forest of Bondy is burning," Victorine heard a man say and, "an experiment with light on Montmartre," said another, his voice trembling with the hope that his words were true. In her ear, the colonel murmured reassuringly, "Don't be afraid, my love. It's only the aurora borealis."

Victorine was not comforted. She was no longer a child to hide in pretty stories. She knew an omen when she saw one. This one, she feared, promised fire and death. She prayed it did not promise her own. Paris might survive triumphantly into a new century, and the mason and his blonde might survive to see its glories, but nothing in La Fée Verte's vision had promised that Victorine, or even La Fée Verte, would be there with them.

~

THE RED LIGHT endured for only a few hours, but some

atmospheric disturbance cast a strange and transparent radiance over the next few days, so that every street, every passerby took on the particularity of a photograph. The unnatural light troubled Victorine. She would have liked to be diverted with kisses, but her colonel was much occupied just now. He wrote her to say he did not know when he'd be able to see her again—a week or two at most, but who could tell? It was a matter of national importance—nothing less would keep him from her bed. He enclosed a pair of fine kidskin gloves, a heavy purse, a rope of pearls, and a history of Napoleon's early campaigns.

It was all very unsatisfying. Other women in Victorine's half-widowed state volunteered to nurse the French wounded, or made bandages, or took to their beds with Bibles and rosaries, or even a case of wine. Victorine, in whom unhappiness bred restlessness, went out and walked the streets.

From morning until far past sunset, Victorine wandered through Paris, driven by she knew not what. She walked through the tent cities, past stalls where canteen girls in tricolored jackets ladled out soup, past shuttered butcher shops and greengrocers where women shivered on the sidewalk, waiting for a single rusty cabbage or a fist-sized piece of doubtful meat. But should she catch sight of a woman dressed in green or a woman whose skin seemed paler than normal, she always followed her for a street or two, until she saw her face.

She did not fully realize what she was doing until she found herself touching a woman on the arm so that she would turn. The woman, who was carrying a packet wrapped in butcher's paper, turned on her, frightened and furious.

"What are you doing?" she snapped. "Trying to rob me?"

"I beg your pardon," Victorine said stiffly. "I took you for a friend."

"No friend of yours, my girl. Now run away before I call a policeman."

Shaking, Victorine fled to a café, where she bought a glass of spirits and drank it down as if the thin, acid stuff would burn La Fée Verte from her mind and body. It did not. Trying not to think of her was still thinking of her; refusing to search for her was still searching.

⁓

ON THE MORNING of October 31, rumors of the fall of Metz came to Paris. The people revolted. Trochu cowered in the Hôtel de Ville while a mob gathered outside, shouting for his resignation. Victorine, blundering into the edges of the riot, turned hastily north and plunged into the winding maze of the Marais. Close behind the Banque de France, she came to a square she'd never seen before. It was a square like a thousand others, with a lady's haberdasher and a hairdresser, an apartment building and a café all facing a stone pedestal supporting the statue of a dashing mounted soldier. A crowd had gathered around the statue, men and women of the people for the most part, filthy and pinched and blue-faced with cold and hunger. Raised a little above them on the pedestal's base were a fat man in a filthy scarlet cloak and a woman, painfully thin and motionless under a long and tattered veil of green gauze.

The fat man, who was not as fat as he had been, was nearing the end of his patter. The crowd was unimpressed. There were a few catcalls. A horse turd, thrown from the edge of the crowd, splattered against the statue's granite base. Then La Fée Verte unveiled herself, and the crowd fell silent.

The weeks since Victorine had seen her on the stage of the Salon du Diable had not been kind to her. The dark eyes were sunken, the body little more than bone draped in skin and a walking-dress of muddy green wool. She looked like a mad woman: half-starved, pitiful. Victorine's eyes filled and her pulse sped. She yearned to go to her, but shyness kept her back. If she was meant to speak to La Fée Verte, she thought, there would be a sign. In the meantime, she could at least listen.

"I am a seer," La Fée Verte said, the word taking on a new and dangerous resonance in her mouth. "I see the past, the present, the future. I see things that are hidden, and I see the true meaning of things that are not. I see truth, and I see falsehoods tricked out as truth." She paused, tilted her head. "Which would you like to hear?"

Puzzled, the crowd muttered to itself. A woman shouted, "We hear enough lies from Trochu. Give us the truth!"

"Look at her," a skeptic said. "She's even hungrier than I am. What's the good of a prophetess who can't foresee her next meal?"

"My next meal will be bread and milk in a Sèvres bowl," La Fée Verte answered tranquilly. "Yours, my brave one, will be potage—of a sort. The water will have a vegetable in it, at any rate."

The crowd, encouraged, laughed and called out questions.

"Is my husband coming home tonight?"

"My friend Jean, will he pay me back my three sous?"

"Will Paris fall?"

"No," said La Fée Verte. "Yes, if you remind him. As for Paris, it is not such a simple matter as yes and no. Shall I tell you what I see?"

Shouts of "No!" and "Yes!" and more horse turds, one of which spattered her green skirt. Unruffled, she went on, her husky voice somehow piercing the crowd's rowdiness.

"I see prosperity and peace," she said, "like a castle in a fairy tale that promises that you will live happily ever after."

More grumbling from the crowd: "What's she talking about?"; "I don't understand her"; and a woman's joyful shout—"We're all going to be rich!"

"I did not say that," La Fée Verte said. "The cholera, the cold, the hunger, will all get worse before it gets better. The hard times aren't over yet."

There was angry muttering, a few catcalls: "We ain't paying to hear what we already know, bitch!"

"You ain't paying me at all," La Fée Verte answered mockingly. "Anyone may see the near future—it's all around us. No, what you want to know is the distant future. Well, as you've asked for the truth, the truth is that the road to that peaceful and prosperous castle is swarming with Germans. Germans and Germans and Germans. You'll shoot them and kill them by the thousands and for a while they'll seem to give up and go away. But then they'll rise again and come at you, again and again."

Before La Fée Verte had finished, "Dirty foreigner!" a woman shrieked, and several voices chorused, "Spy, spy!

German spy!" Someone threw a stone at her. It missed La Fée Verte and bounced from the pedestal behind her with a sharp crack. La Fée Verte ignored it, just as she ignored the crowd's shouting and the fat man's clutching hands trying to pull her away.

It was the sign. Victorine waded into the melee, elbows flailing, screaming like a cannonball in flight. There was no thought in her head except to reach her love and carry her, if possible, away from this place and home, where she belonged.

"I see them in scarlet," La Fée Verte was shouting above the noise. "I see them in grey. I see them in black, with peaked caps on their heads, marching like wooden dolls, stiff-legged, inexorable, shooting shopgirls and clerks and tavernkeepers, without pity, without cause."

Victorine reached La Fée Verte at about the same time as the second stone and caught her as she staggered and fell, the blood running bright from a cut on her cheek. The weight of her, slight as it was, overbalanced them both. A stone struck Victorine in the back; she jerked and swore, and her vision sparkled and faded as though she were about to faint.

"Don't be afraid," the husky voice said in her ear. "They're only shadows. They can't hurt you."

Her back muscles sore and burning, Victorine would have disagreed. But La Fée Verte laid a bony finger across her lips. "Hush," she said. "Be still and look."

It was the same square, no doubt of that, although the café at the corner had a different name and a different front, and the boxes in the windows of the apartment opposite were bright with spring flowers. Victorine and La Fée Verte were still surrounded by a crowd, but the crowd didn't seem to be aware of the existence of the two women huddled at the statue's base. People were watching something passing in the street beyond, some procession that commanded their attention and their silence. The men looked familiar enough, in dark coats and trousers, bareheaded or with flat caps pulled over their cropped hair. But the women—ah, the women were another thing. Their dresses were the flimsy, printed cotton of a child's shirt or a summer blouse, their skirts short enough to expose their naked legs almost to the knee, their hair cut short and dressed in ugly rolls.

Wondering, Victorine looked down at La Fée Verte, who smiled at her, intimate and complicit. "You see? Help me up," she murmured. As Victorine rose, lifting the thin woman with her, she jostled a woman in a scarf with a market basket on her arm. The woman moved aside, eyes still riveted on the procession beyond, and Victorine, raised above the crowd on the statue's base, followed her gaze.

There were soldiers, as La Fée Verte had said: lines of them in dark uniforms and high, glossy boots, marching stiff-legged through the square toward the rue de Rivoli. There seemed to be no end to them, each one the mirror of the next, scarlet armbands flashing as they swung their left arms. A vehicle like an open carriage came into view, horseless, propelled apparently by magic, with black-coated men seated in it, proud and hard faced under peaked caps. Over their heads, banners bearing a contorted black cross against a white and scarlet ground rippled in the wind. And then from the sky came a buzzing like a thousand hives of bees, as loud as thunder but more continuous. Victorine looked up, and saw a thing she hardly knew how to apprehend. It was like a bird, but enormously bigger, with wings that blotted out the light and a body shaped like a cigar.

If this was vision, Victorine wanted none of it. She put her hands over her eyes, releasing La Fée Verte's hand that she had not even been aware of holding. The buzzing roar ceased as if a door had been closed, and the tramp of marching feet. She heard shouting, and a man's voice screaming with hysterical joy:

"The Republic has fallen!" he shrieked. "Long live the Commune! To the Hôtel de Ville!"

The fickle crowd took up the chant: "To the Hôtel de Ville! To the Hôtel de Ville!" And so chanting, they moved away from the statue, their voices gradually growing fainter and more confused with distance.

When Victorine dared look again, the square was all but empty. The fat man was gone, and most of the crowd, all heading, she supposed, for the Hôtel de Ville. A woman lingered, comfortingly attired in a long grey skirt, a tight brown jacket with a greasy shawl over it, and a battered black hat rammed over a straggling bun.

"Better take her out of here, dear," she said to Victorine. "I don't care, but if any of those madmen come back this way, they'll be wanting her blood."

THAT NIGHT, VICTORINE had her maid stand in line for a precious cup of milk, heated it up over her bedroom fire and poured it over some pieces of stale bread torn up into a Sèvres bowl.

La Fée Verte, clean and wrapped in her old green kimono, accepted the dish with murmured thanks. She spooned up a bit, ate it, put the spoon back in the plate. "And your colonel?" she asked. "What will you tell him?"

"You can be my sister," Victorine said gaily. "He doesn't know I don't have one, and under the circumstances, he can hardly ask me to throw you out. You can sleep in the kitchen when he spends the night."

"Yes," La Fée Verte said after a moment. "I will sleep in the kitchen. It will not be for long. We . . ."

"No," said Victorine forcefully. "I don't want to hear. I don't care if we're to be ruled by a republic or a commune or a king or an emperor, French or German. I don't care if the streets run with blood. All I care is that we are here together now, just at this moment, and that we will stay here together, and be happy."

She was kneeling at La Fée Verte's feet, not touching her for fear of upsetting the bread and milk, looking hopefully into the ravaged face. La Fée Verte touched her cheek very gently and smiled.

"You are right," she said. "We are together. It is enough."

She fell silent, and the tears overflowed her great, bruised eyes and trickled down her cheeks. They were no longer crystalline—they were just tears. But when Victorine licked them from her fingers, it seemed to her that they tasted sweet.

Delia Sherman writes fantastical/historical/folklorical/tragical/comical fiction for adults and younger readers, and is a frequent contributor to Datlow/Windling anthologies. Her most recent novels are *The Fall of the Kings* (with partner Ellen Kushner) and *Changeling*. She is the president of the Interstitial Arts Foundation (www.interstitialarts.org), an organization dedicated to art that transcends, bends, blends, and otherwise ignores conventional genre divisions. A long-time resident of Boston, she has recently moved back home to New York City, where she is working on a novel about La Fée Verte and her world.

Dust Devil
on a Quiet Street

Richard Bowes

THE SUMMER AFTER I took an early retirement from the University library, I found myself sliding into my past. I tried to establish a timeline of events from forty years before, recalled old monsters and murders, scribbled phrases like "statute of limitations" and "déjà vu" on pieces of scrap paper. I scanned eBay and Google for pictures of amber rings, wrote "The idle mind occupies itself with inventing connections," on a Post-it and stuck it on my fridge.

It wasn't just me. That summer, the whole city, maybe the whole world seemed to be in a similar mood. Books were all memoirs, every concert was a reunion, every museum exhibition a retrospective, every Broadway opening a revival.

All this first got my attention one morning in June when I came out the door of my building on the corner of Bleecker and MacDougal Streets and found that forty-five years had been erased.

A few old places like the Figaro and Café Wha? have more or less survived as tourist traps. So their signs can always be seen. But that morning long-gone café and bar signs—the Gas Light, The Kettle of Fish, and Rienzi—had all returned. Even the Folklore Center poked its nose out. On the ground floor of my building, The San Remo had come back from wherever notorious old bars go when they die.

On warm, sunny mornings in this neighborhood, someone is always making a movie. MacDougal Street was choked with trailers, a breakfast buffet was set up on tables along the sidewalk, and a prop woman toted a set of bongo drums.

This film I'd heard about. It starred some of TV actors whose names meant nothing to me and concerned a young folk singer, just enough unlike Bob Dylan to avoid lawsuits, in Greenwich Village circa 1961.

That morning, I was on my way over to St. Mark's Church in the Bowery for a memorial service and that set me on a reflective path. Back in the early sixties, Marty Simonson, a couple of other kids, and I would come into the Village from the suburban college where we had been sent to repeat our freshman years, and hang around the old San Remo.

On our first visit, the grouchy bartender looked at our compulsory ROTC crew cuts and asked, "You guys in the army? The army of the squares, maybe?"

We all had to show our draft cards to prove that we were eighteen. But it was my card that got held under a light and examined to see if it was counterfeit. My friends, especially the ones months younger than me, found this hilarious. Later, I suspected it was a special scrutiny.

When the place got crowded the bartender would chase

us off our bar stools, saying, "Beer heads stand back and let the mixed drink customers sit."

One night, one of the regulars pointed out Norman Mailer sitting at a table with an English lady and a guy who looked like he might have been a prize fighter.

That same barfly was the one who told us that the bartender was Jonah Pearl, son of Max. As drama lit majors, Marty and I knew that name. Max Pearl was a legend from the 1920s and 1930s: theater critic, Algonquin Round Table wit, friend of the Marx Brothers. His newspaper column "Pearl of Precious Price" and later the radio show of the same name, introduced first New York and then the nation to banter, celebrity interviews, and bitchy book and movie reviews.

Some say that the homicidal radio personality in the movie Laura is based on Max Pearl. Famously, he once said, "My ambition is to die at the wheel of an expensive car that I don't own in the company of a beautiful woman to whom I'm not married on the grounds of a country club that doesn't admit Jews." And one evening in 1947 he managed to do exactly that.

Jonah Pearl was a surly Greenwich Village lowlife who, we were told, had been to jail a couple of times. We found this fascinating, wondered if it was for possession of exotic drugs, for political activity, or selling forged Jackson Pollocks.

When I discovered a few years later that it was for criminal assault and rape it was no big surprise. By then Jonah had said to me about his father: "The selfish bastard went out in high style and left me with nothing but his cigar bills and some half-assed gibberish about magic." By then, Jonah had also threatened to kill me.

That summer morning I felt a minor dust storm swirl around my legs. I remembered that long ago a friend and I had decided that these swirls of dried leaves and trash were actually the small gods, the spirits playful and malign, of Manhattan.

THE CHARM OF St. Mark's in the Bowery is that it's an early nineteenth-century Episcopal country church complete with graveyard that finds itself located on Second Avenue in the dirty, dynamic East Village.

That morning the church hosted a memorial service for Robin Saint Just. Born Robert Justin in Duluth, Minnesota, Saint Just was the man who discovered subway graffiti art and Blondie. His connection with the Pearls was still just a vague memory at the back of my brain.

When Saint Just died in a fall down the stairs of his building, obituaries and articles on the arts pages showed him in Avedon photos of Warhol's studio and in newspaper pictures of opening nights at the Met, in shots taken at CBGB's and Studio 54. The police found no evidence of foul play in his death and cited a lack of motive. That's because they didn't know Saint Just.

Amid the crowd gathered in the cobblestone church yard, I recognized lots of faces. Wearing dark glasses and scarves were former hippies who were now successful entrepreneurs, men and women who had gone from experimental theater communes to roles as wise-cracking pals in long-running television sitcoms. Along with these were many who looked resourceful but a bit worn and who I knew still lived, apprehensive but wily, in old apartments on ungentrified blocks in neighbor-hoods like this one.

Frankie, the Bug Boy, everybody's favorite connection, was there with Gloria Starrett, the ancient dancer who, leg-end had it, pleasured JFK up at the Hotel Pierre when she was a call girl. They stood with Nick and Norah Grubstreet, my private nickname for a young couple who supplemented their trust funds with hack writing.

"Critic, performer, poet, painter, composer, Robin had his fingers in everything," said Nick.

"His fingers were the least of it," Gloria replied.

Then I saw the Major in one of those wide-brimmed hats English ladies know how to find standing under the portico with some friends. She waved me over.

Barbara Lohr stood gray haired, five foot ten, smiling a bit sadly. Her slight military bearing had led to people calling her Major Barbara which then got shortened to the Major. I had known her for years. Barbara had been a friend, and a close one, of Saint Just.

The Major's parents were actors. Her mother was Tom Brown's kindly mother and Bob Cratchett's wife in movies I had seen on TV as a kid. Her father played gallant young officers who died holding off the Pathans in the Khyber Pass or went down in Noel Coward's destroyer.

In reality he was a sadist and she was a drunk. Or maybe it was the other way around. All this I found out from others. They were the reason that Barbara left London and sought her fortune in America.

The Major writes big fantasy novels about romantic, fiery gay males who toss their long hair and run their enemies through with cold steel, as unlike the behavior of the writer and her partner Marie, two very sensible women, as it is possible to be. Saint Just gave her work serious attention much to the envy of genre writers everywhere.

"His age was reported as anywhere from fifty-eight to sixty-six," said Alan Wick, a minor novelist who looks like an old-fashioned dentist, the kind who once said, "This won't hurt," before ramming in the drill.

The Major murmured, "He was sixty-five. I'm two weeks older than he was."

A side door opened and we began to move toward the church. Saint Just had become an Episcopalian late in life, just like W. H. Auden. The obituaries described him as eclectic. The word plagiarism was used privately. But it was said of Saint Just that when he stole from you, it didn't seem like theft so much as affirmation.

Before going inside, I looked around at the trees and the sun, the world passing by outside the iron fence. A plain black car pulled away from the curb.

Instinctively, I identified the two male riders in sports coats as cops and was reminded of police monitoring a mafia funeral. I guess it was a day for memories and juxtaposition because I also realized that one of them was Jaime, an old lover of mine.

The Major and those of us with her had good seats near the front of the church, two rows behind Saint Just's surprisingly plain daughter from his brief marriage to the actress, Katie Berlin. She sat between her nebbishy husband and Saint Just's brother, a retired insurance executive from Chicago.

"Ah, Tanya Jewell," whispered Alan Wick, and I looked to see a handsome dark young woman with her hair in a small afro come down the aisle. She nodded slightly to the Major. When I looked at Alan for an explanation, he murmured, "The new Robin Saint Just."

Tanya Jewell's good looks were lightly adorned. She had no visible tattoos or piercings. Her white top could almost have been a classic T-shirt. She wore some bracelets and on a chain around her neck was what looked at first like an ordinary plastic ring. That ring caught my attention.

Then the service began with Mozart's *Exultate Jubilante*, which Saint Just had said he wanted played at his funeral. The daughter spoke briefly, and the brother.

Then an elderly curator emeritus at MOMA talked about him. "Robin came to us when he was twenty-two as an intern. Six months after his arrival, Jack Moore—who was then the curator of sculpture—took him on as an assistant. It was still that wonderful time when a bright young person could come to the city and get noticed that quickly."

Alan Wick snorted rather loudly and the Major glared at him.

"Within a few years Jack was dead, as we all remember, and Robin—still in his midtwenties—was able to take over and finish the catalog for the 1965 American Retrospective Show."

Songs with lyrics by Saint Just, the one on the New York Dolls album, the one Marianne Faithful sang, were performed quietly. Somehow the fact that he had songs on a few classic rock albums was almost the last straw when people envied him.

"I'm not Saint Francis and he wasn't me," was one of the lines. "The gods' children touched me and I'm a miracle man," was another.

Then the Major rose and walked to the microphone.

"Robin and I both came to New York in the same week from schools in different parts of the world. It was 1962 and both MOMA where Robin worked and *Harper's Bazaar* where I was an editorial assistant paid about eighty dollars a week. But he had found a place he could afford, the wonderfully awful Hotel Betsy Ross on the outskirts of the old garment district. And within days of meeting him, I moved there, too. In a separate room, of course. Over the years we traveled in and out of each others' orbits, ending up as fellow parishioners here at St. Mark's church."

The Major talked about Saint Just taking her with him when he met Jim Morrison and the Doors. About his finding distinctive graffiti and tracking down the artist Keith Haring.

"His final passing, the way it happened, was not fair, perhaps. He was kind. To me and to many others. And if he wasn't always kind to everyone, well, as he himself said, he wasn't Saint Francis."

I watched as Tanya Jewell and the Major briefly embraced at the end of the service. The ring Ms. Jewell had on a chain around her neck reminded me of Jonah Pearl telling me that all his father had left him was, "Bad memories and a couple of little gee-gaws."

The particular gee-gaw that he described was a very old amber ring with a dragonfly inside. I tried to get a closer look at this one and was aware of the Bug Boy staring my way.

At the end of the service as the crowd dispersed, I went with Major Barbara, Alan Wick, and a few others through the gate and down the stairs that lead to East Ninth Street. It was a fine early June day, warm but not hot. As we hit the sidewalk an imperceptible breeze caused dust to swirl in the gutter.

"Oh, Robin, you can't come with us, I'm afraid," the Major sighed. "In his prime and sometimes later," she said, "Robin really was a kind of small god."

"More like a large, dirty dust devil," I said, taking up the old idea we'd once discussed. She nodded and gave a little laugh.

The Major and Marie live in a rambling third-floor apartment in a building that overlooks the St. Marks Church rectory yard. From certain angles in certain lights, the view from their windows evokes an English village.

Half a dozen of us sat around in the dining room drinking tea as dark as the Major's old oak table, eating scones and talking about Saint Just. Ceiling fans beat slowly and the open windows brought in the sun, the scent of flowers in somebody's garden, and the distant voices of children from the church day care center.

"In the *Times*," said Alan Wick, "someone mentioned all the influences on Saint Just, everyone from e. e. cummings to Fats Waller. Actually all he had was one really big dose of Jack Moore."

Jack Moore was once described as being like an Irish traffic cop standing at the intersection of the written word and abstract expressionism, of modern dance and the morning newspaper.

"Booze and boys had crippled Moore's ability to function. Saint Just was doing Jack's job long before he died. But

I'm not one of those who think little Robin murdered him. Not at all!" Alan Wick said.

The Major shook her head wearily. Jack Moore had supposedly died in a hit and run, clipped by a car over on West Street late one night. Back then what went on after dark at that far end of the Village never got seriously investigated.

The Major said, "Things were changing in the midsixties and Robin was more suited to function in that world. He understood the electronic media and the new music in ways Moore just didn't. He did a lot for many new writers and artists. But as with Moore, the time had come for Robin Saint Just to step aside."

I thought that "step aside" seemed kind of a heartless euphemism for an old friend's fatal tumble.

"Tanya Jewell has an uncanny ability to be in on any scene just before it becomes a scene," said Wick. "Her Arts Zoo will be fabulous for the creative community," he added. "And I don't believe for minute that she pushed Saint Just."

Some in the room approved of Ms. Jewell and her zoo, some didn't. Quite an argument ensued. It wasn't something that interested me much and I guess that showed. When I took my leave, the Major saw me to the door

"Having a steady job means you didn't have to worry about survival like the rest of us," she said. That made it sound like I'd been stuck in storage for all those years. It bothered me enough to tell me what she'd said was at least partly true.

⁓

THE SATURDAY AFTER Saint Just's memorial, I browsed the flea markets along Sixth Avenue. Not so long before, big raucous markets had sprawled for blocks on any weekend. Now ugly high-rise buildings stand on most of the lots and only small remnants of the great carnival remain.

In part I really did need to find a housewarming present for a godchild. Mostly, though, I was looking for Frankie the Bug Boy because I had certain memories and questions about both Jonah Pearl and Jack Moore.

I was happy to find the Bug Boy set up in a small, crowded market in a parking lot on the corner of Seventeenth Street. The location tied in nicely with some things I was trying to get straight in my memory.

This lot was the former site of the Hotel Betsy Ross. I'm not sure when the Betsy got built and didn't notice when it disappeared. Decayed fleabags like it once stood every few blocks in old Manhattan. In the early sixties it was full of people down on their luck: drunks, addicts, drag queens, and the occasional kid new to the city. It was at the Betsy that I'd once spent afternoons listening to the speed babble of Billy B, the young son of a famous junkie author.

In the Bug Boy's booth that day he had a drum set, an almost new bike and microwave, a speaker system, a vacuum cleaner, and a pretty good leather jacket.

"Old hippies rising from the dead and walking into my booth!" Frankie said when he saw me. "I must be having acid flashbacks."

He and I go all the way back to the sixties and the East Village. Bug Boys are what they called kids who were going to be jockeys. Even before I met him Frankie had gotten too tall and so stoned he fell off horses that were standing still.

"Like always, your stuff looks like the contents of some

apartment you just ripped off," I said. He looked a bit of-fended. I'd been told that if you asked him just right, the Bug Boy would bring out from under one his tables the tray of guns he had for sale.

Getting information from him can be a devious, sidewise kind of process. "Hey," I said, and indicated the lot crowded with tents and tables. "This is an historic spot we're standing on."

He nodded. "Yeah, it was weird hearing the Betsy men-tioned the other day. I wondered if you remembered."

"I hadn't even known that this is where Saint Just and the Major stayed when they first came to New York," I said. Then I threw in, "This must be where they met Billy B." It was no more than a hunch but I wanted his reaction.

Frankie paused then evaded. "Lots of people came and went back then, man. I can't remember them all." But he hadn't said no.

"Remember listening to Billy B rap?" I asked him. The son of the great man managed to be gaunt and puffy at the same time. He'd lie on his bed and talk endlessly. "Meth, man, is like a kind of vitamin that makes you smart and let's you see right through walls," he'd say. "That's why junkies are all old and dried up. My old man sleeps twenty hours a day. I haven't slept in a year and a half."

Billy B was a trust fund baby. Both of us, me first then later Frankie, did little errands for him. One day, Billy told me how he felt a kind of mystic kinship for another son of a well-known writer. This guy was looking for someone to do a few chores for him.

This friend lived way west in the Village on a little side street over near the Hudson. When I paid a visit, he turned out to be Jonah Pearl. Only a few years had passed since I'd last seen him but he looked bad. His face was thin and kind of blue, his belly bloated.

I was surprised but he didn't seem to be. He looked at me with disgust and boredom the same way he looked at everything and said he'd expected to see me turn up again. "Sooner or later your type always returns."

Weird encounters pretty much defined my life right then but this one made me uneasy. He offered me a hundred dollars to do a simple job. But I had some hidden reserve of common sense and I didn't take it.

When I next saw Billy B and told him what had happened, he wasn't happy. In fact he stood up and said, "There's a little gun I can keep under my belt in back with my shirt hanging out to hide it and it's not so good for shooting someone but it's the surprise when you think I'm reaching into my back pocket for my wallet to pay you off and I pull out the twenty-two and blow open your face."

I'd left before finding out if he could actually do that. From then on the Bug Boy ran his errands instead of me.

All these years later in his booth at the flea market I asked Frankie, "Did Billy B ever send you to meet someone named Jonah Pearl?"

The Bug Boy looked really quizzical and shook his head. "I don't remember the name," he told me and I was certain he was lying.

I was tempted to ask him something else just to see him squirm again. But at that moment a woman with feathery green hair came into the booth and wanted to look at the drums. With relief, Frankie turned to deal with her.

Walking away I thought about the wastrel sons of notorious writer fathers and it struck me that Max Pearl with his "Pearl of Precious Price" newspaper column and radio show occupied pretty much the same slot in his time as first Jack Moore and then Robin Saint Just did in theirs.

I might have carried this line of thought further, but at that moment, I spotted a possible housewarming gift.

⌒

OTHER MATTERS CAME up: I did a reading and book signing, a family anniversary took me home to New England for a few days. So it was the next weekend before I thought much more about Jonah Pearl and company.

My old friend Marty Simonson had sublet an apartment on Abingdon Square in the Village. He was in town to teach a summer course on stage direction at NYU. Marty goes all the way back to when we were gawky kids first hanging around the Village.

The friendship has endured because he doesn't write and so isn't a rival and I'm not in show business and don't put the arm on him professionally. Some of the people with whom we were in the theater program at school are fairly desperate and ask him for favors he can't grant.

"At my age, in most businesses I'd be enjoying a certain security," he said. "Fortunately I like my work and still get hired. But my finances are kind of shaky. For a lot of my friends, though, they're just plain scary."

That Sunday we had a leisurely brunch and took a stroll. Because of something that was on my mind and certain memories that we shared, I led us down to tiny, quiet Weehawken

Street. It's is a single, short block between Tenth and Christopher but it was almost like I wanted someone with me when I walked down Weehawken.

The west side of the street is the back of a bunch of old riverfront structures. The fronts of these buildings face the Hudson. Over the years, stevedore bars turned to leather bars, maritime supply stores became porn video parlors.

But on Weehawken little has changed. Amazingly, one or two rear roofs still have shingles and there is a flight of wooden stairs going up to a porch on a second floor.

"It has just a touch of an old New England shore town," I said.

Marty had grown up out in Eastern Long Island and saw it, too. "Not the quaint, scenic part with the views. These are the rented rooms where they stick the town drunk and the summer kids who work as waitresses and lifeguards."

I paused and looked up at that second floor porch. The windows were dark and looked as if they might be papered over.

"Remember Jonah Pearl, Max Pearl's son? Tended bar at the San Remo?"

Marty nodded. "He lived up there in an old rundown artist's studio. Years ago, I got sent around to see him."

"About what, buying your soul, renting your ass? You were a wild and enterprising child back then. We were all in awe."

That pleased me. Who doesn't want to be remembered as having been a devil in his youth? Marty waited for my story.

I remembered yellow stains on the walls and the way the place smelled of mildew and cats. Jonah was sprawled on a busted old couch, his eyes yellow and his hands shaking. It was the first time I'd looked at someone and thought maybe they were dying. Behind him, through big, dirty front windows, the sun reflected off the Hudson and the ruins of the old elevated highway cast shadows.

"Jonah talked about his father," I said. "About how when he was a little kid Max had called him a Pearl of no price whatsoever. Jonah didn't meet his critical standards.

"He said nothing much was left after his old man died but, in his words, 'Bad memories and the lucky charms he believed in.'

"He said his old man was more superstitious than any of his admirers would ever had believed. 'Even Columbia University couldn't knock all the fucking Kabbalah out of him,' was how he put it.

"Jonah described to me a ring that looked like a piece of plastic junk but was actually amber and ancient. His father kept it on him all the time; believed his success as an arbiter of the arts depended on it.

"Jonah personally had no use for the thing but he'd rented it out. And the one who wore it had a major career. Max Pearl told Jonah that what looked like a dragonfly preserved in the ring was actually the soul of Callimachus the first critic."

At that Marty laughed out loud. "Who'd have thought that a critic's soul was such a magic and valuable thing?"

And right then on a bright, warm Sunday it did seem pretty funny. So I didn't tell him how Jonah said he needed to talk to the one who had the ring. He said that guy had fallen behind on the rent and wouldn't talk to him.

Jonah said he had a way for me to make money. He was going to point out a man who frequented the neighborhood piers. I was going to pick him up and bring him to a place where he and Jonah could talk.

What I did say to Marty was, "It was about selling my soul and my ass. But in a rare burst of common sense, I chickened out." I also added, "Right around the corner on West Street is the spot where Jack Moore, the critic, got run over."

"Really, you could do tours of the Village!" Marty told me.

As we continued on our way, scraps of paper blew along the gutter. On the other side of the street a guy wearing a polo shirt and sunglasses sat in a car. I recognized him as a cop. I also realized that I knew him.

At the Christopher Street end of the block some shop-worn hustlers lounged on one corner near the door of Badlands, the video gallery. On the other corner, balding, gray-bearded bears, gay guys proud of their body hair and pot bellies, smoked outside the Dugout bar.

Marty paused and mimed his indecision at which way to go. The bears were amused and began beckoning to us. So we stopped in there.

～

AT THE APARTMENT warming a few nights later, I brought a couple of bottles of a good sauterne, the turquoise-green goose lamp from my apartment that the hostess has loved since she was a little girl, and a half dozen rather nice Chinese bowls. As a special present I also brought Marty, who qualified as a minor celebrity.

Selesta and her boyfriend, Sammy, had just moved into a fourth floor walkup on the Upper East Side. Long ago her mother and I lived at the same time in the same apartment on East Tenth Street but with different people. We stayed friends, and years later when Selesta was born, I was named her godfather.

Selesta has a tattoo design on her throat that matches the blue of her eyes. Sammy's full name is Samson. He shaves his head. The two have been together since college. She is twenty-five. He is twenty-three.

It's a good match. In high school, he had an obsessive compulsive disorder. She was bulimic. Now, and it almost seems to follow logically, he is a painter. She is an actress. Both have day jobs but I can never remember what they are. Selesta and Samson have highly developed networking skills.

"Josef, this is my godfather," Selesta told a tall young man with a chin beard. "He writes science fiction."

"That is so cool," Josef said. His eyes never stopped darting around the room.

"This is Marty Simonson. He directed Al Pacino and Claire Danes in *King Lear* at Williamsport last month."

"Awesome!" He focused on Marty.

"Josef has a blog," she told us. The small rooms had begun to fill up rapidly.

"Saturday Night and Sunday Morning," Josef said. Marty seemed impressed. I had heard of it, even looked at it.

Old family friends arrive early and stay a very short time if they are hip. I sat for a while on the double bed and watched young people come through the front door and kiss Selesta and Sammy.

Marty sat next to me. Josef said, "I started 'Saturday Night and Sunday Morning' writing on Sunday the things I'd seen the night before. Now I do it every day. I've got sponsors and everything. You'll be on it tomorrow. What's the most important thing you've done in the last three months?"

Before Marty could reply, the door opened again and a small entourage came in. At its center, simple and elegant was Tanya Jewell. She smiled and hugged the hostess and host. I saw she wore a T-shirt with Art Zoo lettered on it and a picture of the Mona Lisa in a cage.

"Tanya!" Josef, awestruck, abandoned us.

Marty was curious. "The new Saint Just," I told him. Ms. Jewell looked around the apartment and missed nothing and nobody. I was impressed by her absolute self-confidence. As Serena led her toward us, I finally got a good look at the soul of Callimachus imprisoned in amber.

I hoped Marty wouldn't notice and regretted saying anything to him. I remembered Jonah Pearl saying he'd kill me if I ever told anyone.

⌒

OTHER EVENTS INTERVENED in my life. A friend's mother had died that winter and I went to New Jersey with her to help inventory everything in the house. I attended a Speculative Fiction Convention. It was a late-July night with a big moon in the sky the next time I walked down Weehawken Street.

By then, though, I had done some research. I'd learned that Jack Moore wrote his first important reviews a month or so after Max Pearl and the wife of a Park Avenue society doctor were discovered wrapped around a tree on an exclusive Fairfield country club's gold course, in a car "borrowed" from a diplomat at the fledgling United Nations. Moore's own death had taken place, as nearly as I could piece together the past, a few weeks after my final encounter with Jonah Pearl.

As a writer, my insights and suspicions about what goes on around me tend to be retrospective. Forty years after the event, I was certain Jack Moore was the one for whom I was supposed to be bait. With all his other problems he must have skipped the rent on the ring. With him gone, Pearl obviously found someone else to take the lease.

Not long after Jack Moore's supposed hit and run, an artist, campy and obsessed, began a whole series of paintings of the death: the body sprawled on West Street, being loaded into an ambulance, on exhibition at Campbell's Funeral Home with mourners weeping. Saint Just wrote a much discussed piece for the *Times* arts pages on critics and publicity. The sixties were a mad and alien world when I thought about them.

On Weehawken Street on a summer night in the early twenty-first century, voices rose and fell like waves, music blasted and ceased when doors opened and closed. A couple of young guys in shorts and tank tops that showed off their tattoos went past me arm in arm. I walked down the block, turned and faced what I still thought of as Jonah Pearl's building.

All around the front door and across the windows of what was once Pearl's apartment were strips of yellow crime scene tape. The cop I'd seen parked here the last time I'd been down this block was Phil. Years ago when he was young and I was a lot younger than I am now, he was the first cop partner of my boyfriend Jaime.

That night on Weehawken Street I walked down the block and asked a hustler and a bartender at the Dugout what had happened. They had told me about the police taking out the floor boards, lowering them down through the second story windows

That reminded me of the time twenty years before that I had first seen Jaime. It was on First Avenue in the East Village. We were both part of a crowd watching a crew from the Police Property Office at work dismantling the floor of a bar.

The Keg of Nails was the name of that place, left over from the days when those blocks were part of Little Italy.

The story that emerged in gossip and later in the papers was that a multiple hit had taken place in there decades before.

They disposed of the bodies but hadn't washed out all the bloodstains. Then someone confessed and the floor got taken out to be used as evidence.

My immediate take was that back when Frankie the Bug Boy ran errands for Jonah, he must have brought Jack Moore right to the building on Weehawken Street. Moore had not left the place alive. They'd killed him there then dumped the body on West Street to be run over.

⌒

ONE NIGHT THE next week or maybe a little later, I got a call. "Phil tells me you're hanging around in bad places," Jaime said. It was the first time we'd spoken in years. He asked me to meet him at a place I knew.

When I came out the front door of my building, I found the August night illuminated and people standing silent and expectant like the witness to a miracle in a Renaissance painting. In the crowd I saw Selesta and Sam and a group of their friends.

Under the lights, an actor wearing jeans and a T-shirt in the manner of the young Brando, paused in front of the Café Figaro and called, "Allen, Allen Ginsberg."

"Cut," someone said. The actor was hustled away, technicians began to move, the audience relaxed. Selesta came back into focus and recognized me.

"We were going to call and see if you wanted to come out for coffee," she said and I was impressed by her polite lie. "Then we saw the film crew and Jared Michaels and realized they were filming that Kerouac movie."

Josef, of Saturday Night and Sunday Morning, was with them, looking at the crowd in search of celebrities. He had referred to me briefly in his blog the day after we met. Mostly he wrote about Tanya Jewell and about Marty.

He described Ms. Jewell as saying that the Arts Zoo would open in East Village in September. She told him it was a chance for people to really see the artists in their midst. "Men and women willing to spend their lives below the poverty line because of their love for what they do."

Josef had asked her if it was true that all the participants would be naked and in cages.

"In cages, yes," she had said. "But in the clothes they wear when they're working."

Marty had then described to her the crowd at the Bear Bar which contained a nice sprinkling of writers, musicians, visual artists. "The zoo should have a bear cage," he said and Ms. Jewell had seemed interested.

When I had read the blog I remembered that the more

I stared at the ring she wore, the more it had looked like a plastic gumball machine prize.

That night on MacDougal Street, the kids planned to stand there and wait for Kerouac to reappear. I realized that the Village was really just a theme park: Beatnik World, maybe. I said good night and went on my way.

Jaime was parked in front of a hydrant over near Sixth Avenue. He was dressed in sweatpants and a Yankees T-shirt, bigger, beefier than I remembered. His hair was still dark but thin now on top. The smile was the same. We sat down in that coffee shop on Fourth Street where the cops go.

I had iced tea. He used skim milk and NutraSweet in his coffee. We talked a little bit. I knew he had two kids. He told me that now it was four. I told him I was retired. Then he said, "Phil tells me he saw you a couple of times recently."

"I'm surprised he remembered who I was."

"It's something you learn to do in this line of work. He says that you're making his job more difficult by hanging around a site he's investigating and asking the bystanders questions."

"There's a building I remember from a long time ago. Before I knew you even. I was thinking about a guy I knew who lived there and who was very mean and very crazy. Seeing it gutted reminded me of the first time I ever saw you."

"The Keg of Nails." He smiled thinking about it.

I remembered Jaime that night, alert, and aware of himself in ways a straight guy isn't. He had turned and seen me looking at him. One thing led to another and we went back to the apartment where I lived then.

"That night on Weehawken Street, I figured they were looking for bloodstains," I said.

"From whoever you knew that lived there how long ago?"

"Forty years."

"That'd be one cold case."

For a moment I thought of asking him why he had staked out Saint Just's funeral a few months before. But Jaime rubbed his eyes and I saw how tired he was.

When he spoke it was in the tone of a cop telling a civilian to move along. "What's going on over on Weehawken's got nothing to do with whatever you're talking about. Phil works Lofts and Safes now. Stolen goods. Not homicide. Phil's a good guy. Knew a bit about us and never mentioned it.

"You know I thought about you and me quite a few times before Phil called. I don't tell anybody about it but I got no problem with what we did. And you were nice, you know, showed me how to take exams, never spoke down to me or tried to twist my head around. You said you're retired now? I could use some of that. You maybe need something to do. Volunteer. Maybe teach.

"There's dangerous guys involved in investigations like Phil's working on. Stay clear of it. I'd feel bad if something happened to you."

ON A SEPTEMBER Sunday with the first hint of fall the Major and I followed the signs and arrows down Saint Mark's Place to the Arts Zoo. A swirl of dried leaves frisked about us like a playful puppy and it almost seemed stupid to wreck an old friendship with accusations of voodoo and murder. But I wanted to let her know what I knew.

The Major talked about her summer, a book signing tour

in the Midwest, a vacation in Nova Scotia with Marie. Then she asked how mine had been.

That was my opening. "I've been thinking about Jonah Pearl and the past ever since the day of the memorial service."

"The past is very alive right now," she said and indicated the swirling leaves. "Look at the dust devils."

"We must have been very stoned when we made that up."

The Major looked a bit amused, a bit affectionate, at the tricks my memory was playing. "It wasn't a case of us making it up. You told me about those being the small gods. You spoke about it very seriously. Looking and watching over the years, I realized you were right. You were a strange young Celtic poet back then. I think all those years working at the library took something out of you."

I said, "Did Saint Just have that amber ring with the dragonfly on him when they found him at the bottom of the stairs? The one Tanya Jewell wears around her neck?"

"No, but it was among his effects. Not many people knew this but Saint Just had been sick for a while with early onset Alzheimer's. I gave the ring to Tanya. And, yes, I'm sure it violates some protocol of his will. But she admired him a lot and it had no innate value. And it gives her confidence. She's very young. Like Saint Just was."

"Jonah Pearl called it the Callimachus ring. Max Pearl got it from God knows where. Jack Moore wore it until Jonah killed him and took it back. That's when Saint Just got it. And you."

Her expression changed to one of concern. We had reached Tompkins Square. The Actors Cage was set up on the east side of the park. The crowds were large. People bought tickets and stood around the old-fashioned zoo fences.

Inside on a large stage a dozen actors auditioned all at the same moment in a cacophony of Shakespeare and Mamet, Hammerstein, and Sondheim. A dozen others down near the fence mimed waiting tables: taking orders, carrying trays, picking up tips. Some were young but a lot were in their fifties and sixties. In a corner an older woman mimed coming downstairs to a real mailbox. She opened it and pulled out bills and an oversize eviction notice.

In silence we watched the performers and the crowd. Then the Major said, "When you first came to Manhattan you were like the rest of us struggling to survive, to create. Some of us became casualties of drugs and sex. Some fell under the spells of various magics.

"I didn't think you'd survive. You did, though. Someone got you that nice little job, and you held onto it for all these years and got a nice little pension.

"Lots of the rest of us didn't have that luxury. We had to live by our wits and the grace of the local gods. Not pretty. Not nice in many ways. A lot of us haven't much to show for all those years. That's what The Art Zoo is all about."

The Painters Cage that contained an art gallery and a big studio with a good north light was on the west side of the Park.

Just inside the fence men and women sat on pavement with their art for sale. The prices were a few dollars for each. They had cardboard signs that read, "Please buy my work I have no medical insurance and no home."

The Musicians Cage was set up in a school yard on Avenue B. A steel band had just finished playing. As we approached, four musicians in rehearsal clothes scattered at kitchen tables and on folding chairs around the yard began to play Oliver Messiaen's "The Quartet for the End of Time."

The Major and I weren't walking as close as we had before. I said, "The ring was yours to give, wasn't it? Billy B felt an affinity for Jonah Pearl. I'll bet Jonah felt one for you. All of you were children of crazy artists. Did he give it to you and Saint Just? Did you buy it from him? He died in a nursing home. Someone must have given him money?"

"I commit witchcraft, robbery, and murder and what did I get out of all that?"

"Saint Just's praise is what launched you."

Neither of us spoke or paid much attention as we passed the Bear Cage in a small vacant lot on Avenue B.

She shook her head and looked disappointed. "If I'd ever thought of killing anyone, I'd start now with you. If any or all of this was true, what would prevent me from eliminating you?"

"Because, if anything happens to me, there's a letter that will get delivered to a cop I know." It wasn't true but I thought it was a nice touch.

The Writers Cage was down on Houston Street. Balloon sellers and popcorn carts ringed the bars but this wasn't as popular as some of the other exhibits.

"I'm not afraid of the police," said the Major. "It's time that we parted for a while." As she turned away, she added, "I think you might devote a little of your time to this project." The swirl of leaves was still with us. "It will please the gods."

The Bug Boy was there wearing a hat that said ZOO KEEPER and selling tickets. He obviously had overheard and understood the last part of our conversation.

From inside the cage came a clatter of keyboards. Writers in their pajamas or their underwear wandered around looking for grants in hollow logs, jumping up to try and grab the contracts hanging just out of reach on the branches of trees. Nick and Norah Grubstreet were dressed in Prada pajamas looking very amused.

Alan Wick in his shorts spoke on a phone and seemed all business. But when another writer rattled the cage door and found it locked, his expression changed to a veiled anxiety that didn't seem rehearsed. Along with everyone else, I'd heard how the Amazon numbers zoomed on Wick's small press story collection after he was profiled on National Public Radio when the Arts Zoo opened.

Tanya Jewell was there speaking to a TV reporter. The Major was at her side and the amber ring was at her throat. She was someone who could have pushed Saint Just down a flight of stairs.

She said, "This is about the artists who are a major reason for this city's being a tourist attraction. We're bringing attention to creative people in late middle age and older who have minimum resources and providing publicity and entertainment at the same time."

Leaves stirred in the gutter, spiraled and blew over my shoes. I tried to step away and it happened again. Paper blew against my leg. Out of the corner of my eye I saw Jaime's car drive past. I wondered if these might be the dangerous people he had warned me about.

The Bug Boy stepped up next to me and whispered in my ear, "You're going around asking questions making everybody all uneasy. And look at how upset you got all the little spirits. You think they're angry that they died? Don't be crazy man. They all prefer it the way they are."

We were next to a door in the cage. "The Major's even more pissed at you than she was with Alan Wick. You need to do what he's doing to make her happy. Everyone wants you inside."

A spiral of dust blew in my eyes. The cage door opened. The Bug Boy and someone else had my arms. Through dust and tears I saw Alan Wick jump up. But I knew that before he could get out, the door would clang shut behind me.

Richard Bowes has lived for most of his life in Manhattan. Over the last twenty years, he has published five novels, including *Minions of the Moon*, winner of the Lambda Award, and *From the Files of the Time Rangers*. His novella *Streetcar Dreams* won the World Fantasy Award, and his story "There's a Hole in the City" won the South 2006 Million Writers Award for Fiction. His most recent short fiction collection is *Streetcar Dreams and Other Midnight Fancies*. Other recent and forthcoming stories can be found in The Nebula Awards Showcase 2005, Postscripts #3, Electric Velocipede #10, Horror: The Best of the Year, 2006, Fantasy: The Very Best of 2005, So Fey, and The Coyote Road: Trickster Tales.

To Measure the Earth

❧

by Jedediah Berry

*She dwelt on the highest peak of the Catskills and had charge of the doors of
day and night to open and shut them at the proper hour. She hung up new
moons in the skies and cut up the old ones into stars.*

—DIEDRICH KNICKERBOCKER

SPRING 1890

ROEL GOT OUT of bed before the fireflies had quit
their nighttime signaling. He took his hat from the
bedpost, strapped on his wooden right leg, and went downstairs to stoke the fire.

Netta had never been able to sleep through the thudding
of her husband's leg on the steps, and the steps creaked, each
one. She threw the covers aside and went to the kitchen to
make their breakfast of blood sausage and buckwheat cake.
They ate without speaking, because they had a rule about
that. Then they went outside to load the cart with things the
spirits wanted.

They packed worn left boots, broken chairs, clean under-
clothes, fingernail cuttings, a bucket of ash, peach stones, and
leftover buckwheat cake. Netta almost said something when

Roel added three sacks of Indian corn to the pile, along with an alarm clock and two wool blankets. That was more than they'd ever sent over, and the blankets would be missed come winter, assuming they hadn't starved by then.

Netta went to chop firewood, and Roel drove the cart down the rutted trail that skirted the fields. To one side, the light of a waning moon fell on pale shoots spotted with disease. On the other, the spirits had hung their lanterns in the pines. The lights swayed and guttered when the wind blew, but did not go out.

Beyond were the lightless mountains and the stark slope called the Wall of Manitou. Some fool had built a hotel up there when Roel was a boy, and other fools from the city still came by steamship, then by train, and then by stagecoach to pass a few weeks on that windy, cloud-dampened peak. With his good eye he could see them on clear days—the men in their top hats, the ladies in their bell-shaped dresses—gliding along behind the tall columns of the hotel façade like clockwork figures. But none of the guests were awake at this hour, and the hotel was a dark lump in the sky.

The mule knew where to stop. Roel got down and took some of the offerings from the cart, set them in a pile on the spirits' side of the trail. He sprinkled ashes over top of the pile. Then he rode on, and did not look back.

After three more stops, nothing was left except the corn, the alarm clock, and the blankets. Roel had come to the worst part of the fields, where the earth was turned to swamp. Nothing grew here but onion grass and ostrich fern. On the other side of the trail was a broad meadow. The lanterns hung along its edges were dimming as the morning brightened.

Roel removed his wooden leg and took out the tobacco and pipe hidden in it. He smoked until the sun came over the trees. Then he strapped the leg back on and gathered the last of the offerings in his arms. He said, "You don't see the ghosts of dogs when they play in the snow," and walked into the meadow.

The lanterns brightened a moment and went out.

Roel left bundles of corn among the roots of the trees, making sure not to look into the woods. The soil under his feet felt like any other, but he could smell that it was different. The land his grandfather cleared had gone sour. This land was rich and old, and anything could grow here. Anything would.

At the far end of the meadow, he spread a blanket on the ground, as though for a picnic. He didn't sit on it, though, only wound the clock and left it there. He laid the second blanket at the center of the meadow and set a bowl on it, then filled the bowl with pieces of red sugar candy from his pocket.

The mule's name was Mule. He understood little of what Roel was doing, but he wanted no part in it, and Roel had to drag him down off the trail. He chuckled and said, "Come on, your children will thank me for it."

He piled stones into the cart, stopping now and then to adjust his leg. Some of the stones were too heavy for one man to move. Those he left in the dirt.

He had circled the outer edge of the meadow once when he noticed the spirit sitting on the blanket at its center. Roel had known a spirit would come, but the shape of the thing surprised him, and when he saw its face he nearly cried out to it. That was mistake enough—the spirit saw that Roel saw. It put a piece of candy in its mouth and said, "It's good. How did you get Mom to use the cinnamon?"

Roel knew better than to answer a question like that, and went on with his work. But his hands were shaking and the next stone slipped out of his fingers. The spirit crunched the candy in its mouth and watched as Roel bent down, got the stone up against his shoulder, hoisted it into the cart.

The spirit rose from the blanket and walked toward him. "Looks like you could use some help," it said.

Mule made an unhappy sound in his throat. Roel remembered something his father used to say to vex him, and he asked the spirit, "Is it as hot in the summer as it is in town?"

The spirit closed its eyes and frowned, then went back to the blanket to think about that.

Roel circled the meadow once more, gathering stones, while the spirit sat and ate candy. The sun reached the top of the sky and the fog lifted. The spirit stayed, though, and the longer Roel worked, the closer he drew to its blanket.

When the candy was gone, the spirit said to Roel, "All you have to do is ask me to help, and I'll help. Some of those stones are too heavy for one man to move."

"They aren't bothering anyone," Roel said. When he looked up, the spirit was standing right in front of him. The boy the spirit was wore nothing on his feet, but his feet were clean. He was shirtless, and stood with his chest thrust forward. His hair was brown and dirty; it hung down over very blue eyes.

Roel said, "Do you walk to school or bring your lunch?"

The boy ignored that. "Why don't you ask me to help you? Just say my name and ask."

Roel coughed to keep himself from speaking. He lifted another stone into the cart. The meadow was almost cleared.

"You sent all the field hands home," the boy said. "You think it's a job we can never finish together. But you have to stay a long time now. You can't claim a meadow and leave it."

Roel lifted the last few stones into the cart, then took up the mule's reins and began to lead it back toward the trail. But the boy stood in front of him, put his hand on his chest. "Dad," he said, "please stay."

The hand was warm, and Roel realized how cold he was, despite the sun, despite the work. And why not stay? The meadow was as good a place as any. The soil there was rich and old. He could stay with the boy and sit on the blanket with him. He could smoke his pipe and maybe have some peace, and when the sun went down they would watch the spirits light their lanterns in the trees. All these years, and Roel had never seen the spirits light their lanterns.

He just had to say the child's name. He knew it better than he knew his own.

At the far end of the clearing, the alarm clock began to ring. The spirit stepped away from him, its face pale. It put its hands over its ears and shouted, "What is that? It's horrible!"

The sound had nudged Roel from his daze. "I'm going home," he said. "You'll have to turn it off yourself or wait until it winds down."

The spirit spat at Roel's feet and ran off. "It's horrible!" it said. "You're horrible! I hate you!"

Roel led Mule onto the trail and back toward the house. He walked for a full minute before the alarm was silenced. Then there was no sound at all. The offerings he had left at the side of the trail were gone now. Out in the pines, the lanterns lit as he passed. Roel didn't look at them. He did not look back.

⁓

WHEN ROEL CAME into the kitchen, Netta was at the table, asleep with her head hanging over the back of her chair. Both her hands were wrist-deep in a bowl of bread dough.

Roel checked the stove. He stirred the coals with a poker and added a few pieces of wood. Then he tilted his wife's head forward and took her hands out of the bowl. She had big hands, bigger than his, and they were cold. He held them to his mouth and breathed on them, licked off some of the dough.

Netta's sleeping sickness had come on soon after their wedding, when he'd moved her from town out to the farm. He had learned it was better to let her sleep, let her wake when she was ready to wake.

He took a deck of cards from their hiding place in the seat of his chair, played a game of solitaire. He lost quickly, shuffled, and started over. He was losing again when Netta woke.

She frowned at the cards and set the bowl aside. The dough had risen while she slept. She got up to fix their dinner, and Roel gathered the cards, put them back under the panel in the seat of his chair. "Where's Louisa?" he asked.

Netta said, "You saw a spirit today."

She always knew too much when she woke from one of those sleeps. Roel grumbled, which meant he didn't want to talk about it.

Netta set bowls on the table and ladled stew into them. She asked, "What was its name? We have to know its name if we're going to figure out what it wants."

Roel ate a few spoonfuls and said, "Doesn't that girl eat? Is there such thing as a boarder that doesn't eat your food?"

"You cleared that meadow," Netta said. "Tell me what the spirit looked like, at least. Head like a garlic clove, or a melon? Were its feet webbed? Did it have bird's wings?"

"No," Roel said. "Nothing like that." He finished his dinner in a hurry and went into the parlor, lit the lamp. He took his grandfather's journal out from under the family Bible and set it on the table, opened it to the pages from 1841.

February 20. Indian corn at the roots of the older trees distracts them while we work. More lights along the border tonight, strange sounds from the well. Wind picking up.

February 21. Sophie looking better this morning, but weak again by sundown. She finished her quilt and I finished the whiskey.

February 22. Woke late. Colder today, stronger wind. Sharpened tools and baked a pie.

Netta was standing in front of him, her arms crossed. She knew he couldn't read while she stood like that.

"It was a boy," he said, without looking up. "It looked like a boy, that's all, and I want to forget about him."

Netta stopped herself from saying something. She went back into the kitchen and filled a bucket with water, took that and a scrub brush upstairs to a little room at the end of the hall. Inside was a perfectly made bed, a trunk, and on the floor a pair of small boots.

It was the cleanest room in the house, but Netta got on her knees and began to scrub. She worked with both arms, pausing only to drag the bucket closer as she went. When she came to the boots she set them aside and scrubbed the floor beneath them, then put them back in their place.

She worked until she heard Roel come thumping up the stairs, heard the bed creak under his weight. Then she dropped the scrub brush into the bucket and went to the door at the back of the room. She could hear Louisa in the attic, singing one of her forgetting songs. The words sounded to Netta like rules for a game too dangerous to be worth playing.

> *Sun come up, fetch a pail of water.*
> *Moon come up, scatter out your bones.*
> *The king is in his wooden shoes,*
> *Walking on the mountain.*
> *The moon is in his mountain shoes,*
> *Walking on your bones.*

Netta did not go all the way up the stairs, only far enough to poke her head up through the floor. She and Roel called Louisa the boarder only because she'd always been called that, and because none of them had a better word for what she was.

The girl wore the same blue housedress she'd been wearing for two weeks; she was seated at her desk at the far end of the attic. She had a book open in front of her. It was the primer that Netta had made.

Louisa said, "Your boy speaks for those others now."

Netta looked down at her hands. They were red and puffy from the work.

"I miss him, too," Louisa said. "But I'm trying to forget more than one name."

"What if there was no boundary anymore?" Netta asked. "What if we let the fields go, let the house go, too?"

Louisa closed the book and ran her hands over the cover. "We'd need a new map," she said.

SUMMER 1890

JUST SOUTH OF what had been the beet patch, a young man wearing a sack suit and bowler hat stepped out of the woods and onto the trail. He took a long canvas bag off his shoulder and laid it gently on the grass, then brushed himself off, taking special care to remove all the burrs from his striped trousers. Next he took a compass from his pocket, looked at it, looked at the hotel on top of the mountain, and shook his head.

His name was Cyrus Makely, and he was lost.

The trail edged fields of sickly vegetation, one crop verging indiscriminately upon another. If not for the ribbon of smoke rising from the chimney of the farmhouse, he would have thought the place was abandoned. He hefted his equipment and followed the trail toward the house, passing a caved-in barn, and something that might once have been a chicken coop.

The house was built of the yellow stone he had seen used in the older Dutch homes in town. But this building's gable roof was sunken, its latticework broken and bare. The house was slumped to one side, staring at itself in the green-rimmed pool to the east—or was it the southeast? All his readings had been off since he stepped into those woods, and now the sun was nearly touching the top of the mountain. Cyrus thought again that he should have taken his father's advice and applied for the post in Tarrytown, closer to New York, to civilization.

He climbed the steps and crossed the creaking porch to the door. It swung inward at his knock. He nudged it farther and called into the dim hall beyond. No answer, but at the opposite end of the house he saw a room bright with orange light. He walked over wide black floorboards to a cluttered kitchen, warm with steam from a kettle over the fire. On the table, baskets of strawberries, raspberries, and red mulberries were encircled by heaps of tomatoes, cabbage, bush beans, muskmelon, and ears of Indian corn. Here was a great block of cheese, a loaf of black bread, a bowl overflowing with cherries, crystals of red sugar candy clinging to pieces of string.

How hungry he was, and on the table an empty plate! He plucked strawberries from the basket, tore pieces of bread from the loaf, cut chunks of cheese and set them on the plate. Then he grew impatient, and put the food straight into his mouth instead, using his fingers to push slices of musk-melon over his tongue, taking cherries by the handful and spitting out the pits.

He was reaching for more when a girl in a dirty blue housedress stepped out of the pantry. Cyrus got up and stepped away from the table. He swept his hat off his head and tried to apologize, but his mouth was full.

The girl's hair was black and straight, and Cyrus thought

she must be part Iroquois, though he had never seen their women, only a few of their men laying railway track along the river. "Sit," she said. She walked past him and took a pitcher from the shelf, poured water into a cup.

Cyrus swallowed the food in his mouth and sat down. "My name is Cyrus Makely," he said. "I was lost."

The girl pushed the cup into his hand. "You still are."

The water was clear and cool. He quickly finished the cup, and the girl refilled it from the pitcher. "You must be tired," she said.

He was tired. And the air in the kitchen was so warm and still. It felt like a little world of its own, separate from the whole of the earth, complete in spite of it. He felt he could sleep right there, sleep for a very long time.

But then he remembered his employers, Mr. Pennell and Mr. O'Hern, and his employer's employers, Mr. Mairs and Mr. Lewis, and their client, Mr. Beach, the owner of the Mountain House. They were going to build a train, a new kind of train to go straight up the mountain. But none of the work could begin until Cyrus brought them his measurements. For a land surveyor, getting lost was a very poor excuse.

He stood and faced the girl. She had been so kind, surely she would understand that he was expected elsewhere. He would ask her the way to town, offer to come back and pay for the food he had eaten.

She came closer, stood so her nose nearly touched his cravat. She whispered, "There are rules, Cyrus Makely. I saw you come out of the woods. You've eaten in this house and I know your name."

A woman came into the kitchen from the garden door. Her thick gray hair was gathered in a bun at the top of her head. She had large hands, and in one of those hands was an ax, the blade smeared with blood and feathers. She was the most terrifying thing Cyrus had ever seen.

"I caught one," the girl said to her.

Cyrus ran. In a moment he was out of the kitchen and away down the hall. But his escape was blocked by a man who stood on the porch on one leg. His other leg, a thick wooden post with a great black boot mounted to one end, was in his hands.

From the hallway, the girl shouted, "Roel, no!"

With a thoughtful-sounding grunt the one-legged man heaved the muddy boot in the air and swung it as Cyrus had seen railroad workers swing hammers at spikes. It was a remarkable display of balance, and the boot struck him squarely on top of his head.

⌒

Cyrus Makely dreamed he had to memorize the names of twenty tribes of savages. If he succeeded, the chiefs would tell him how to measure the earth using only water, a thimble, and a piece of string. If he failed, they would pluck out his eyes and make them into toys for their daughters.

"I know so few of your names," Cyrus admitted.

"Only think of a map," one of the chiefs counseled him. "Your people name places for what they killed there."

FALL 1890

ON CLEAR MORNINGS, the mountains looked so close that Cyrus felt he could reach out and touch them, could burn his hand on those wild red ranges. He liked to linger in his room as long as he could, breathing the cool air from the window, listening to the crows in the old barn, counting the boarder's footsteps on the floor above. He would wait until he heard Roel's leg on the steps, then dress and go downstairs to breakfast.

By the time he returned from his work in the fields each day, the lights of the hotel were gleaming on the peak. Seeing them made him feel he had forgotten something, something important. But then the spirits lit their lanterns in the pines, and looking at those lights made him forget his forgetfulness.

"Don't stare too long," Louisa once warned, so when he did look at the lanterns, he counted to twenty and turned away. He did a lot of counting. Sixty-eight days that he'd lived with Roel and Netta. Thirteen steps from the landing to the ground floor. Eleven times Louisa had looked at him. Six that he'd heard her speak.

When she did say anything to him, it was to warn about the dangers on the farm. It was bad to walk alone in the fields past the old barn. Worse to wake Netta from one of her sleeps. The little boots beside the bed stayed where they were. And when Louisa had to enter or leave the attic, he should step into the hall so she could pass through the bedroom without him there.

He remembered standing with her in the kitchen, once, and her face was close to his. She seemed to want something of him, then. He wasn't sure he'd ever known what it was, but he wished he could remember.

~

IN THE PARLOR one night, he came upon a stout old book left open to a series of journal entries written in dull brown ink.

May 2. Warm and clear. Mended the fence and cleaned the chicken house.

May 3. Went to town today. Bought powder, but didn't see anybody I wanted to see. They asked after Sofia and I told them.

May 4. An Indian girl came out of the woods. She says she used to live on the mountaintop, but she had to leave when men came and built their roads on it. Says she was some sort of queen up there. I've made her a room at the top of the house, and she'll do cooking and cleaning in exchange. I asked her if that was the sort of work a queen could get used to, and she said she wanted to forget the good things. I told her this was the right place for it.

May 5. Went along the border this morning. Figured out they like: scrap wood & metal, buttons, sweets, worn boots. Do not like: worn clothes, day-old bread, jam.

~

ROEL CAME INTO the room and found him reading. "My grandfather cleared this land," he said, "though the house is older." He showed Cyrus a map of the farm, pointed out the black square where the house stood, the boundary winding its way through the wilds. "The fields were bought from the natives for twenty beaver pelts, two casks of rum, five rifles, and a knife for each of the braves. It's cost us more than that, in the end, but we need that border, if only to pretend there's something that divides."

Cyrus knew what he meant, and knew better than to ask. On his first night in the house, after Roel had struck him with the boot on his wooden leg, Cyrus woke in the little room at the end of the hall. Netta brought him tea and sweet cakes, and Roel, twisting his hat in his hands, stood in the doorway and apologized as best he could. "I mistook you," was what he said.

Then, in the morning, Netta presented him with his bowler hat—she'd mended the tear on the top with black felt. All the wood in that room was gleaming in the sunlight, and Cyrus, still unfamiliar with the rules, had asked her why it was so clean there.

"Our son William was running out of ways to hurt us," she said. "This was his room, and this was where he found one more way." Her face did something funny then, and she sat down on the polished floor and went to sleep.

ROEL AND CYRUS worked a long day in the farthest field. They were silent through the morning because of the rule they had, silent through the afternoon because by then they were used to the quiet. When the cart was loaded with as much squash, turnips, and beets as Mule could pull, they sat on a rock and smoked a pipe together.

Men were working out on the Wall of Manitou. Below the hotel, the slope bore a great vertical scar, a black trench between ridges of red trees, and every minute another tree fell and was dragged down the mountain.

Seeing this, Cyrus felt a strangeness come over him. The stone was beneath him, Roel's pipe smoke was in the air, yet he knew he was not in the field with Roel, not on the farm at all. He was on the mountainside with those other men, checking their work against a map he had somehow made.

Roel saw Cyrus squinting, saw his hand shaking a little when he took the pipe. But Cyrus didn't say anything about it, and Roel didn't ask.

The strangeness lessened as they walked Mule back along the marches. Netta's stew helped, and so did a few hands of cards with Roel. But when Cyrus went upstairs, he fetched the canvas sack from under the bed and laid its contents over the mattress.

He'd brought this sack downstairs one morning, and asked if it was something the spirits wanted, but Roel had broken the rule to say to him, "You'd be an idiot to part with your tools, Cyrus Makely."

His tools? He touched each of them, trying to understand. There was an instrument that looked like a telescope, another he recognized as a magnetic compass, a little book full of numbers and charts. He put them back under the bed and went to the window. The lanterns were back in the pines.

ON THE LAST night of the harvest, Louisa came into Cyrus's room without knocking. He got up to leave but she blocked his way and looked him in the eyes. It was the twelfth time she had done so. She said, "You have work to do," and Cyrus thought, seven.

She took his shirtsleeve and led him to the attic door. He had put his ear to it, once, to listen to her singing, but he had never dared to open it. Now she opened it for him and took him up the stairs.

The attic was lit with the yellow glow from the lanterns outside. The light reached everywhere, making long mazy shadows over the rafters. In the farthest alcove was Louisa's room—a mattress on the floor, a chest of drawers, a desk. Louisa lit a candle and Cyrus saw a book, a page dominated by an ornate letter F. Below was a drawing of the sun setting on—or rising over—a broad meadow. *F is for forget*, the legend read.

"I've been learning my letters," said Louisa.

Cyrus flipped to the first pages and read aloud, "A is for absence. B is for bulwark. C is for ca . . . cac . . ."

"Cacophony," Louisa finished. "Netta made it for me. The more I learn, the more I forget. The alphabet helps a lot. But it's time for you to remember some things, Cyrus Makely. There isn't much for you and me in this world together until I finish my forgetting and you finish your remembering. Do you understand?"

He was too bewildered to speak, too afraid that he would say the wrong thing and be marched back downstairs. He asked, "Does it have to do with your mother? Was it her mother who came to this farm from the mountaintop?"

She frowned and shook her head. "Questions distract,"

she said. "Truth, now. You've forgotten how to use your instruments."

She stood close to him, just as she'd done that day in the kitchen. "You were going to help build a train," she whispered. "They've started without you. It will go straight up the side of the mountain, drawn by cables. You told me about it in your sleep, when you first came here."

He rubbed the top of his head with his hand. "A new kind of train," he said.

Louisa kissed him. It was a careful kiss, but Cyrus didn't mind. He thought: *One*.

She stepped back and looked at him, waiting as though for a transformation of some kind. And Cyrus remembered. Remembered the steamship ride up the Hudson, remembered landing at that odd little town on the creek: the boardinghouse above the tavern, the drunks in the street who argued over which of them owned the fattest hog. Then the long trip up the mountain with other guests of the hotel (how they'd complained about the jouncing stagecoach!), his meeting with Mr. Beach on the promontory, their plans for the elevated railway.

"It's beautiful on the mountaintop," he said to Louisa. "I'll take you there. We'll stay at the hotel and walk the trail to the waterfall, and when we come back there'll be dancing in the ballroom. There is nothing like the view. You can see three states from up there. Or is it four? I guess it depends on whether you count this one."

"I count none of them," Louisa said. "Do you remember how to use your instruments?"

"Triangles," Cyrus said, surprised and a little giddy.

"Triangulation. You have to look at the same thing from two different places. That's how you know where it sits on the earth."

"Good," she said. "But there are rules, so listen close."

⸺

A YOUNG MAN wearing a sack suit and a bowler hat walked the trail along the fetid fields, a canvas bag slung over his shoulder. He went to the only place on the farm where anything grew. The meadow was emptied of its crops now, and only brush and stalk remained.

Cyrus checked his compass and saw that north was keeping true. He took the tripod out of the bag and set it on its feet, placed the theodolite on top. It was a clear day, and even without it he could see straight across the fields. He made some notes, then peered through the lens. There was the caved-in barn, there the old chicken house. He also saw, coming toward him over the field, a young boy, shirtless and barefoot.

When Cyrus looked with his naked eye, the field was empty. When he looked through the theodolite again, the boy was only a few feet away. "Do you need some help?" the boy asked.

Cyrus reached into his bag and pulled out a small pair of boots. He'd broken a rule when he brought them. He tossed them onto the ground, and once the boy had them on and laced, Cyrus could see him plainly.

"I do need your help. Do you think you can help me see it the way it was before? Before your great-grandfather cleared the fields?"

The boy was happy with his boots. "What's your name?" he asked.

"I don't remember," Cyrus said.

The boy stopped smiling. "Liar," he said. "Bed-stealer. They don't love you, you know. She doesn't love you."

Cyrus shrugged and made some more notes. "It's still morning," he said, "so we probably shouldn't be talking. We're not allowed to talk in the morning."

"That's a stupid rule," the boy said. He held his chin up, and Cyrus could see the red line beneath it. He went on with his work while the boy paced back and forth beside him, getting impatient. "Do you know why they made that rule?" he asked.

Cyrus shook his head.

"It's because of me. It's because we always argued in the morning."

"What about?"

The boy shrugged. "I don't know." He looked suddenly bashful. "What's it like, now?" he asked. "In the morning, I mean. Without me there."

Cyrus looked out over the fields. "It's quiet," he said. "Your mom makes breakfast. She looks at your dad like she's mad about something, and he pretends not to notice. But it's warm in the kitchen, and the kettle's on the stove. Sometimes you can hear the boarder upstairs, singing."

The boy looked where Cyrus was looking. "Has Louisa finished her forgetting yet?" he asked.

"Almost."

The boy bent down to clean a speck of mud off his boot. "I guess I could help you," he said. "I wish you would tell me your name, though."

Cyrus didn't respond, but when he next looked through the lens, the lifeless fields were gone. In their place he saw one great meadow, green and shadowed by a few tall pines. The sun was at its edge. It was the meadow from Louisa's book, and he still couldn't tell if the sun was rising or setting.

⁓

ROEL AND CYRUS took the cart into town, stopping often to move fallen limbs off the road. No one had been this way in a long time, and there were a lot of limbs to move.

When they arrived at the market, it was no longer morning, and Roel said, "I have something for you." He reached under his seat and pulled out his grandfather's journal. "I've read it a dozen times, but maybe you can make better sense of it."

Cyrus opened the book. He's seen several parts of it, but now he turned to the last page and read the entry for September 29, 1843:

What a fool I've been! They don't light the lights. They are the lights.

He closed the book and set it beside the other things in his bag, then hopped down from the cart. The map was in his coat pocket; he unfolded it and showed it to Roel.

Roel blinked at the paper and it shook in his hands. "Why did you do this?" he asked.

It wasn't the question Cyrus expected. Why? Because Louisa wanted it, because all three of them wanted it, he'd thought. He said, "So you can stop pretending. So you can talk in the mornings again."

Roel got down off the cart and stood close to Cyrus, began to unstrap his leg. "I knew you from the start," he said.

Cyrus took a step back and Roel swung at him, but his eyes were watery and he missed. "I didn't mistake you," Roel said. He hopped on his one leg, and with his next swing he fell to the street. Tears were on his face.

"My boy!" Roel shouted into the bricks. He said to Cyrus, "I knew what you were from the start."

Cyrus avoided the eyes of the gathering townsfolk. Roel tried to pull himself up with his leg, but fell again. He was still on the ground when Cyrus turned and started walking faster.

Winter 1890

It was too cold to sleep in the attic, so Louisa spread her blankets on the kitchen floor near the stove. She would tend the fire through the night, then make breakfast before the others woke. While Roel sharpened his tools and Netta read or patched clothes, Louisa knitted. She often forgot what she was doing, though, and once she made something that was a sock at one end, a cap at the other, and a scarf in the middle.

She made a game out of counting the number of times Netta nodded off each day. The woman spent more time asleep than awake now. She still cooked and cleaned, but she did it all with her eyes closed, and not very well. She talked in her sleep, too. One day she asked Louisa, "Do you remember when I was a little girl, and you told me how you used to cut up the old moons into stars?"

"No," Louisa said. "I don't remember that."

They put Mule in the pantry, and he was happy to lie there with a sack of potatoes for a pillow. He was old, though, and when Louisa went to feed him one morning, she found him dead. It took all three of them to drag him out into the snow.

LOUISA OFTEN THOUGHT of the land surveyor. His new map was hung in the parlor, and he'd given her his compass before he left. She thought maybe she could use it to find him, but it must have been broken. It always pointed in the same direction.

On sunny days, she strapped on her skates and went out to the pond. The sweep of the blades over the ice made her feel she was forgetting something, and that made her smile, though she didn't know why.

It was on one of those days that she saw Roel shoveling snow off the front steps, saw the boy walk out of the woods and right up to the porch. He wasn't wearing a shirt, but he didn't seem to mind the cold. "Can I help you now?" he said.

Roel leaned forward on his shovel, closed his eyes. He was quiet a long time. "Yes," he said.

The boy kicked snow with his boot, waiting.

Roel said, "Yes, William, you can help now."

Later, she found their prints in the snow leading away toward the woods. She went inside to tell Netta this, but Netta was asleep on the stairs.

⁓

LOUISA WAS IN bed one morning, sitting up with a book on her lap. She stayed in Netta's room now. Roel had been gone three days, but at night Louisa heard the thump of his wooden leg downstairs. The rhythm was too quick, though, and she thought someone other than Roel must have been wearing it.

Netta was asleep and seemed happy to stay that way. She talked a little but wouldn't eat, and appeared most content when Louisa read to her. She hadn't opened her eyes since Roel left.

Louisa read, "H is for happenstance. I is for indisposed. J is for jinx."

She heard a knock at the front door and the noise startled her from bed. She couldn't remember the last time someone had knocked. She went downstairs to answer it, smoothing her dress with her palms.

A young man stood on the porch, hat in hand. The snow was gone, and a carriage was waiting in the yard.

"I thought I would never get my job back," Cyrus said. "But it turns out they're building trains everywhere these days."

"Why are you here, then?" she asked.

He fiddled nervously with his hat. "I forgot my compass," he said.

SUMMER 1899

DESPITE HIS FAMILIARITY with the railway, Mr. Makely found the ride up the mountain unsettling. It was the groaning of the iron cables that troubled him—they seemed always about to burst. Mrs. Makely, however, didn't mind that at all. She turned round and round in her seat, looking for the best view of the valley.

It was their anniversary. A few nights before, he had found her in the sitting room of their town house, reading the old journal Roel had given him. Over her shoulder he read

May 8. The Indian girl's a decent cook. She wouldn't tell me her name, said she needs a new one anyway. I told her she could have my mother's, and Sophie's old blue dress, too. When she finishes forgetting things, she says, she'll start to grow old. I told her not to hurry.

"Such strange people," Louisa had said. "Who were they?"

He caressed her shoulder. "I'm not sure I could tell you," he said.

On the stone promontory in front of the hotel, Mr. Beach's sons had mounted a great electric spotlight. It served some practical purpose, but management allowed the guests to use it to play games of tag with steamboats on the river twelve miles away.

"They look like boots with cigars stuck in them," a drunken guest explained.

When Mrs. Makely's turn with the spotlight came, Cyrus pulled a notebook from his pocket. "I did some calculations," he said. "If you aim it a little to the left, about fifty degrees below the horizon, you should be able to touch the old farmstead."

Either she didn't hear him, or didn't understand. She

pointed the great finger of light at the river and almost immediately found a steamship. The boat flashed its own light, as if to signal surrender, and the other guests on the promontory cheered.

"I caught one," she said.

Jedediah Berry's stories have been published in journals such as *Fairy Tale Review*, *3rd Bed,* and *La Petite Zine*, and he writes book reviews for *Rain Taxi*. Another story is forthcoming in the Datlow/Windling anthology, *The Coyote Road: Trickster Tales.*

He is an associate editor for Small Beer Press in Northampton, Massachusetts, and also serves as an associate editor of *Conjunctions*. He recently completed a novel, *The Manual of Detection*, about a file clerk who must outwit a pair of homicidal twin brothers and a beguiling ex–fortune-teller in order to solve a mystery involving sleepwalking criminals and dream detectives.

A Gray and Soundless Tide

Catherynne M. Valente

THIS IS MY skin. This is my skin; take it from me.

SHE USED TO wander up and down the strand crying that, barking it like a fishwife with a hip-basket full of cod. I remember her that way, her stride like a prayer, a plea, her hair plastered wet and snarled against her waist, against a dress so thin it was more a hazy dream of what a dress might be than linen or wool. She walked, paced, clutching a gray bundle to her chest. Sometimes she would thrust it at passersby, who shrunk from her as though she held out a dead child in her arms.

It was winter, and a scrim of salt and ice lay like bones on the sea-battered road—it was winter, and I was bringing home four fat fish, half-frozen and wrapped in brown paper, when she thrust that pitiful gray thing at me.

It stuck to my hands in a moment, mottled and rubbery, sliding over my wrists as though looking for a way in, a way around. It pulled at me, and I meant to pull away, I meant to give her a coin and keep my eyes on my feet and my fish, but it pulled at me, like water, like warm, sweet water, and I looked up at her.

"This is my skin," she said, "take it from me." Her eyes had no irises—they were all pupil, bottomless black, and her skin had no real color: she was nothing but gray and dark, pressed roughly as pages, one against the other. Her hair was strung with ocean-slime; its curls left green tracks across her calves.

"Take it," she whispered, and her hands closed over mine, the skin moving between us, writhing like a well-fed animal.

I don't know why I took it—why of all the women who walk that pockmarked road in the mornings, arms full of fish and beef and needles and wax, I took her bundle from her, I put my arm around her, and stumbled, just a little, as she fell into me, wild and exhausted as a near-drowned cat.

⌒

FOR DAYS, SHE said nothing. I brought her home, stray-dog-she, and my husband looked at her with eye-whites gleaming. He sighed, took her bundle away and hid it up under the rafters in the rear room, near the damp straw.

"That is where it goes, Dyveke," he said quietly. "Didn't you ever read a book? Don't let her find it."

"She wanted me to have it," I mumbled. She was quiet as a blue-shelled mussel in the tide, standing between us like a scolded daughter.

She sat watching the fire every night. Rain spattered against the windows and her skin dried. She leaned her head against the walls, as if listening, always listening. My feet came home mud-slashed each day; hers were always white, so white, as if she had no blood in her. I washed the slime from her hair in a tin basin, and she let me touch her, placid as a pool, her skin cold and yielding. Under it, she was beautiful, like a scrubbed length of sun-bleached wood.

She ate my salted soup, but she would not touch meat, not the smallest fish or fowl.

At night, she lay between us like water, a stream flowing between two mountains. I lay my arm across her waist, and as I wandered toward sleep, I seemed to sink into her, as though she were made of sleet and sand and nothing more. She lay between us, infant-hunched, and her hands curled around her hair at night, so that she woke crying, pressed against me, pulling pale her own scalp. The linen was damp with her tears, damp and salty, as if she dragged the sea with her into our bed.

I did not press her—she haunted my house like a ghost, but I did not ask even her name. I liked her there—her smell, her silent shuffling on the floorboards. I gave her a blue dress belted in white, and braided her hair in the mornings. Once, she pushed a strand of my dull red hair behind my ear, an almost mothering gesture—but that was all she gave me. All she gave me until the rain stopped and the snow came soundless against the door.

My husband went to sink a line into the ice, and bring up fish like a jeweler's fist of silver. We did not go out. She sat nearer to the fire than she ever had, and the light played on her skin, red hands over her face, blood moving underneath skin that had never been warm, never, in all these months.

She did not look at me when she spoke, and her voice was like shells crushed underfoot.

"I wanted to be kept," she whispered. "I wanted to know what it was like. All the others, it was so easy for them—a wide-knuckled hand appeared in the water and pulled them up by the hair. Or they slid out of themselves in sight of a sailor, who caught it up between his fingers—and those skins shone in the sun! Air strung through with fire! It was so easy, and they came running back into the surf with black-eyed babies, black-eyed babies with fat little hands. Then the fists would come breaking through the waves again, and haul up the children, and the screams, the screams were swallowed up by the cold current—my father, Dyveke, my father pulled me up out of the salt and the sea and my mother's breast when I was so young I couldn't yet open my eyes in the sunlight."

She stared into the fire, and her hands were washed in red.

"He raised me up to be a good girl, after a fashion. He called me Silja. He called me his darling girl, his pup, his lovely. And every day he took me out on his boat, which stunk of entrails and watery blood and which always needed a new coat of paint. Every day he took me out and we hunted the seals. He taught me to throw his great harpoon—so long and heavy that I almost fell overboard into the water with its weight the first time I hefted it. He shook me against the side of the boat and told me for the hundredth time never to go in, never to go into the water, never to let myself fall. And he steadied my arm, and with his strong hands on mine, brown and brine-streaked, smelling of whiskey and salmon's blood, I threw it after a dark shape cutting the sea in two. He was proud when he roasted that wet flesh in the night; he cut it for me into neat little pieces, and made sure I ate every bite. It tasted rich and sour, like sweet butter gone rancid in the heat. He patted my head; I was such a good girl. His Silja, a natural fisherman, just like him. The seals fueled our lamps, oiled our leather, kept us warm.

"One morning, when I was thirteen, he woke me when the light was a coughing spatter of gray across the flat sea, and in the wet fog he bundled me up, and with the harpoon we climbed into the boat. He had sighted a seal, he said—a great spotted black cow with flippers like oars. We tracked it through the thin-clouded noon and into twilight—that terrible twilight, with the moon like a wound in the sky! The seal's head broke the foam just before us, a smooth stone bobbing up from the depths. He guided my arm as always, and I smelled his familiar sharp smell.

"I wish now it had been harder than it was. The harpoon slid out of my sure grip, and stuck into the broad back of the seal, that strong, flaring back, rippling in the last light. Blood slid black into the sea. My father hauled the corpse into his little boat, staggering with the weight. He shoved it, whisker by belly, into a canvas sack, and knotted a rough rope over those depthless eyes.

"That night he sent me to fetch whiskey from the tavern while he cooked our day's catch. I brought it sloshing in a bottle of coppery glass, and again he cut my meat for me, smiling, his yellowed teeth snatching the light of the low fire. We ate without talking, and again the meat was rich, rich but somehow sour, and I thought for the hundredth time that I did not really prefer seal, and wished my father hunted squid or cod instead. But in the night, in the sweat-ridden night, I felt sick, so sick, somewhere deep in the center of me, as though I would vomit up my heart. I crawled from my bed and my sealskin covers, trying to find the basin in the dark—and in the last bloody embers I saw the sack that had brought home the great black seal.

"I do not know why I went to it, Dyveke—it was nothing more than a dead seal, like all the other dead seals that waited for skinning in the corners of our house. But I went to it, and I opened the knots of the rough rope, and I did not cry out, for all the voice had left me.

"In the limp canvas was a woman, her flesh carved open and raw, long strands of black hair plastered with blood, her slim hips cut open like the wings of some strange insect—and open and staring, open and staring, those black, depthless eyes. I rocked backward on my heels, breathing in slashes, keening, clutching at my elbows."

I stared at her, her own dark eyes, dark as dying, eyes that never blinked, even as she began to rock back and forth in my old rocking chair, just a little, touching her fingers to her forearms.

"My father caught me up in his arms then, and I shrieked, but no sound came. He smoothed my hair and crooned in my ear, slurred and slippery:

'Now you'll never leave me, you'll never leave, my pretty Silja. I chased her all these years and finally, finally I caught her—she couldn't stay away, you know, she kept swimming around, close to the harbor, trying to see you. I seized her out of the tide, the tide like a bridal bower, years ago, and she gave me a daughter, she gave me such a pretty girl—the baby just slid out of her, and there was no blood, no blood at all, only seawater. But then one morning she was gone—just gone!—like she had never deepened the bed. But I found her, I found her, just like I found you, and now you'll never go, you'll never run back into the sea to find her, because they wouldn't take you, no, no, you've eaten their flesh, just like us, the rotten, stupid fishermen they lie to, they lie and lie and abandon, whores, whores on the harbor or under it, there's no difference. Oh, my Silja, now you're mine, my own daughter and not hers, not hers, and you'll never leave me, never, never.'

"He kissed my hair and stroked it, whispering, his hands hot on my belly, wrapped around me, and I tried to tear away, away from him like paper ripping, but he was so strong. I beat him with my little fists, crying silently and clawing, until he finally let go and I ran, I ran so far, out of the house and down the road, past the tavern and the market, and my stomach folded over on itself, but I kept running, I kept running until I reached the sea, and the moon was on it like an eye. I leapt into the froth and waded out until the sand gave way beneath me and I let myself fall into the dark. I didn't know whether or not I would drown, and I admit—Dyveke, I admit it, I was sorry when I felt my skin stretch and open, when I felt the water rush over new flesh, when my mouth narrowed and became a muzzle, and my limbs disappeared into a long black body, spotted and sleek."

"But, then . . . why would you ever have come back?" I choked through a throat thick as wool. "Why did you walk back and forth like that, trying to give your skin away?"

Silja spread her hands, her pale, wide hands that were not unlike the fringe of a seal's flippers.

"He was right. They would not take me. I swam beside them but they would not speak; I barked in the moonlight but they would not answer me. They could smell it somehow, what I had done, and even when we sat on the desolate rocks in our women's skins, they stared at me through stringy black hair, silent, accusing.

"But I didn't know, Dyveke. You have to believe me, I didn't know." Her voice snagged on the air and tears began to slip down her cheeks.

Carefully, as if reaching out to pet a wild fox, I folded her into my arms—she weighed nothing at all. "Of course you didn't know," I murmured, "how could you know?"

"This is the only story selkies have," she said, her lips against my neck, "It is all they know: how to be kept, how to be found, how to escape. It was so easy for them, but somehow the sailors and the fishermen and the drunken men looking for whores on the boardwalk could smell it, too. They did not want my skin. I couldn't have a story; no one would come near me, they could see my mother hanging off of me like a mourner's dress.

"Except you. You didn't see her. You took my skin from me, and you kept me, and you warmed me between your body and his all through the rain."

⌒

SHE LAY BETWEEN us like water, and slept in my arms. Every now and then I pulled her hands from her hair, and she did not cry in her sleep. Over and over, I whispered her name:

Silja.

Silja.

⌒

IN THE MORNING, she was gone, and my husband lay in my arms like a changeling. She left nothing behind her—she had brought nothing with her to leave. A few stray pieces of straw lay on the floor of the rear room.

⌒

IT WAS A long while before I stopped setting a place for her, before I stopped seeing her hunched over the fire every time I blinked. For a while I cursed my husband that he did not hide the skin better—he only holds me until I am quiet, holds my head to him and asks again, so gently, if I have not read books. I whisper her name into his chest:

Silja.

Every morning I go to get fish, fish wrapped in brown paper, their moisture seeping through into my sleeve. I stand on the strand where she walked, waiting for her to begin her old cry. She is not there, but the air that carried her still seems to hold her shape. She escaped; and sometimes I think that this will be enough, that she is surrounded by black-eyed sisters with fat pups at their teats, listening to her story with glistening eyes. Sometimes I think that she is alone, deep in the cold, dragging her mother's corpse behind her, and no one will hear her, no one will take her tale from her like a skin.

I look for her every day; I look out over a gray and soundless tide, and I think—yes, that is her, that dark head cresting the waves. That is my Silja, and if I wait, if I can only wait long enough, she will come walking up onto the sand, the ends of her long hair leaving green tracks across her calves.

By the time I get home, my boots are sopping with mud, mud and melted snow.

Catherynne M. Valente is the author of The Orphan's Tales series, as well as *The Labyrinth, Yume no Hon: The Book of Dreams, The Grass-Cutting Sword*, and two books of poetry, *Apocrypha* and *Oracles*. She lives in Norfolk, Virginia with her husband and two dogs.

Concealment Shoes

❧

Marly Youmans

Princess Owl was twitching her ears, one at a time.

Her dignity had been assaulted and torn into interesting small tatters that made the Arnold children laugh.

"Did you see—"

James, the youngest, rolled on the floor, making a sound that his fourteen-year-old sister Beatrice recognized as chortling, though she'd never heard such a thing before. It made her laugh the harder.

"She was flying!" Beatrice shouted, wiping her eyes.

It was true; the Princess Owl had been flying, and in the most undignified manner. She had stamped on rainbow after rainbow, pinwheeling until she seemed a dark-and-tawny storm. Her tail was puffed with excitement.

The cries lured their mother to the door.

"Ouch! You're stabbing my poor ears with needles," she said. "Beatrice, you're so shrill! What was funny?"

They thought it a bit dramatic. Grown-ups were like that: dramatic over stupid things.

"The Owl, she—"

James leaped, whirling about until he collapsed on the floor.

"What?" Their mother was laughing at him now.

"The rainbow-caster," Beatrice said, pointing to the window where she had fastened the gift from her now-faraway friend, Rose.

"Oh! Well, she looks offended," her mother said. "Deeply offended."

The Princess Owl was gazing into the middle distance without blinking, her golden eyes perfectly round and innocent. The feathery boa of her tail was curled over her toes, and only a slight twitch of the ear betrayed any interest in the prismatic lights that were taking angelic glides across the ceiling. At her feet, more of them made a teasing, slow slippage.

As the sun increased, she cocked her head to look as the bars of color began flying to and from the turning prism.

"Look at her face," James whispered.

The Owl was giving tiny jerks of the head, as though gripped by a bout of cat-chiropracty. Her skin rippled. Up on her feet as if by magic, she swooped sideways and pounced on a rainbow; it colored her paws for an instant before sweeping away. The crystal blazed like a star, and the lights began their carousel slide to and fro.

"Poor kitty," their mother said, but she didn't make them stop laughing. "Quit tormenting the cat and come help."

But they didn't want to help their parents and Francis, who were doing nothing more interesting than lugging boxes and emptying out the contents. Half the floor space in the old cookhouse, soon to be the playroom, was obliterated by stacks of cartons. An enticing jungle gym for cats, they bulked almost to the ceiling. Princess Owl, indignant once more, surged from box to box until she was high above them.

"She's going to jump on us," James howled. "She's up on the cliffs, and she's going to attack." He wrenched an imaginary set of pistols from his hips and began shooting with both forefingers at once.

"No, she's not. But she does look like she might. She wants to leap on the ceiling," Beatrice said.

The Princess Owl sprang into the air, her paws barely brushing a rainbow before it shot back toward the prism. She landed splay-legged on the brink of a carton, shook the look of confusion from her face, and began grooming her tail as though nothing at all had happened.

"Come on," Beatrice said. "Let's go explore."

They squeezed behind the mass of boxes, pressing close to the walls and stopping to look out of the rear windows.

"That's probably where the cookhouse garbage got tossed," Beatrice told her brother. "That's what Dad said. We can do digs there and find old busted pottery and clay marbles and stuff."

"We could tear up the whole yard."

"Yeah."

But now the lawn blazed with snow, and it hurt their eyes everywhere but in the blue shadow from the cookhouse.

They kept going, the wallpaper catching against their

clothes and ripping a little, though they didn't pay attention. The tunnel around the walls ended close to a door into the mudroom and kitchen.

"We never had a mudroom before."

"It's a Yankee thing," Beatrice said. "The North is a very dirty place, did you know that?"

Yes, he knew it; he knew everything, or else it went into his mind quick, like a wink, so very quick that James thought that he surely must have known each new piece of information already. This was something that annoyed Beatrice. Now in third grade, James believed that he knew enough, and that it was time to stay home with Mama and quit bothering with school. It disturbed him that his mother had a different idea. She worked at home; why couldn't he?

"Let's play hide-and-seek." James didn't wait for his sister to agree but charged off yelling, "Count to twenty!"

Beatrice glanced at the Owl, who was still parked on top of the mesa of boxes but had relaxed into the meatloaf position, paws pulled under and tail swept close to her body. A ruff of fur stood out around her head.

"You adorable, stupid cat," she whispered.

Princess Owl blinked at her, looking for all the world like the Sphinx, ready to pop an unanswerable question.

Darting from the room, Beatrice moved swiftly around the house, scaling the steep back staircase that climbed from the kitchen and weaving in and out of the upstairs rooms. Nothing. She avoided the master bedroom, where her parents and Francis were at work. In the case of her older brother, this was an astonishing fact, suggestive of dire threats or the discovery of powerful foreign magics. Later on he would be sure to blame her for not tugging trunks and cartons around the house, though the mere thought of it gave her a dizzying sensation of light hysteria. The towers of boxes with their secret tunnels made her feel younger, as if she could play and play and never get tired of winding through a secret world.

"Beatrice?"

When she heard her father's voice, she plunged down the front staircase, leapfrogging the last five steps to land by the enormous, squat newel post that resembled a black chess queen. Now she was in the oldest portion of the house. Soon her parents would have a bicentennial party; they'd already decided, though they didn't know exactly how old the house was. Beatrice thought that this was rather silly. What if they didn't like anybody in Templeton, or nobody liked them?

She kicked off her shoes. James could be right in front of her, creeping through one of the crooked passageways between moving boxes; she'd never know. She held her breath and listened: nothing but a faint ringing in her ears and the low voices of her parents from upstairs.

"James?" Usually the name would make him squirm and laugh out loud, and then she could catch him. But it had been a long time since they had played hide-and-seek. He didn't make a sound.

The wide boards of pumpkin pine felt silky against her socks. She tiptoed through the living room, past the fireplace that plunged into the cellar where it metamorphosed into something gigantic—a hearth of boulders with elephantine walls and a Dutch oven, all whitewashed. The guest room had already been set up with the brass bed where her grandmother had been born and the bird's eye maple furniture that had belonged to an aunt of her mother's. She peeked behind the bed and an upholstered chair but found nothing but a few Styrofoam peanuts.

Back in the center hall, she glanced both ways and veered through the butler's pantry to the dining room. She could feel James close by, a bundle of energy about to explode and give himself away.

"Oh, James, James, Jamie-boy," she cooed. They were not much of a family for nicknames. Nicknames were for Yankees who couldn't be bothered with saying a person's whole name, their mother said. She hated it when they called her "Sue" instead of "Susanna." Of course, their father was a Yankee, so he had a nickname. "Tom." They didn't mind, if that was what he wanted.

She grazed her fingers along the big Empire buffet with the three tassels tied to keys for the three doors. Some of her father's antique toys were already in the display case a few feet away. How silly! James hadn't had any underwear this morning, but the toys had already been unpacked. In fact, her little brother—wherever he might be—was wearing the black jeans and long-sleeved shirt that he'd had on a day ago.

She crawled over boxes that had been heaped against the paneled door. In the corner was a built-in corner cupboard. After opening the bottom, she knelt down but found nothing inside but a moth flung on its back, legs crimped in death. She let her fingers bump along the tops of two steam radiators under the windows, and stopped to peer outside at the dollops of snow on rectangles of holly and privet. Her mother was going to grub up the shrubs, come spring, and put in a cottage garden. What had been the point in making an old house look like the suburbs? Beatrice shrugged, staring at the thick green shoots visible through crystals of ice. No suburbs here, and they were as close to downtown as it was possible to be. Nobody was going to get confused, even if there was a row of shrubs as uniform in size and shape as so many meatballs.

She clambered over more boxes and reached the closet with the bench inside. That was the chimney corner, where people used to curl up to keep warm in the winter. You'd open the door and maybe find an old man snoozing in his nightcap, a child sprawled at his feet. That's what her mother had said. Beatrice felt half sure that she would see exactly that and scream. But it was also in her mind that James was huddled under the bench. Probably they would both let out a yell when she flung open the door.

Her fingers fluttered along the edge, feeling for a knob behind the stacked cartons. When she drew open the door and peered in, she could have sworn that she heard a faint titter of laughter. Yet there was nothing inside but darkness and more of her father's toys on the shelves.

"Little rat," she said, closing the door, her heart pittering fast.

Crates and boxes were wedged against that end of the long fireplace, so she backtracked until she found a spot where she could slip through a gap. She popped out near the center of the fireplace. It was the oldest one in the house, with an immense opening inside a heavy mantle and surround. The firebricks had been plastered over and painted black in the front. In the rear, two centuries of smoke had left its patina.

She skimmed her hand along the top of the screen. It was cold, and she could feel air trickling across her fingers. Her parents had brought the black steel guard with them when they moved—a heavy thing, with a cutout pattern of the Shaker tree of life.

"James!"

She bent, peering over the screen. There was her little brother, his fingers clamped over his mouth and his hazel eyes looking as round and excited as the Princess Owl's.

Throwing up his hands to shield himself from attack, he let out a piercing cry. He squatted, looking from her to the darkness above him.

"There's something in the chimney!"

"What? Let me see."

Beatrice pushed aside the screen and knelt on the hearth, craning to look. On the bricks underfoot lay a trapezoid of painted board. She suspected that her little brother must have knocked it from the shaft. Her parents wouldn't be pleased to find heated air escaping up the chimney.

"Where? I don't see anything." She flicked a curled-up spider from her jeans.

James had backed into the far corner and was looking fixedly overhead.

"There," he whispered.

"You give me the creeps." She dusted her hands together and gingerly stood up inside the chimney. Her brother put his arms around her. "Hey, stop that. Don't shove."

She could see what he meant now. There was a shelf built into the shaft, and an object resting on it. And there was something pinned to the bricks just above.

"Bats." James moaned, clutching her tighter.

"No, it's not bats," she said in disgust. "People don't have bats in their houses." Still, she paused with her hand upraised.

"Yes, they do. They fly out at night."

"What's on the shelf is a lot bigger than a bat. Even a vampire bat. And it's got a handle. But I don't know about the other ones. . . ."

She picked up the fallen panel and pried at the two objects fastened to the wall, jumping backward as they tumbled and slapped against the hearth.

"Dead bats!" He moaned again, pulling the hem of her sweater over his face.

For an instant she thought he was right. They certainly looked like the desiccated bodies of animals. She leaned over and stared at the flattened objects.

"Get your head out of my clothes, you idiot. It's shoes!"

Oddly, James made not the smallest objection to being called an idiot. He crouched and examined a leather sole.

"Are you sure that's a shoe?"

"Yes, a big shoe and a tiny shoe. Now let me get the other thing." Poking the corner of the board beneath the handle, she lowered a black bag onto the floor.

Her brother had been testing a shoe with his fingertip.

"Whatever it is, it's dead."

"Shoes, silly." Beatrice was examining the clasp on the bag. "Should I open it?"

"No!" The voice of alarm made her feel more confident.

"Why not? It's awfully dusty."

"Because something might come out!"

"Like what?"

"Centipedes," James said in a sepulchral voice.

Beatrice grinned at him. "You should see your face."

"Okay, open it then." He struck a pose of ghoulish fascination, hunching his back and lifting his hands like claws.

The bag yawned open.

James let out a short, sharp screech.

⸱

"NOTHING BUT A dirty old newspaper, a doctor's bag, and some shoes."

A day later, Beatrice still felt let down.

"Let's go to the lake. Mama said I could, if you come with me, and I don't wade in the water." James gave her the look she called "the face of imploration."

His sister laughed at him and agreed. They had arrived in town at Easter, but the days were still cold, with ice turning to slush on the lake. The pair sat on the pew in the mudroom, tugging on their rain boots and light Southern coats. Come next winter, they would have to get proper gear, all miracle fibers and feathers.

They raced down the alley and across Lake Street, where slate stairs led to an overlook by the water's edge. Glimmerglass lay open at its heart, with islands of ice wandering across the gap. James plopped a stone through the rotten ice close in, then sat on his heels to examine the shingle beach.

"Look, there's treasure."

"What?" Beatrice bent over, scanning the ground. "I bet those are polished shards of brick, two hundred years old."

Her brother held up a handful of the rounded, porous stuff, pale orange. "Look, there's flowers."

Sure enough, she saw chips of cobalt blue blossoms and brown transfer-ware and ovals of lake glass, burnished and smooth. Meltwater from tiny crystal towers of ice glazed and deepened the colors.

"I know," she said. "Let's make the stump over there into a fairy table. We'll leave gifts for the fairies."

It pleased them both, and for some time they hurried back and forth between the shore and a stump that lay under the shadow of a low bank and trees. Once James caught his sister by the hand and asked, "Is that a fairy?" He jerked his head toward the red withies that were springing up from the shallows where the lake beach joined to the riverbank.

"What?" She let her gaze drift along the thicket and the waves lapping at the foot of the stems. "Oh. That's not a fairy. Just a tiny old lady."

Whatever she might be, the figure was trundling their way. The two stopped what they were doing until Beatrice remembered that it was rude to stare, and she pushed James toward the beach. They knelt on the pebbles, gathering more fairy treasure.

"Hello, hello," the stranger called, nodding at them. She was wearing a dress that hung shorter in the front that the back, covering the tops of her wellies, and over it was buttoned a quilted jacket like something Beatrice imagined that a woman planting shoots in a rice paddy might wear. The girl straightened, and James darted behind her for refuge. The old woman smiled as if amused by his shyness. "You're new in the village, aren't you? Prentiss Cottage, I'd wager."

"Yes ma'am," Beatrice said.

"They told me that you'd found shoes in the chimney. Is that right? Yes? Isn't that wonderful!"

"But how do you know about that?" Beatrice let the lake glass slip from her fingers.

"That's how things work in a village, you know. One word, and news flies around the lake."

Her hair looked rather like James's after a restless night, except that it was white where his had darkened to gold. But the crown stood up in the same intractable way that would not be laid to rest by water or comb or a dab of gel. Her eyebrows were also white, and her skin was very pale; she was altogether colorless aside from the washed-out lavender of her eyes.

"Are you—"

Beatrice gave a little cat-twitch; she had had the impulse to ask the woman whether she might be—what?—an albino, a witch, a fairy?

"Oh, I'm sorry. My name's Catherine. My husband says I can't remember my own name, but there, you see—I can. He just teases me because I always forget to introduce myself when I meet someone. So they go off not knowing—"

James had moved slowly to the front, hanging on to Beatrice for security but gawking at Catherine. At this juncture he announced his own name and his sister's; then he held out his hand to show a burnished lozenge of glass the very color of her eyes.

"For you," he said. "I'm good at finding treasure. I found the shoes."

"Well," Beatrice began, "actually you—"

"I found them," he repeated firmly, with a short stab of a glance at his sister. "Nobody would've seen them if I hadn't been hiding in the fireplace. Here," he said, "this is for you." He deposited the lavender glass on Catherine's palm.

"Thank you. How lovely."

"I found the shoes," he said. "I did."

Beatrice was annoyed with him, but she felt sure her mother would have said to ignore it, especially when meeting someone new.

"Fine," she said, giving him a pinch.

"Ow!" He cut his head back, quick, throwing the word at her.

Beatrice shook herself free of his hand and stepped closer. "Do you know why there were shoes? They were old and squashed and dark from soot."

"Didn't they tell you? That's a weird thing, you know, but then the village is a curious place . . ."

She rocked back on her heels, looking out at Glimmerglass. An ice floe wandered past, in search of somewhere to moor.

"Nobody told us anything."

"All right, then, I'll tell you. What about you," she said, addressing James. "Are you a brave, bloodthirsty boy, or not?"

"Sure I am," he said, though his voice sounded uncertain to Beatrice.

"They all of them are," she said comfortably. "Love nothing better than going out to shoot some poor grouse or rabbit. In my time, the boys loved to box and fistfight. But they don't let them any more, not until they're eighteen and shipped off to some raging desert. Let's see. Shoes. Oh, yes, the concealment shoes."

Her glance fell on the fairy table, and she narrowed her eyes. "What's that, then?"

"Presents for the fairies," James said.

She gave him an appraising look. "Fairies are as cruel a lot as boys or men. I suppose you can stand the truth."

Beatrice shivered in her light jacket, wishing that she'd worn a second sweater underneath. "What do you mean?"

"A long time ago, before our ancestors came over in ships to torment the free-ranging Indians and to be scalped or kidnapped in return, before they thought to settle here and scratch a living from the ground and fence it in—I mean way back, before anybody in Europe thought to make black marks on white paper—the people used to sacrifice one of their own kind when they built their dwellings of boulders and fitted stones. They'd dump the body in the foundation as a charm to keep stone on stone. But it didn't take, did it? Because now those prehistoric sites are ruins."

"But what about the shoes?" James stood on one foot, his arms akimbo, like a water bird. Ice bird, thought Beatrice.

"I'm getting there, don't you worry. That's pretty barbaric, isn't it? After some eons of blood, they quit slaughtering a human victim for house glue. They'd sacrifice chickens or cats—"

"Not Princess Owl!" James blurted out the words.

"A long time ago," Beatrice said.

Catherine must have been cold, because she began tugging a length of cloth from her sleeve. When she'd pulled out several yards of thin black stuff, she wrapped it about her head and throat.

James whispered to his sister. "Was that magic?"

But to the girl's eyes, the small, elderly personage seemed changed, and now resembled some long-ago woman from across the sea. A *babushka*, she thought. Baba Yaga flitted through her mind. The slush and ice grated on the shore, swinging back and forth with the waves.

She picked up the conversation as though there had been no pause. "No, they won't hurt your cat. Since then we've gotten more civilized. But for a long time builders still put offerings in the walls and chimneys—cups and gloves, spoons and toys. Shoes most of all. I've heard it said that shoes were to kick the witches out of chimneys." She made a sour face. "Not very friendly to the poor biddies, were they? What's sure is that worn human relics were good against uncanny things—could ward off the evil eye. See, house repairers find the charms near windows and doors and among the roof rafters or in chimneys: holes where something could worm its way in. Like in your Prentiss Cottage. Oh, they're lovely old creatures, these cottages in the village. They're alive, you know. Full of spunk and personality. You can hear them breathe and creak, and when the wind gusts they lift up as if they might be dreaming about flying. Then afterward they settle slowly until you can hear the faint *ping*! of a pin falling into place."

Beatrice curled her toes inside the rain boots. They felt numb, but she wanted to hear the rest.

"Shoes," James prompted.

"Think about a shoe. Think about slippers that you'd have on every day. Maybe the only pair you owned, and the leather would mold to your feet. There would be a bump where your bones were irregular, and creases and tucks would form all around, snuggling against your skin. Think how personal a shoe is."

"I suppose a kind of memory of your steps would be there, in the wear on the heels," Beatrice said.

"That's right. So it would have your history and your shape—it would be a kind of image of you, made by your own body. You'd put one in the wall like a piece of your spirit, set it up to guard the way. And there the shoe would be, always vigilant."

The wandering floe had returned, wobbling off to the west, slapped by the waves. Beatrice watched it depart.

"But we don't have our shoes anymore," James told her.

"What do you mean?"

"Daddy carried them to the museum, and somebody wanted to keep them and study them for a while."

"Is that true?" Catherine turned to Beatrice, who nodded.

"Four in all—two out of each chimney. They'll return them afterward," she said.

"Your father must put them back! It's not right; it's not safe. Those shoes have been guardians for two centuries now. Oh, I must have a word with him—"

The old woman pulled the shawl close around her head, mumbling to herself, and hurried away without waiting for the children. They watched as she hauled herself up to the steps of the platform that overlooked the lake and began slowly ascending the stone staircase to the road.

"How funny," Beatrice murmured.

James scampered to the fairy table, his hand-me-down boots flapping, and inspected their arrangements.

"We need some more glass," he announced.

"No, we'd better go home," his sister said. "We might miss something. What will that Catherine woman tell Daddy? We'd better go listen and find out." She didn't entirely approve of the way Yankees made free with their first names. At home in South Carolina, she had always called her parents' friends "Miss Anne," "Mr. Gerald," "Miss Marjorie." It was a habit falling into abeyance all through the South, but it lingered in certain old-fashioned places, especially those lacking a university culture. She felt a pang of longing for her grandmother, safe in the white house with its live oaks and isles of ferns.

"I'm cold," she added.

"I'll race you to the alley." James bent at the knees as if to launch himself forward at her word.

The alley was an old stagecoach run. They liked to think that the coaches had wheeled past, just beyond the garage.

"No, don't. I'm too cold." She trembled, climbing the stone stairs, but at the top she changed her mind. "Beat you home!" she cried out, darting across the street and along a sidewalk made jagged as a frozen sea from frost heaves and the roots of trees.

James burst into full cry, pounding after her and gaining as they turned the corner.

OUTSIDE, THE SNOW blew slantwise past the lamppost, and pitchy streamers of cloud rippled in front of the moon. A lid of night had slipped across half of its staring orb.

"It's like a story," Beatrice said dreamily, her arms wrapped around her knees. Snug in a new flannel gown, she sat gazing out the window. "See the lamppost, with its crown of snow? A faun might appear. Or a girl searching for strawberries under the drifts. Or the Snow Queen, with boys on sleds tied behind her sleigh. The neighbors said this is spring, but see—little ice ferns are creeping across the windowpanes."

"Maybe it's always winter here. Did you ask?" The boy's delicate face looked pale and golden in the light shed from a lithopane lamp. "Beewish," he said, using his baby name for Beatrice, "I'm afraid."

She drew back, her eyebrows lifted and mouth open in a mocking "O."

"Don't scare me!" James threw himself forward, tackling her, his legs churning against the coverlet. He hid his face against her shoulder.

"All right, all right—stop it!"

But Beatrice didn't mind. It was pleasant to be in this nook in what would be her bedroom. All around loomed the cartons, but Francis had quarried out the center so she and James could sleep inside a cave. And he had even left gaps so they could see the snow sliding by the lamppost. He wasn't such a bad brother, she thought—not when he wanted to be nice, anyway.

"Everybody's asleep." James hid his face in his pillow, letting out a squeak of dismay. Their mother had found her wardrobe jammed with toys, and now they were barricaded in by a motley ring of animals—an armadillo, a Siberian tiger, furry snakes, sharks, pink monkeys with red eyes that were leftover from Valentine's Day, sea and river otters, a peacock, a pair of hedgehogs. . . . James loved small creatures more than either of his siblings had. But he'd been frightened when his mother had suggested that the scratching in the walls might mean mice or voles, and even more so when she added that the jutting portion of the wall was where the upper level of the chimney had been plastered up, long ago.

"They're dead to the world. All that awful unpacking."

"He'll guard them," James proposed, holding up a grizzled wolf puppet.

"I'm going downstairs," Beatrice said, her eyes glistening in the lamplight.

He dove deep in the bag and used the pillow as a stopper. "No, don't leave me!" The words were muffled by feathers and sleeping bag.

His sister jeered at him. She wrenched the pillow from his grasp and threw it high in the air. A few down feathers floated free, and a fingerling of draft from the windows sported with them, urging one out the door.

"I'm going—"

"Wait, wait for me!" James's head popped out of the bag, his hair wild.

"Put on your slippers. Mama said nails from the floor boards might hurt our feet."

The feather was still adrift in the hallway. Boxes, many of them half-ransacked, had been shoved against the wall and balusters.

The Princess Owl shot by them, her eyes glowing and tail bristled.

James jumped sideways. "She's meowing at something!"

"No, she's just doing that weird throat noise she makes when she's stealing a glove or socks. She's probably got one in her mouth."

That made James laugh, though he claimed that he had glimpsed legs wriggling in her jaws as Princess Owl plummeted down the steps. Sometimes they found balled-up socks, fresh from the laundry, in a trail from bedroom to kitchen. The Owl loved the fall, when the chest of scarves and gloves emerged from its summer hiding place; she had learned to open the lightweight lid and slip out a glove.

"The movers didn't do a very neat job of packing." Beatrice peered into a large box holding a tangle of ties, a few sweaters, and a jumble of her parents' shoes.

The shoes made James think about the encounter by the lake.

"I wish we still had those shoes in the chimney," he said. His voice sounded woeful; it echoed in the upper hall. "I wanted the tiny red shoe with the fur inside. And can't we turn on a light?"

"No. That Catherine woman told Daddy the reason there was just a child's shoe and a man's shoe in each one is that the wife died before this house was finished. The chimneys were probably built last, when the mason had time for them."

James stared, gripping her sleeve.

"Don't look so bug-eyed," Beatrice said, jerking her arm away.

"You mean she died here?" The question ended on a high-pitched note.

"Hush. There aren't any ghosts. Mama said she wouldn't buy a house with ghosts."

"But there are ghosts all around," he persisted, "like in the stone house across the street. And at Greenbriars—the haunted picture."

"Yeah? And we're right by the old hanging ground, too. Who cares? Other people's ghosts are interesting. They're like thumbprints on a piece of glass—they're not real, just an image from a long time back. Like the ghost of a movie."

"How do you know?"

I make it up, she thought. She padded along the hallway, glancing into the rest of the boxes. Rumpled sheets and towels, books, and art supplies had been flung haphazardly inside.

"Come on. There's enough moonlight to see." She tossed the faint crescent of a smile over her shoulder as she slipped down the stairs.

James made a choking noise and fled after her, catching her nightgown at the waist.

"Look. They forgot—"

The paneled front door was ajar. Nobody locked their doors much in Templeton—that's what their new neighbors had told them. But she didn't like the idea of anybody walking in without so much as a rap of the lion's head that served as a knocker. The moon poured through the crack, radiating the towers of cartons with its pallor.

"The living room," James whispered, pointing inside.

Stripes of light showed at the half-closed inner shutters. And snowflakes were filtering from the black maw of the fireplace, spinning out into the center of the room and floating up. The flue must be not quite sealed, Beatrice thought. Her father had showed her how to open and shut it, just after he restored the board in the dining room chimney. All the upstairs fireplaces had been closed up in the last century. The snow looked luminous in the darkness; James sprang catlike into the room, hopping and catching one, two, three snowflakes on his tongue.

Though she meant to tell him to stop, Beatrice found herself dodging through the boxes and leaping after the shining stars.

"They taste really good—like the moon." James gasped, giving a quiver of pleasure as a large star kissed his lips.

But the moon would taste like stone, Beatrice thought, but she didn't say so. She was caught up in the chase; when she snatched one in her hand, it turned to a sprinkle of glittering dust.

Her brother was crouched on the hearthstone, looking up.

"What's the matter?"

"I spy a monkey," he whispered; "picking stars out of the sky with his fingers and cracking them between his teeth. Like lice. Or star fleas."

"What? Let me," Beatrice crawled across the firebricks and gazed up through the barely open flue. There was something that looked like a monkey—she could see it perched on the edge of the chimney, hands groping at the air. She grasped the handle and jerked. The flue let a shower of bright flour and black grains and soot tumble onto their upturned faces. Before their eyes teared up, they glimpsed the monkey—if monkey he was—as he gave one flashing, red-eyed glance downward and bolted, his tail lashing the air.

"Ow, ow—that hurts!" James thrust at his sister in the dark, and she slapped his arm.

"I'm sorry, honest. Be quiet!"

They shook out their nightclothes, and Beatrice raked her hands through her brother's hair. Ash and sparkling dots of light sifted onto the hearth at their feet.

"It was a monkey, wasn't it?"

"I suppose," she answered, though she didn't think so. Whoever heard of a monkey with red eyes? Just before her own teared up, she had felt a yawning fright. Now she peered back up the shaft. Nothing but night sky and stars, more dazzling than the ones at their old home. Not so many lit-up houses here, she remembered, to make the sky go pale and washed-out. "Let's check if we can see anything on the roof."

James looked obstinate but followed her, first giving a final jump and catching a last star on his tongue.

"Lemon drops," he murmured.

The brick floor between the porch pillars was clear of snow. From there to the street took only six steps. The world was pristine, dusted with a fluffy fresh inch. Farther down Main Street, Beatrice thought that she could see flowering trees, their candelabra cups holding up the loose snow. But maybe that was just a trick of the light and the new snow that had made the spindly trees in the backyard resemble brush strokes on a Japanese scroll. She loved all things Japanese, particularly sushi and manga and karate, and soon she would be going for zen do kai lessons with a sensei in Cherry Vale: the name sounded pleasantly Japanese, though it was the site of a famous massacre of settlers.

She wasn't afraid; already she had decided that the night played tricks on eyes. James lingered behind the glass panes of the outer door, his face a panic.

"Come on," she mouthed to him, hands on hips, and he slipped outside, leaving a flurry of prints in the snow as he scuttled headlong, colliding with her body and hugging her tight.

"It's cold."

"Who cares?" Beatrice said the words automatically but shivered all the same, her arms around her brother as she inspected the roofline and the tops of the two big chimneys. "Everything looks so black and white. But I don't see anything out of place."

She let go, wheeling to face the bridge. Drawn by a strangeness in the landscape, she hurried forward until at last James chased after her.

"Look at the water," he called.

The river and lake, barely sealed by a film of ice, were emitting beams that arrowed up slantwise more than head-high. Past the hanging ground, the curving line of the channel was made visible for half a mile, shimmering in the trees. Behind the houses, Glimmerglass resembled a cauldron of white fire, its spears of light rising to meet the stars.

James tugged at his sister's arm, at once entranced and longing to go home, but she crossed the street and went as far as the bronze plaque on the bridge before turning.

She was shaking with cold and a little uneasy at being out, yet reluctant to leave. No cars had passed in a long time; no tread disturbed the pavement. They walked up the center of the street toward the cottage.

As they passed the set-back wing that had been the cookhouse, James caught sight of something strange in the curtainless window. The rainbow-caster was moving.

"I didn't know it could work on moonlight." Beatrice stopped, watching the prism under the gears and solar panel as it jiggled in slow revolution.

It was James who dashed to the window, standing in the bed of winter stalks and pressing his face against the panes.

"Come see!"

Moon bows flashed and fled in swinging circles, sweeping over the towers and flying along the ceiling.

"There are so many of them." It was puzzling. Beatrice was sure there were far more than she had ever seen in the day.

"They go on out, but they don't go back to the crystal," James said, taking her hand. "It's protecting us. The good guys are light, like the stars."

"How can that be? Let's go inside." She was colder than she had ever been in her life. Her feet felt like stone. *Like pieces of moon*, she thought dreamily.

"Angels?" He asked, but nobody replied.

Rounding the front of the house, Beatrice paused to put a hand on the lamppost. She looked over her shoulder and glimpsed the open door and the moonlit boxes and parcels standing like a glowing city in the hallway. The snow was starting to blow slantwise again, looking like flakes of white fire where it passed athwart the lantern. Separate stars had lodged in the fluting of the lamppost, terribly cold against her palm.

"I know what you're thinking," James said, staring at her.

"Maybe," she whispered.

Scampering past the post to jump into the street, he whirled about, then flopped down in the fresh snow to wave his arms and make an angel.

"Fear not! I bring you tidings—"

"Funny sort of angel you'd make." Beatrice put out her tongue, but the snow here tasted only of water and distance and sky.

The boy gently waved his arms, gazing at his sister with her hair decked in snowflakes. Despite being chilled, he felt happy. She hadn't spent this much time playing with him in years, and his heart seemed curiously light, like a moon bow sprinkled with stardust. Though he was groping for how to say it and couldn't, he felt precisely as though the little moth of him had flown up into the sky and danced with the twinkling stars.

He looked away from her, at the cottage where they would live from now on, and for the first time it looked to him like somebody's home—like his home.

"The house likes my angel," he said. "I saw the wind make snow fly from the top like a pair of wings when we came outside. Now it's looking at me. See? There are its eyes, and the porch roof is its nose, and the door is its mouth, and the roof's a hat and the chimneys are—"

"Get up. You'll get sick."

Lying inside the snow angel's embrace, he didn't answer but stared up, his mouth ajar. She followed his gaze. The sudden intake of breath plunged like a blade in her throat.

Something half-transparent lay cauled around the chimney, a creature of smoke and darkness. The thing seemed to Beatrice to be one of the great wyrms of fairy tale, but devoid of their scaly, hot shine. Once a flicker of flame lit the face and might have been an eye. The body coiled round and round the stack, anchoring itself or perhaps guarding the spot. But it didn't say one thing. Boiling upward, the creature displayed a long snout and a tongue of fire. In the manner of cloud-pictures, it began to shift and become more human looking, though with great flapping ears that threatened to bear the head away. The arms were streamy filaments, barely visible against the stars. Mounting higher, it wavered and arced downward, peering into the shaft.

Then, gyring above the cottage and slowly elongating into a spear of smoke, it shot into the chimney and disappeared.

"I closed the flue," Beatrice said, her arms tight across her chest. "I closed it." But all the time she was thinking about how the stars had gotten in, even though she had seen her father give a final thrust to the handle and heard the grate and clang of metal.

Perhaps the angel lying in the street whispered in his ear and gave the boy a message of wisdom; who knows?

He sat up. "Shoes," James said. "Shoes. One for each of us."

They tracked snow into the warm hallway and halted at the living room door. Wobbling moon bows had navigated a path from the former cookhouse but were quivering and dying as they neared the hearth. A few shining stars lay scattered on the floor. Like an immense war-banner in tatters, ribbons of the creature were squeezing through a crack and flowing from the flue, gathering into a single fabric in front of the mantle.

"Yank off your shoes and throw them."

Who said that, neither could remember later on.

The cold, wet slippers sank through the river of smoke, dividing its dark pour into five main tributaries.

"Upstairs," Beatrice cried.

For once they didn't vie to reach the top, each trying to knock the other away, but charged up the stairs as one.

"The box—with the ties and shoes—"

"Here—"

James's hand closed over his father's lawn mowing shoes, battered white and black sneakers, stained green. Beatrice grappled longer, hurling shoes aside until she found her mother's favorite leather flats, so often worn that the heels had been rubbed to papery thinness.

"Our slippers—"

They plunged back down the staircase. In the living room, the mass of smoke was collecting itself into a puddle on the ceiling. A wavy line of moon bows was lifting into the air, punctuated by a few asterisks of snow.

Beatrice hesitated. "It smells bad in here. Like rotten eggs."

"I don't mind." James dashed to the hearth to retrieve their slippers, crouching low without looking up.

A clattering from the dining room across the hall panicked them; rushing to see, they discovered the board tumbled from the chimney and an oily smoke drooling into the room. The Princess Owl blurred past with a small whistling creature in her jaws. She vaulted a carton, rocketing toward the cat door in the kitchen.

"Shove them in place," Beatrice called.

One of each shoe was thrust onto the shelf in the chimney, and the long, froggy tongue began withdrawing, then stopped, as if testing the air.

"Francis." James grabbed his sister's arm. "Catherine said one for each person, and we don't have any for him." He held a shoe and a small green slipper against his chest, his face intent.

"Right," Beatrice said. "Let's get them."

The thing from the living room was floating in the hall now, its red, beadlike eyes rolling in its puzzle of a head. Crushed fragments of bows and stars dropped from its jaws and littered the boards with moonshine.

She ducked underneath its body, reaching for her brother's hand.

"Hold up your shoes," she whispered, towing him behind. The smoke shot upward, as easily as water splashing downhill, and pooled on the ceiling outside the children's bathroom. It began groping for a path into the chamber, stretching until it blocked their way. The door to Francis's room stood on the other side. There was a second entrance from what would be James's bedroom.

"No!" She was blocked by boxes once again. *A demon*, she thought. *It's a demon, a stealer of—what? souls? bodies?*

"It's all right. I've got a secret path to Francis." James stretched out a hand to lead her, and she took hold and followed. The last gap was almost too small for Beatrice, but by dint of hard shoving, she managed to squeeze between cartons and through the barely open door between the bedrooms. All of the boys' things were stacked in the adjoining bedroom, and so Francis already had a refuge with a bed, dresser, desk, and bookcase. Smoke must have been spiraling from the keyhole of the door between his room and the bathroom while Beatrice was struggling through the barrier of boxes; now, as she searched her brother's closet, the last thread of smoke pulled free from the lock's eye and was reeled into a floating yarnlike ball that immediately began to manifest face and throat and torso. Once fully knitted together, the head moved in a snaky fashion.

James lay at full length, scrabbling around under the bed for shoes.

"How'd he get so much junk here already? I can't find any."

"There's got to be the ones he had on."

Beatrice leaned over her older brother. Francis was co-cooned in a quilted blue spread, only his head showing. Under the shadow of the demon, his coarse hair shone richly gold, and his cheekbone was dusted with a glitter of moth dust—as if one of the glowing snowflakes had kissed him there, leaving some frail blessing. She looked at his face with the high forehead and strong jaw and beautiful lips, the long lashes on the lids over the hidden blue of his eyes, and she felt love for him: just that simply it came, like water gushing from a fountain.

"He makes me so mad sometimes," she said aloud, in a pleading voice, waving her mother's leather shoe and her own black slipper between the being of smoke and Francis.

Her brother's mouth was ajar in sleep. The creature sank nearer, heavy with ooze, until finally it lay snuggled on the boy's body. Slowly it began dragging itself, floppy as a rag doll, toward the face. Beatrice batted at the cloudy flesh with the shoes. An odor of burned custard wafted across the room. Though it flinched, the thing went on drooling along the neck and then lapping onto the cheek. A tendril flicked outward and felt around, like a tiny arm, though she slammed it with both shoes. Just as she managed to push that probe away from his lips, a whip of smoke lashed upward and dropped inside the open mouth.

"Quick, quick—"

"I'm trying," James called. He was now entirely hidden under the bed, and could be heard slapping the floor, scooting aside books and papers and clothes. "If he knew, he'd clean up his room—"

"Hurry!" Beatrice struggled to thrust the smoke away and yank the rope of darkness from her brother's lips. Her fingers slipped right through, and only the shoes could dam its steady flow a little. The stuff had thickened and reminded her of lava.

"I've got a pair!" The boy jolted up from the far side of

the bed, ricocheting off the night table and bedpost as he leaped, a penny loafer in each hand. "Ouch! Not all that old, but they're stinky."

"Oh, good—"

She grabbed one of the shoes and began twisting the smoke around it like a strand of cotton candy around a paper cone. The demon flesh came spurting from his lips with surprising ease, and the end popped out of Francis's mouth all wet and dripping, with a resounding thwock!

"Gross!" James whispered the word, sticking out his tongue afterward.

But he was too busy patting at the body with several of the remaining shoes to talk. The thing drew back from the touch of the now-united family of shoes when Beatrice joined in, shoveling the smoke with the three she awkwardly held.

Except for Francis, again breathing deeply, and the soft slapping of the shoes against one another, the room was silent. The body of smoke became a black dog with eyes of magma; it became a firecat bristling with sparks; it became a gargoyle vomiting smoke; it became a souplike, smoldering gloop that neither of them could name. Last of all it pulled inward and formed a dense orb, slightly tacky from the moisture that had been inside Francis.

After that, it would shrink no more but stayed a semi-solid.

"What do you think? Roll the ball into a shoe?" Beatrice paused, looking at her little brother.

It was a signal moment of his boyhood: he felt it so. James grinned, feeling sweaty from the fear that was now passing away but also good—expansive, pleased that his sister had asked him for advice.

He picked up the sphere, bounced it on his palm, and plopped it into a loafer. Seeing a penny on the floor, he leaned over.

"Heads. That's lucky." He slid the coin into the penny slot on top of the shoe, and the dark thing compacted on the wrinkled inner sole seemed to quiver.

"That's really smart. Did you remember how Catherine told Dad that people used to put money in the walls some-times?"

He shrugged, smiling and clearly pleased with himself.

The two tiptoed downstairs, the collected shoes piled hig-gledy-piggledy in a basket Beatrice had spotted in a corner of the bathroom. The penny loafer with its burden went into the living room chimney with those already in place, and the remaining five were arranged on the shelf built into the dining room chimney. Afterward, they spotted a flashlight in a box marked SOCKS and shone it up the shaft in the living room. A jet-black amoeba no larger than a woman's hand was creeping up the firebricks. "It looks kind of cute," James whispered. The flashlight jiggled in his sister's hand. "Not," she said, poking him in the ribs. They waited until the crea-ture was lost in gloom before shutting the flue and making sure that not even a chink was left open.

"Nobody ever woke up," James said.

"Too tired, I guess. All that lifting and unpacking."

"We saved them, didn't we? Let's go to bed. And tomor-row we can find that Catherine. Was she a witch?"

"She wasn't so strange after all. Not compared to this." Beatrice peered outside at the snow before shutting and locking the front door.

Pinpricks of light speckled the pumpkin pine boards. She bent and placed her palm against the dots. When she lifted her hand and inspected it, she smiled.

"Moonshine."

"We ate the stars," James said, marveling. He took his sister's hand, and she squeezed his fingers, but not too hard.

The Princess Owl burst past them, hurtling up the stairs.

He stared in surprise. "Did you see that?"

"It must be almost daylight." Beatrice began climbing the steps as the cat leaped gracefully onto the hand rail.

"I'm going to like this house." James yawned uncontrollably as he trailed after his sister. He blinked sudden moisture from his eyes and looked up at the Owl, now perched directly above him.

The cat's quick, neat mouth had closed on a patch of prismatic light, its colors caught halfway between a moon bow and a rainbow. Like a victory pennant raised in the very teeth of defeat, the bow fluttered in the jaws of Princess Owl, tinting her fur and round eyes with the enchantment of those leaf-green dreams with violet shadows that flare up just before the gold and rosy dawn.

Marly Youmans is the author of a collection of poetry and five novels, including two fantasies: *The Curse of the Raven Mocker* and *Ingledove*. Originally published by Farrar, Straus & Giroux, both were reprinted as Firebird paperbacks in the fall of 2006. Her novellas and short stories have recently appeared in *Argosy 3* and *4*, *Fantasy Magazine*, *The Year's Best Fantasy & Horror 2006: Nineteenth Annual Collection*, and other magazines and anthologies.

The Guardian of the Egg

Christopher Barzak

M Y SISTER WAS the girl with the tree growing out of her head. You've probably heard of her. You might have seen her on TV. Her picture was plastered all over the place for a while. That shock of wheat ruffling around her face like a great golden mane, the weeping willow tree growing out of the top of her head, her skin white as chalk and smooth as porcelain, those tiny tiger lilies that grew between her eyelashes. And all of those geese she kept under her mossy cloak! A freak show, really. I understand why everyone thought she might be working with a foreign government, or that she'd been irradiated by the local nuclear power plant. But, really, she was just another ordinary teenager under all of that flora. I know because she was my older sister.

Hester was a straight A student. She was going to be class valedictorian. No one was really surprised. She wore white stockings and old-fashioned sweaters with pearl buttons.

The girls at school used to make fun of her because of how she dressed and because of how smart she was. Also maybe due to the fact that she had braces and bad acne, and her hair might have been styled better, and she had a habit of looking down at her feet shuffling through the hallways. She bumped into people a lot because of this. I was two years younger, in the tenth grade. I pretended not to know her. It was easy to do that because she never saw me in the hallways. Her head was always pointed toward the floor.

When the tree started growing out of her head, it was springtime. Only a few more months of school remained before she'd graduate and go off to college. At first, you could look right at her and not notice the tree, unless you got close and examined the part down the middle of her hair. After a few weeks, though, it was the size of a flower blooming, a little weeping willow. Kids started to call her Daisy Head Maisy, and they'd laugh and elbow each other when she walked by. Hester didn't pay them any attention, although I'd shrink back into the hollow of my locker whenever I saw her coming, those weeping willow branches swaying back and forth like a grass hula skirt.

Hester didn't seem to mind the tree. In fact, when she discovered it, I remember the strange grin on her face, like she'd found forgotten money in one of her pockets. She seemed so excited that she parted her hair down the middle instead of on the side, as if she wanted people to notice it. She walked with her head held high. She looked a bit like maybe she thought she was better than everyone. I remember asking, "Hester, why don't you get scissors and cut it off?" and she winced as if the very thought was repulsive.

"I like it, Stephen," she said, tilting her head one way, then the other, while she looked at the tree from different angles in the mirror.

"It's gross, Hester," I said, and she narrowed her eyes and said, "I don't expect you to understand this. Maybe you're even a little jealous?"

I couldn't believe what I was hearing. She sounded slightly religious, flipping her hair over one shoulder, then the other, examining the tree growing out of her cranium as if it were a pair of earrings. I'd never seen Hester so concerned with a mirror.

My parents took Hester to a neurologist and then to a psychologist, to ease some of their worries. The neurologist said the tree couldn't be removed because its roots grew directly into her cerebrum. She'd suffer brain damage if we fiddled with it. "And anyway," he said, "it doesn't seem to be hurting her." The tree roots conducted electrical currents, just like the other nerves in her brain. The psychologist said Hester was remarkably sane, considering she had a tree growing out of her head. "She's coping quite well," he told my parents, and all my mother and father could do was raise their eyebrows and nod.

OUR HIGH SCHOOL decided to graduate Hester early. The school board said they didn't want any problems. "Besides," said our principal, Mrs. Merriman, "everyone knows Hester is the smartest student in her class. Graduation would have been inevitable, wouldn't it?" She shook hands with my parents briskly, then asked her secretary to see that all the forms were properly filled out.

Reporters and talk show hosts stalked the sidewalks and fast-food restaurants of our formerly quiet town. Paparazzi flashed pictures at innocent young girls who happened to be wearing their hair in a ponytail. Ponytails soon became stylistic suicide due to the first-glance similarity they shared with a tree growing out of a girl's head. This frustrated and angered many female athletes who liked to put their hair up while they jogged or played softball. Now they had to brush their hair out of their eyes as they dribbled or leaped hurdles. Because my sister was the reason for their troubles, the female athletes petitioned for her to move out of town. The petition never made it through the court system, though. A judge threw it out on account that you can't petition people to leave town. They have to do something wrong first, he said, and Ada McGowen, our school's best volleyball player, said, "Oh yeah? Well what do you call someone who grows a tree out of her head? I'd say that's pretty wrong, wouldn't you?"

Hester seemed oblivious to the troubles her tree caused. She said, "Really, Stephen, my tree isn't the problem. Those people create their own messes. They'd just like to think my tree is the reason."

She seemed very wise and old when she spoke like this. In fact, Hester didn't seem like Hester after a while. I would search her face as she wandered through our tiny backyard, running her fingers through the water in the birdbath, cupping the water in her hands and releasing it, the sun glinting through the water as it ran back into the bath, and sometimes I couldn't even recognize her as my sister. She seemed larger than she used to. Majestic, even. This was when her skin turned pale and chalky, and overnight her hair changed from silky blond to a shaggy, golden wheat. This was also when my mother stopped Hester as she passed by the hall where our parents measured us each year on our birthdays and placed a pencil mark where the top of our heads met the wall.

"Hester," my mother said, "come back here a minute."

My mother took a pencil from the mug that sat next to our telephone. She marked the wall with a thin line, even though she'd already done the same thing three months earlier, on Hester's seventeenth birthday. Hester stepped away from the wall this time and my mother shook her head, her eyes widening.

Within three months, my sister had grown nearly four inches.

〜

I DON'T KNOW how to describe Hester before her changes started to happen. She was Hester, my older sister. She was plain and awkward and bad at conversation. You wouldn't invite her to a party. You wouldn't ask her to a dance. You probably wouldn't want to have a locker next to hers, either. You could become strange by association if you spent too much time near her. Hester didn't have any friends, and neither did I, but I had none because of Hester. Because of my embarrassment for Hester, I never brought anyone home. I'd meet Alex or Ryan or Chelsea at the movies, or the mall, or else at a coffeehouse or the park. They never asked about my family, and I never asked about theirs. We were conspirators in covering up our own pasts. We respected each other's secrets, never prying or becoming curious. We knew our own secrets weren't that interesting, and what pain we harbored no one else would understand. We wouldn't find each other's problems to be problems anyway, so we never asked what they were.

It was unavoidable, though. After Hester started to change, after the town itself started to change, and the media slipped into our lives, everyone discovered we were related. I was now "the girl with the tree growing out of her head's" brother. You might have heard someone call me by that name. You might have read a reporter quote me wrong in any variety of news articles or docudramas, and I never approved of the actor they chose to play my part in the made-for-TV movie, *Wild Thing*. He was uncouth, and my hair isn't even blond. I never wear hiking boots either. That was a dramatic affectation dreamed up by the director, most likely. But people started recognizing me anyway. I could no longer exist anonymously. Suddenly my identity was more Hester than Stephen was ever Stephen. When people saw me, they thought of Hester.

"How is your sister?" they'd ask. Or else, "Is Hester still growing?" Or even, "Tell your sister her sort doesn't belong in our town."

I'd nod and twitch a little at the people who held violence toward Hester in their hands. They seemed unforgiving, as if she'd done something to personally affront them. The postman in particular became decidedly spiteful. "You should get someone to start landscaping this crap," he told me one afternoon in the summer. I looked to where he was pointing and saw vines growing around our mailbox. He pulled some vines away from the lid, stuffed our mail inside, then snapped the box shut.

"Sorry," I said, as he stalked down the driveway. But all he did was flick me the back of his hand.

⁓

AS SUMMER WORE on, Hester spent more and more time outside, in the backyard. My parents installed a small above-ground swimming pool, and Hester would lounge on the deck with her feet curling into the blue water. I swam along the floor of the pool and watched the shadows from the light above rippling along the bottom. I watched Hester's toes flick back and forth above me. Tiny roots grew between her toes, like potato tubers. They soaked up the water and Hester soaked up the sunlight, like a plant photosynthesizing.

Hester was now at least eight feet tall, a giantess by all standards, and she continued to grow without pause. One day, my father hired a lumber company to bring us a truck full of lumber, and over the course of a few days, he fenced in our front yard and backyard. The fence stood twelve feet tall, a virtual fortress. "There are too many people in our business," he grumbled, looking up sheepishly at Hester, then back to the work at hand. Hester winced each time the hammer met the nail, but she never said anything. Eventually, she looked down at her feet and walked back to the house, back to her bedroom, ducking her head under each door frame.

⁓

NOT MUCH LATER, the first of the geese arrived. It was a large bird, sleek and sidling up to everyone's legs, but especially Hester's. Soon *only* Hester's. It followed her around like a zealot. If someone raised a voice to Hester (which I often did in argument, even if she *was* over eight feet tall) the goose would flap its wings threateningly, hiss and puff up its feathers. I called the bird names like Brunhilda and Marta. I called it the Viking Bird, the Assassin, the Bodyguard. And eventually Hester asked me to, "Please desist in offending the poor creature. It doesn't have a name like we do, Stephen."

"I was *joking*," I told her, and she said, "*I'm* not." The discussion began and ended with Hester folding her arms across her chest in warning.

"Ice Queen," I muttered as I walked away.

"I heard that," she shouted. "Do not think your willfulness goes unrecorded!"

I stopped short, shaking my head in disbelief. Finally I said, "Are you protesting something, Hester? Because if you're protesting something, why don't you just say so, and protest, instead of acting all weird?"

Hester winced. I raised my eyebrows and waited. She didn't say anything, so I turned and left her there, wincing.

IN OUR TOWN, every street had five lampposts lining it. There was a town square with a gas station, a grocery store, and a Super-Mart, which came three years ago, set itself up like an overnight circus, and began selling everything from household cleaners to underwear. We no longer traveled into the city for art supplies, books, birdseed, or to have our automobile's oil changed. It was a self-sufficient community. Children attended three schools: one for elementary students, one for the middle grades, and the last for high school. We were raised to be good, decent people, who knew what it was to be practical, what real work was, and how to one day raise our own children with these same values.

If our town had ever had any failing, the flaw was in our environment. Within a span of three years, most of our trees had been cut down. Dutch Elm disease invaded, infested, and because of this, shade in the summer was a commodity. We had few birds, since birds and trees go together, but occasionally we'd see them pass overhead. The last refuge for our trees was the town park, a mile wide and long, where they enjoyed a small pond and a cannon used in World War II. Also a small memorial wall engraved with the names of all the men from our town who died in one of the wars stood in the shade of our remaining elms.

But all that began to change after Hester began changing.

⁓

ONE MORNING, I woke up angry from a dream of eight-feet tall geese that nipped at my ankles. When I rubbed the sleep from my eyes, I realized it was the fern brushing its lacy leaves against my feet. The fern had been growing beside the foot of my bed for nearly a month, coming up between the floorboards. I'd tried to remove it, pulling it up by its roots, but it only grew back within a few days, a persistent reminder that things were not right in the world. Ferns should not be growing in bedrooms, unless they are potted. Vines should not grow over mailboxes, unless the mailbox is in a jungle outpost. Tiger lilies should not grow in place of a girl's eyelashes. There are rules in this world. I told the fern this myself, but it pretended not to know what I was talking about.

Suddenly I heard Hester's geese in the backyard, and her voice ringing out for them to fall in behind her. When I looked out my window, I saw her back turning the street corner with a line of ten geese following. I decided to follow as well.

They didn't go far—to the park, only a few blocks away from our place. There the geese wandered aimlessly, seeming without true purpose, just like real geese. I watched Hester slip into the pond and begin washing her face, her hair. The pond could have held twenty children, but Hester filled the whole thing. It looked like a water hole with her inside it. I was going to call out to tell her she shouldn't be out alone like this, that there were still crazies around who would rather see her disappear than take a bath in this pond, but I stopped when I saw her rise from the water, look furtively from side to side, and step into the little grove of trees near the pond.

I followed in secret, casting my own furtive looks over my shoulder. I felt like a spy, capturing enemy information. What's going on in that head of yours, Hester? I wondered.

Besides a tree growing, that is.

I came down on the other side of the trees, in case Hester had placed one of the geese by the pond as a lookout. She was hiding something—that much was obvious. Luckily, the park was well groomed. "Managed," is how the grounds-keepers referred to it, so there was no underbrush to rattle through, which might have alerted Hester. There were well-trod dirt trails, and little flower gardens between trees, everything patterned like an English garden. I ducked from tree to tree, my back pressed against the bark so Hester wouldn't see me. I felt invigorated by my own cleverness. I was primal and silent—I thought maybe I should try hunting. And then, all at once, I came upon Hester kneeling down in what appeared to be an "unmanaged" section of the grove.

Here were brambles and thorny bushes, vines creeping up the sides of trees that grew wild with branches; there were ferns and wild flowers growing along the forest floor—and it did seem like a forest, not a park at all. There were even rings of mushrooms. I was waiting to see a fairy arrive. Hester knelt down on a patch of moss near the base of a large weeping willow. The weeping willow that grew out of her head swayed above her and the weeping willow that grew in the grove swayed along with it, but there was no wind. Hester picked something up from the mushroom ring in her pale white hands, and as I snuck closer to see what it was, a branch broke beneath my feet. I had grown too comfortable sneaking through the managed sections of the park, clear of debris and noisy branches. My dreams of big game hunting evaporated as suddenly as I'd dreamed them.

Hester's eyes snapped open. She lifted her head and looked at me as if I were one of the crazy people who left death threats on our answering machine. "Stephen!" she shouted in surprise, staggering up from her kneeling position. The fear in her eyes reminded me of a deer caught in headlights, even though I hadn't seen a deer in our town for at least five years. I thought she was going to run, but she didn't. "What are you doing here?" she asked instead.

"I'm sorry, Hester" I said. "I was going to call out, but then you came inside here. What is this place? What are you doing here?"

"Don't worry about it," she said, her face firm. "It's a secret, so don't tell anyone you saw me here. Not even Mom and Dad."

I raised my eyebrows. "Do you seriously think I'm going to leave here, say nothing, and *not* try to find out what it is you're hiding?"

"I'm not hiding anything," she said. "I'm protecting something. There's a difference."

"Sometimes you have to hide something to protect it," I said. "Come on, Hester. You can trust me. I won't tell anyone. Promise."

At that moment she peered down into her cupped hands at whatever she was holding. Then she opened her hands a little and lowered them so I could see.

She was holding a grayish colored egg. It was about the size of a football, but in Hester's hands, it appeared to be the size of a chicken egg. Blue spots polka-dotted its surface. "An Easter egg?" I asked, which was the first thought that came to me.

Hester nodded. "Yes. But not how you're thinking."

"What then?"

"It's not an Easter egg, really," said Hester. "Just sort of. It's bringing something back to us. Something dead is coming back again."

I reached out to stroke the egg, but Hester pulled her hands back as soon as I made a move toward it. "No!" she shouted. "You can't touch it, Stephen. No one but I can touch it."

"I wasn't going to hurt it!" I shouted back. "Don't be so bossy, Hester!"

"I'm sorry. It's just that those are the rules. Only me, Stephen. Only I can touch it. I'm its guardian. I'm the guardian of the egg."

"What are you guarding it from?" I asked, and Hester looked over my shoulders, then from left to right, as if there might be unseen presences eavesdropping.

"From them," she said. "From the people. If anyone knew about the egg, that it was the cause of my changes and all the other changes around here, they'd destroy it. Just like they do with everything else."

"Why not keep it at the house then?" I suggested.

"Because that's the most likely place to look. If I keep the egg somewhere public, they'll never find it. People always look where they're not supposed to be looking. If I keep it where anyone could find it, they won't even think to come here. Also, the egg needs a place with trees and clean water. The park is growing stronger now."

It was true. The park was slowly but surely being overtaken by a new growth of trees and wild flowers. A surge of underbrush and brambles grew over and between trees like the strands of a spider's web.

"But is this a *good* thing?" I asked. "How do you know the egg isn't evil?"

"Because I know," said Hester. "I just know, Stephen. You'll have to trust me."

Both of us had asked for trust from the other. This was something new to my relationship with my sister. We'd barely held a conversation before this one, except to argue and put each other down. Suddenly I felt like we understood each other, had jumped over the preliminary forgiveness rituals and gone straight into a deep and meaningful friendship. I wasn't ashamed of this feeling. I wasn't ashamed of Hester anymore either, even if she *was* over eight feet tall, white as a clown, and covered with vegetation. I knew to trust her, as she knew to trust the egg, and so I did that, and went home with her that morning, and said nothing to anyone about her secret.

Hester's growth became more problematic as each month passed. At eleven feet tall, she was quickly becoming visible to the outside world again. My father's fence would keep her from prying eyes and cameras for only a few more weeks. Also, we had no clothes that Hester could fit into, and autumn was chilling us into a sudden December. My mother went to the Super-Mart and ordered yards and yards of a stretchy orange fabric, then sewed it into a shapeless dress for Hester. "You'll grow into it, honey," she said, and ran her fingers through my sister's yellow-brown hair. Kernels of wheat clung to Hester's shoulders. Now that the sun grew weaker, Hester's hair fell out in shocks of dried brown wheat.

"It's a little flimsy," Hester told my mother. She lifted the hem of the dress and said, "The wind will cut right through."

"A coat then," my mother said, and rushed back into her sewing room.

Several days later she emerged with a white cape made from bed sheets and lined with flannel. "I'm sorry it's not a coat," said my mother. "I didn't have enough material."

Hester tied the cape around her neck. She looked dashing, like a superhero. She thanked my mother and didn't complain about her makeshift clothes, nor that she had to go barefoot. She knew her changes were costing our parents a small fortune.

Hester spent the winter inside the house, sleeping through most of it, curled up in the dining room. She seemed to be hibernating, waiting. Her breath came sparsely, but it kept on coming. Her geese flew south when the cold months arrived, and I wondered if they would return when it grew warmer, or if they would find other idols to worship come next summer.

Sometimes my parents and I would be in the living room, watching TV, snow falling gently against the picture window, and Hester would utter something incomprehensible from the dining room. I once asked her questions while she slept, whispering into her ear, "What's happening now?" to which Hester replied, "There are two creatures here with me. They sit in my tree and throw down apples for me to eat. I tell them to save the apples, I'm not hungry, but they keep throwing them anyway."

"What do they look like?" I asked.

"I don't know," said Hester. They're in my tree. The tree growing out of my head. They're above me. I can't see them."

"Tell them I see them," I whispered, even though I saw nothing in the tree growing out of Hester's head. It lay across the dining room floor, brown and withered, only the trunk still looking strong and alive.

Hester was silent for a moment. Then she finally spoke again. "They say you are lying. They say to tell you to stop meddling in their affairs. You are not the guardian of the egg! Be patient, they say. Some day you, too, may be important."

WHEN WINTER DIED, and spring came to melt the snow piled in our yards and tree limbs, Hester finally awakened. My mother was cooking breakfast for my father before he left for work. She scraped eggs around in a frying pan and I stood beside her, spooning wheat flakes into my mouth. The eggs sizzled and foamed in the frying pan. My mother was telling me about a dream she'd had the night before.

"There were all these people in it," she said. "They all looked familiar and strange at the same time. You were in it, and so was Dad, and Mr. Jackson the school janitor—he was there too. And Ellen Darby, next door, she was trying to give me a pitchfork. We were in a forest, but our clothes were weird. Rustic. We all looked like farmers and farmer's wives, bonnets and linen dresses. I kept shouting for you and your father to run before we had to start farming, but you wouldn't listen. You already had a hoe in your hands."

Before I could laugh at my mother, a groan came from the dining room. My mother turned the heat off the eggs and we ran to the next room to find Hester pushing herself up from the floor. She was having difficulties. Her weeping willow was wedged in one corner of the dining room, and she couldn't back up far enough to dislodge it. "Help," she sobbed when we entered the room. "I'm stuck!"

My father decided to take extreme measures. He went to the garage and came back with the chainsaw. Hester screamed when he pulled its cord and the chainsaw began buzzing. "I won't hurt you!" he promised. Quickly, efficiently, he slipped the saw through several branches, and they fell to the floor in a pile of dust.

Hester opened her eyes after he shut the saw off. "Is it over?" she asked, and my mother patted Hester's rump and told her everything was okay. We took the patio doors off their sliding tracks, and Hester squeezed out into the sunshine. She took a deep breath, and the wheat framing her face lifted toward the warmth. "Finally," Hester whispered, still kneeling on the back deck in the puddles of newly melted snow. "It is time," she said. Whether she spoke to us or to some unseen audience, I couldn't tell. But soon a dark V-shape appeared in the sky, distant but coming closer, and within moments Hester's geese landed in our backyard, milling about, nibbling her ears, her fingers, as she stroked them.

IT WASN'T MUCH longer before the entire town was bursting with spring again, and the rain was falling, falling, bringing up beds of forgotten flowers. The trees budded, unfurling leaves like banners in only a few weeks. I saw a deer—a buck—one day on my way home from school, loping through the park, which was nearly unrecognizable anymore. The park had grown an unruly amount of trees around its perimeter, like the wall of thorns in the Sleeping Beauty story, and no one dared enter its darkness any longer. Children told stories about witches living in the grove at its center. Before the park became a forest, our witch stories were always set in the house of some old lady nobody liked. It was a strange phenomenon to see a story leave the comforts of our houses, our streets and cul-de-sacs, to take up residence in the new forest.

Hester was busy. She paced the backyard, chewing her fingernails with a look of constant worry, while her geese flew in and out of the yard on what seemed to be missions. One would leave and another would land and waddle up to Hester to report its findings. Hester would kneel down and press her ear to the goose's bill in order to hear its secret messages. New saplings rose from the wet ground all across town. They grew thick and strong, branching and rebranching over the course of a few weeks. Bushes and brambles sprang up between them. Ellen Darby found a large thicket of blueberry bushes in her backyard. She set a sign out by her driveway that said FRESH BLUEBERRIES, PICK YOUR OWN!

My mother told me one morning, "Don't go to school, Stephen."

"Why?" I asked.

"Because Hester is in trouble. I drove past the town hall this morning on my way to the Super-Mart. There were a lot of people there already. They were in the parking lot with picket signs. They were shouting horrible things about Hester. They say the property value is declining, that it's because of her. I don't want you near that crowd, understand me?"

I nodded and she patted the back of my head.

My father stayed home from work that day, too. All of us gathered in the backyard. We grilled steaks and skewers of vegetables. I chased the geese around the birdbath, splashing them with water. It was good-natured fun, and they loved it. Hester could see this, so she didn't chastise. She leaned against the fence with her knees tucked up to her chest. She sighed a lot, and ate a lot, and seemed anxious. So did my parents, but they did their best to hide their anxieties. They were both good at doing that, and as their child, I appreciated their tact and skill at covering up their own problems. I had my own problems, and anyway, children shouldn't have to worry about their parents. It's supposed to be the other way around.

Toward evening, when the sky purpled and the wind started to buck, Hester told us she was leaving. Somehow we'd all been prepared for this and weren't surprised by her decision. My mother resisted only once with an, "Oh, honey, don't talk like that." But Hester shook her head. My mother lowered her face and said no more. She just nodded.

"I won't be going far," Hester told us. "Just to the old park, the new forest. I'll be safe there. You can come visit me sometimes. Later, though, after everything has settled."

This cheered my parents a bit. They went to Hester and hugged her arms, her legs, tried to fit their arms around her neck. They cried a little, then retreated to the house.

I was about to say my good-byes, too, but Hester spoke before me.

"Stephen," she said, "I need you to come with me. You'll have to keep watch for a few days. If anyone tries to find me in there, you'll have to stop them, or else everything will be ruined."

"This is my job, isn't it?" I asked.

"Yes," said Hester. "You are the guardian of the guardian of the egg. Please don't let me down."

I nodded gravely. I would protect her under any circumstances. In a matter of minutes, I collected my whittling knife, rope from the basement, and my BB gun. I felt like an action hero gearing up for battle. Mel Gibson, Arnold Schwarzenegger—why didn't the director of *Wild Thing* approach one of *them* to play my role?

We left for the park later that night. In the darkest hours, our town was silent except for the sounds of crickets whirring, night birds cooing, and the strum of frogs in their secret places. Hester's geese flew our route before us, then circled around to report that the way was clear. An unmarked white van was parked several houses down from ours, but the driver was slumped against the window, asleep from too much waiting for Hester. We followed the geese through the vine-covered streets until we arrived at the park, where Hester slipped into a dark sliver of space between two towering elms. As soon as she passed between them, she disappeared. I couldn't even hear her rustling in the branches. A moment later her long pale arm stretched forth from the dark place and her fingers curled inward, motioning for me to follow. I took hold of her pinky and Hester pulled me inside her realm.

The quiet of the suburbs I'd heard as we slipped through the streets of our town would have sounded like a parade in that forest. I heard nothing there but wind in the trees and the gurgle of a nearby creek. Hester loomed large above me. Her breath came heavily, as if she were anxious. Suddenly she started walking at a fast pace, pushing through the treetops, which swayed and snapped back into place behind her. The ground beneath my feet trembled at her step. I clasped the hem of her orange dress to my chest and followed as close as possible so I wouldn't get caught in the backlash of branches. And in this way, crashing through the forest, we found our way to the grove at its center.

Tiny lights awaited us in the grove. They shimmered in the dark, floating through the night like miniature Japanese lanterns. As one passed by me, I heard a slight buzzing sound, a hum like a bee as it skims your ear in summer. I looked at Hester, who stood in the center of the grove already. The glowing creatures circled her, lit upon her face, her hair, her shoulders, upon the weeping willow growing out of her head. She held her arms out at both sides and turned in a slow circle, a smile of pure pleasure washing over her.

The trees in the grove towered over Hester, unlike some of the smaller ones at the border. If I squinted here among these giant elms and maples, she looked to be the right size again. For a moment, she looked like the old Hester, the girl who was once so awkward and quiet, books clasped to her chest protectively, ready to bump into anything if it meant avoiding other people. Hester still avoided people, but now it was for different reasons: now Hester shrank from the burdens of civilization in order to accomplish a task so mysterious even I didn't know all the reasons for her secrecy.

"Here," she murmured, talking to herself really. She stood upon a small hill, and I saw that she held the egg in her hands once again. A pale stream of silver moonlight spilled over her, illuminating the trees ringing the hillside. She slipped the egg into one of the pockets of her orange dress, then bent down and forced her fingers into the earth. She groaned, struggling, flexing her muscles. The wheat of her hair rustled over her shoulders, against the small of her back. The weeping willow tree growing out of her head swayed with her exertion. Finally she pulled up a tab of earth and continued pulling until she'd pulled up the grass and sod of the hillside in one long strip.

"It's up to you now, Stephen," she said, wiping the sweat from her pale brow. The glowing creatures circled her as if they were planets orbiting a sun.

"Don't worry, Hester," I told her. I trotted up to her and she bent down and lifted me into her arms. "You're so big!" I said, truly realizing it for the first time. Since she'd started changing, I never actually allowed myself to touch her. I was happy to touch her now. She was still my sister. She was still Hester underneath all that flora. I wished I'd hugged her more often when she was still five foot seven, and I could reach my arms all the way around.

Hester placed me gently back on the ground, then laid herself down in the hole she'd created. She pulled the strip of grassy sod under her chin like a blanket. She was getting comfortable in the hillside, wiggling her toes at one end, shrugging her shoulders at the other to make more room. She retrieved the egg from her pocket a moment later. Then, holding it between her forefinger and thumb, she placed it inside her mouth. She swallowed, and the egg traveled down the column of her throat and disappeared from my sight forever.

"Take care, Stephen," she said, blinking soberly. Then she pulled the quilted earth over herself entirely and disappeared as well.

I MAINTAINED A defensive position in the days that followed. Hester's geese helped to guard the perimeter of the grove where Hester had buried herself in the hillside. The geese patrolled the outer borders, reporting to me at varying scheduled hours during the mornings, evenings, and in the night. I didn't understand their bluster, but I sensed that their posts were well watched. Only once did I feel an impending threat to the grove, and that came on the fourth night of our vigil, just when I thought things were going to be okay.

Brunhilda, the Viking goose, suddenly appeared in the grove at sunset, her wings fluttering anxiously, her bill filled with an alarming honk. She led me through the forest until we reached a blind of brush that she'd selected as her vantage point. I kneeled beside her in silence and waited, and then all at once I heard the sound of men moving through the forest, snapping branches beneath their feet, grunting, sometimes cursing. More than one voice. Perhaps three, maybe four. All male, deep, and rough.

I looked down at Brunhilda, gave her the signal for our agreed upon plan of action, and she nodded gruffly and waddled out into the woods, awaiting the men. Once they reached us, she flew up into their faces, landed, jogged away from them for a moment until she was sure they were following her, and then took once again to air.

I caught only a glimpse of them. They were dressed differently from each other: one in flannel and blue jeans, another in a business suit, and also the postman. Two of them had guns, a handgun and a rifle. The postman held a baseball bat, and slapped it lightly against the palm of his hand. Two shots rang out immediately. "Blast her!" the postman shouted. When the silence of the woods resumed a moment later, he ran forth like a dog to see if he could retrieve Brunhilda. He returned to the other men shaking his head. "Missed her," he said, "but she's just up ahead." On hearing this, they began to track Brunhilda once again.

It didn't take much longer to capture them. Brunhilda executed our plan brilliantly, leading them to a pit Hester had dug for us before burying herself. We'd covered it with weak branches and leaves and pieces of brush. The men ran over it, the branches broke beneath their weight, and they fell twelve feet into the earth.

What other disturbances we faced were minimal. Other geese had scared off trespassers simply by surprising them, jumping out of their hiding places and chasing them out of the park. A week passed, and no more incidents occurred, and I decided it was time to venture back to town.

This was a trickier proposition than I thought, though. The town was no longer the town I remembered. As I slipped through the two towering trees that Hester had guided me through, it became apparent that the roads were no longer drivable—trees broke through the pavement, tumbled the sidewalk slabs this way and that. Vines grew over street lamps, filtering their light so that it felt like you were underwater, like swimming at the bottom of our pool in the backyard.

I found home eventually. My parents cried when they saw me, circled me in their arms and held me close. "We were so worried, so worried," my mother sobbed. "Where is Hester?" my father asked. I told them she was safe, that she was in the old park, that she said to tell them she loved them, but this was a call she could no longer ignore. They nodded, but I could tell they didn't understand. "Where did I go wrong?" my mother asked no one in particular. "Was it all those years of Brownies and Girl Scouts?" my father pondered.

We toured the rest of the town—or what remained of it— later in the week. Whatever Hester and her egg were up to, it had changed our home from its original refined layout into a riot of wild things. A wellspring sprung up in the electronics department of the Super-Mart, ruining the TVs and computers and stereo equipment on the shelves. Deer roamed the strip mall parking lots, which now greened over with thick grasses and wild flowers. Our school found itself surrounded by oaks so tall they appeared hundreds of years old. Bird song filled the air. The chatter of squirrels. Overnight our town population tripled, but no one human moved in.

Soon after Hester's metamorphosis reached its final stages, many of the people of our town packed their belongings into their SUVs and minivans and drove off to other towns outside of Hester's influence. A few people stayed, though, and some newcomers arrived. It was a small settlement, and we lived off what the land provided, and tried not to over-extend it or ourselves.

My parents decided to stay in the hopes that, one day, Hester might come back to us, a regular girl again. Actually, it was my mother held this hope. My father only indulged it from time to time. I myself felt that Hester wasn't really gone. She was all around us, in the air and in the earth and water. I could smell her, feel her chest rise and fall as I walked the forest to visit her hillside, I could hear her voice on the wind and in the gurgle of the streams. I saw her face, just once, in the still surface of a small lake. I was fishing, and then I wasn't. I was watching my reflection in the water instead, thinking, Hester, Hester, show yourself, give them a sign. They miss you so.

Hester's face swam up at me then, floating just under the water. She smiled, tilted her head at a quizzical angle, waved, then swam to the bottom again.

The tree was no longer growing out of her head. Her body had returned to the young woman's body I remembered. I wondered if perhaps she had been showing herself occasionally to my mother and father, and that these brief visitations kept them here in the hopes that she'd return one day for good.

SOMETIMES AT NIGHT, when my mother sews jackets and darns socks and mends buttons, when my father gathers firewood and guts fish for our dinner, when we're all home and the forest seems satisfied and restful, I go out to Hester's hillside, where the glowing creatures congregate in uncountable numbers—hundreds of them swarming the grove, faster fliers than most birds, brighter than most fireflies. I go out there and sit on the hillside with a book—sometimes school textbooks, sometimes an old paperback crime novel or a fairy tale—and I read aloud to Hester and the glowing creatures. They hover over my shoulder, perch upon my head or on my legs, folded Indian style, and when they are still I can sometimes make out their faces, tiny and almost human, their eyes slightly slanted, their ears slightly pointed. They no longer hum like bees when their wings are at rest. Quiet and rapt, they listen to the adventures of detectives, or to the mishaps of children lost in the woods, abandoned by their parents. They listen to stories of terrible witches who live in Victorian houses, not in forests at all, and wonder at the utter strangeness of automobiles, airports, high-rises, factories, subways, and cell phones, only to return from these visions of a world not their own, hearts eased, home again.

Christopher Barzak grew up in rural Ohio, lived in Japan for two years teaching English near Tokyo, and recently returned to the United States. His stories have been published in magazines and anthologies, including *The Year's Best Fantasy and Horror*, *The Mammoth Book of Best New Horror*, *Trampoline*, *Realms of Fantasy*, *Nerve*, *Lady Churchill's Rosebud Wristlet*, *Pindeldyboz*, *The Third Alternative*, *Strange Horizons*, *The Journal of Mythic Arts*, and *So Fey*. His first novel, *One for Sorrow*, is forthcoming from Bantam Books. He is currently completing his second.

My Travels with Al-Qaeda

Lavie Tidhar

I KEEP GOING BACK to the disaster areas:

Poet as war correspondent, words like tracer bullets
Lighting up the sky
Shouldering memory like a backpack and marching into
The battle fields of time.

If I could make you see:
I hand you a poem like a pair of field-glasses—

Words like a flock of bullets
A pride of artillery
A gaggle of grenades
Quick after-images of impact burning through your retina

Imprints scribbled by star light and camp fire and kerosene stoves
Poems of permanent semi-darkness.

I was in Dar-es-Salaam when the American embassy blew up
And in Nairobi a week later
Watching the circle of underfed Kenyan soldiers as they surround-
ed the building
Like a chastity belt over a virgin who was no longer innocent.
The building, shell-shocked, caved-in, deformed
Had finally managed to blend with its surroundings

No longer American, it was now just another collapsed dream,
Easily sharing a crumpled roll-up with a scratch-card tout
Or a taxi driver
At the corner of the pock-marked road.

—THE AMERICAN EMBASSY IN NAIROBI, LIOR TIROSH (1998)

IN THE SUMMER Dar-es-Salaam is even less attractive than usual: the August heat squats over low buildings and stains with sweat the pages of the African Writers Series paperbacks sold from a cart outside the hotel. Black ink smudges Ngugi wa Thiong'o's *Devil on the Cross*; in a small tearoom near the harbor Alyson sits with a mug of milk tea and a box of matches that rattle between her fingers. It is 10:44, August 7, 1998.

Alyson feels nauseous; she threw up in the hotel earlier, a thin, pale liquid sluicing between her teeth into the small chipped sink. She has malaria, and the Lariam is giving both of us intense, vivid dreams that leave us sluggish and uncertain when we wake. She tries to read, but the paperback slips from her fingers and lands on the floor, disturbing dust. She sips from the tea and shudders despite the heat.

I watch the old clock hanging above the small kitchen door; a black, one-eared dog lies asleep beneath it. I take the matches from Alyson and strike one against the size of the box, putting a Malawian *Life* cigarette in my mouth. The night before I dream of Brueghel's *Icarus*, the boy falling from the heavens while everything around him turns away: in my dream the fall is silent and the boy's face is filled with ecstasy like a bungee-jumper at Vic Falls. We stand and watch his fall together, Alyson and I, holding hands on the shore, and I recognize the place instantly: it is the Dar harbor and the ship sailing calmly away is the Zanzibar ferry, as cumbersome and ungainly as a sow.

The clock ticks, and it is 10:45. Somewhere in the distance, a car explodes, and people die.

(Manager's son, Hilltop Hotel, Nairobi): Khalid Saleh

> *You know, this is like a train station. People come and go. I've not seen any of them. It's a very busy place, and you could have definitely noticed. Usually cleaners come to clean every day. We don't allow people to go with the keys, so if there were anyone who was assembling a bomb here, it could not have been done here, definitely not, (I am) 100-Percent (sure).*
>
> —FBI Transcript, 1998

⸻

PERHAPS IT STARTS, if it starts at all, in July 2005 in London, when Alyson gets on the train to go to work in Farringdon, via King's Cross.

I'm asleep while Alyson is on the train. I dream of the Hilltop Hotel, of the single bed we lie on, faces close to each other's, of breathing in Alyson's patchouli. I dream that in the adjoining room one of the bombers is currently sleeping. He lies on his back on the narrow bed and dreams of being in London, getting on a packed commuter train, going about his business via King's Cross. He turns in his sleep, makes eating noises that go unheard through the wall separating us.

Alyson and I kiss. She closes her eyes when we do. I fall asleep with my arm around her and dream of her getting on the train. It's July 7, 2005, in London. It's July 7, 1998, in Nairobi.

Somehow, we are caught between these two summers, and the seasons freeze.

⸻

ALYSON ARRIVES IN Nairobi from London in the beginning of summer. Night covers the tarmac as if trying—or so it seems to her then, the transition from Europe to Africa only beginning its metamorphosis—to hide the city's flaws, its cracked roads, its flaking paint, dusty Cola stands, and bag thieves. She takes a black cab (she remembers thinking how strange it was, seeing a London cab in such a place and wondering how it got there) to downtown Nairobi, where the cab stops outside the hotel. The driver's name is Martin Ayub; Alyson thanks him as she pays and he smiles at her before driving away. Alyson shoulders her small backpack and goes in, where she pays for a single room at the Hilltop Hotel.

The room has a view of the street outside: lying on the bed she sees a white backpacker with long, dirty-blond dreadlocks buying a scratch card. He is smoking a cigarette while clutching a coin between his fingers, and it glints under the street lamp. Evidently unsuccessful, he drops the card to the ground and turns around, lifting his head, and their eyes meet.

I LOOK UP and see the girl in the window. She has large eyes that seem soft against the hard glare of the street light.

We meet again over breakfast at the hotel's shabby dining-room. There are other people there: maybe, I think, one of them is Mohamed Rashed Daoud Al-Owhali, or Mohammed Odeh, or Wadih el Hage, or Khalfan Khamis Mohamed: I must see them, perhaps to say hello to, as I pass room 102 or 107, but if I do, I never know. They seem to trickle through our lives without leaving stains, seeping harmlessly through this serene scene of young backpackers and rundown businessmen.

Alyson and I talk. Where are you from? Where have you been before Nairobi? Where are you going to?

Mombasa, we both answer the last one, and smile, and our hands touch between my coffee, her tea.

When we leave the hotel it is two days later, and we

disappear like moisture drying on glass, evaporating without leaving traces. Like bomb-makers.

⌒

IN MY TEL Aviv hotel in 2004 I think of bomb-makers as I look at the small, jacketless hardcover I buy from a shop on Dizengoff Street. It is a worn book of poetry, by an Israeli writer I have never heard of. His name is Lior Tirosh. I stand the book on its spine and let it open of its own accord. Pages know where they have been most read, and the book, *Remnants of God*, opens to a page a short length away from the end. Alyson is away, on holiday in the Sinai with a friend, sunbathing on the shore of the Red Sea. I'm working. We've been apart a week.

The poem the book opens on to is called "Wires and Charge," and I read it as I wait for sleep, while *Die Hard* flickers silently in the background.

The place where we first kiss
is, in all likelihood, gone:

destroyed by the army, the police, various terrorist organizations;
I have not been back to Jerusalem to check.

just a public bench,
hard wood warming in the fading sunlight like an old cat, peeling paint—

overlooking the cemetery on Mount Zion
and, somewhat nearer, a children's playground.

when darkness approached we sat like suicide bombers
touching lips together

like wires and charge
exploding.

THAT NIGHT IN Dar, Alyson throws up again in the hotel, then lies beside me, her small frame shivering against my back. She falls asleep slowly, while I lie awake and listen to the cries of the *muezeen* calling for the evening prayers. We have seen no newspapers, heard no radio: we are wrapped in each other's misery, a shared malarial dream, and when I fall asleep at last she is waiting for me. Her face is pale in the light of dying suns, and the city at our backs is a ruin, tall minarets spinning between them a torn web of impossibly thin walkways. The cries of the *muezeen* echo inside the dream, rising from the minarets of this nameless, impossible city. Maybe this is the foundation: I find myself searching, more and more, for a base, a starting point, a ground zero. In modern Arabic, the word is Al-Qaeda: and I wonder what they, too, are looking for, and if they'll ever find it.

I turn as I think this, the wind suddenly cold against my bare arms. I'm wearing a T-shirt, and I realize it's like the ones Alyson tells me about when she gets back from Afghanistan: the Nike sign, and underneath a drawing of an AK-47 and the legend in Arabic that says, simply, Osama.

There is a lighthouse farther down the shore and as I turn I see the light come on, shining cold through crystalline walls. There is a figure standing underneath, face cowled; robes shake in the wind, and for a moment it seems that the figure is dancing.

⌐

WE SEEM TRAPPED in the dream, and in time. It moves, not linearly any more but sideways, and we are shunted with it, juggled like marbles on a carved, ebony bawo board, shunted from moment to moment, between the holes and the cracks. Time has become a videotape on which Clint Eastwood shoots the bad guys again and again only for them to come back when the tape is rewound. And those moments, frozen amber memories, define us, border us in. Dar, Nairobi, Ras-al-Shaitan, Kabul, London. A litany of years, a rosary of months, a Kaddish of numbers.

We remember them before they happen and yet we continue to be bounced between them as if we are trapped in an American pinball machine.

Martin Ayub (Nairobi Cab Driver):

> *They could assemble it, knowing the people here don't know much about bombs. You see most of the people here they are mechanics and all these other people (types of professions). So if people come with the bombs and start assembling (them), nobody would know that this is a bomb.*
> —FBI Interview Transcript, 1998

SUMMER IS THE time for bombs. It is 2005 and the Americans are all over Kabul. Alyson is in Afghanistan for an NGO training course; our phone call is cut off by helicopters flying above her hotel. After we talk she stands alone on the Soviet concrete balcony of her room at the Intercontinental. From

up here, high on the mountain slope, she can see all of Kabul
spread before her like a dirty blanket. She watches the legless
wheel themselves around on boards of wood, and the little
children in the streets who have taken over the city's economy.
It is a sweltering forty degrees and the hot water tap in the
bathroom is dripping, turning the air to steam. Alyson watches
Al-Jazeera on the old cumbersome television on the dresser,
and *Rambo*. Later, she goes down to the buffet meal by the
pool, where a large, well-fed American tries to chat her up.

It's August 16. As Alyson sits in the hotel a helicopter crash
near Herat kills seventeen Spaniards. In the north it's poppy
harvest time: soldiers capture several tons of opium and burn
them on a bonfire, and for a short time it seems everyone in
Afghanistan is simply stoned.

IT'S OCTOBER 7, 2004, and I wish I was stoned. It's getting late. I have switched off the television and Bruce Willis's
John McClane fades away just as he is about to kill two
terrorists. I stand by the window and look at the Tel Aviv
skyline and the hint of blue sea, and listen to the traffic move
far below. I think of picking up the book again when the
phone rings.

It is my father. I switch the television back on. Bruce Willis is gone, and in his stead is a news bulletin. Confused images and loud presenters, and no one knows exactly what's
going on, but for two things: there have been bomb attacks
in the Sinai, and I can't get hold of Alyson.

BUT SHE IS always there: and from Dar we take the bus back to Nairobi, and the long, hot journey across narrow roads sends us both to sleep.

She rests her head in the space between my shoulder and neck, her breath hot against my skin. She dreams, and in the dream she is alone on that distant shore and the minarets are gone, torn down and ground to dust, and in their place is a new city, of low-rising white stone and trees. On the empty beach a bonfire burns, sending sweet, intoxicating fumes into the air, and she breathes them in and thinks of Osama.

~

NEAR RAS-AL-SHAITAN, the Devil's Head, Alyson lies on the dusty woven rug on the sand and looks up at the stars. A girl beside her assembles a Bob Marley from three King Size skins into a conical shape, tears the roach from the top of the *Rizla* packet. The girl lights up and passes the joint to Alison. She doesn't know where the dope comes from. Perhaps Afghanistan.

She feels a tremor, so slight it is possible she imagines it, but it is followed by the sound of sirens. As the tourists lying on the beach stand up, there is the sound of an explosion. The blue ganja smoke rises and threads into the dirty-black smoke that begins to blow from farther down the beach, and the joint is soldered to Alyson's lips as she rises with the others. At that moment she is reminded of her dream, the ruined city by the shore, the cowled figure wreathed in shadow. It's Mr. Man. It's Mystery Man. For a moment the explosion clouds form a smiling face through the darkness, and stars sparkle through its hollow eyes.

More black smoke billows up into the sky as, a kilometer down the beach, a man has blown himself up with a soft wet sound and people die.

‿

PEOPLE DIE; TAKE Yeats, or Auden's eulogy of him. Is death really dark and cold? It had seemed to me, seems to me now, as I wait in the hotel room in Tel Aviv and ride the bus to Nairobi and hold her hair while she pukes in the hotel room in Dar, that the death we had seen, the death we see, again and again in our burrowing through time, is hot and humid and rank, the sun beating with little mercy on our browning bodies and makes us shell clothes like the pods of peas or the outer layers of onions. That death, *that* death, always comes in the midst of a never ending summer, like an unwanted family guest who arrives unexpectedly and refuses to leave. Alyson remembers the sight of the burned-out car rammed into the Taba Hilton Hotel on the Egyptian side of the border, and the tan brown legs that protruded like two upturned fingers from the wreck. Disembodied, existing independently of a body, unworthy of being called a corpse.

And she thinks, inexplicably, of love.

‿

I AM ALWAYS away when they happen. Always apart from her, not able to hold her, not able to share the near-escapes. In London, I am asleep as the blast rips through the tube carriage on the Piccadilly, and in the Sinai I am a country away, holding helplessly to a phone. In Dar and Nairobi we were only tourists; by Ras-al-Shaitan we've become participants.

‿

ALYSON WATCHES ME with her hands wrapped around her mug of tea. They are malarial pale despite her brown tan from Zanzibar.

I watch the old clock hanging above the small kitchen door; a black, one-eared dog lies asleep beneath it. I take the matches from Alyson and strike one against the size of the box, putting a Malawian *Life* cigarette in my mouth.

Alyson watches me and thinks of the night before, when we make love in the sluggish heat and fall asleep under the slow revolving fan hanging from the ceiling. She dreams of a boy falling from the sky, and in the dream the boy's face is filled with horror. She tries to focus on the boy but, with the logic of dreams, she then sees a horse scratching itself against a tree, and by the time her attention returns to the skies the boy disappears.

She watches the clock above the kitchen door.

The clock ticks, and it is 10:45. Somewhere in the distance, a car explodes, and our half-life begins.

Lavie Tidhar grew up on a kibbutz in Israel, lived in Israel and South Africa, traveled widely in Africa and Asia, and has lived in London for a number of years. He is the winner of the 2003 Clarke-Bradbury Prize (awarded by the European Space Agency), was the editor of *Michael Marshall Smith: The Annotated Bibliography* and the anthology *A Dick & Jane Primer for Adults*, and is the author of the novella *An Occupation of Angels*. His stories appear in *SCI FICTION, Chizine, Postscripts, Nemonymous, Infinity Plus, Aeon, The Book of Dark Wisdom, Fortean Bureau*, and other magazines and anthologies, and in translation in seven languages.

Chandail

~~~~~~~

Peter S. Beagle

LAL SAYS. CAPE Dylee is not like other places.

Yes, it does resemble Leishai, Grannach Harbor, and the Karpache headland in being almost perpetually cold and misty, clearing only when the shrill *laschi* winds of late summer dispel the haze for a little while. Myths and legends—gods, even—always seem to be born in such places, possibly because one's vision is generally so clouded. But Cape Dylee is different, all the same.

My full name is Lalkhamsin-khamsolal. In other times and lands I have been known by such names as Sailor Lal, Swordcane Lal, Lal-Alone, and Lal-after-dark, but all that was very long ago. Now I am older than I ever expected to be, and I live here, in this desert hut, and I tell stories, which is what I was always meant to do, and people come far to hear them, as you have. Listen to me now, listen to an old woman, and perhaps I will make you very wise. Perhaps not.

Cape Dylee is indeed different from all other peninsulas isolated at the backside of nowhere, and not merely because of the fishermen's boots and trews and hooded capes for which it has become known. Cape Dylee is where you find the *chandail*.

No, they are altogether of the sea. I, too, have heard the tales that have them walking on land like men, but this is fable. As many legs as they have, and not all of them together capable of supporting their great soft bodies out of water. They *can* climb, slowly, but surprisingly well, employing all four of those finny arms to haul themselves up on any jutting bit of rock, or even a wharf now and then. Origin of the mermaid legend? Naked half-women languidly combing their hair to lure poor sailors and fishermen? You have never seen a *chandail*.

They are not shapeshifters, *chandail*, though it is easy to see why folk believe them so. Ugly, yes, marvelously horrific; yet if you look at them long enough, sometimes something happens to your sight, and you can actually see them becoming beautiful right before you, so beautiful that your eyes and mind hurt together, trying to take in such splendor. And yet they remain exactly what they are—dankly reeking multilegged monsters, like some grotesque cross between a jellyfish and a centipede. One knows that . . . one always *knows* that . . . and yet more than once I have forgotten to breathe, watching that impossible alteration, feeling my eyes filling with tears that I cannot lift a hand to brush away. Do *they* know—do they realize what is going on in the humans who stare at them so helplessly, repelled and yearning by turns, watching them ripple and shift like rainbows? Some days I think one thing, some days another.

You cannot ever tell from their faces. Oh, yes, they do have faces, in a sort of way; indeed, there are moments when they look heartbreakingly not quite human, nearly resembling plump-cheeked children, except for the huge slanted eyes (which are not really eyes) and the little parrot beak. Then—so subtly that you cannot tell where the transformation starts and ends—all features slide away, drift out of proportion into a shapelessness that the eye can never name or contain. What do they look like when that happens? Like clouds. Like massive, fleshy clouds, swollen with storm and stink. When the wind is right, you can smell them before you see them.

No, they cannot speak. They do not need to.

On Cape Dylee they say, "Ask advice of a wind in the grass—go to a rock-*targ* for comfort—but heed no word of the *chandail*." Not that they chat with humans in words; you hear them inside. No, not in your head—I said *inside*, making pictures in your bones and belly and blood, pictures that you *feel* in the way that you feel who you are, without having to study or remember it. They can impart a wondrous truth in this manner—a truth that lives as far beyond language as I live beyond the place where I was born—or they can picture you such a lie that the word itself has no meaning, a lie you will forever exalt over the truth, knowing all the while, every minute, what it is. Believe this—oh, for your soul, believe it. *Lal says*.

Being a storyteller myself, I have been drawn all my life to this thing the *chandail* can do; yet I am no closer to understanding its nature, or theirs, than I am to knowing, finally, what I am *besides* a storyteller, and a wanderer, and . . . someone my mother would not have liked very much. What I do know certainly is that the *chandail* are neither sea monsters nor magicians, nor mind readers, as those to whom the exact name matters so often assume. You might call them soul readers, if you choose. It is no more accurate than the other words, but it will do.

The fishermen there have more ancient legends and superstitions about the *chandail* than they have about fish. Depending on where you drink and with whom, you can hear that the First *Chandail* fashioned a world before this one of ours: gloriously beautiful, by all accounts, but crafted all of water, which was no problem until the Second *Chandail* made the sun. More wondrous yet, that must have been for a while, what with the new, new light bending and shattering so dazzlingly through those endless droplets—a rainbow creation, surely. Except, of course, that it melted away, by and by, and sank back into empty dark until the world we know came to be. I have been told, over many a tankard of the equally legendary Cape Dylee Black, that the *chandail* grieve still for that lost wonder, and would gladly call it back to drown ours, if they could. A sailor I know tells me that he can hear them planning in the night, in the little waves that chime and murmur against the sides of his ship. He says that they will never give up.

Another tale has it that the *chandail* could speak once, when they were first born, at the beginning of things. They were given the waters of this world for their dwelling by the fishermen's god, Minjanka, who instructed them not to be greedy, to share the catch with their neighbors, and always to warn the humans when they sensed a storm coming. The legend says that for a time the *chandail* did as they were ordered; but presently they become restless and mischievous, and began sending the fishermen off with word of vast shoals of herring and *lankash* and roe-laden *jariliya* to be found along the south shore, while they gorged themselves giddy half a mile west. In the same manner, they would divert the fish from their usual sea-roads, teasing and cozening them to flee this unseen predator, or swarm in search of that promised prey. Fish are quite naïve, and lack humor.

The same could be said for gods, I have often thought. Minjanka grew angry at this and took speech from the *chandail*, which was a mistake, more of a mistake than perhaps even a god could have known. Silent and patient, forced to find some other way of communicating, the *chandail* learned to lie in pictures, in images—in waking dreams—and found themselves newly able to deceive human beings to a depth and a degree that words could never have achieved, while the great Minjanka remained as ignorant as a fish. Gods can send dreams themselves, but they cannot eavesdrop. Always remember this; it's the only true privacy we have. *Lal says*.

I am not sure, even now, whether the *chandail* actually understand the difference between our flawed reality and the perfection of falsehood. Why should they, when we ourselves hardly do? See now, I tell the old stories, and train a young disciple to tell them as they should be told, as she will tell them after me. But no one knows better than I that what I teach through those tales, is not truth, not as you and I know what that word is supposed to mean. My truth is told through illusion, through fraudulence, through purest mendacity—why should it be any different with the *chandail*? In that way, if in no other, we may be kin.

They are sociable, in their way: it is not uncommon for a *chandail*—or several, for that matter—to follow a boat for days, keeping pace effortlessly while they babble to the crew in outlandish hallucinations, flooding them with antique gossip of the sea lanes, with uncanny fancies and foreshadowings, with memories most likely not their own. But they feel like our own—oh, that they surely do, even if one knows better. They *feel* like the memories we should have had, the dreams that belong to us, though we had no hand in their shaping. Even now, merely speaking of them, a dozen lives later, I can smell those memories. I can taste them.

I was very young when I met the *chandail*—at least it seems so to me now. It came about some time after I parted from the man I ever afterward called *my friend*, the wizard who took in, and sheltered, and trained, and loved (though he never once used the word) a child newly escaped from slavery and half-mad with terror. I had no desire ever to leave him. Indeed, I pleaded against it with all my heart. But he judged it time, and there never was any arguing with him. So I bundled what I owned, along with the gifts he gave me (not all of which needed to be packed up, or could be), and I set off along the road he recommended, which in time took me to Leishai, on the west coast. He always knew what I needed, that infuriating old man.

At Leishai I found work on a fishing boat called simply *The Polite Lady*. I was at home on that pitching, yawing deck the instant I set foot there, as though I had been bred and raised fishing day and night for *jariliya* and never coming ashore, like the families I used to see in the bustling harbor of Khaidun, where I was born. I did what I was told, scrubbing and shining, patching and sluicing down, and when I was ordered to lend a hand with the halyards or the anchor or the nets, I did that, too, and felt as though I had come home. No . . . no, I do not mean that, not as it sounds. I already knew that I could never go home.

I was stolen and sold when I was very young. I never saw my family again. Perhaps they sought me and still do; perhaps they shrugged. The one thing I know is that they never found me. I was sure that they would, for a long time.

When that passed, between one moment and the next—I was cleaning fish at the rail, just abaft the galley, as I recall—then I became Lal, there on the spot, Lal-Alone. Nothing dramatic about it; hardly even any sorrow or pain. All done, that, all gone over the side with the fish guts, gone with the salt spray wind-whipped across my face. I barely noticed, to tell you the truth.

But the *chandail did*—at all events, they began calling to me that same night. Coincidence it very well may be. I am only telling you what happened.

It may have been only one *chandail*—you never do know—but at the time there was no way I could have believed that a single creature could overwhelm me so with visions of my parents and the lost life already so far behind me. I dropped all the fish and sagged against a bulkhead, weeping as I never had—*never*—when certain things were being done to me. Because these were no ghostly, wispy, transparent glimpses of scenes remembered wrongly: no, these were real, and more than real—beloved faces and voices and bodies, all pressing so close, so desperately joyous to have me back at last. My little brother's nose was running, as it always was, and my mother was already fussing with my hair, and my father called me Precious. He had other pet names for his other children, but I was Precious.

It was not an illusion. Whatever I know today about the powers of the *chandail*, I will die believing that it was no illusion. *Lal says*—oh, *Lal says*.

And yet . . . and yet, even then I did know that it could not be—that they were not real here, in this place where I was, alone on *The Polite Lady* with my blood-slick fish, my shipmates, and the featureless, slow-heaving sea. I tried to tell them. With my arms around as many as I could hold—and I felt and bumped and smelled them all—I cried out to them, "Go away, I love you so, go away, *go away*!" But they stayed.

It was the Captain who finally came to my aid. She was a stocky, red haired, middle-aged woman, an easterner who spoke with the strange, thick Grije accent that seems to swallow half the vowels. She marched through the crowd around me as though they were none of them there—which, of course, for her they weren't—and she lifted me roughly to my feet with one calloused brown hand, saying, "So, so, girl, and now you have know *chandail*. Welcome aboard."

I could not speak for the tears. The Captain took me down to her cabin—no more than a bunk that she had for herself, while the rest of us slept in hammocks—and she gave me a full schooner of barleywine and waited patiently until I grew quiet, only sniffling a little, before she said, "They will do it again. You must accustom."

"No," I said. "No, I cannot bear it. I will have to get off, get off the boat."

The Captain smiled. "Then no fishing ever here, no

fishing anywhere near—you will go east, where folk talk like me, and no *chandail*. But you like here, yes?"

I nodded. I was sold east, the first time, and I swore before all the gods of my people that I would never in my life return there. I did, though, later on.

"So," the Captain said again. "So you learn not to listen. *Must* learn," and she caught me by the wrist, peering hard into my face with her hard blue eyes. "*Chandail* mean not much harm, not much good either. To them, our minds like—" she groped for a word—"like toyshop, like a playroom, our minds. Everything they find," and now she made a gesture and a face as though happily tossing invisible objects into the air with both hands, "play. You understand? All for *them*, no matter the rest, no matter us. You cry now—listen, we all cry over *chandail*, one time. One time, no more. You understand?" She waited until I nodded again. "Got to be, or we can't live. No cry no more—back on deck now, best thing." She slapped my shoulder heartily, and we went up together.

But I cried a good deal more before I finally became immune to the sendings from the sea. The worst of it, in a way, was not the faces, wracking as it was to feel myself surrounded again and again by all the loves of my amputated innocence, knowing beyond any self-deception that even though I could actually touch and hold them, I could not *touch* them, if you see what I mean. That was bad enough; but my particular horror was of the *places*—the sudden dazing visitations from gardens I had toddled through, woods where I had slipped away from my brothers, giggling happily to myself as I heard them shouting for me; the wharves and harbors where the sea-wonder had first taken hold of me. I was a long time learning not to see *them*, those hideaways of my heart. But the Captain knew. I did learn, like the others, because I had to.

And in so doing I came to hate the *chandail*, as I do not think I have ever hated even the ones whose hands and faces still wake me most nights, after so many years. Because at least those are long dead, all of them—someone else got Shavak before I found him, but I missed no others, for all the comfort I had of it—while these images daily and nightly brought back both the joy and the horror and despair of my childhood, and there was no revenging on that, nor ever would be. And the very worst thing was that I, like others, came to *desire* those visions, even as I loathed and dreaded their coming. As the Captain had said, the *chandail* were playing with me, in me, and I knew that I would forgive Shavak, and even Unavavia, before I forgave them.

In the years that followed, I traveled the sea, left the sea, came back to it, left it again . . . and so it has gone for me until more recently than you might think, to look at me. I'm done with the sea now—or it with me—but somehow in those days, journey as I might, I was never really away from it. Sooner or later, there I'd be, Sailor Lal once more—passenger, pirate, or crew, it made no matter. And so, will-I, nil-I, I have had some dealings with the *chandail* in my time.

And I would hate them still, bitterly, heartlessly, mercilessly, without compassion, in that way of hating that does no one any good, except for a thing that happened when I was *not* a sailor, but a plain paid . . . until I was hired to hunt down an undeniably bad man in Cape Dylee. Yes, I found

PETER S. BEAGLE

him, but that is not part of this story. What matters is that, having earned my fee, I was indulging myself somewhat, allowing myself a full night spent wandering the waterfront taverns before I set off for home the next day. Yet for some reason—perhaps because of a nagging doubt that the man was that much worse than I—no amount of ale, wine, or that vile but curiously captivating fish sauce the folk there call a liqueur had the least effect on me, much as I wished it. Near sunrise, then, I was as dead-sober as I'd been when I walked away down the long wharf, grateful for the kindly absence of the moon. Now, with the tide well on the ebb, I forced myself precisely back over my sandy footprints to see whether or no it had taken the body with it. Always so much simpler for everyone, for that to be the case.

Well, this time the sea had struck a bargain with me, as it has done once or twice since. The tide had indeed accepted my offering, but left for me, in return, an enormous pulpy mass of tangled—legs? Or were they vines? Strands of bladder-wrack?—four separate appendages that might almost be arms, each crested along its ropy length with a line of tiny, useless-looking fins; the whole dominated by a bulbous, more or less conical head with no recognizable features, except for the dainty little beak in the center. Not to mention the dizzying aroma, like an entire shoal of dead fish, all by itself. I had never seen a *chandail* close to before.

At first I was sure it was dead, because I saw, not only the blood dark on the sand under it, but the short spear half-buried in one of the still, flabby sides. It was a two-pointed stabbing lance, the kind the Cape fishermen use in shallow water—but I could not fathom why anyone with any sense would be hunting so plainly inedible a beast, nor what a *chandail* could have been doing so near shore. I came slowly closer in spite of the stench, in spite of the fear licking coldly along my nerves; not because of anything that helpless mass could possibly do to me, but out of a sailors' belief that a *chandail* can continue its making and sending—its *playing*—for some while after death. This is completely untrue, of course, and I knew it at the time. But it didn't matter, standing there with one foot in the sea and that great dead thing washing back and forth against it as the tide began to turn—nothing about it then to make you cry with wonder, I promise you. I wished that it would come to life for a moment, so that I could kill it again, and I bent and tugged the fish-lance out of its body, meaning to stab it once or twice, just for myself. I was a fine hater in those days.

And then it moved . . . and it *was* alive, though only the least bit so. It made a kind of floundering heave, slugging its helmet-shaped head like a horse fighting the reins. It pulled itself almost erect, turned blindly this way and that; then pitched over on its side once more, with the tiny, trusting sigh of a child falling asleep in a familiar place. I had expected a rush of blood to follow my removal of the lance, but there was almost none. The thing lived, that was plain enough, and either I ended it once and for all, or I took responsibility for keeping it alive. It's not important whether I yet abide by the ancient ethics of my people, I know what they are. *Lal says.*

Why did I make the choice I did? As long as it has been, I ask myself that question still. Perhaps my conscience was troubling me over the man I'd killed a few hours before—I have always had the most inconvenient conscience for the life I have lived—but much more likely it had to do with that first curious exchange at the water's edge. Somewhere in my long-gone child soul, there must have been a buried belief that it is bad *dree*—bad luck, you would say, bad business—to reject a gift from the sea. Abominate it or not, the wretched creature was mine.

And I hadn't any notion of what to do with it. The deep wound in its side had stopped bleeding altogether, but the *chandail* had shown no other sign of life after that one brief flurry. I stood over it (you don't ever get inured to the smell, but your nostrils go numb after a time) and wondered what to do. If there's a physicker in the world understands the innards of a maybe dying *chandail*, I've not met him, no more than I've again been that close to a living one: so close that I could see the fringes all along the undersides of the four arms quivering with the tide. They look very like hair, but it is thought that they serve the *chandail* as eyes in some way. I couldn't tell whether the motion meant that they were seeing, or not. I couldn't tell anything.

"Talk to me," I said aloud. "Here I am, talk to me."

I readied myself, bracing my mind—well I knew how to do it by now—against the shock that always comes with the first explosion of the *chandail* into their . . . playroom, as the Captain called it. But nothing happened. There came no apparitions, no impossibly responsive mirages such as I was bitterly accustomed to—only a silence in myself fathoms deeper than the mere absence of sound. Feeling almost as deep a relief, and something somehow absurdly close to guilt, I had begun to move away when there came a picture so tenuous, so frayed and shadowy, that I would never have recognized it as the sending of a *chandail*. As it was, in the darkness I could barely distinguish the figure of a woman, myself, bending over a huge inert form and lunging a swordcane blade into it, hard, over and over, all the way to the wooden hilt, on and on. The woman even twisted her wrist at the end of the thrust, as I always do.

Beyond the least doubt, the creature was begging me to kill it.

And I could not.

No. Before you even open your mouth, *no*. Mercy had nothing to do with it. Quite, quite the contrary. I could find no mercy in myself for a suffering *chandail*, but only cruelty of the purest sort, as I know better than many, and knew at the time. They had, at their whim, made my mind their theater, their sporting arena—very well, here was a chance, long overdue, to make one hurt as I had hurt when the creatures summoned my father from my heart to call me "Precious" again. And I need do nothing at all to cause this pain, nothing to alert that ever so self-conscious conscience of mine—nothing but to savor the beast's agony for as long or as little a time as I chose, and then walk away. How much more innocent could raw revenge possibly be?

But I couldn't do that, either. And I tried. *Lal says*.

I must tell you that it was one of the more interesting discoveries I have ever made. To have spent much of my youth, and all of my adult life, learning to kill more and more efficiently, with less and less pleasure, because pleasure gets in the way, and then to realize that even your taste for retribution has its limits . . . as I say, it was an interesting moment. I whispered, "I will help you," feeling the words rake the back of my throat as I dragged them out of myself. "What must I do?"

No response for another long while, with the *chandail's* sides not stirring in the least, and then the same image over again, exactly: me with my swordcane vigorously putting the thing out of its pain. I said, louder now, "No. No, I'm not going to do that. Tell me how I can make you well." And all the gods in their idiot secrecy know that I never intended to say any such thing.

Silence. Night and silence, and the tiny giggles of the waves. The *chandail* was still alive—of this I was doggedly certain—but I knew enough to know that it could not long survive in the shallows, half out of the water. The first lunatic step, therefore, must be to tow it as far to sea as I could— which, considering that I had neither a boat nor a rope, seemed likely to prove troublesome. Not insurmountably so, however: in a tumbledown shed, located in an isolated corner of the harbor, I came across a derelict but service-able fishing smack, just small enough to be managed by a lone sailor. I left a good portion of my assassin's wage atop a heap of ragged nets, skidded the boat down to the water, and warped her around to where I had left my malodorous charge. Having halyards and a tiller to manage was, as always, a dear comfort, and kept me from concerning myself with my own astonishing foolishness. Not altogether, but almost enough.

The *chandail* had not moved an inch, as far as I could see; but when I tried to bunch a few of its legs and bend a cable around them, then it suddenly began to struggle, hard enough to make it plain that I had no chance of rigging any sort of towline without the bloody thing's cooperation, moribund as it undoubtedly was. I splashed furiously away from it, aware that daybreak was near, and disinclined to be caught with someone else's boat, expensively borrowed or not. The *chandail* sank back into somnolence, but not before I felt a tremulous suggestion that it would drown if dragged through the water by its legs. Once I had reversed the rope and managed to find a way to snug it safely under the great bloated head, all went so swiftly and smoothly that it took me some while to realize that my old tormentor and I had communicated most matter-of-factly, to our mutual benefit. I found the thought disquieting, and put it out of my mind.

Away then, and out of the harbor with the sun and the little dawn breeze, sails nearly as limp as the *chandail's* sides, and me tacking this way and that, desperate to make a little headway before someone recognized the boat, let alone what I was hauling. But no one did; and by the time the dripping red sun had climbed high enough to grow yellow and small, I was beyond sight of Cape Dylee. Even so, I cracked on as much sail as I could handle, convinced that the *chandail's* one hope lay in its deep home, out where such small crafts as mine rarely venture, with good reason. I spied a weak patch in the caulking, and lashed the tiller down while I reinforced it as I could with what I had. *Teach you to steal boats you don't know,* I thought. How many more such weaknesses might there be below the waterline?

The *chandail* itself seemed none the worse for being employed as a sort of sea anchor to windward. If anything, it appeared even a bit revived by the rush of water through its . . . gills? Even today, I know exactly nothing about how the *chandail* breathe, mate, and reproduce (I never could be certain whether mine was male or female), nourish themselves—well, fish, I know they eat various small fish—let alone how and when they die, in the normal way of things. I regret that now, but at the time I was much less interested in such affairs than in, first, seeing this one *chandail* healed and whole, and, second, trying to comprehend why its survival should matter so much to me, when I had loathed the entire species so fiercely for so long. In those days, it annoyed me mightily not to understand myself. I felt it a weakness, a luxury that I could not afford. I feel differently now.

When the wind dropped, near sunset, I took in sail, threw out an actual anchor, and fixed myself a barebones meal, the boat being well stocked for its size with several days' worth of salt fish and ship's biscuits. I sat on a hatch cover to eat, staring down over the stern at the *chandail* floating passively just to starboard, looking oddly like a flower in the fiery sea, with all its legs spread out around it like grotesque petals. It raised two of its arms rather feebly, in what could have been a shaky salute, but which more likely meant that it was studying me very intently with those eye-hairs on the undersides. I waved and smiled at them. I said to them, "Yes, this is indeed me. Who are you?"

Nothing, for a long moment; nothing but the fading cries of a few seabirds and the deep whuff of a *panyara* briefly surfacing a few yards to port. Suddenly a very small girl, no more than perhaps eight or nine years old, was standing beside me: so present, so entirely human, so *there*, that I actually offered her a biscuit before realizing what she was.

The *chandail* had ransacked my mind for some equivalent of its own identity, and presented with me with—no, not myself at her age; the thing knew better than *that*—but with a child who had bright blue eyes, a firm little mouth and chin, and a sprightly, self-confident carriage that I must have seen somewhere and somehow remembered. She was barefoot and wore the simple wraparound garment that most folk wear south of Grannach. The *chandail* pay great attention to detail.

I asked her name, and she told me. I could not have repeated it then, let alone now, but that was how I learned that the *chandail* do have individual names, which I had doubted. I said, as I had said before, "How can I help you? What must I do?"

Her voice was somewhere between a croak and a chime. She said, "Why do you help? You do not want to help. I know."

I was some while replying. I said finally, "It is something I have to do. I cannot tell you why. But from this moment, you will stay out of my memories—is that understood? One other creature appearing on this boat—one single vision of *anything*, anything at all—and I promise you that I will cast off the line and leave you to die here, and never look back. Is that understood?"

The girl uttered a low, rough chuckle: curiously chilling, coming from that small throat. "Very well," she said, "and what can you do about *this*?" She turned abruptly, loosening her single garment, and I saw the purple-lipped gash that took up so much more of her body than it had of the *chandail's* great loose bulk. There was no blood, but I know the smell of rotting tissue. I'd have thought salt water would have done the infection some good, as it usually does with humans, but this was looking worse than when I had found the *chandail* helpless in the harbor. I asked the girl, "What happened to you? Who did this?"

The child shrugged, as lightly as a much older woman dismissing an importunate lover. "A fisherman. He was angry." I could picture the rest of it easily enough: some heartbroken deckhand, taunted one time too many by visions of vanished beloveds—as I had so often been—stabbing downward with the one weapon ready to hand, finding flesh and twisting the two-pronged lance as viciously as he could, until the *chandail's* flailing struggles snatched it from him. The girl added casually, "There will have been poison on the tines."

"Yes," I said, for I knew of many such attempts, usually futile. I said, "I lived awhile in the South Islands. I have some skill."

She did not answer. Her image thinned and flickered—just for a moment, but it made me aware that the *chandail* was weakening steadily. I looked from her festering wound back to the creature lying so serenely in the darkening water. If it had had an expression I could read, I would have said that it appeared resigned, neither avoiding nor approving its fate. I turned to the child again and asked her, "If I heal you, am I healing . . . ?" I could not quite finish the sentence, and there was no need. The girl nodded. I said, "Well, then."

I had only a very few salves and unguents with me, and none that would likely ease an injury such as hers. South Island cures are mostly a matter of the hands, anyway, of something that happens between one's hands and oneself— or one's soul, call it what you choose. I have never been able to explain it, nor to teach it to anyone else; and it does not always come when I call, if you understand me. But when it does work, I have seen it make bodies change their minds about being dead. *Lal says*.

"I must meditate now," I said. "We will begin at first light." The little girl nodded again, and was gone. I sat where I was for a long time, watching the thready infant moon rise, and the *chandail* stirring only with the stir of the tide. I thought about the South Islands, and the woman there who taught me the little I know of healing. Lean and bare and twisted as an old winter branch, yet she had a laugh to set butterflies dancing, and a way of being kind that one only noticed long afterward. To this day, I call her into my heart, or at least try to do so, on the rare occasions when I need to summon what I learned from her. She died many years ago, but I still sometimes pretend no one has yet told me.

The little girl was there precisely at sunrise—no, a bit before, it was, because I remember the sky being a cool, pale, translucent green behind her. She did not speak, but turned and let her dress fall, exposing the *chandail's* wound on her slender brown back. The smell was stronger than it had been only a few hours ago. I breathed it in deeply, as you have to do with South Islands healing. You have to take the pain all the way in.

"This will not hurt," I told her, "but it will feel very peculiar. And it will take a long time—perhaps all day, perhaps days."

The girl laughed again: that deep old laugh that could not belong to her. "*I* will feel no hurt," she said, "whatever you do." At my direction, she stretched out on the hard deck, facedown, and I put my hands on the raw, oozing laceration and asked my long-dead teacher to be with me. I stretched my fingers as far as I could, from one edge of the wound to the other, not actually measuring its length and width, but only to let them spy out the battlefield before them. Then I simply waited for the feeling to come: the familiar sensation of near-boiling water flooding through my wrists and forearms and out of my body altogether, leaping all fleshly boundaries to pour itself over and into whatever suffering was calling it. I never felt that I was master of any healing that happened— nor did my teacher, as she often told me. I was merely grateful to be its conduit, its channel. Its river bed.

But not that day. And not the next, nor the one after that. South Island healing comes when it comes, caring nothing for mere need. If I had needed more evidence that the *chandail* was dying, it was there in the little girl's behavior each day: not so much in her words, which were always terse and calm, but in the way she held herself, in the tension of the muscles I was so vainly kneading, and the increasing chill of her skin. I could do nothing for her but wait; there was no way that I could find by myself into either the *chandail*'s mystery or my own. Nothing to do but wait, with an unreal child fading under my futile hands, and the creature itself slipping lower and lower at the cable's end each day. I caught fish, yellow and blue, and patched the hull as best I might, and drank raw red wine, of which there was considerably more on board than there was water. It comes when it comes.

The *bruach* came first.

There were two of them, which is unusual. *Bruach* are

solitary scavengers—and cannibals, to boot, as likely to turn on each other as on a dead whale or stranded *lankash*. They are more like eels than like anything else, I suppose, except that they run as much as twenty feet in length, and fear nothing, because nothing but a bruach would eat one. As a rule, they wait for their prey to die on its own, but not always.

The girl saw them first: the two long, swift swirls to left and right of the *chandail*, and then the sheep-snouted gray heads—sheep with teeth like sharpened little pegs—rearing high to get their bearings and submerging again. She gave one soft cry and vanished between my hands, leaving me clutching foolishly after her. The *chandail* shivered in the water.

The *bruach* imitated her in their eerie, twittering voices, as though mocking her fear. I searched frantically for a bow or even a throwing ax, my swordcane being of no practical use just then. The galley finally yielded up a couple of decently balanced carving knives, and a butcher's cleaver as well. I have fought for my life with less, although at the time I couldn't remember when. I scrambled back on deck, and prepared to do battle.

By choice, they go for the belly, gnawing their way in, dining on the fatty organs, and often laying their eggs in the ruins. I leaned over the low railing, gripping my knives, praying for each sheep-head to rise above the waves just once more. When one did, I cocked my arm just so, as an old soldier who was drunkenly kind to a slave child taught me to do, and made sure to follow through from my legs. The head did not come all the way off, but close enough.

The second *bruach*, distracted by the sudden explosion of near-black blood, romped in the sticky ripples for a few moments, gnawed briefly on its late companion, and then turned its attention back to the *chandail*. I threw the second carving knife, but missed. The *bruach* dived deep, beyond my sight, but I knew that it would turn and straighten itself in the darkness, and begin to spin along its whole length, faster and faster, until it came hurtling up under the *chandail*, hard enough to knock it out of the water, using its leverage to grip and twist and bore through the toughest hide into the helpless body. I hefted the cleaver without much hope of hitting anything, if I should somehow be granted a second chance. It felt like a stove lid in my palm, and the handle was loose.

But as the *bruach* surged toward the surface, the *chandail* moved. Just a bit, no further than a slight eddy might have pushed it, but enough so that the *bruach* missed its mark, as I had mine. The *bruach* broke water, instead of flesh, looked around unhurriedly, making no connection between its partner's death and me at the rail of the fishing boat—they are dull beasts—and turned to dive for a second strike. But the *chandail*, rolling halfway onto its side, struck out feebly with a pair of its arms, not stunning or even jarring the *bruach*, only holding it *still* for one brief moment, no more than I needed. This head did not come off, but it did make a very satisfying sound when it split. The cleaver was better balanced than I had thought, after all.

The girl did not reappear on board until near sunset. I sat on deck and watched the same yellow and blue fish I had been eating nibbling daintily at the bodies of the two *bruach*. My right shoulder ached from having hurled the heavy cleaver with all my strength, while my mind ached even more from puzzling over my reason for being where

I was, doing what I was doing. After a time the *bruach* began to sink, and I prayed that others of their kind would not come and discover them, because I had nothing else to throw. I was so distracted that I almost failed to notice the child when she did return.

She was different—not drastically so, but unmistakably. There was at once a greater solidity about her, and a certain new clarity as well; even her eyes seemed to have changed from an indifferent, washed-out blue to something close to the color the sea would be again, when the blood was gone. She said, in that strange voice of hers, half ragged with age and pain, half clear as snow-water, "Thank you. You saved my life."

I said nothing. She continued, gently and innocently. "And now you are wondering why you should ever have done such a thing."

"Yes," I said. "Yes, I am."

"Because I am your memory," the little girl said . . . the *chandail* said. "I am the secret place where you hide it all— the beautiful room you cannot bear to enter—the cave where the monsters live—the dreams that make you dread sleep. You know this, Lalkhamsin-khamsolal."

No one had called me by my rightful name for a great many years. I was not even aware of having leaped to my feet, nor of shaking my head until my hair stung my eyes. I do not think I was screaming, but my throat hurt as though I had been. I said, "*No*. No, you are no part of me. You are parasites, like the *bruach*—no, worse than the *bruach*—and I despise you all, make no mistake. If I saved you, it was out of pity, as one or two others have had pity on me in my life. Nothing more. Nothing more."

The girl remained as serene as though I had soberly agreed with her. She said, "Despise us—hate us, if you will—but consider. What you are is also what you lost—what was taken from you—and if I and mine did not keep the key to that room, would you be fully yourself? Would you even truly exist?"

In her half-smiling child's mouth, my name sounded foreign and faraway, not connected to me at all. I said only, "You have a wound to treat. Come."

She laughed then, and lay down for me to try my poor backcountry curing one more time. The infection was worse, the stench brought back places I wish I had never seen . . . but the feeling was there, too, at last, rushing down from my shoulders, hurrying so hungrily toward the need that it seemed almost to stumble over itself on the way. The rotted skin sloughed away under my hands as I put them directly on the lesion, and I sensed the *chandail*'s suffering draining back into me, as it should if the healing is working right. There was pain, but it was happening a long way off, to someone who was at once me and not-me. I cannot say it any more clearly than that. I did nothing—only touched, and closed my eyes.

When I opened them again, the sky was black and starless, with no smallest rag of sunset left. The girl vanished, as she always did, and I went below to my bunk, where I lay awake the rest of the night, brooding over what she had said to me. It was at least a change from the dreams.

In the morning I could see no real difference in the wound, beyond a certain suggestion of knitting around the edges— most likely wishful thinking on my part, for the smell and suppuration were definitely unaffected. I told the girl that South Island healing is unpredictable and rarely instantaneous, that I would not give up until she was well, however long a time it might take. She answered simply, as she lay down, "It will not be long," and left me to take that how I would.

In the three days that followed, the power that coursed between the *chandail* and me never faltered; but the undoing of the damage that the fisherman's two-tined lance had wrought was a wearier business than I had ever dealt with. At times I convinced myself that the wound was smaller and cleaner looking, and that the creature itself was plainly stronger; at others, it seemed dreadfully obvious that the *chandail* was not only failing, but that my treatment might very well be hastening its end. Even at my most hopeful, I never dared cut or loosen the cable, our only other connection, for fear that the creature might slip silently down out of sight, as the two dead *bruach* had done, too weak and damaged to stay afloat on its own. There came to be nothing else in the world but the same sun pouring down on us each day, and my little boat swinging in the same slow half-circle between sea and sky, between the *chandail* and me. I fished and swam, and drank my red wine in the evenings, and watched the stars flickering through the waves, quick as fish themselves. It was very peaceful, and there was no time.

Of real speech between us—between me and the *chandail* speaking through her—there was very little. As I have said, the creature seemed utterly unconcerned with its own life or death; and whatever pain it truly suffered, I never knew. But we did actually converse, now and again, through the little girl, and I slowly gained a sense of the cold and fearless arrogance under my hands—and something else, as well: something almost like a teasing desire to be known, to be understood, to be *seen* by a human being. I remember that once I asked her, "Why do you amuse yourselves with our grief? We have never fished for you, never harmed you in any way—we could not, even if we wanted to. Why do you toy with us as you do?"

She had the grace to look surprised by the question; or it could have been a trick of the light on the water. "But what else are you here for? Of all beings on the earth, your folk alone were created especially for us, for our own particular delight. Have you kept me alive only to make you understand this?"

I did not trust myself to answer her. What she had told me was no more than I had feared, suspected—indeed, *known*, somewhere in myself where I rarely visited. The Captain had told me truly: the *chandail* did what they did in perfect simplicity, with neither malice nor pity, quite simply because we belonged to them. What particular delight could they have drawn, after all, from the memories of fish? The nightmares of *panyaras* or the *bruach*? The gods I was raised to worship never promised human beings their entire eternal attention, but neither did they advise us that we were to be forever the playthings of creatures with eyes on the underside of their four arms. I spoke no more for the rest of the day.

Then, on the cool, bright morning of the third day, it was she who posed a question. As though we were in the middle of an ordinary chat between friends, she asked suddenly, "And what harm have *my* people ever done *you*? Where is the great evil in bringing your memories to life for a little while? Where is our wickedness, that you hate us so?"

I cannot say how long it took me to find words—no, to remember language at all. I said, "You don't know? You really do not know?"

I will always think that she actually blushed—though, obviously, that couldn't have been possible. She said, "We have not given it much thought, I admit that. Nor are we likely to—I am speaking honestly to you. I am asking for myself, and no other." And that was how I learned that the *chandail* were indeed individuals, with their own desires and curiosities. Few believe me yet, after all this time. *Lal says*.

I told her why we hated them. I told her, I think, for hours—all the while trying as hard as I knew to transmit healing through her illusory body to the monster likely dying off my starboard bow. She listened in silence, never interrupting once—that would be a human sort of thing, after all—and when I was done at last, she did not speak for some time. Only when I was resting for a little, soaking my hands in seawater—South Island work is painless, but your hands get so hot—did she finally say one word, "Interesting."

I gawked as dumbly as any astonished yokel. She said, "I have never known a human being. This has been extremely interesting for me."

I forgot everything I ever knew about healing in that instant. I thought of the first time the *chandail* had had all their way with me, and I remembered the Captain, and though I directed my words at a little girl, I was speaking directly to the thing she was. "You know *nothing* of me. You know nothing of us—nothing—and you never will, because you have always been too busy raping our memories, sporting with our hearts, without thought, without even the notion of pity. No, forgive me, I must take that back. The truth is that you know everything about us but what we are—everything but what it is to have those memories, good or bad, cherished or denied . . . or dreaded. You need a heart to understand that, and a soul, and your kind have neither." I was shouting into her face, just as though she were real.

And for the smallest moment she responded as though she were, and I had my one true meeting with the *chandail*. Her tranquil, expressionless blue eyes darkened with anger—or it might have been disbelief, or perhaps even sadness. She said, "You are quite right—we have no hearts, not as you and *your* kind would understand them. But souls . . . souls we do possess. Whether *your* kind would call them so or not." A truly human voice could never, surely, have conveyed such contempt as I heard in her soft, lilting words.

I did not want to talk to her—to *it*—anymore. I gestured with my head for her to lie down on the deck again, and she obeyed. The great gash on her back looked far more hideous than it had the first time I had seen it, and no gainsaying that it stank like a slaughterhouse. I understood one thing at least then, very suddenly. I said, "I have been no use at all, have I? All this that I have done—tried to do for you—*nothing*, from the beginning. You have been dying every minute since that lance went into you, is that not true?"

The girl turned her head slightly to look back at me over her shoulder. "If you were no help, you did me no further hurt either. As I have said, it was interesting, and I was . . . curious. As I am about death." Her voice had become a placid mumble; she might have been drowsing in the sun.

I stood with my hands on her, still feeling the heat vainly

racing down my arms into the wound, as though the healing were stubbornly refusing to admit its futility. My anger was gone, and every other feeling seemed to have flown with it. I had difficulty, not only in finding something to say, but in remembering what individual words meant. I managed finally to mumble clumsily, "I've never known South Island healing to fail."

"Not on humans, perhaps." She looked at me as she always had, from somewhere I had never been. She said, "I told you to kill me."

"It was not in me to do," I answered. "Killer as I am."

The child laughed her strange laugh, for the first time in some while. "I am grateful that you could not. I would not have cared to die where you found me, wallowing in the filthy shallows. This is better."

Neither of us spoke for a long time after that. I went on working mechanically on her injury as though my efforts still mattered, while she continued calmly sunning herself. At last I asked her, "Should I loose the cable? Is that what you wish?"

She shook her head. "Not yet. I can no longer swim, and that is a bad thing for us, a dishonor. Besides, I have"—she hesitated briefly—"something to do. A gift."

"Not for me," I said, as quickly as I have likely ever said anything. "Forgive the discourtesy, but I have had well more than enough of your *gifts* in my life. If you mean to say farewell, we can simply shake hands, and each say *sunlight on your road*. No gifts."

The girl's smile lifted the corners of her eyes, but not her mouth. She said, "Oh, you will like this one, I assure you. The word of a *chandail* undoubtedly means little to you, but it has some worth even so. Trust me, Lalkhamsin-khamsolal."

That was the second time she called me by my name, and the last. I neither nodded agreement nor shook my head. Only waited.

"Shake hands, is it?" she said. She reached out then, but did not take my hand, merely touched it—an instant's fiery tingle, and she was gone. And Bismaya was there.

Bismaya ...

I had not seen her since a certain afternoon on a riverbank when we were children, but this Bismaya was full grown, and pregnant, heavily, clumsily so, carrying herself with the weariness of a woman who has long since lost hope of ever *not* being pregnant. Her plain, broad face was lined and sagging, and her beautiful skin, richly dark and always smoother than mine, had aged to the color of wet slate. I would have known her in any guise, at any distance. I would have known her in my sleep, in the darkest and most dreadful of the dreams into which she sold me, my cousin, my dear deadly playmate. I will know her after death.

The *chandail* had outdone itself. Unreal as Bismaya had to be, she still paled with the motion of my anchored boat, and swayed slightly as it rocked in the swell. Bismaya had never had any sort of a stomach, even on the wobbly little rafts we used to make with boards and logs and *janshi* vines. I remember everything about Bismaya.

She was so occupied with being bewildered, frightened, and queasy that she did not see me until I spoke her name. Then she turned, stared, and tumbled awkwardly to her knees, whispering two words. "Lal. Please."

I used to imagine her saying that, begging me for mercy

before I tore her to pieces, one slow piece at a time. Gods, how many times had I put myself to sleep with that vision? How many times did I call it up to shut out what was being done to me? And here it was—here *she* was, helpless on her knees before me—and here *I* was, dumbstruck, horror-struck, knowing that it could not be happening, not like this. Even the *chandail* cannot do this.

You see, the sendings of the *chandail* look and feel absolutely accurate, perfect to the smallest detail strained out of your recollection, your imagining. They can touch you, and you can touch them; they can chatter endlessly of memories only you—and so they—could share; indeed, they often call up people and places and events that you had completely forgotten, for good or ill. What they cannot do is hear what you say to them and respond to it—they cannot *listen*, not to words, not to eyes or bodies. Bismaya could not possibly have seen what she so plainly saw in my face.

And yet the little girl had said of her gift, "Oh, you will like this one." As false as any *chandail* vision, this one, surely, but illusory in a completely different way. I managed to mutter, "Oh, get *up*, you stupid slut, get up," and Bismaya tried to rise, but her belly gave her so much trouble that I had to fight the impulse to help her to her feet. We faced each other in silence. She said finally, "You look well, Lal."

"Slavery agreed with me," I answered. "Rape has kept me young."

I spoke quietly, but Bismaya cringed away from me, catching hold of a railing to steady herself. "There was never a boat," she whispered. "All the dreams, every night, every night, but never on a boat. I will wake from this—I *will*." But her eyes knew better.

"The best is not to sleep," I said. "Take my word for it."
She saw the *chandail* in the water then, and gave a little cry
of boneless terror: seeing one of them without warning does
have that effect. I said, "You *are* dreaming, Bismaya. I cannot harm you, and I would not if I could. Now that I see
you, the idea of it—the dream that cradled my heart every
night for so long—seems silly and meaningless." She actually
bridled at that: the same Bismaya who would rather have
been flogged in the market square than ignored. I went on,
"But I need to know something, and I think you need to
tell me." She belched suddenly, as pregnant women will, and
then looked horribly shamed and mortified. I savored the
old bitter taste of the word for the last time before I let it
leave me. "*Why?*"

She stammered and coughed, looking everywhere but at
me. I said, "Later I heard that you received money enough
to buy that singing bird you coveted so. Was that really the
way of it, then?"

Bismaya shook her head, still not looking at me. Her hair—
dusty graying shadow of the comb-defying black wilderness I
remembered—hid her face when she finally replied to me. "It
was your eyes. I could not bear your eyes."

I think my mouth actually dropped open. She said timidly,
"Lal, you always had such beautiful golden eyes—always, from
the first—and all I ever had was these muddy brown ones.
They're too small, and the lashes are just stubby, and I wanted
so much to have eyes like yours. I couldn't sleep for envying
you, do you understand?" She made that maddening helpless
twittering gesture with her hands that she used to make when
explaining why some new disaster wasn't her fault. "I couldn't

stand to see you, Lal, every single day. You remember how it was. How we were."

First up in the morning, first over at the other's house to play and laugh, and gobble breakfast, and swim in the river, and make up long, long stories about the adventures our toys had together. . . . Bismaya went on, talking faster now, "I had to be rid of you—I had to make you go away, do you understand, Lal? So I wouldn't be *thinking* about you all the time." She stopped abruptly and stilled her hands, spreading them with something resembling dignity. "That was why. That was all."

I was suddenly very tired. There was nothing here for me: not retribution, not solace, not even poor old useless justice—nothing but a foolish woman whom all my hating had not made worthy of hatred. Had she been there in the flesh, I would still have . . . but how do you strangle a ghost? Beat a ghost to death? Claw out the stupid eyes the ghost so hungered to trade for yours? Instead I asked, "When is your baby due?"

"In two weeks' time. So they tell me." Changing the subject made her voice firmer, and strengthened her stance as she faced me. "My ninth, would you believe it? It would have been the eleventh, but we . . . lost two of them." I dislike people who cannot bring themselves to say *died*, but the pain in her eyes was as real as she—I had to keep reminding myself—was not.

I wanted to look away from her, so that she would vanish, as the *chandail*'s specters always did if I could ignore them long enough. It astonished me to hear myself saying formally, "I grieve your grief" to her, and I deliberately undercut any suggestion of sympathy by adding pointedly, "but you clearly lost no time in finding replacements." Bismaya winced visibly. I was glad.

"This one will be the last," she said. I must have made some sort of derisive sound, because her voice changed, becoming harshly flat in a way that I had never before heard from fluttery Bismaya. "This one will kill me."

I stared at her. She smiled a strange, almost exultant smile. She said, "I know this. I welcome it."

"No," I said. "No, you can't know such a thing certainly." But women can, and I had seen the look of her body and her face too many times on others not to recognize it, whether I would or no. There was nothing to say, so I said, "The child?"

"Oh, the child will live." The smile sidled wider. "It's healthy and strong—I can feel it—and my husband will have a new wife to raise it before the earth has settled on my grave." She mentioned his name. I recalled it, and his chubby face as well, from our shared childhood. She said, "So there you are, Lal. There you are. It is all to you, in the end."

"Nothing is mine," I said. "Victory, vengeance, the triumph of patient virtue—none of it worth a minute's waiting for. In a moment you will wake, when the *chandail* wearies of its play with us, and so will I rouse from my own old dream, and neither of us will ever awaken so again. It is over, Bismaya."

"Over?" she cried, stepping toward me for the first time. "Over for *you*, perhaps!" Marriage, or motherhood, perhaps, or simply the imminence of death—had given her distinctly more spirit than I recalled her ever possessing. "Lal, for every night you suffered for the wrong I did you, I promise you that *I* have spent *two* nights of weeping, of writhing in shame and horror inside my skin, hating myself as I hate myself now—of wishing I could die, welcoming it—"

My hands came up at my sides of their own accord, curled fingers beckoning death; if she had been solid flesh, they would have been on her throat, choking that insect whine to cinders. Very well, I was not—I *am* not—entirely free of Bismaya, after all. "You could have looked for me," I said. My own voice sounded like someone else's; it could have been an old man's voice. "You could have bought me back. As much money as your family had."

"I was a little girl!" She seized my hands, touching me for the first time with hands that felt like dead leaves. "I had done a terrible, evil thing, and I was afraid to tell my mother and father! I was afraid!"

I pulled free of her. I said, "I was a little girl, too."

After that we only stared at each other, until it occurred to me that the *chandail* might easily have died by this time, without my knowledge. Surely she would have vanished instantly, if that were so—but what if she did not? Which would be the true Bismaya then? The illusion stranded here with me, or the body trapped in her own bed, swollen with life, empty of spirit? I turned from her and looked over the side at the massive hulk floating so inertly at my cable's end. There was no way to be certain whether it yet lived. I called to it loudly—no response—and then threw an empty ship's biscuit tin to splash beside its head. Nothing.

"Excuse me for a little," I told Bismaya politely. She gaped as I swung myself over the side and went hand over hand down the cable to drop into the sea only a foot or two from the *chandail*. Close to, even half under water, the huge eyeless head still loomed over mine, and the jumble of limp legs was like one of those vast seaweed tangles that snare and drown ships much bigger than mine. Bobbing in the slow swells, I lifted the cold tip of one—more than that would have been beyond my strength—looking for the fringe of eye-hairs underneath. No way of telling whether they were open, of course; all I could do was hope to rouse whatever fading attention might linger there still. I said, or perhaps only thought—what difference now?—"Enough. It is enough."

The *chandail* did not stir. I gave up then, really, but I tried once more anyway. "I do appreciate your gift. Knowingly or not, you have lifted a great stone from my heart, and I thank you for it." I hesitated, and then added, "Sunlight on your road." Not that I truly cared—not exactly—but it is what we say.

Whether my words had anything to do with it or not, the *chandail* moved then. No more than a sluggish heave, granted—by comparison, its behavior in the oily shallows of Cape Dylee harbor was that of a spring lamb—but it lived, and for one last tremulous moment it began doing what they do, if you look too long: rising and flowing into radiantly misshapen beauty, the beauty of the *chandail*; shifting, not its shape, but its spirit, somehow, burning there on the water, casting its own light on the road it was taking. I said once again, "Enough," and I swam away and climbed back up the cable.

Bismaya was pacing the deck, rail to rail, left hand squeezing and twisting the fingers of the right, as she always used to do when fearful of being scolded. When she saw me, she wrinkled up her nose in her old annoyance at my messy habits. She said, "Phoo, you're all *wet*, don't come *near* me," exactly as she would have said it—did say it—when I was seven, and she was six and a half. Idiot compassion roused in me for an instant, but I smacked it on the head and it lay back down again.

"You are going home," I said. "I hope you are wrong, and that this baby will not be your death." And I did hope that, in a way that I do not think was any less genuine for being so cold.

She gave me that eerily triumphant smile once more. "Oh, it will. No fear."

I wanted to comfort, not her, but myself. I wanted to tell her, "Bismaya, live or die, we are quits. I cannot remember why you took up so much of me for so long." But it was not true, and never will be, and I did not want my last words to her to be a lie. So all I said in the end was, "Good-bye, Bismaya. I send my best greeting to your family." And she was gone.

I felt the *chandail* go very quickly after that, but I never looked up. I stayed on deck the rest of the day, patching the mainsail and the little jib, caulking and filling where I could, and salting down as many fish as I could catch. At sunset I cut the cable, and watched the creature slide away into the deep gray-green where I still think I will go one day, even though you find me here in this white-bone emptiness. Then, with the moon rising, I hoisted sail and set off for the place where I was living at the time. There is nothing at all to say about the journey, except that all the long way I was never once visited by any *chandail* come to play with the pieces of my life. I never have been again.

And that is all there is to the story you have come such a long way to hear. There is nothing to add—except, perhaps, that I did go home one day, many, many years later. There I learned that Bismaya had indeed died in childbirth, and that her husband had indeed remarried, and was himself long dead, as were my own parents. I found her grave, and stood by it for a time, waiting to feel something, anything—rage or triumph, or even watery compassion. But all that came to me was an ache in my left knee, almost as old as I—we both fell out of a tree, playing outlaws in its high branches—and a memory of the two of us spying on Bismaya's older brother and his sweetheart, hoping to see them . . . doing what, I wonder now? Kissing, I suppose; I really remember only the giggling together, which we would barely manage to smother before a glance at each other would set it off again. Her brother caught us, of course, and chased us all the way to the river—we had to dive in to escape him.

A week later, she sold me. No, it was nine days. I grow forgetful.

So, then? Have I told you anything you did not know before you came to me? Do my old eyes discern something besides attentive cleverness in those eyes of yours? No, do not answer—what my listeners take away with them on the journey home is their own concern and none of mine. Ah, but I did speak of wisdom, did I not? Very well, in that case I will tell you the one thing I know for certain. . . .

Wisdom is uncertainty. Wisdom is confusion. Wisdom is a heartless trickster healing my heart, my worst enemy drawing pity up out of my lifetime of hating, like sweet water from a long-dry well. Wisdom is knowing nothing, and not even knowing how you feel about knowing nothing. Wisdom is finding joy in bewilderment, at the last. At the last. *Lal says.*

Peter S. Beagle was born in 1939 and raised in the Bronx, in New York City, just a few blocks from Woodlawn Cemetery, the inspiration for his first novel, *A Fine and Private Place*. Since then he has built a world-wide following with magical novels for both adults and children, including *The Last Unicorn*, *Tamsin*, and, most recently, *Summerlong*. His short fiction has appeared in a variety of publications, including his 1999 collection *The Rhinoceros Who Quoted Nietzsche*. In addition, he has written numerous teleplays and screenplays, and is a gifted poet, lyricist, and singer/songwriter.

"Chandail" is part of Beagle's "Innkeeper's World" tapestry, which began with his novel *The Innkeeper's Song*, returned with the stories in the collection *The Magician of Karakosk* (also published as *Giant Bones*), and has been the setting of a continued series of works ever since.

Down the Wall

Greer Gilman

STILT-LEGS SCISSORING, SNIP-SNAP! the bird gods dance. Old craneycrows, a skulk of powers. How they strut and ogle with their long eyes, knowing. How they serpentine their necks. And stalking, how they flirt their tails, insouciant as Groucho. Fugue and counterfugue, the music jigs and sneaks. On tiptoe, solemnly, they hop and flap; they whirl and whet their long curved clever bills. A sly dance, a wry dance, miching mallecho. Pavane. They peacock, but their drab is eyeless, black as mourners, black as mutes. They are clownish, they are sinister, in their insatiable invention, their unending. Like the frieze in a Pharaoh's nursery, like the knotwork in a chthonic gospel. In and out, untiring as wire, they weave a thorny hedge of selves, and in their eddering, enlace their eggs, their moonish precious eggs. They gloat. And they go on. Like viruses, mere self-engendering more self, they replicate. They tangle genesis in their inexorable braid.

~

THE BIRDS ARE phosphor in a box. They sift and sift across the screen; they whisper. They are endless snow or soot, the ashes of the old world burning. Elsewhere fire. The hailbox whispers, whispers. There is no way to turn it off. No other channel but the gods. All day and night it snows grey phosphor, sifting in the corners of the air. The earth is grey with ash.

The children watch the box, they sprawl and gaze. They're bored, locked in so many endless days. Mewed up. Where's out? they ask. When's never? Why? Their mam clouts and pinches, slaps and spells and grumbles, twisting bacca in a screw of paper. She's a wad of it, torn leaf by leaf away. Time sometime to get another book, ward and spell to steal it. Smoke it. Time enough. See, paper's upworld. Outwall. Paper swirls about the open streets, abandoned to the gods, all scrawled with stick-dance; paper's layered, scrap on gaudy scrap, on upworld walls. It's slagheaps in the towers of the burning world, the Outwith, where the Old Crows breed. And their nests are sticks and souls.

They take souls fool enough to wander outwall, under sky. The sots that stumble from the trances of the underground. The wardless and unwary. Blink, blunder, and they're snatched. Like her awd man. Kids' father. "Blind drunk," she tells them, scornful. "Pissing out a window."

She twitches at the curtains, net on net against the talons of the numinous. Their seine is grey with ashes, hung with toys: green headless army men and dolls' eyes, wired, blue. The window is brick. "Bad enough here, down t'Wall," she says. "Living here. Gettin in wi' this lot." Mouth snecked and her eyes like iodine.

Boy's mazy.

She takes the girl to dancing class, up Mrs. Mallecho's. And pays good brass for it. Smoke. Spellcards. Takes her both ways, proper, through the twisting maze of ginnels, and locks to do, undo, at every trance. Quells beggars with a look. In the cloakroom, in among the downy girls, she plucks at her daughter's bits of swansdown, pluming out her tawdry dress. Tufts at her shoulderblades. Gosslyn. She'll do. Girl dances lovely, well she'll give her that. Not like that Dowsa Fligger, silk stockins til her arse, and all them gilty bits ont never never. They says. Off her auntie's bed, more like. Dancin' on her back. Oh, she's fly, is Mrs. Theek. Gosslyn's mam clamps down a round comb, fanged and feathery, to crown her daughter's hair; she screws her handkerchief and spits and scrubs.

Girl's fratchety.

The mothers watch from the margins, fierce, aspiring, appraising: their arms crossed, bags clutched, their mouths like paper cuts. They acknowledge haughtily with lifted chins: so much, no more.

"Mrs. Leathy."

"Mrs. Fligger."

"Mrs. Fligger."

"Mrs. Theek."

The hatchlings dance.

⁓

AT HOME, BEHIND the jaded couch, her children whisper. They have doorsteps and dark jam to munch; they have a bulwark of pillows. They have stubs of crayons and the wall. From behind them, they can hear the godbox and the skulking music. Lunar tunes. And rising keening over that, a melancholy roar and drone, a pibroch with the fear note in it. Their mam's doing Wednesday, she feeds the Oover north-northwest: three fag ends, a catseye marble, tea leaves. Widdershins: a doll's shoe, a snarl of hairpins. East: a coin. It molochs them all up. West by south: she ties, unties her pinny, back to front, the old one with the faded poppies.

"Black," the boy says. "They must be black. And shriking."

The girl is twirling a plastic ball on her palms, full of heavy water, bright plastic fish. The water whorls and rights itself. "Black's used up." She thinks. "There's *holes* there. Outwall." She swirls the ball; the fish dither.

"There's rain," he says.

The girl's heard tell of it, old Pudfoot with his bottle, muttering. Like slanting wires, he says: but not a cage, like music someways. Or a dancer in nailed boots, she says: they've heard it on the tin-roofed trances, hurried by. Sometimes it sleeks in at the corners, seeking with its slow tongues, twining. And they're not to touch it, and it chokes on dust.

"There's turnings," says the girl.

Slowly their drawing grows, cracked eyries and a maze of faces. The wallpaper's scrawly like the godbox, but brown: all over and over, all the same. Crawlies and blotches. They've turned them into strange things: winged cats, birdheaded women. Owls with horns. Upworld things. A leafgirl by a hedge of bones, tossing up a golden ball. A hurchin boy, astride a cockerel. All pictures from their mother's stash, all smoke.

⁓

DOWN THE WALL, down the end shop. The boy waits until the Mrs. sees him, sleeving on the glass case that his breath has clouded. Fly cakes. Bacca. There's a babby in there, under glass. Goss says. She says it's Outwith, it can talk and fly. The boy rubs and peers. The black comes off in wrinkles. Ghostly, he can see his own face, in among the things to sell. Tin birds. Cards of hook-and-eyes. Pale buns. The ladies talk.

"Mrs. Spugget."

"Mrs. Pithy."

Her shop smells of sour milk and smoke and bacca, drowsy sweet; of mops and cabbages and fennel-at-the-door. And mice. There's holes down there. Worn lino, brown like her toffee, on the sour splintery boards. He once found a bird-sweet in a crack in a corner. Dusty licorice.

". . . down Howly Street . . ."

"Large white and a tin of Brasso. Snatched?"

"Jumped. One and three."

The bell rings to make the birds scatter.

"Mrs. Pithy."

"Mrs. Spugget."

"Mrs. Harpic."

"Mrs. Pithy."

Their hair's done Saturday. Grey snails and gilt snails, criss-cross with iron pins. His mam jabs them in, she's holy.

". . . gone Outwith. In her nightdress. . . ."

Sharp chin quirks at him. ". . . kid . . ."

"That one? Hears nowt. Pane shy of a glasshouse." Fat

chin creases, as she leans and whispers. ". . . far gone, she were. Her mam, she took and . . ."

Far gone. He sees the lost girl, in among the towers and the sticks of crow's nests, searching for an urchin bairn.

~

MR. HAWKLESS THE trancer got snatched. They hurry by his corner with the slashed spells, with the tins forlornly jangling. They burn fennel. Mr. Snipe is the trancer, and he helps the kids cross.

~

MARRI FROM DANCING'S gone. Her hook is bare, and the mothers silent, their eyes like awls. Stitched mouths. They preen their daughters savagely, as if their frou frou were meringue, to beat. Still whiter and glassier, girls turn in the mirror. Spun fantasies. Pavlovas. None adroop: all stiff as sugar in their tinseled frills. Blackstick Mrs. Mallecho stumps up and down their line. White silence, like a cut before it fills with blood, spills over. But it never bleeds, the girl thinks, posing in the First Ward. Clack! goes the woodbook, and the dancers pirouette. The music thumps and sniggers. The mothers' will is like a cage of wires, strung with dancers, bright as beads. They tell them like a rosary, an abacus of souls. They were five twos; they will make three threes.

~

NIGHT. MATINS. FROM her clutched grey bag, the mother takes a soft soft piece of paper, wrinkled, scented, like a cheek held up to kiss. Green coin. She pleats it, snips it—there, a chain of craneycrows, as wick as if their own quick legs had scissored them. Just on time, the tune beginning as she lights the paper, lets it go: a flaring and a lace of ash. She marks her sleeping children: eyelids, palms.

⁓

THE GIRL DREAMS of the stitch witch, putting children in her bag. She prods them as she picks. She's made of stuffing, grey stuff like the Oover's belly, and her mouth's sewn shut. There's a black thread and a needle dangling from her lip, a tangle like a raven's beard. She gluts on souls. Behind the railings, there are children crouching—Goss among them, hiding—in a heap of cushions stitched with rain. It twangles as they shift, they burrow. Ah, she's hunting for her ball, her shining ball, before the witch can take her. Down she gropes, amid the slather, deeper still. Then it's changed, the dream, she's riding rantipole with Marri, whirling round and round, and up and down, hold tight! until she breaks away and flies. The air is full of girls like leaves.

⁓

THE BOY WAKES in the night. There are Old Ones storming; he can hear the hurl and crackle in the air: not sound but fury. Something that restrings your bones. His mam is standing turning toward it. Tuning. She is blue in the godlight.

⁓

MORNING. THIN AND blue, lit flickering by the box. Their mam's doing Thursday. She slamps her irons down and

grutches; spits and dabs. The air's full of scorch and muttering. The chairs are hung with ghosts, themselves outspread
and suppliant. Vests. Petticoats. Rue's shirts. There's rows of
eggshells on the sills, all filled with ashes and with milk.
Thwick! Thwick! She jabs the milk tops with her nail, pours
out a measure to the Old Ones. Milk swirls on the step. She
will string the silver, hang it jostling in the doorways.

"Rue." His sister's breath, not sound but stirring. Warm in
his ear. It tickles. "Rue. I've getten keys."

"Goss?"

The girl's far ahead in the trances, counting turnings. Her
thread is words.

"Goss. Wait." The boy calls after. "Is't dead?" There's a
black thing in a runnel, stark. The girl turns back and prods
it. Bone and wings? It slacks from its bent ribs. Nobbut wire
and cloth. She grins. "It's a dolly god, I think." She pries it
from the drain, awry and sagging, twirls it. Sword falls open
into cup.

Rue laughs. "It's drunk," he says, and makes it stagger.

"Go on. Yer have it, then."

It pecks along the tunnels, rattles on the railings, swishes,
scything down a host of shadows. It pokes at bins. Now and
then, it twirls and wobbles, with a loose-stayed shimmy, like
the Widow Twanky in a swoon.

Below them, they hear voices, children calling, running feet.

"Goss?" Tiled and echoing, a trance in a maze of trances.

"Sneck up." She's biting at her lip and peering. What way is Out? They're in a bridge above another passage, grinning with stained tiles. Dank water drips. It sidles over posters, over tilework scrawled with birds. Smashed lamps. Dark arches, cages full of coils and wheels and shards. Ratscuttle and the stench of ancient piss.

Round the bend, a soft voice calls. "Off to yon rant?"

They stiffen. Goss yanks her brother round behind her.

"Leggo."

"Hush. Nobbut an awd busker. I'll fend."

A beggar sits against the wall, knees up and watchful, idle. In their path. A tin whistle in her dangling hand, a bowl between her feet. Her clothes are like herself, her pelt; her jacket's hairy on the inside, black, and rustling with paper. And she smells of ashes and of rain. A little penknife of a smile, all bone and flick, her long eyes hidden in her shaggy greyblack hair. "Where's thou bound?"

"Out," says Rue, and draws his dolly, which slacks open, gaping foolish; but Goss steps up to her with silver, got groping in the Oover's belly. "Leave us go."

The beggar quirks at the bowl. The silver falls among small things, silver. "What's that to me? Is't thine?"

Goss lifts her chin. "Is't yours? All that lot?"

"Nay, all theirs as leave. And not until."

There's odd things in the bowl, thinks Goss. Spectacles. A torn-up photograph. A tooth. A torch, all eaten up with rust. A heap of long red hair. The beggar scrabbles in the bowl, hands back the coins. "Owt else?"

A handful of crayons. The beggar finicks through them. Bluegreen. Redviolet. The stub of black. She measures

Gosslyn with a glance. "All this? Thou's overdrawn thysel."
As if the dole were kingdoms.

"What I has."

They're taken; then the beggar turns to Rue. He's got
the dolly god hooked over his shoulder, and he's turning
out pocket fluff. Three black birdsweets and a marble on
his sticky palm. Blue clouded, with a fleck like a falling leaf.
That, too. The beggar holds it to her eye, shakes back her
hair to squint. And laughs.

No riddles this time. "Put up thy brolly. I'll not eat thee."

"Dolly brolly." Rue's delighted.

"Gerroff wi' yer. Left, left, down close and top o't stairs."

As they turn, she calls out, mocking, "Did tha want thy
change?" And flicks a bit of chalk at Gosslyn. It skitters, spinning on the tiles, and veering, rolling toward abyss. Goss
darts for it before it's lost. They hurry on.

They can see the turnstile now, the lightspill on the stairs.

～

AMAZED AT THE wind, they stand: high tumult and the
ragged moon. "Will't *hatch*?" says Rue. Turning round, heads
back, they stare. Cloud, red beneath with burning. Wrack
and scurry backlit by the scatheless sailing moon. Unfath-
omed cliffs of tower, sheer and derelict. Unwarded streets.
Leaves paper litter rising. Whirl and flacker in a ghostly
dance. They've not felt wind afore. Goss laughs, whirling
widearmed. Rue scuffles and twirls, he surges through the
leaftrash in a glorious roar and crackle, swashing with his
stick. They spin themselves giddy. They are catseyes, whorled
with shadow, wound with moon.

They've fallen down. Clouds towers leaves wheel round them.
A voice calls. "Crows!"
Another, "Here's inwits for yer supper. Crows!"
"Hey, crows!"
They are laughing.

THERE ARE CHILDREN in the dark. They run by night: a shifting crew of mortals. Old and young, they're driven by a fey mood, a sudden quick desire to shake the fear, to dance unwarded under heaven. Back of law. They bring no wards, no form of worship to their tryst, evading death by chance, by offhand magic: a patchwork of tinkering and brilliant dodges, crazy risks. Chancers, they call themselves. Some run a moment, whirled away like moonclocks; others, crazed or clever, live a night, two nights, a week of dancing.

There are shadows in the moon: huge knots of hawklike darkness, sheering. As they turn, they catch the moonlight, glint and vanish, skyblack into sky. They are bright beneath, with women's bodies; they are cold, with starless wings. No rise and wheeling of the dance in them, no scrawl of stars: all timeless and unstoried night. Cloud coils from them, un-silvering the moon. Their breath is tarnish, is forgetting. And their talons—ah, they rend the soul. They take.

CLOSE NOW, THE running and the calling start, from street to street, from shadow into shadow, in and out of light. Rue and Gosslyn stagger up and after, witch-led, drunk with air.

The world swerves sideways, lurches them at walls. The brolly bangs and bruises, tangles in their feet. The voices mock and rally. *Tigged last! Telled witch of yer!* A twitch, a tug at skirt or sleeve. Whirl round and no one. Whispering. And there, a white face, round a corner? Gone. Phantasmal creatures loom, elude them, dwindling into junk. And all around them tunes the bedlam jazz band of the wind. Scritch and jangle. Howl and hurly. Scrape and clattering and sough. A clang on a skeleton of stair, above; a sheet of paper, burning, falling. See, it's eyed with cinders, blinded one by one. An ash. It's nothing in Rue's hand. Goss feels a soft slap on her cheek. Another. And another. No one, pattering, and all around. They stand, astonished, in the briefest lash of rain.

They've come into a wide square, set with shattered baulks of stone: a great cat with a muffled head, a riven owl, a witch in flinders. There are fires here and there, some leaping and some embers, ashes. Some long cold. And some a-building: leaves and boxes, doors and drawers and random trash. Children heap frail crazy towers: sticks stacks crows' nests, all to burn. Some run with brands, they leap and whirl them in a swarm of sparks. They write great fading loops of spells. Three drag a gnarled branch to the fires, its dry and leafy fingers clagged with tins, as many as the rings on a witch's hand. And still it scrabbles, rakes for more.

Warily entranced, Rue watches, edges round them, keeping hold of Goss. She stoops for a bit of paper, torn and scattering. No images. All scratches, black as birds. She lets it go.

A dark lad's hurling dustbins down a flight of steps, with a bang and clangor and a long-drawn rumbling. Whuff! He lights one, lofts it blazing with a trembling hollow roar; and howling, casts it down in ruin. Children rush to kick and scuffle at the spill of embers, stamp them out.

Leaning close in the curl of newel at the broad stair's foot, two girls play cat's cradles with red yarn. They pick their crosses carefully, perplex and intricate. Undergo; then overturn.

Children tumble from a carapace of engine, with its soft maw sprung to wires, and its shattered eyes. They're all in flutterings of rags, torn and knotted, with their coats turned inside out. They've ashes on their faces, tins of pebbles in their hands. Mute as ghosts, they prowl and shake their rattles.

All alone, a small child huddles on a step; he rocks and sucks the ragdoll babby at his cheek. But his lullaby's from elsewhere, voices in the dark. "Lay down, my dear sister . . ."

Still in shadow, Goss and Rue slip by.

In a sidestreet by a railing, by a tree scant of leaves, a knot of children call and chant. They are whirling clapping in a game.

> *Tell B for the beast at the ending of the wood*
> > *Good night, Good night*
> *Well, he eat all the children when they wouldn't be good*
> > *Good night, Good night, Good night*

AND "GOOD NIGHT," the voices cry in antiphon, like birds; as if there were a greener world indwelling in these streets. A wood. Their city's crowded, crowned with visionary trees. There's no way in; they weave themselves a hedge. Goss lingers for a moment, drawn and doubtful; Rue tugs her on.

Still others turn a rope, and leap through it in turn. Brown legs, scratched legs. Jauncing plaits. In turn there is no one jumping, but they call the dark, they bid it in. The rope whips round and round, slapping at the stones.

Not all are children. A man in a soft hat and a muddy suit, unshaven, stands and shouts. At nothing, at the sky. Not angry, thinks Goss. Amazed.

The rope slaps to their chant, his chant.

    "Babylon is fallen."
              "Is fallen."
                    "Is fallen."
    "Babylon is fallen."
        "To rise no more."

By a shattered window, by a lamp, a boy kneels, dark amid the glittering. He keeps to the fringes of the light, penumbral; coming closer, they can see he's thin and fairish, scowling, with bent mended specs. He's working at something. A cosmos of black wire, all in tension, with a long spiring tail. It glitters blackly; it jangles. He shakes the long coil of it, and leaves rags paper dance.

Goss says, "What's that for?"

"Catching crows," he says. "Summat I thought on."

"What *day*?"

"Yer must be inwits," he says, tilting his scarred glasses. "It's nights here Outwith. All as it comes." They can see his scabbed knees, his scarry fingers. Stained burned slashed. Soft hair like flocking, whitey-brown. "There's all sort of chancers runs. Some clever and some mad. There's ranters and goners—" He nods at the shabby man. "And guisers—them wi' ashes. Then there's howkers and tigs, and there's ticers. What I is. A niner, come daybreak."

"Ticers?" (What do they do? Could I?)

"Get by. Call crows. Get round 'em." He lights the kite's tail of his strange device; for a moment now his face is eerie, ambered from below. "Happen talk with them." He pinches out his spill.

And as the shadow stoops, he cries, "Run, will yer!"

The man falls open-armed, ecstatic.

They run.

Behind them comes a whirring and a cry. The shock embrittles them, turns all their blood to branching ice. Blindly they stumble on until Rue falls, tripped up on his brolly. Goss muffles him against her breast, she strokes the black frost from his hair. They crouch, as still as rats. No shadow of the bird strikes, wheels, returning to her prey. After a time, Goss dabbles at his scrapes, then at hers; she wipes his streaked and snotted face. Her own. Then they share what she has left: a scrawny orange. Cradling, she snuffs at it before she breaks it open. Pith and bittersweet and curving.

It was beautiful, the bird.

They wander on, at random, turning down this street, that crescent, past the naked windows and the empty rooms.

A shout. Boys snatch the brolly, toss it high above his sobbing reach, the fury of her nails; they hurly down the street, thwacking it at tins and bottles, quarreling; until the tallest leaps and hooks it to a high bar, where it dangles, all agape and stark.

They vanish.

Rue and Goss gaze up. It's hanging from a gate of iron, in

a wall. They clamber up and flail at it with sticks; at last they knock it down.

Beyond the gate's another square, but silent, sheeted all with moon. No fire and no games. Stones cracked with weeds. And stony, too, the white girl crowned with leaves, with leaves and flowers in her stony lap. Her fountain's dry.

Rue slips between the rusted bars, undoes the latch for Gosslyn. They go in.

But there's someone there, behind the circle of the stony dance, her grove of girls: another girl, a real one, in a night-dress and slippers, squatting on her heels. Quite a grown girl, thin and ginger, with a cat's curly smile. Her cardigan won't button round her middle, but her freckly arms and legs are thin. She's drawing on the paving stones with chalk, white and red. They've seen her with her mam's brood, down the Wall: jerking stragglers howling after, wiping noses, soothing, fratching. Goss glances at her belly.

"Mrs. Stemmon?"

"Not Mrs." She chalks another line. "Outwith, I's Phib."

"Goss. Yon's Rue."

"Know yer. Hey up, brat."

Scrape goes the ferrule. "What is't yer drawing?"

"Snakes and ladders." Nodding at Goss, she holds out a bit of chalk. "Halfs?"

Goss fumbles at her pocket. "Got a bit."

Laddery as stockings, what Phib's drawn, with blotches in it, red as poppies, red as blood. As if they'd scattered as she ran.

Kneeling on the pavement, Goss chalks angles, spirals, mazes round and round them. They are holes, doors, houses; they are earth and heaven. White on black. They make a grammar as they go. Halt runes becoming terse and supple, turning to a rime, a rant, a summoning. No more her mother tongue: new heaven and new earth. Her line's a labyrinth, her thread of moonlight, winding on the spindle of the moon. She draws it down.

Hawklike, darkness knots itself and stoops: not fury but a fall of chance. The air's like black glass shattering. Rue whirls the umbrella, heavy suddenly with wind. He's staggered, but he holds it fast with both hands, blown askew. It wrenches at him, bucks and judders on the pavement, scraping stone; it leaps and bellies out. For a breath, its bones are lightning and its web is sky. Its godcrow sister cries to it; she wheels and counters, and the white thread snares her. Goss draws it tighter still, until the jess must snap, the falcon strike. She's drawing on its dark, she's drawing on the night itself. The chalk is crumbling. What she writes with it are stars and clouds of stars, ascendancies in nightfall. With the powder of her end, she sets them dancing.

THE MRS. LOOKS about the bare room, the scrubbed wall, with her shrewd embittered eye. The box still flickers with its frieze of birds, still gloating on their eggs. Leave that. There's another, always. Got her bacca, got her hairpins. Smokebook. Feather dress and comb. She folds away the last wards in her cheap case, snecks the latch. Unhooks the mirror from the wall. Cord's coiled, Oover's gutted, nets are drawn. She'll get herself another place, then. Somewhere further down t'Wall. Deeper in. Then. Long time since she's had a make. Last man

were sackless. Got her brats, but. Thankless. And t'last afore him.
Time sometime to get another. Screw him. Time enough.

She broods.

Greer Gilman's novel *Moonwise* won the Crawford Award
and was short listed for the Tiptree and Mythopoeic Fantasy
Awards. Her novella, *A Crowd of Bone*, won the World Fantasy
Award in 2004. Set in the mythscape of *Moonwise*, it is the
second story in the Ashes cycle, a triptych of variations on a
winter myth. The first story, "Jack Daw's Pack," was a Nebula
finalist for 2001. She is working on the third.

A graduate of Wellesley College and Cambridge University, and a sometime forensic librarian, Gilman lives in Cambridge, Massachusetts, and travels in stone circles. She recently
gave a paper on "Shakespearean Voices in the Literature of the
Fantastic" to the Shakespeare Association of America.

Femaville 29

Paul Di Filippo

LA PALMA IS a tiny mote in the Canary Islands, a mote that had certainly never intruded into my awareness before one fateful day. On La Palma, five hundred billion tons of rock in the form of an unstable coastal plateau awaited a nudge, which they received when the Cumbre Vieja volcano erupted. Into the sea a good portion of the plateau plunged, a frightful hammer of the gods.

The peeling off of the face of the island was a smaller magnitude event than had been feared, but it was a larger magnitude event than anyone was prepared for.

The resulting tsunami raced across the Atlantic.

My city had gotten just twelve hours' warning. The surreal chaos of the partial evacuation was like living through the most vivid nightmare or disaster film imaginable. Still, the efforts of the authorities and volunteers and good samaritans ensured that hundreds of thousands of people escaped with their lives.

Leaving other hundreds of thousands to face the wave.

Their only recourse was to find the tallest, strongest buildings and huddle.

I was on the seventh floor of an insurance company when the wave arrived. Posters in the reception area informed me that I was in good hands. I had a view of the harbor, half a mile away.

The tsunami looked like a liquid mountain mounted on a rocket sled.

When the wave hit, the building shuddered and bellowed like a steer in an abattoir euthanized with a nail gun. Every window popped out of its frame, and spray lashed even my level.

But the real fight for survival had not yet begun.

The next several days were a sleepless blur of crawling from the wreckage and helping others do likewise.

But not everyone was on the same side. Looters arose like some old biological paradigm of spontaneous generation from the muck.

Their presence demanded mine on the front lines.

I was a cop.

I had arrested several bad guys without any need for excessive force. But then came a shootout at a jewelry store where the display cases were incongruously draped with drying kelp. I ended up taking the perps down okay. But the firefight left my weary brain and trembling gut hypersensitive to any threat.

Some indeterminate time afterward—marked by a succession of candy-bar meals, digging under the floodlights powered by chuffing generators, and endless slogging through slimed streets—I was working my way through the upper floors of an apartment complex, looking for survivors. I shut off my flashlight when I saw a glow around a corner. Someone stepped between me and the light source, casting the shadow of a man with a gun. I yelled, "Police! Drop it!" then crouched and dashed toward the gunman. The figure stepped forward, still holding the weapon, and I fired.

The boy was twelve, his weapon a water pistol.

His mother trailed him by a few feet—not far enough to escape getting splattered with her son's blood.

Later I learned neither of them spoke a word of English.

One minute I was cradling the boy, and the next I was laying on a cot in a field hospital. Three days had gotten lost somewhere. Three days in which the whole world had learned of my mistake.

They let me get up the next day, ostensibly healthy and sane enough, even though my pistol hand, my left, still exhibited a bad tremor. I tried to report to the police command, but found that I had earned a temporary medical discharge. Any legal fallout from my actions awaited an end to the crisis.

I tried being a civilian volunteer for another day or two amidst the ruins, but my heart wasn't in it. So I took the offer of evacuation to Femaville 29.

⁓

THE FIRST WEEK after the disaster actually manifested aspects of an odd, enforced vacation. Or rather, the atmosphere often felt more like an open-ended New Year's Eve, the portal to some as-yet undefined millennium where all our good resolutions would come to pass. Once we victims emerged from the shock of losing everything we owned, including our shared identity as citizens of a large East Coast city, my fellow refugees and I began to exhibit a near-manic optimism in the face of the massive slate-cleaning.

The uplift was not to last. But while it prevailed, it was as if some secret imperative in the depths of our souls—a wish to be unburdened of all our draggy pasts—had been fulfilled by cosmic fiat, without our having to lift a finger.

We had been given a chance to start all over, remake our lives afresh, and we were, for the most part, eager to grasp the offered personal remodeling.

Everyone in the swiftly erected encampment of a thousand men, women, and children was healthy. The truly injured had all been airlifted to hospitals around the state and nation. Families had been reunited, even down to pets. The tents we were inhabiting were spacious, weather-tight, and wired for electricity and entertainment. Meals were plentiful, albeit uninspired, served promptly in three shifts, thrice daily, in a large communal pavilion.

True, the lavatories and showers were also communal, and the lack of privacy grated a bit right from the start. Trudging through the chilly dark in the middle of the night to take a leak held limited appeal, even when you pretended you were camping. And winter, with its more challenging conditions, loomed only a few months away. Moreover, enforced idleness chafed those of us who were used to steady work. Lack of proper schooling for the scores of kids in the camp worried many parents.

But taken all in all, the atmosphere at the camp—christened with no more imaginative bureaucratic name than Femaville Number 29—was suffused with potential that first week.

My own interview with the FEMA intake authorities in the first days of the relocation was typical.

The late September sunlight warmed the interview tent so much that the canvas sides had been rolled up to admit fresh air scented with faint, not unpleasant, maritime odors of decay. Even though Femaville 29 was located far inland—or what used to be far inland before the tsunami—the wreck left behind by the disaster lay not many miles away.

For a moment, I pictured exotic fish swimming through the streets and subways of my old city, weaving their paths among cars, couches, and corpses. The imagery unsettled me, and I tried to focus on the more hopeful present.

The long tent hosted ranks of paired folding chairs, each chair facing its mate. The FEMA workers, armed with laptop computers, occupied one seat of each pair, while an interviewee sat in the other. The subdued mass interrogation and the clicking of keys raised a surprisingly dense net of sound that overlaid the noises from outside the tent: children roistering, adults gossiping, birds chattering. Outside the tent, multiple lines of refugees stretched away, awaiting their turns.

The official seated across from me was a pretty young African-American woman whose name-badge proclaimed her HANNAH LAWES. Unfortunately, she reminded me of my ex-wife, Calley, hard in the same places Calley was hard. I tried to suppress an immediate dislike of her. As soon as I sat down, Hannah Lawes expressed rote sympathy for my plight, a commiseration worn featureless by its hundredth repetition. Then she got down to business.

"Name?"

"Parrish Hedges."

"Any relatives in the disaster zone?"

"No, ma'am."

"What was your job back in the city?"

I felt my face heat up. But I had no choice, except to answer truthfully.

"I was a police officer, ma'am."

That answer gave Hannah Lawes pause. Finally, she asked in an accusatory fashion, "Shouldn't you still be on duty then? Helping with security in the ruins?"

My left hand started to quiver a bit, but I suppressed it so that I didn't think she noticed.

"Medical exemption, ma'am."

Hannah Lawes frowned slightly and said, "I hope you don't mind if I take a moment to confirm that, Mr. Hedges."

Her slim, manicured fingers danced over her keyboard, dragging my data down the airwaves. I studied the plywood floor of the tent while she read my file.

When I looked up, her face had gone disdainful.

"This explains much, Mr. Hedges."

"Can we move on, please?"

As if I ever could.

Hannah Lawes resumed her programmed spiel. "All right, let's talk about your options now. . . ."

For the next few minutes, she outlined the various programs and handouts and incentives that the government and private charities and NGOs had lined up for the victims of the disaster. Somehow, none of the choices really matched my dreams and expectations engendered by the all-consuming catastrophe. All of them involved relocating to some other part of the country, leaving behind the shattered chaos of the East Coast. And that was something I just wasn't ready for yet, inevitable as such a move was.

And besides, choosing any one particular path would have meant foregoing all the others. Leaving this indeterminate interzone of infinite possibility would lock me into a new life that might be better than my old one, but would still be fixed, crystallized, frozen into place.

"Do I have to decide right now?"

"No, no, of course not."

I stood up to go, and Hannah Lawes added, "But you realize, naturally, that this camp was never intended as a long-term residence. It's only transitional, and will be closed down at some point not too far in the future."

"Yeah, sure," I said. "We're all just passing through. I get it."

I left then and made way for the next person waiting in line.

⌒

THE TENTS OF Femaville 29 were arranged along five main dirt avenues, each as wide as a city boulevard. Expressing the same ingenuity that had dubbed our whole encampment, the avenues were labeled A, B, C, D, and E. Every three tents, a numbered cross-street occurred. The tents of one avenue backed up against the tents of the adjacent avenue, so that a cross-block was two tents wide. The land where

Femaville 29 was pitched was flat and treeless and covered in newly mowed weeds and grasses. Beyond the borders of our village stretched a mix of forest, scrubby fields, and swamp, eventually giving way to rolling hills. The nearest real town was about ten miles away, and there was no regular transportation there other than by foot.

As I walked up Avenue D toward my tent (D-30), I encountered dozens of my fellow refugees who were finished with the intake process. Only two days had passed since the majority of us had been ferried here in commandeered school buses. People—the adults, anyhow—were still busy exchanging their stories—thrilling, horrific, or mundane—about how they had escaped the tsunami or dealt with the aftermath.

I didn't have any interest in repeating my tale, so I didn't join in any such conversations.

As for the children, they seemed mostly to have flexibly put behind them all the trauma they must have witnessed. Reveling in their present freedom from boring routine, they raced up and down the avenues in squealing packs.

Already, the seasonally withered grass of the avenues was becoming dusty ruts. Just days old, this temporary village, I could feel, was already beginning to lose its freshness and ambiance of novelty.

Under the unseasonably warm sun, I began to sweat. A cold beer would have tasted good right now. But the rules of Femaville 29 prohibited alcohol.

I reached my tent and went inside.

My randomly assigned roommate lay on his bunk. Given how the disaster had shattered and stirred the neighborhoods of the city, it was amazing that I actually knew the fellow from before. I had encountered no one else yet in the camp who was familiar to me. And out of all my old friends and acquaintances and coworkers, Ethan Duplessix would have been my last choice to be reunited with.

Ethan was a fat, bristled slob with a long criminal record of petty theft, fraud, and advanced mopery. His personal grooming habits were so atrocious that he had emerged from the disaster more or less in the same condition he entered it, unlike the rest of the survivors who had gone from well groomed to uncommonly bedraggled and smelly.

Ethan and I had crossed paths often, and I had locked him up more times than I could count. (When the tsunami struck, he had been astonishingly free of outstanding charges.) But the new circumstances of our lives, including Ethan's knowledge of how I had "retired" from the force, placed us now on a different footing.

"Hey, Hedges, how'd it go? They got you a new job yet? Maybe security guard at a kindergarten!"

I didn't bother replying, but just flopped down on my bunk. Ethan chuckled meanly at his own paltry wit for a while, but when I didn't respond, he eventually fell silent, his attentions taken up by a tattered copy of *Maxim*.

I closed my eyes and drowsed for a while, until I got hungry. Then I got up and went to the refectory.

That day they were serving hamburgers and fries for the third day in a row. Mickey Dee's seemed to have gotten a lock on the contract to supply the camp. I took mine to an empty table. Head bowed, halfway through my meal, I sensed someone standing beside me.

The woman's curly black hair descended to her shoulders

in a tumbled mass. Her face resembled a cameo in its alabaster fineness.

"Mind if I sit here?" she said.

"Sure. I mean, go for it."

The simple but primordial movements of her legs swinging over the bench seat and her ass settling down awakened emotions in me that had been absent since Calley's abrupt leave-taking.

"Nia Horsley. Used to live over on Garden Parkway."

"Nice district."

Nia snorted, a surprisingly enjoyable sound. "Yeah, once."

"I never got over there much. Worked in East Grove. Had an apartment on Oakeshott."

"And what would the name on your doorbell have been?"

"Oh, sorry. Parrish Hedges."

"Pleased to meet you, Parrish."

We shook hands. Hers was small but strong, enshelled in mine like a pearl.

For the next two hours, through two more shifts of diners coming and going, we talked, exchanging condensed life stories, right up to the day of disaster and down to our arrival at Femaville 29. Maybe the accounts were edited for maximum appeal, but I intuitively felt she and I were being honest nonetheless. When the refectory workers finally shooed us out in order to clean up for supper, I felt as if I had known Nia for two weeks, two months, two years—

She must have felt the same. As we strolled away down Avenue B, she held my hand.

"I don't have a roomie in my tent."

"Oh?"

"It's just me and my daughter. Luck of the draw, I guess."

"I like kids. Never had any, but I like 'em."

"Her name's Izzy. Short for Isabel. You'll get to meet her. But maybe not just yet."

"How come?"

"She's made a lot of new friends. They stay out all day, playing on the edge of the camp. Some kind of weird new game they invented."

"We could go check up on her, and I could say hello."

Nia squeezed my hand. "Maybe not right this minute."

I GOT TO meet Izzy the day after Nia and I slept together. I suppose I could've hung around till Izzy came home for supper, but the intimacy with Nia, after such a desert of personal isolation, left me feeling a little disoriented and pressured. So I made a polite excuse for my departure, which Nia accepted with good grace, and arranged to meet mother and daughter for breakfast.

Izzy bounced into the refectory ahead of her mother. She was seven or eight, long-limbed and fair-haired in contrast to her mother's compact, raven-haired paleness, but sharing Nia's high-cheeked bone structure. I conjectured backward to a gangly blond father.

The little girl zeroed in on me somehow out of the whole busy dining hall, racing up to where I sat, only to slam on the brakes with alarming precipitousness.

"You're Mr. Hedges!" she informed me and the world.

"Yes, I am. And you're Izzy."

I was ready to shake her hand in a formal adult manner.

But then she exclaimed, "You made my Mom all smiley!" and launched herself into my awkward embrace.

Before I could really respond, she was gone, heading for the self-service cereal line.

I looked at Nia, who was grinning.

"And this," I asked, "is her baseline?"

"Precisely. When she's really excited—"

"I'll wear one of those padded suits we used for training the K-9 squad."

Nia's expression altered to one of seriousness and sympathy, and I instantly knew what was coming. I cringed inside, if not where it showed. She sat down next to me and put a hand on my arm.

"Parrish, I admit I did a little googling on you after we split yesterday, over at the online tent. I know about why you aren't a cop anymore. And I just want to say that—"

Before she could finish, Izzy materialized out of nowhere, bearing a tray holding two bowls of technicolor puffs swimming in chocolate milk, and slipped herself between us slick as a greased eel.

"They're almost out of food! You better hurry!" With a plastic knife, Izzy began slicing a peeled banana into chunks thick as Oreos that plopped with alarming splashes into her bowls.

I stood up gratefully. "I'll get us something, Nia. Eggs and bacon and toast okay?"

She gave me a look which said that she could wait to talk. "Sure."

During breakfast, Nia and I mostly listened to Izzy's chatter.

"—and then Vonique's all like, 'But the way I remember it is the towers were next to the harbor, not near the zoo.'

And Eddie goes, 'Na-huh, they were right where the park started.' And they couldn't agree and they were gonna start a fight, until I figured out that they were talking about two different places! Vonique meant the Goblin Towers, and Eddie meant the Towers of Bone! So I straightened them out, and now the map of Djamala is like almost half done!"

"That's wonderful, honey."

"It's a real skill, being a peacemaker like that."

Izzy cocked her head and regarded me quizzically. "But that's just what I've always been forever."

In the next instant she was up and kissing her mother, then out the hall and raising puffs of dust as she ran toward where I could see other kids seemingly waiting for her.

Nia and I spent the morning wandering around the camp, talking about anything and everything—except my ancient, recent disgrace. We watched a pickup soccer game for an hour or so, the players expending the bottled energy that would have gone to work and home before the disaster, then ended up back at her tent around three.

Today was as warm as yesterday, and we raised a pretty good sweat. Nia dropped off to sleep right after, but I couldn't.

Eleven days after the flood, and it was all I could dream about.

⁓

ETHAN WAS REALLY starting to get on my nerves. He had seen me hanging out with Nia and Izzy, and used the new knowledge to taunt me.

"What's up with you and the little girl, Hedges? Thinking of keeping your hand in with some target practice?"

I stood quivering over his bunk before I even realized

I had moved. My fists were bunched at my hips, ready to strike. But both Ethan and I knew I wouldn't.

The penalty for fighting at any of the Femavilles was instant expulsion, and an end to government charity. I couldn't risk losing Nia now that I had found her. Even if we managed to stay in touch while apart, who was to say that the fluid milieu of the postdisaster environment would not conspire to supplant our relationship with another.

So I stalked out and went to see Hannah Lawes.

One complex of tents hosted the bureaucrats. Lawes sat at a folding table with her omnipresent laptop. Hooked to a printer, the machine was churning out travel vouchers branded with official glyphs of authenticity.

"Mr. Hedges. What can I do for you? Have you decided to take up one of the host offerings? There's a farming community in Nebraska—"

I shook my head in the negative. Trying to imagine myself relocated to the prairies was so disorienting that I almost forgot why I had come here.

Hannah Lawes seemed disappointed by my refusal of her proposal, but realistic about the odds that I would've accepted. "I can't say I'm surprised. Not many people are leaping at what I can offer. I've only gotten three takers so far. And I can't figure out why. They're all generous, sensible berths."

"Yeah, sure. That's the problem."

"What do you mean?"

"No one wants 'sensible' after what they've been through. We all want to be reborn as phoenixes—not drayhorses. That's all that would justify our sufferings."

Hannah Lawes said nothing for a moment, and only the

minor whine of the printer filigreed the bubble of silence around us. When she spoke, her voice was utterly neutral.

"You could die here before you achieve that dream, Mr. Hedges. Now, how can I help you, if not with a permanent relocation?"

"If I arrange different living quarters with the consent of everyone involved, is there any regulation stopping me from switching tents?"

"No, not at all."

"Good. I'll be back."

I tracked down Nia and found her using a piece of exercise equipment donated by a local gym. She hopped off and hugged me.

"Have to do something about my weight. I'm not used to all this lolling around."

Nia had been a waitress back in the city, physically active eight or more hours daily. My own routines, at least since Calley left me, had involved more couch-potato time than mountain climbing, and the sloth of camp life sat easier on me.

We hugged, her body sweaty in my arms, and I explained my problem.

"I realize we haven't known each other very long, Nia, but do you think—"

"I'd like it if you moved in with Izzy and me, Parrish. One thing the tsunami taught us—life's too short to dither. And I'd feel safer."

"No one's been bothering you, have they?"

"No, but there's just too many weird noises out here in the country. Every time a branch creaks, I think someone's climbing my steps."

I hugged her again, harder, in wordless thanks.

We both went back to Lawes and arranged the new tent assignments.

When I went to collect my few possessions, Ethan sneered at me.

"Knew you'd run, Hedges. Without your badge, you're nothing."

As I left, I wondered what I had been even with my badge.

~

LIVING WITH NIA and Izzy, I naturally became more involved in the young girl's activities.

And that's when I learned about Djamala.

By the end of the second week in Femaville 29, the atmosphere had begun to sour. The false exuberance engendered by sheer survival amidst so much death—and the accompanying sense of newly opened horizons—had dissipated. In place of these emotions came anomie, irritability, anger, despair, and a host of other negative feelings. The immutable, unchanging confines of the unfenced camp assumed the proportions of a stalag. The food, objectively unchanged in quality or quantity, met with disgust, simply because we had no control over its creation. The shared privies assumed a stink no amount of bleach could dispel.

Mere conversation and gossip had paled, replaced with disproportionate arguments over inconsequentials. Sports gave way to various games of chance, played with the odd pair of dice or deck of cards, with bets denominated in sex or clothing or desserts.

One or two serious fights resulted in the promised

expulsions, and, chastened but surly, combatants restrained themselves to shoving matches and catcalls.

A few refugees, eager for stimulation and a sense of normality, made the long trek into town—and found themselves returned courtesy of local police cars.

The bureaucrats managing the camp—Hannah Lawes and her peers—were not immune to the shifting psychic tenor of Femaville 29. From models of optimism and can-do effectiveness, the officials began to slide into terse minimalist responses.

"I don't know what more we can do," Hannah Lawes told me. "If our best efforts to reintegrate everyone as functioning and productive members of society are not appreciated, then—"

She left the consequences unstated, merely shaking her head ruefully at our ingratitude and sloth.

The one exception to this general malaise were the children.

Out of a thousand people in Femaville 29, approximately two hundred were children younger than twelve although sometimes their numbers seemed larger, as they raced through the camp's streets and avenues in boisterous packs. Seemingly unaffected by the unease and dissatisfaction exhibited by their guardians and parents, the kids continued to enjoy their pastoral interlude. School, curfews, piano lessons—all shed in a return to a prelapsarian existence as hunter-gatherers of the twenty-first century.

When they weren't involved in traditional games, they massed on the outskirts of the camp for an utterly novel undertaking.

There, I discovered, they were building a new city to replace the one they had lost.

Or, perhaps, simply mapping one that already existed.

And Izzy Horsley, I soon learned (with actually very little surprise), was one of the prime movers of this jovial, juvenile enterprise.

With no tools other than their feet and hands, the children had cleared a space almost as big as a football field of all vegetation, leaving behind a dusty canvas on which to construct their representation of an imaginary city.

Three weeks into its construction, the map-cum-model had assumed impressive dimensions, despite the rudimentary nature of its materials.

One afternoon, tired of constantly accompanying Nia during her exertions in the tent full of exercise equipment, I drifted over to the children's site. Her own angst about ensuring the best future for herself and loved ones had manifested as an obsession with "keeping fit" that I couldn't force myself to share. With my mind drifting, a sudden curiosity about where Izzy was spending so much of her time stole over me, and I ambled over to investigate.

Past the ultimate tents, I came upon what could have been a construction site reimagined for the underage cast of *Sesame Street*.

The youngest children were busy assembling stockpiles of stones and twigs and leaves. The stones were quarried from the immediate vicinity, emerging still wet with loam, while sticks and leaves came from a nearby copse in long disorderly caravans.

Older children were engaged in two different kinds of tasks. One chore involved using long pointed sticks to gouge lines in the dirt: lines that plainly marked streets, natural features, and the outlines of buildings. The second set of workers was elaborating these outlines with the organic materials from the stockpiles. The map was mostly flat, but occasionally a structure, teepee or cairn, rose up a few inches.

The last, smallest subset of workers were the architects: the designers, engineers, imagineers of the city. They stood off to one side, consulting, arguing, issuing orders, and sometimes venturing right into the map to correct the placement of lines or ornamentation.

Izzy was one of these elite.

Deep in discussion with a cornrowed black girl and a pudgy white boy wearing smudged glasses, Izzy failed to note my approach, and so I was able to overhear their talk. Izzy was holding forth at the moment.

"—Sprankle Hall covers two whole blocks, not just one! C'mon, you gotta remember that! Remember when we went there for a concert, and after we wanted to go around back to the door where the musicians were coming out, and how long it took us to get there?"

The black girl frowned, then said, "Yeah, right, we had to walk like forever. But if Sprankle Hall goes from Cleverly Street all the way to Khush Lane, then how does Pinemarten Avenue run without a break?"

The fat boy spoke with assurance. "It's the Redondo Tunnel. Goes under Sprankle Hall."

Izzy and the black girl grinned broadly. "Of course! I remember when that was built!"

I must have made some noise then, for the children finally noticed me. Izzy rushed over and gave me a quick embrace.

"Hey, Parrish! What're you doing here?"

"I came to see what was keeping you guys so busy. What's going on here?"

Izzy's voice expressed no adult embarrassment, doubt, irony, or blasé dismissal of a temporary time-killing project. "We're building a city! Djamala! It's someplace wonderful!"

The black girl nodded solemnly. I recalled the name Vonique from Izzy's earlier conversation, and the name seemed suddenly inextricably linked to this child.

"Well," said Vonique, "it will be wonderful, once we finish it. But right now it's still a mess."

"This city—Djamala? How did it come to be? Who invented it?"

"Nobody invented it!" Izzy exclaimed. "It's always been there. We just couldn't remember it until the wave."

The boy—Eddie?—said, "That's right, sir. The tsunami made it rise up."

"Rise up? Out of the waters, like Atlantis? A new continent?"

Eddie pushed his glasses further up his nose. "Not out of the ocean. Out of our minds."

My expression must have betrayed disbelief. Izzy grabbed one of my hands with both of hers. "Parrish, please! This is really important for everyone. You gotta believe in Djamala! Really!"

"Well, I don't know if I can believe in it the same way you kids can. But what if I promise just not to disbelieve yet? Would that be good enough?"

Vonique puffed air past her lips in a semicontemptuous manner. "Huh! I suppose that's as good as we're gonna get from anyone, until we can show them something they can't ignore."

Izzy gazed up at me with imploring eyes. "Parrish? You're not gonna let us down, are you?"

What could I say? "No, no, of course not. If I can watch and learn, maybe I can start to understand."

Izzy, Vonique, and Eddie had to confer with several other pint-sized architects before they could grant me observer's status, but eventually they did confer that honor on me.

So for the next several days I spent most of my time with the children as they constructed their imaginary metropolis.

At first, I was convinced that the whole process was merely some overelaborated coping strategy for dealing with the disaster that had upended their young lives.

But at the end of a week, I was not so certain.

So long as I did not get in the way of construction, I was allowed to venture down the outlined HO-scale streets, given a tour of the city's extensive features and history by whatever young engineer was least in demand at the moment. The story of Djamala's ancient founding, its history and contemporary life, struck me as remarkably coherent and consistent at the time, although I did not pay as much attention as I should have to the information. I theorized then that the children were merely re-sorting a thousand borrowed bits and pieces from television, films, and video games. Now, I can barely recall a few salient details. The Crypt of the Thousand Martyrs, the Bluepoint Aerial Tramway, Penton Park, Winkelreed Slough, Midwinter Festival, the Squid Club. These proper names, delivered in the pure, piping voices of Izzy and her peers, are all that remain to me.

I wished I could get an aerial perspective on the diagram of Djamala. It seemed impossibly refined and balanced to have been plotted out solely from a ground-level perspective. Like the South American drawings at Nazca, its complex lineaments seemed to demand a superior view from some impossible, more-than-mortal vantage point.

After a week spent observing the children—a week during which a light evening rain shower did much damage to Djamala, damage that the children industriously and cheerfully began repairing—a curious visual hallucination overtook me.

Late afternoon sunlight slanted across the map of Djamala as the children began to tidy up in preparation for quitting. Sitting on a borrowed folding chair, I watched their small forms, dusted in gold, move along eccentric paths. My mind commenced to drift amidst wordless regions. The burden of my own body seemed to fall away.

At that moment, the city of Djamala began to assume a ghostly reality, translucent buildings rearing skyward. Ghostly minarets, stadia, pylons—

I jumped up, heart thumping to escape my chest, frightened to my core.

Memory of a rubbish-filled, clammy, partially illuminated hallway, and the shadow of a gunman, pierced me.

My senses had betrayed me fatally once before. How could I ever fully trust them again?

Djamala vanished then, and I was relieved.

⁓

A HERD OF government-drafted school buses materialized one Thursday on the outskirts of Femaville 29, on the opposite side of the camp from Djamala, squatting like empty-eyed yellow elephants, and I knew that the end of the encampment was imminent. But exactly how soon would we be expelled to more permanent quarters not of our choosing? I went to see Hannah Lawes.

I tracked down the social worker in the kitchen of the camp. She was efficiently taking inventory of cases of canned goods.

"Ms. Lawes, can I talk to you?"

A small hard smile quirked one corner of her lips. "Mr. Hedges. Have you had a sudden revelation about your future?"

"Yes, in a way. Those buses—"

"Are not scheduled for immediate use. FEMA believes in proper advance staging of resources."

"But when—"

"Who can say? I assure you that I don't personally make such command decisions. But I will pass along any new directives as soon as I am permitted."

Unsatisfied, I left her tallying creamed corn and green beans.

Everyone in the camp, of course, had seen the buses, and speculation about the fate of Femaville 29 was rampant. Were we to be dispersed to public housing in various host cities? Was the camp to be merged with others into a larger concentration of refugees for economy of scale? Maybe we'd all be put to work restoring our mortally wounded drowned city. Every possibility looked equally likely.

I expected Nia's anxiety to be keyed up by the threat of dissolution of our hard-won small share of stability, this island of improvised family life we had forged. But instead, she surprised me by expressing complete confidence in the future.

"I can't worry about what's coming, Parrish. We're together now, with a roof over our heads, and that's all that counts. Besides, just lately I've gotten a good feeling about the days ahead."

"Based on what?"

Nia shrugged with a smile. "Who knows?"

The children, however, Izzy included, were not quite as sanguine as Nia. The coming of the buses had goaded them to greater activity. No longer did they divide the day into periods of conventional playtime and construction of their city of dreams. Instead, they labored at the construction full-time.

The antlike trains of bearers ferried vaster quantities of sticks and leaves, practically denuding the nearby copse. The grubbers-up of pebbles broke their nails uncomplainingly in the soil. The scribers of lines ploughed empty square footage into new districts like the most rapacious of suburban developers. The ornamentation crew thatched and laid mosaics furiously. And the elite squad overseeing all the activity wore themselves out like military strategists overseeing an invasion.

"What do we build today?"

"The docks at Kannuckaden."

"But we haven't even put down the Mocambo River yet!"

"Then do the river first! But we have to fill in the Great Northeastern Range before tomorrow!"

"What about Gopher Gulch?"

"That'll be next."

Befriending some kitchen help secured me access to surplus cartons of prepackaged treats. I took to bringing the snacks to the hardworking children, and they seemed to appreciate it. Although truthfully, they spared little enough attention to me or any other adult, lost in their make-believe, laboring blank-eyed or with feverish intensity.

The increased activity naturally attracted the notice of the adults. Many heretofore-oblivious parents showed up at last to see what their kids were doing. The consensus was that such behavior, while a little weird, was generally harmless enough, and actually positive, insofar as it kept the children from boredom and any concomitant pestering of parents. After a few days of intermittent parental visits, the site was generally clear of adults once more.

One exception to this rule was Ethan Duplessix.

At first, I believed, he began hanging around Djamala solely because he saw me there. Peeved by how I had escaped his taunts, he looked for some new angle from which to attack me, relishing the helplessness of his old nemesis.

But as I continued to ignore the slobby criminal slacker, failing to give him any satisfaction, his frustrated focus turned naturally to what the children were actually doing. My lack of standing as any kind of legal guardian to anyone except, at even the widest stretch of the term, Izzy, meant that I could not prevent the children from talking to him.

They answered Ethan's questions respectfully and completely at first, and I could see interest building in his self-serving brain, as he rotated the facts this way and that, seeking some advantage for himself. But then the children grew tired of his gawking and cut him off.

"We have too much work to do. You've got to go now."

"Please, Mr. Duplessix, just leave us alone."

I watched Ethan's expression change from greedy curiosity to anger. He actually threatened the children.

"You damn kids! You need to share! Or else someone'll just take what you've got!"

I was surprised at the fervor of Ethan's interest in Djamala. Maybe something about the dream project had actually touched a decent, imaginative part of his soul. But whatever the case, his threats gave me a valid excuse to hustle him off.

"You can't keep me away, Hedges! I'll be back!"

Izzy stood by my side, watching Ethan's retreat.

"Don't worry about him," I said.

"I'm not worried, Parrish. Djamala can protect itself."

The sleeping arrangements in the tent Nia, Izzy, and I shared involved a hanging blanket down the middle of the tent, to give both Izzy and us adults some privacy. Nia and I had pushed two cots together on our side and lashed them together to make a double bed. But even with a folded blanket atop the wooden bar down the middle of the makeshift bed, I woke up several times a night, as I instinctively tried to snuggle Nia and encountered the hard obstacle. Nia, smaller, slept fine on her side of the double cots.

The night after the incident with Ethan, I woke up as usual in the small hours of the morning. Something urged me to get up. I left the cot and stepped around the hanging barrier to check on Izzy.

Her cot was empty, only blankets holding a ghostly imprint of her small form.

I was just on the point of mounting a general alarm when she slipped back into the tent, clad in pajamas and dew-wet sneakers.

My presence startled her, but she quickly recovered, and smiled guiltlessly.

"Bathroom call?" I whispered.

Izzy never lied. "No. Just checking on Djamala. It's safe now. Today we finished the Iron Grotto. Just in time."

"That's good. Back to sleep now."

Ethan Duplessix had never missed a meal in his life. But the morning after Izzy's nocturnal inspection of Djamala, he was nowhere to be seen at any of the three breakfast shifts. Likewise for lunch. When he failed to show at super, I went to D-30.

Ethan's sparse possessions remained behind, but the man himself was not there. I reported his absence to Hannah Lawes.

"Please don't concern yourself unnecessarily, Mr. Hedges. I'm sure Mr. Duplessix will turn up soon. He probably spent the night in intimate circumstances with someone."

"Ethan? I didn't realize the camp boasted any female trolls."

"Now, now, Mr. Hedges, that's most ungenerous of you."

Ethan did not surface the next day, or the day after that, and was eventually marked a runaway.

The third week of October brought the dreaded announcement. Lulled by the gentle autumnal weather, the unvarying routines of the camp, and by the lack of any foreshadowings, the citizens of Femaville 29 were completely unprepared for the impact.

A general order to assemble outside by the buses greeted every diner at breakfast. Shortly before noon, a thousand refugees, clad in their donated coats and sweaters and jackets, shuffled their feet on the field that doubled as parking lot, breath pluming in the October chill. The ranks of buses remained as before, save for one unwelcome difference.

The motors of the buses were all idling, drivers behind their steering wheels.

The bureaucrats had assembled on a small raised platform. I saw Hannah Lawes in the front, holding a loud-hailer. Her booming voice assailed us.

"It's time now for your relocation. You've had a fair and lawful amount of time to choose your destination, but have failed to take advantage of this opportunity. Now your government has done so for you. Please board the buses in an orderly fashion. Your possessions will follow later."

"Where are we going?" someone called out.

Imperious, Hannah Lawes answered, "You'll find out when you arrive."

Indignation and confusion bloomed in the crowd. A contradictory babble began to mount heavenward. Hannah Lawes said nothing more immediately. I assumed she was waiting for the chaotic reaction to burn itself out, leaving the refugees sheepishly ready to obey.

But she hadn't counted on the children intervening.

A massed juvenile shriek brought silence in its wake. There was nothing wrong with the children gathered on the edges of the crowd, as evidenced by their nervous smiles. But their tactic had certainly succeeded in drawing everyone's attention.

Izzy was up front of her peers, and she shouted now, her young voice proud and confident.

"Follow us! We've made a new home for everyone!"

The children turned as one and began trotting away toward Djamala.

For a frozen moment, none of the adults made a move. Then, a man and woman—Vonique's parents—set out after the children.

Their departure catalyzed a mad general desperate rush, toward a great impossible unknown that could only be better than the certainty offered by FEMA.

Nia had been standing by my side, but she was swept away. I caught a last glimpse of her smiling, shining face as she looked back for a moment over her shoulder. Then the crowd carried her off.

I found myself hesitating. How could I face the inevitable crushing disappointment of the children, myself, and everyone else when their desperate hopes were met by a metropolis of sticks and stones and pebbles? Being there when it happened, seeing all the hurt, crestfallen faces at the instant they were forced to acknowledge defeat, would be sheer torture. Why not just wait here for their predestined return, when we could pretend the mass insanity had never happened, mount the buses and roll off, chastised and broken, to whatever average future was being offered to us?

Hannah Lawes had sidled up to me, loud-hailer held by her side.

"I'm glad to see at least one sensible person here, Mr. Hedges. Congratulations for being a realist."

Her words, her barely concealed glee and schadenfreude, instantly flipped a switch inside me from off to on, and I sped after my fellow refugees.

Halfway through the encampment, I glanced up to see Djamala looming ahead.

The splendors I had seen in ghostly fashion weeks ago were now magnified and recomplicated across acres of space. A city woven of childish imagination stretched impossibly to the horizon and beyond, its towers and monuments sparkling in the sun.

I left the last tents behind me in time to see the final stragglers entering the streets of Djamala. I heard water splash from fountains, shoes tapping on shale sidewalks, laughter echoing down wide boulevards.

But at the same time, I could see only a memory of myself in a ruined building, gun in hand, confronting a shadow assassin.

Which was reality?

I faltered to a stop.

Djamala vanished in a blink.

And I fell insensible to the ground.

I awoke in the tent that served as the infirmary for Femaville 29. Hannah Lawes was sitting by my bedside.

"Feeling better, Mr. Hedges? You nearly disrupted the exodus."

"What—what do you mean?"

"Your fellow refugees. They've all been bussed to their next station in life."

I sat up on my cot. "What are you trying to tell me? Didn't you see the city, Djamala? Didn't you see it materialize where the children built it? Didn't you see all the refugees flood in?"

Hannah Lawes's cocoa skin drained of vitality as she sought to master what were evidently strong emotions in conflict.

"What I saw doesn't matter, Mr. Hedges. It's what the

government has determined to have happened that matters. And the government has marked all your fellow refugees from Femaville 29 as settled elsewhere in the normal fashion. Case closed. Only you remain behind to be dealt with. Your fate is separate from theirs now. You certainly won't be seeing any of your temporary neighbors again for some time—if ever."

I recalled the spires and lakes, the pavilions and theaters of Djamala. I pictured Ethan Duplessix rattling the bars of the Iron Grotto. I was sure he'd reform, and be set free eventually. I pictured Nia and Izzy, swanning about in festive apartments, happy and safe, with Izzy enjoying the fruits of her labors.

And myself the lame child left behind by the Pied Piper.

"No," I replied, "I don't suppose I will see them again soon."

Hannah Lawes smiled at my acceptance of her dictates, but only for a moment, until I spoke again.

"But then, you can never be sure."

Paul Di Filippo lives in Providence, Rhode Island, with Deborah Newton, his partner of thirty years, a chocolate cocker spaniel named Brownie, and a calico cat named Penny Century.

Since 1995, he's had twenty-one books published. If and when he manages to reach twenty-five books published, he's giving himself a nice fat party.

His story collection *Shuteye for the Timebroker* was recently published by Thunder's Mouth, and the trade paperback of *Top 10: Beyond the Farthest Precinct*, Di Filippo's graphic novel, will be published DC Comics.

Nottamun Town

❧

by Gregory Maguire

T HESE THINGS COME together in Edward Haile: A childhood snuffing out—whoosh, gone—and a bulkhead of memories and associations that suddenly stand by themselves, the bas-relief without the scaffolding, and will it hold—and the light of the Lord God Almighty of the Israelites, the God who put the awe in awful and the terror in terrible, revealing Himself at last, again, lo these thousand or two years, to be the force that is yet going to outlast the brave moral genius of Jesus.

Which is to say, precisely, what?

An arc of light through the flat predawn black of the Alsatian tableland. A conversational remark of artillery following. A scream: high-pitched, metallic, an unmusical glissando, a down-swooping chromatic blur of hemi-demi-semiquavers in the treble clef. Before he knows which way to turn, which way is the safe way, the munition hits its mark. The taste of breakfast turnip arises ahead of the blood in his esophagus. His companion-at-war, Grahame Ross, is a flat figure pasted onto the two-dimensional backdrop. Grahame is up, in marionette jerks, like an image from the Biograph moving pictures. Edward sees the frame of image catch in the wheeling pins of the machinery of a vision, emblazon itself on his eyeballs—in an instant it will flame up from the heat of such attention. Blood black as bile stutters forward from inside him, as if mounting steps toward the air. Sound is bowing elliptically through his being; he is aware of sound but cannot hear it.

"Oh Christ oh Christ," says Grahame, "Eddie lover, Eddie chap." Edward cannot answer, he cannot feel Grahame's arms bolstering him, couching him toward the grave. The land rises slowly, a seeping pool of soil to suffocate him. The blasted trees dangle their broken limbs at a more precipitous angle, as if away from him, leaning back, offended at the smell. He has crapped his trousers, but no matter. The earth laps at the back of his knees as if his trousers are gone. A strange sensual tickle, like a lover, like Ma Clare bathing him in a porcelain basin on the deep windowsill of the house in Hampstead Garden Suburb. There are some words, "My Shepherd walks on water, My Shepherd walks on sea, On tempest tossed to search the lost, and bring him back to Thee . . ." "Oh," says Grahame, putting his hand flat on Eddie's chest, five fingers spread out against the blood, no more than a spiderweb erected to hold back a geyser. "Do not sing those coarse vaudeville hymns," says Mrs. Clive Haile coldly to Ma Clare, "you'll turn him weak." "Turn him loose," says Ma Clare under her breath, "one way or the other." "I'll turn you loose, and it's back to the potato patch," says Mrs. Clive Haile, sweeping from the room. Or perhaps that last remark was not spoken, but etched in the air by arching eyebrows. The sun pours through the window more warmly into the bath when his mother has left them safely alone. Or maybe Wedward has peed the warmth there himself.

Ma Clare sighs, reaches for a towel with one hand while steadying Edward with the other. She smells of lavender water and some sharp vegetable scent, not so much pretty as real. A wooden soldier, drowned and swollen from many maneuvers that ended in bath water, comes dripping up with Edward, clutched in his hand, as Edward is made to stand, and roughhoused with a towel in ways that hurt and ache so deeply that he will forget about it until he is on his way to war, and braves himself to intimacy, and remembers it for the first time.

Ma Clare dismisses the pieties of the hymnody of the First Reclaimed Mission Church, and she delivers herself of an older bequest. For a warm good woman she is given to melodies in minor keys. She keens to Wedward:

> In Nottamun Town, not a soul would look up,
> Not a soul would look up, not a soul would look down.
> Not a soul would look up, not a soul would look down,
> To show me the way to fair Nottamun Town.

Who knows where she learned this one? The soul raised on a penny faith, hemmed in by murky codes of sin and un-reliable grace, finds its comfort where it can. Edward catches the double-edged tone in her voice. He moves the soldier up and down in his hand, looking up and down, as if to disprove the song: Not a soul would look up, not a soul would look down. Except the toy soldier, who is going through the indistinct landscape, the mothy, fog-shrouded lowlands, looking for Nottamun Town.

The master of the Prince Regent primary would never look up or down when he lectured his boys. He would stare from his place on the dais, hands tucked in the sleeves of his gown, and drill his eyes through a spot in the back wall. He would utter remarks of contempt, would fire questions through the air above their heads and see which boys would leap to sacrifice themselves first to respond. Edward, who had wanted to please, to make his mother proud, to be Ma Clare's good little Wedward, had not been able to join the school of little dragoons, urgent in their need to answer. He had needed more connection from the master than this. He had needed an expression, an address, a personal comment. "It seems young Haile, alone of our number, cannot volunteer an answer," said the master, but he spoke to the wall, not even to the other boys. "Would the young Haile care to take himself to the cupboard, there to sit until he can summon up some enthusiasm for our activities?" Edward had scarcely known what this meant. Ma Clare had always spoken directly, and his mother had absented herself almost completely. This practice of sideways address was befuddling. Only the whispered translations of his fellow students told him what to do. He exiled himself behind the bookshelves and found his bladder had betrayed him again.

In Nottamun Town, not a soul would look up,
Not a soul would look up, not a soul would look down.

Grahame was gone, Grahame Ross, of the (so Grahame had said, laughing) Cheapside Rosses; Grahame of the bitten lower lip, the private penchant for early Renaissance paint- ings of martyrs, the untrainable roll of hair the color of tea spilling from under the lip of his helmet. Grahame Ross of the secret pact, the daring eyes, the translator from the High Modern Poetics of Rupert Brooke's "the rough male kiss of sheets" into the vernacular of a more common tongue. Grahame was gone, drained away, as if never been. Edward moved without him, not so much inconsolable as beaten from within by a sense of lost opportunity. For Edward wasn't moving forward, but backward, to the time before Grahame had jostled him in the queue at the induction cer- emony, the time before friendship began.

Edward settles his eyes on the indistinctness. The geography of war? Is he moving out over the terrain they have recently retreated from? Is he carrying a white flag of surrender to the Huns? There is no light nor is there the comfort of darkness, in which at least one can hide. Everything is the color of things reflected in steel. Everything is blank with indecision. If you could call this a tree, this thing here, it drips with water, or congealed fog; it loses itself in vitreous globs out of a lack of intestinal fortitude; it can't be dignified with a name like tree. Its branches, sorry things, go out of focus if you try to train your eyes on them. There is nothing fine and proper like a tree smell about it; it smells like smoke aggravated by water. It has leaves, or something like leaves, but they are ghosts, they are paper, they are thin as the vellum pages tipped-in to protect colored prints in expensive volumes.

The landscape not of memory but of forgetting. There is

not even a good word for the opposite of memory: *Memory* is precise, concrete, a contract of a word; *forgetfulness* is a patched up word, jerry-rigged and clumsy, unlocking nothing; and *amnesia* forgets its own meaning. But this is a terrain of amnesia then, a place that forgets it is to refer distinctly to someplace else. The ground is more cake than earth. It settles under the foot as if unsure how ground is supposed to behave. It is neither green with grass nor brown with soil but a kind of shadow-color. Edward will kick it. He will kick color into it. But his foot does not want to kick.

Here is a rock. "Show me the way to fair Nottamun Town," says Edward. The rock looms, vaguely higher than broad, vaguely treacherous. Edward has the feeling it has spoken before, something like "It seems the young Haile, alone of our number, cannot volunteer an answer." But it does not choose to speak again. Against such silence, at some deep level, has Edward first chosen to go to war, long before Europe had tickled itself into a mood for annihilation. Had Edward an implement of war with him now, he would shoot the rock in its face. But he seemed to be walking without guns, without mortars, without a truncheon or a sword or even a brick to hurl.

"I rode a big horse," sings Ma Clare, "that was called a grey mare.

"Grey mane and grey tail, grey stripes down his back.

"Grey mane and grey tail, grey stripes down his back.

"There weren't a hair on him but what was coal black."

Ma Clare drips the sponge on Wedward's back as she sings "grey stripes down his back." Now there is no sun, it is dusk, another bathtime. Ma Clare is angry at something, and singing to hide it. Singing, she shares it with Edward. He doesn't think to ask what, or why. He pops bubbles into the water from behind; they tickle as they trace up his skin; he laughs at his prowess. Ma Clare keeps singing.

She stood so still, she threw me to the dirt,
She tore my hide and bruised my shirt.
From stirrup to stirrup I mounted again
And on my ten toes I rode over the plain.

Ma Clare thrusts her soapy fingers down between Wedward's ten toes, one at a time, rubbing with the face flannel. He has fallen in the pond in Regent's Park. They are not in Hampstead Garden Suburb, this is Devonshire Terrace. The air is colored with the dust of Queen Anne redbrick, rosy with the late summer sunset. He is having his bath very late. There is a party down below from which he is invited to absent himself. He doesn't care. Ma Clare cares, and not even for herself, for him. He senses all this without words, and doesn't thank her for her pity. Thinks it weak of her to mind, really. He doesn't mind. He'd rather be in the bath, and have her sing, and the sky go all pink, as if the streaky sunset clouds are leaking blood into the watery air.

The big horse that was called a grey mare. It trots forward out of the foggy nothing at him, but without the warning echo of heavy hoofs on sternly resisting soil. The thing comes at him sideways, almost like a circus animal, resisting the task, knowing it needs to anyway. He sees with un-blushing clarity that it is briskly male in the undercarriage, though a mare, in some indefinable way, regardless. The only thing that surprises him is his own lack of shock at this. He reaches a hand for her mane. He knows horses, he has ridden the grounds at Millscott House in Gloucestershire; on his best borrowed lady, She, he has crossed the fields eastward to view the white chalk horses cut in the Chiltern Hills. She is stabled at Sir Philip Lenox's farm for Edward's amusement when he comes down from London or from Cambridge over holiday.

Edward reaches for the moth-colored beast, to grab its mane, to ride it somewhere that is less unsure of itself. "You are making a fool of yourself, Mother," he says. The mane cannot be grabbed; it dissolved under his grip. He tries again. "Sir Philip is married and so are you." "You have become a prig," says the creature. "How dare you apply your schoolboy morality to the conditions of my life? You have no right and I am offended." He tries to encircle the neck with his arms, to drag the head down, so he can look in its eye. He would feed it if he could, to substantiate it. "Everyone talks," he says coldly, "Sir Philip's wife taking a cure in the Riviera, and you seen on his arm in every venue! Not enough that you should disgrace his wife and your husband, but what about yourself?" "Talk grace and disgrace, my own son, to me?" says she, rearing back. "You should take it kindly that I do not set out to embarrass you, my boy, but only achieve that by accident. I am a stronger force than you are, and will not tolerate such condescension." It is the foyer of the house, which house, the one with black and white marble tiling, and an Arts-and-Crafts wallpaper, ferns and white peonies improbably entwined. The house in South Ken? She is furious. She dashes a vase to the floor for the sound of shattering crystal. Summer roses in a thorny tangle, and green water pooling toward the Turkey carpet. "For you I gave up what I did, that you might not be a bastard, at any rate," she says, "what means your opprobrium to me? You've inherited your father's small morals, worse luck. I had hoped you'd be smarter." She raises her long face and snorts at him, steps on the carpet several times, pawing it. Her flanks twitch; the grey tail twitches. She reaches forward to munch out his heart as if it were an apple he was offering. Her teeth rake against his shirt, draw stripes on his skin; he falls back against the stairs. He makes to mount her and lead her out of the hall, but she dissolves beneath him, and he settles down on the ground, his ten toes barely touching, like a child trying to get down from a chair. There is no black and white tiling, only the ground to wade through, thick as toweling still wet from the laundry.

Ma Clare at the laundry, finding him some clean pants and a vest. He is naked. The steam of the flatiron against hot wet cloth pleases him. It is winter outside and he needs his clothes. Ma Clare is older but he is still young, still Wedward, still before the age in which memories slot themselves, falsely or correctly, in some sort of chronological order. Ma Clare's face is bruised with disapproval. Of him? Of his mother? Of something else? He has never cared to ask. From whom was he to learn such caring?

> Met the King and the Queen and a company of men
> A-walking behind and a-riding before.
> A stark naked drummer came walking along
> With his hands in his bosom a-beating his drum.

Edward pulls himself forward in his grey world. Shapes emerge again, this time more recognizably human, less rock-like, though still without apparent features. A King and a Queen, stiff as marble monuments, as the stone effigies that dawdle, frozen, in all the church porches and circuses and memorial avenues in Westminster. No particular King, no Queen, just them: the King and the Queen. He is dour and distant. She is privy only to her own thoughts, but her lips look well exercised in edicts, complaints, appointments, dis-approvals.

They step down from a plinth that turns out to be a stair, or a ledge maybe?——the bottom of the rank of steps at the Albergo at San Guillame, in the leafy lap of the lower Rhaetian Alps. A lake beyond. Edward is what, ten, twelve, fifteen?——odd how, so soon, it melds together, becomes dif-ficult to distinguish. A waiter withdraws a bottle produced by the local vineyard because it just, somehow, won't quite do. Mrs. Clive Haile sets her profile to a profitable angle against the green escarpment. Sir Philip Lenox lights a pipe, draws on it with vigor, busying himself so he doesn't need to add anything to the remarks. Edward is naked again, and at the age when it most bothers one, the age when physi-cal changes blur through the comfortable envelope of the child body like cancers, infections, mold. He is dangling a foot in the lake. His uneasiness though derives from what his mother is saying, not how vulnerable he is. She doesn't seem to notice, nor does Sir Philip even wrinkle a brow in disap-proval. They are both too busy not noticing to notice.

"Don't be bizarre, of course you can't stay here, you have your studies," says Mrs. Haile. "I can learn Italian," says Edward, though listlessly, as he knows this battle is already lost. "Think of Dante, think of Virgil." "Think of Virgil indeed; think in Latin," says Mrs. Haile. "Think what would be said if you were to stay here, and we were to deprive you of a proper English education. Think how poorly I would be judged. It's out of the question. Whyever would you bother me with such a notion?" "The hills," says Edward, opening his palms, "the lake." The things he cannot say: I am only ten, or eleven, or fourteen. I am not old enough to live in a different country from my mother. "Winifred," says Sir Philip Lenox, "are we to engage the carriage this afternoon or can I send snaggletoothed Paolo to Sondrio to find me some riper tobacco? This dry shred to hand is more original than sin." Around Sir Philip Lenox and Mrs. Clive Haile are arrayed the ranks of the employed, including, somewhere, faceless in the crowd, Ma Clare. They almost edge Edward into the lake. "Besides," says Mrs. Haile, turning to watch the swans glide near, looking for broken bits of old bread, "I'm thinking of Alexandria for the winter, and that would never do for a boy. Unhealthy. No, there's nothing else for it but you are to return to Sussex Tuesday week."

The swans are beautiful and treacherous. The nakedness is suddenly a bit of a problem; an older boy now, he protrudes in an obvious, graspable way, and swans can be vicious. He tucks his hands against his thin chest, and his heart beats with alarm. The smoke of Sir Philip's pipe rises like campfires in the Alsatian dawn. "As if enough had not already been said," says Mrs. Clive Haile, "Sir Philip is joining me. We will steal across the desert on a single camel and approach the pyramid in the purple night, and lie down in the shadows, and in the sight of agelessness, which alone understands such things, we will commit our crime against propriety. You are hardly welcome there." Edward backs up. Surely she could not have said these words? The swans take on an aggressive expression. But his heart thrums too loudly and scares them off. The lake is gone; the King and Queen are gone. The world is made of moth-eaten cotton. Here is a field, bereft of particularity: a stretch of grey without depth or dimension, like a chevron of fabric pinned up on a theatrical flat. The sky is made of the same color, drooping; the road, yet again grey. Where are the Huns, where are the Frogs, where are his compatriots? Where is his commander, his flag, where is his Grahame? Why does he have a drum and who is he signaling?

Where is the woman who could interfere with this? The one for whom Edward was nicknamed Wedward? The one who by walking into his life might displace, for once and for all, the central authority of a certain Mrs. C. H.? The woman for whom the fumblings with Grahame could prove to be only lovely mistakes, earnest accidents, the woman who would stand on two feet as Ma Clare had stood, but this time Edward would be adult, ready and willful. It has not seemed to be the primary aim of life, such a love, but to be wandering this grey landscape without knowing even what to look for! A shame. A failure of his proper English education.

He is beating a drum in his bosom.

They come, though, whether he is calling them or not; they come to his side, a forest, a grove of individuals without name or feature, a mob of the impossibly dim. A throng, a population. They come, a serried rank of the dead, or of the never-to-be-born. They come, ten thousand offspring of his loins down the next several centuries, the nameless, faceless, uncarved souls now being cut out of possibility by his death. Or maybe they are merely the older personae of the soldiers now being cut down this very dawn, on this tired sweep of farmland-gone-hell, with the artillery still booming beyond vision and the blood staining the broken stalks of winter wheat.

> *Sat down on a hot and cold frozen stone,*
> *Ten thousand stood round me yet I was alone.*
> *Took my heart in my hand to keep my head warm.*
> *Ten thousand got drowned that never was born.*

THE MORE HE is with them, the more his world returns; it is now an even arrangement. The ghosts stand in the wheat, wraiths as the wet light breaks east, visible before they disappear, before he does. "But with you?" he cries, or means to, "go with you? Or stay here? And which is which, which is the country of the dead? For I can no longer tell." They will not answer him.

> *In Nottamun Town not a soul would look up.*
> *Not a soul would look up, not a soul would look down.*
> *Not a soul would look up, not a soul would look down*
> *To show me the way to fair Nottamun Town.*

The last ebb begins, but which world is to replace which? Or is there a blanker blankness to which to return, in which to dissolve? He is nearly no longer he, he is pulsing edges of vapor parting for the realer limbs of wheat among which his body has fallen.

The world resolves—

My Shepherd walks on water, My Shepherd walks on sea,
On tempest tossed to search the lost, and bring him back to Thee.

It is not Ma Clare singing this time. Ma Clare used to stop at that line and go back to the beginning. This voice meanders on, shakily, through exhaustion and determination.

So when I founder blindly, And when I lose my way,
Oh Shepherd come and find me wherever I should stray—

The sky throbs, the edges of the worlds retreat from each other, the drum that is pounding becomes again his heart. It is Grahame singing, thinking that Edward is lost, thinking that Edward's soul has gone. It is Grahame, not knowing that this hymn has majestic credentials in the annals of Edward's brief life. It is Grahame saluting the puckering nibble of death with the first bit of religious tripe that comes to mind. It is Grahame, this time, being the Shepherd, bringing Edward back, though Edward doesn't yet have the strength to tell him so. He lies in Grahame's arms, as the pain begins to assert itself. He closes his eyes. The thing in his eyelids is not visions, not music; it is the blooming rose of mortal agony. He blesses it, this one time only, and keeps on living.

Gregory Maguire is the author of over twenty books for children and five novels for adults, including *Wicked*, the inspiration for the Broadway musical of the same name, *Confessions of an Ugly Stepsister*, and *Son of a Witch*. His forthcoming novel for children has a working title of *The Tooth Trade: Or, What-the-Dickens*. His short fiction has appeared in *The Green Man*, *The Faery Reel*, and other anthologies.

Maguire lives with his husband and their three children outside of Boston.

Yours, Etc.

Gavin J. Grant

She was writing to one of the dead girls again while he walked around the house. He walked solidly, stolidly, muddily, froggily. He was lost in a wordless daydream where words came up with his steps, lost their meaning, bled into others. He was lost but he knew where he was going. He had passed the front door—the outside light on, he knew what was on the other side. So now thought four left turns. Four more left turns, he thought, and the front door would appear again. But he knew his house was not square, that he could not take four more lefts unless he acquired the dead girls' ability and began walking through walls. He walked and walked and the dead girls did what they always did. Nothing.

His wife had finished writing and was chopping some-thing in the kitchen when he passed the windows. He knew she couldn't see him through the night-black glass. He imagined it was onions that she was chopping but the word became something else. Bunions. Blisters. Corns. Vegetables that grew off the corpse. Mushrooms, always it came back to mushrooms. Was there nothing else that grew off the rot? He would take his flashlight and look under the hedgerows.

He stopped walking. The ghosts came a little closer. He had neither flashlight nor hedgerow. He grew neither mushrooms nor corn. He was an empty man with an empty garden. His father told him he had a beautiful lawn. He didn't know why his father would say that. A team of men came once a week and took care of it. Made the lawn green, short, rolling. Sometimes his wife talked to them on the phone for hours and they'd come back again and again until whatever it was she wanted was done.

She'd pretend she wanted something new. Perhaps some landscaping. She'd scatter catalogs and her voice would grow deep with longing. Her calls were always returned.

She'd moved him out of the house without him really noticing. He was tied up at work. Or, wearing a tie and working. Then his home office had been moved from the back room to the basement and then out over the garage. He'd liked that. Until the first winter.

It wasn't that the house was done in chiffon or some other unrecognizable substance. It had been Crate and Barrel. Then Williams-Sonoma. Then she'd moved away from mall stores. She kept ahead of his position, his credit cards. She said it was important for their house to look the part. He thought maybe it would be nice to look the part of a beach bum in Jamaica for a week. She told him they couldn't afford it even as he was wondering if a resort in Jamaica was really all he could imagine.

He'd given up on the garden when the cupola went up. He'd enjoyed getting into his old trousers—which she'd probably thrown out—and getting dirt under his nails.

It was winter and he was walking widdershins around the house, and he was aware now that it wasn't the first time he'd done it. Light from the windows washed over him, spilled over him, slicked him down, sucked him in, and spat him out. He crept, he leapt, he kept his balance. And all the while his wife was writing to a dead girl. He had taken off his shoes. His trousers were wet where he had been sitting under the pine tree near the front door. He had left his shoes there. He crept out from under the tree and crept around the house. Everything was different, new parts were sore, when he went around hands and knees. Every five steps, shuffles? he tried to meow like a cat. He heard rustlings around him and knew it was the dead. He was pulling all his history behind him, tying them in knots around his house like a fishing line with more tangles than straights.

⌣

HE LIVED IN a house and he drove a car and he worked in an office. When he was a child he had been raised by raccoons at night, feral cats by day. When he was a child he had built a sleeping platform in the trees and stayed there summer after summer. He did not remember his childhood rightly. He remembered the roads melting softly in the sun and he thought about global warming and how perhaps the roads would melt and sink into the earth. He had loved the outdoor world and now Monday through Friday he might never step outside, other than walking to and from his car.

So now he walked around the house. He could not walk around his neighborhood. The roads had no sidewalks. The cul-de-sacs and gated communities did not welcome walkers. There was an asphalt path around the lake. His garden, so controlled, so manicured, was all his wildness now.

⁓

A DEAD GIRL had moved in with them, once. It wasn't anyone they knew. Just a dead girl. The husband hadn't been as good at seeing ghosts then. He couldn't hear when she explained why she was there. Couldn't hear what she said to his wife. He could barely see her. He didn't know how or why she had died. But his wife knew; she could see all of these things.

That was why they had moved. The two of them were rattling around their McMansion by themselves but it was newly built when they bought it, and his wife said it would take years for a ghost to work its way in.

He could tell his wife where the ghosts' late night murmurings were becoming entangled in a fir tree. But he didn't tell her about the line of history he was walking into the ground around the house. He couldn't.

At their old house, the dead girl had been persistent. This was why his wife still wrote to her. He thought she missed her. He knew the dead girl missed his wife. He could feel the dead girl coming closer. Or, that could be cold. His body felt it differently now. Old age. Death's winged Cadillac hurrying near.

He reminded himself he could feel and it didn't have to be only the dead girl's tiny steps. But she *pushed* through the ether and he felt the vibrations.

His mother had always called him sensitive and he had laughed it off. He was a jock. A smart jock, able to work in an office, but still a jock. He was fully rounded. More so then than now, he thought. More so now than then, too.

⁓

He was walking around the house again, circling, drawing the ghosts into his path and away from the house when he saw the antlers in front of him. He lifted the antlers and put them on his forehead. He bent forward to take the weight on his shoulders. He had to keep watching the ground in case he tripped. He had to watch the mulch he'd spread by the wall. He had to watch the mud he had made walking around the house.

"The antlers are a gift from Herne the Hunter," the dead girl said. She was there walking beside him. If he looked straight at her he could see her shrinking back through time. But she only went so far. Back to her birth, forward to her death. There was an emptiness where her future should have been. That was part of her bespecteredness. The missing, slightly plump fifty-two-year-old teacher she would have been. The annoyingly perky cheerleader with the B+ average.

She told him she haunted her own future looking for herself, and when she couldn't find it she would come back and tell him what she missed about herself. And when she was bored with that she might tell him lies about himself, about everyone he knew.

She was dead and so knew things he could not know so he could not tell what were lies, what weren't.

"The Hunter loves you because you live in the city but you're walking the darkness," she said.

She said, "You should be glad to be loved by the Hunter." And, "The Hunter doesn't love anyone so you should be careful."

He walked and walked. He had a pedometer sitting in his briefcase and he imagined it unhappy at being unable to count his steps.

The girl said she hated herself for the things she had never done. And it wasn't sex or drugs or drinking. She boasted unconvincingly of doing her share of partying. She hated not having ever had a dog. Not taking the hostess job at Vegedilla's when she had the chance. Not dyeing her hair any color ever but New Summer Sun.

He wore the antlers all that night and his shoulders sank into knots. He found his shoes under the fir again. He went in the back door, ducking into the house. His wife had gone to bed. He considered all the places he could sleep. On the couch. In the basement. In a guest bedroom. In his office. But he loved his wife and wanted to sleep with her. He thought she would not mind the antlers.

In the morning he left before his wife was up. He wore the antlers to work and no one said anything. He began to get used to them. He wore them home and when he went out that night to look at the stars he bent his head back carefully and breathed deeply of the air. He was conscious of his neck straining and he tipped himself backward but he could not make himself fall. Instead he began to walk around the house again. Wearing his antlers and tying the ghosts into his tread, he walked and walked around the house.

⁓

DEAD GIRLS RAN in his family but he hadn't known this until they had gotten one of their own. The dead run in every family but no one ever wants to talk about it. They'd been married, the husband, the wife, in a tiny ceremony because that's what they wanted. He'd thought. She had no siblings and his brother had moved to Alaska. His brother was a high-school teacher. He taught physics and in his spare time he made vodka. "Two hundred gallons a year," he used to tell the man every time they talked. They didn't talk much anymore. The man's brother had sent them a case of homemade vodka as a wedding present. It was somewhat thoughtless in a way the brother couldn't have known: alcohol was implicated in many of the woman's pen pals' deaths. The man didn't tell his new wife about the present and she never missed it. He asked his brother not to mention it. So his brother didn't come to their wedding.

But history was never gone. It was always popping up, recycling itself into the present.

One of his wife's pen pals was alive. She had been a friend in college and now she was in prison. They'd been sorority sisters. After a party in their sophomore year, the man's wife—although they did not meet for years, he knew the story well—had declared she would walk back to the sorority house. This had been the early nineties and Seattle was repudiating grunge, full of riot grrls and empowerment and defense classes; so mostly safe. The future letter-writer's friends decided to drive, and the letter-writer gave them a few pithy phrases and walked off. She arrived home safe (as she always did, even in her junior year abroad when she lived in Hui-San and did many things she never told anyone about). But her friends did not return. Her friend who was now in prison was the quieter of the three and decided she was best suited to drive. But as she was going around a long curve she drifted over the line into the next lane and ran her Ford Explorer right into a high-school student's Honda Accord. The student was returning from her job waitressing at a pizza restaurant. She was killed instantly, and the wife writes to her to this day. The dead student doesn't answer. The wife sends the letters to her friend in prison. Her friend was sentenced by a hanging judge so she'll be in prison for a while. Her friend reads the letters, and sometimes writes back to the wife.

HIS WIFE LEFT him a note this morning that said, "The landscaper says they're going to lay down traps and see if they can catch whatever's leaving those tracks around the house." He had thought his footprints were clear.

HE OFTEN DREAMED of the ghosts, of the years lived and those missed. Then in the morning his wife would tell him about the same girls.

SINCE WE'RE ALL always dying she also wrote letters to herself. Some of them she had mailed years ago and they would arrive when she wanted them to. When they used to live in the city she had sent postcards to the two of them here in this echoing new house. He hadn't believed her then.

She only writes to girls. She says that she hardly claims to understand men in life—and she stretches up and kisses him on the cheek—and after that . . .

She gives a roll of her shoulders that later, when he is walking around the house, he tries to replicate. When he can't quite get it he blames the weight of the antlers.

He never reads her letters. Once she starts writing she doesn't stop until she seals it up, puts it out for the postman to pick up the next day. Sometimes he's been tempted by the postcards but he cannot cross the line. She has never offered (but why would she?) and he cannot ask.

She writes to a girl she knew in high school. He watches football sometimes with the girl's brother. The world is smaller than he expects, sometimes. He loved the girl back then but everyone did. This was in the seventies, a different age. The girl was another car crash ghost. His wife didn't put return addresses on her letters because she didn't want the ghosts finding them. He didn't tell his wife this girl's ghost was passing her years quite happily in her brother's apartment.

He finds he is suddenly taken with inexplicable exhilaration. He is having a moment. He feels that the top of his head may have flown off. He is near to laughing, expects that if he looked up he would find that the antlers will have stuck to the ceiling. But he daren't look because his brain would spill out. He clenches his fists and looks at his stubby fingers going white. He is paler than the ghosts. And this calms him. As his fingers relax, the top of his head drifts slowly back down. The ghosts are colorful and he is not.

⸺

LATER WHEN HE is walking around the house he is afraid of happiness taking him. What if the top of his head flies off? There is nothing to stop it getting away. He keeps his hands on his head while he walks around the house. The rut is getting deeper. If his hand were free he could point to it and say *I made that*. But he knows he won't. He is walking down the side of the house along the ornamental fence the neighbors put up. It is about twenty feet long. Neither house has any pets. He has seen the grandchildren next door play around the fence so it serves the purpose of amusing them. He would like to take his chainsaw and cut it down. But he hasn't touched his chainsaw in years. He thinks he should be able to say he isn't even sure if he has a chainsaw but it's not true. He could list the contents of his garage. The troop of gardening men take care of everything. He wonders if they would cut down or remove the fence. He wonders where they are from. At work there's a partner from Ecuador, maybe she could tell him. But he knows he will never ask the gardeners or the partner. It is too late. He should have asked his wife where they were from years ago.

He feels as if his life is full of these moments when he realizes it is too late. To ask. To do. To cut down. To be someone that he is not now. A ghost of his impossible present is raging toward the fence pulling it out stake by stake. He watches the ghost and knows that this is a terrible thing. Not pulling out the fence, not being stupidly angry, not doing anything else but letting this ghost out of himself. Ghosts see or smell or leech onto other ghosts. He knows there are some ghosts here but so far his wife does not. If he attracts more ghosts they will have to move, to run away again. She cannot live with all the ghosts that would come. But he cannot look away, cannot ignore the ghost and make it go away. This ghost is not another dead teenager. This is his own self. He likes the ghost's shirt. It is white like his but has a subtle stripe. He hates that he noticed. This ghost is stronger than he is. This ghost will take him over and push him out of his life. He must look away. He wrenches his gaze away. The path is in front of him. He must walk around the house. His long nights of walking will save him. He must tie the present into itself. He must, for his wife. For himself. He must make this the world he lives in and not let the ghost overpower him. He is crying.

Around the next corner he trips over a rainspout. He has never seen it before. His ghost is pushing him out. He closes his eyes and insists that the rainspout is not there. There is a plant here, he thinks. He damns himself for knowing nothing about his own garden, for stopping caring, removing himself from his own life. He can *see* the plant and the way it had been trained up the wall on some kind of wooden frame. *Wisteria* on a *trellis*. He could hear his wife talking about it as they stood just over *there*. He faced where they had been standing. His wife was solidly in his memory but he could not picture himself from the front. His parallel ghost comes around the corner. He is clean and tidy and has a tie on. The man was pleased to see that the ghost is wearing an ugly box-patterned sweater. The ghost was grinning in a horribly toothy manner and his ears were trembling. The man smiled.

His wife would never go for a bucktoothed fool like that. He tipped over from the waist and tried to touch his toes. His feet were on the ground and the ground was worn down. This trough is the depth of his heart, his work. His ankles are level with the ground. This was something he had done, something he had to do.

He stood, put one foot in front of the other. His ghost was gesticulating and exploding. You have no power, he thought. I will not see you I will not write to you I will not give you a second thought. This was not the ghost of himself that he feared. This ghost had no strength. By not fearing this ghost he gave strength to the other ghosts. But he did not know what else to do.

He turned from the ghost, walked around the house. When he came back around, the ghost had disappeared.

IT WASN'T THE first or last ghost of himself he'd seen. His favorite hadn't ever gotten old because he'd died young. Apparently he was a gigolo or courtesan or pirate or had died at a Halloween party. The man never knew. This ghost had appeared to him on his wedding night. The man really didn't want to see him there but the libertine ghost had been enjoying himself with the ghost of the man's wife and the horror of that and the hidden flask of vodka the man had partaken of had combined into a night of fucking and love-making that he felt he had never quite managed to rise to again. So he loved that ghost even if he insisted on his own life and not giving it over to the ghost.

He'd known other people who lived in the shadows of

their own demons, real or imagined, but not a ghost of themselves. He missed his brother's vodka more than he missed his brother.

⁓

ANOTHER DEAD GIRL. A black girl who'd died a couple of years ago. He'd liked her even though they'd barely met. She was interning at one of the offices on his floor and they'd met at some kind of building maintenance meeting. She'd been taking notes and he'd passed her a note suggesting that she not bother. But he'd remembered being young and disconnected and knowing that he knew nothing and having to pay attention to everything. So he wasn't surprised when she gave the slightest shake of her head and kept on taking notes. He'd liked her compact, quick handwriting. He wished he had an assistant as smart. He thought she was pretty but she was so young that it did not go beyond that.

He met the intern in the building cafeteria. He had realized he'd seen the girl there before. She was usually in a group of four or five young women her own age. Sometimes she was on her own; she always had a paper or a magazine. Something to keep her busy and make her unavailable to the dirty old men like him. But when he saw her eating salad one cold February day he couldn't resist stopping by and talking to her.

She put her copy of the *Times* away and shuffled over on the curved bench enough to denote an invitation. He sat far from her and thought they both enjoyed talking with someone quite unlike themselves.

He saw her now and then and sometimes they ate together.

Once or twice he took her out for a coffee—she liked her coffee unsweetened and without milk. He horrified her by telling her that she should enjoy it while she could because the only way he could drink it that way was if he had Rolaids with him.

His wife thought the intern was a stand-in for a daughter or a lover. But she laughed when she said it.

In May the intern told him her internship was over at the end of the month. He remembered to give her his card and told her if she was interested in joining the firm after college, or if there was anything he could do, to give him a ring. But a week or so before she left—after the office manager had sent around an e-mail about the intern's departure and to come by for cake on Thursday afternoon—a week or so before that, she'd died.

He'd never found out how. He was surprised how upset he was. His wife told him again about her stand-in theory and he had said sure, maybe there was something in that. Both of them knew she didn't mean it. She was just talking, helping him fill the empty space until he got used to the girl's death. He thought about the girl a lot and realized that she had been alive to him, she'd encapsulated a universe in a way that he felt many of the people he knew didn't. He'd believed in her in a way he didn't believe in other people.

He didn't ask, but later he realized his wife had been writing her letters for years.

~

HIS WIFE HAS dark hair with a streak of white in it that leads from her temple back to her right ear. Sometimes when she colored her hair it took on the color until she next showered and it went back to white. She said she'd always had it and it always drew his hand. He loved the way it looked even though he knew it had nothing to do with her. It wasn't fancy or affectation. He knew she had not had it when they met. He did not know when it had appeared. Perhaps when she realized the ghosts were following her. It wasn't in her childhood pictures, but he had never carried out a forensic examination of her photographs to find its first appearance.

THE ANTLERS LASTED until autumn. He was used to them by then. The dead girl hadn't been around for a couple of weeks. He'd been walking around the house at night and working away during the day. His wife had been planning a trip to see her cousin's new baby and the dead girl appeared beside him and told him if he went he couldn't keep the antlers.

"The horned god has many aspects," the dead girl shouted over whatever she had playing on her earphones. It was a whisper, a shout. "If you go with your wife, the Hunter there might not remember—that's not the right word, but you know—remember that the Hunter here gave you the antlers. I'm just saying it probably wouldn't go well."

The husband stopped walking. He was deep in his trench. This was the first trip his wife had planned since they had moved into this bare mansion. The first trip since she had fled the ghosts that had taken over their last house. The house they had bought after years of saving and worked on every weekend for so long he would have lost many sets of antlers if he had had them then.

The dead girl is shouting something at him and he is scratching the antlers.

Their first house was so different from their first home: his apartment in the city which she had moved into and slowly made into a new thing: theirs. The ghosts were too busy in the city to notice her. It was only later when they bought their first house that the ghosts had realized how lovely, how tasty and sweet she could be for them. They followed her, buried into her habits, tried to eat of her life, and he hadn't believed her until one day he saw them, too. So they left the house that they had spent so much time on but that never became a home. He had a short time when he thought the ghosts had been left behind.

He took off the antlers and laid them on the ground. He immediately missed them. He was so short. So base. So uninteresting; ghostlike. He had walked around his neighborhood and scraped the velvet off the antlers on all his neighbors' trees. He had enjoyed watching them find his marks.

"Your loss, asshole," the dead girl shouted at him and picked up the antlers. She walked into the space beside and away from him.

~

HE'D ASKED HIS wife about her letters once and she had said: Long, long ago when the world was young and before there was paper or shopping malls or road rage there were the living and the dead and the sea and the sky. The dead had the sea and the living had the sky and land hadn't been invented yet.

When the bodies of the living wore out they would kiss

one another, kiss on one cheek, kiss on the other, more kisses for the loved, the family—it all took a long time but they were in no hurry—and they would tidy up their lives and drop down to the sea and they would never be seen again.

One eternal morning the living decided they were tired of flying and that they would set down on the sea. There was no word for doing this, which was hilarious and exciting. None of the living had ever seen what happened to those that were tired and gave up the sky. The living gathered together and the first among them dropped to the sea. All followed. The first living ones to touch the sea died instantly. Those coming down from above saw the first people touch the sea and watched as their bodies went under. The living did not understand that those who had touched the sea had immediately joined the dead. They thought the first among them were flying through the water the way they all flew through the air. They could not see the dead coming up from the depths. They could not see the ghosts of the newly dead leaving their bodies, trying to fly above the water, trying to stop the living from joining them.

And the bodies of the living—there were thousands upon thousands of them—settled deep in the sea as they fell and piled up and up until there were so many the living could drop from the sky and stand upon the dead.

Then the living who stood upon the dead understood what had happened. And they wailed and ground their teeth and drove their elbows into one another's sides and bit one another and gouged their unhappiness upon their skins and they stopped others from going into the water. And most of the living flew back into the sky and vowed never to return, never to see water until they were ready to die. But some of the living did not leave. They stayed there and lived upon the bodies of the dead. And among those who stayed was an even smaller number who, when they touched the bodies that touched the water, could see the dead and the ghosts below. And since all that they stood on were the bodies, they could always see the ghosts. And the ghosts would see that they were being seen and the ghosts tried to follow those living that could see them.

And it has been the same ever since.

SHE WAS HIS wife. He believed in her in the same way he believed in dentists, hybrid cars, the logarithmic tables he had memorized as a boy.

HE WALKED AROUND the house and he walked under the plank he had placed over his trench so that they could still use the front door. He had removed the flagstone path when his walkway became too deep. He had walked around the house for a year. More. He had walked through winter and spring, down summer and autumn. He had walked through a presidency, a Super Bowl, and an Olympics. Through a promotion, through the antlers. His trench was as deep as he was tall.

The ghost he had hidden from his wife was there. The ghost of his wife—one he hadn't recognized she was so alien to him, the one with the three girls and the rolled-over SUV with no seat belts—was there. He could feel the ghost of himself—the ghost of himself in this world—walking with him. Hundreds of himself walked behind him. He thought he might catch up with himself. But he could not walk fast enough. And he walked and walked around the house.

⁓

HE WAS WATCHING television and she was writing again. He was in his office battling their health insurance and she was writing again. It was her birthday and at the Tex–Mex place she liked, all her friends had their straws in a Meg's Massive Margarita and they were waiting for her before they could all drink and she was writing on the napkin. The dead girls were coming closer and she kept writing, hoping to keep them back.

He drove to work and he trailed a string of heartbreak and bad haircuts and torn-up Valentine's Day cards to draw away the ghosts but they had her scent and each night when he returned his wife looked a little older. She knew they were coming even if she could not see them yet.

She was being surrounded and knew it but didn't know it. He was building a wall in reverse, digging down with his life and energy and his walking night after night. She knew it was him but didn't know why. She'd talked to her gardening team and told them not to disturb his project. He knew she thought he was losing himself.

The ghosts thought they would get past him, they thought he was cutting away her privacy and letting them in. He let them come closer, let them follow him around and around and down and around the house. They twisted around him as he walked. They obsessed over the prints his bare feet left. They did not know that he was building a trap for them.

His wife was talking about Colorado and New Mexico. Places high and far away. Switzerland. She asked him about transfers and started watching his company's job boards. He did not tell her because even then he was not fully sure. He walked and drew the ghosts down into his dry moat and thought perhaps he and the house were becoming stronger.

He would not disappear. This was his wife. This was his life. This was his path around his house. His home. This was his city. His country. He had begun with the ghosts and he had made his way past them.

He climbed out of his trench. His clothes were muddy, his bare feet going numb and blue with cold. He looked back down and saw the roaring tornado of ghosts. He could see the letters his wife was writing next year and the year after, already arrived and whirling in around the ghosts. Being read and eaten and absorbed and loved. He was certain that he and his wife would not be leaving. They would live in this house for long years to come.

There were ghosts of himself and his wife in possible futures and some of them were better and some of them worse.

He walked back around the house and for the first time he walked clockwise. He went deep into the garden away from the house. All lights were on in the house and they lit his way. He picked up his shoes and socks from under the fir tree. He walked beside his trench, back around the house. He rang the front door bell. The door opened and his wife was waiting. She had a pen in one hand and with her other hand she took hold of his and they walked into their house.

Gavin J. Grant's stories have appeared on *SCI FICTION*, *Strange Horizons*, and in *Polyphony*. With Kelly Link he runs Small Beer Press, publishes the zine *Lady Churchill's Rosebud Wristlet*, and co-edits the fantasy section of *The Year's Best Fantasy & Horror* (St. Martin's Press). He lives in Northampton, Massachusetts.

The Mask of '67

❦

by David Prill

OUR HOLLYWOOD STAR comes home. You know the drill. Small-town girl makes it big, returns to her priceless past to grin and bear the locally crafted gifts and blessings.

It began at the train station, where all decent homecoming stories begin. The station is usually a yawny place, Pete the ticket man, Griff the baggage man, the usual loafers laying odds on the arrival and departure times. Crazy times would have been more the ticket.

But on the day she came back, we small-towned it up like hadn't been seen around here since the sesquicentennial. The Fire Hall Band. Banners. Clowns. Politicians. Ice cold . . . well, you get the idea.

⌐

WELCOME HOME, BETTY LYNN Ballmer!

The train harrumphed to a stop at the station, which had gotten a facelift a couple years ago as if preparing for this very day. A trainman hopped off and set up a step on the platform, at the door to the passenger car. A red carpet would have been in order, too, that's how good people felt.

The crowd seemed to crane forward as one when the passengers began getting off the train. Even the single men who lived in the apartments above the storefronts leaned out of their windows, bare tattooed arms resting on the sills, cigarettes burning low, wise guy looks on their unshaven faces. Those that disembarked from the train gaped at the crowd, heard the news, turned, and joined right in. This was a community cause. A point of celebration.

Shouldering his way right up to the front was Big Jim McDiffie. He had dated Betty in high school, he the big football quarterback, she the head cheerleader. They were the homecoming royalty. He had even given her a ring.

Now Big Jim looked like he had a couple of footballs tucked under his shirt. He took a run at a nearby community college after graduation, before scrambling back to town for good. He had worked at Wally Beamer's Olds dealership out on the highway for fifteen years, before getting fired last month for drinking while test driving. Divorced once. A couple of grown children, long gone, their calls coming mostly on major holidays.

When Betty Lynn appeared, standing there on the top step in all her strange splendor, the band lost its breath, their

last notes a strain. The air left the clown's shoes, balloon animals ducking for cover in a squeaky panic. The crowd was
too crowded to get away, the hubbub dropped to a hush, and
you couldn't hear anything, quiet as death on the outside, a
mad rushing on the inside. In their heads, see. You could see
it in their eyes. They didn't want to look, but they couldn't
look away neither.

How could you not look?

You're expecting that million-samolean smile, those land
of sky blue waters eyes, that hair of a tawny stallion.

And you get . . .

A metal mask, on that cheerleader head.

It wasn't exactly a goalie mask, or a mask you might see
on a burn victim, it was almost a work of art. An off-trail
combination of the sleek and the medieval. Intersecting
loops around that lovely homecoming head. The sunlight
glinted off the metal, and as she turned her head it was like
she was blessing the crowd with some beams from beyond.

You couldn't really see her face, so maybe it wasn't Betty
after all, an optimistic few hoped. It could have been anybody behind that metal mask. Hopefully someone who disembarked in error, who intended to get off the train a few
stops down the tracks, at a town with a more freakish pedi-
gree than ours.

But that dress, white and frilly, just like the one in *Rainbows over Innsmouth*. And her long hair, rumpled as it was by
the mask, right out of *At the Mountains of Merriment*.

Oh, it was Betty all right. She exuded Bettiness. Since she
had become a near-star, we had studied her form, her posture, the way she walked, the way she brushed her teeth,

everything about her. She was the most excellent person ever to come out of our town. The world knew about us through her, we thought. We thought about her a lot. We thought we knew her better than she did herself.

Sure there were gasps. Of course there were cries. Was there a scream? So it would seem.

She just stood there, beaming on everyone.

And then the crowd did something funny.

It stopped being a crowd.

It broke up as fast as a Hollywood couple, a subconscious instant poll, everyone going this way and that, back to whatever they would normally be doing on a beautiful Saturday afternoon. Mowing the grass or playing kittenball or maybe even going out for an ice cream at the Big Swirl. Anything to get some normal-feeling vibes back into their bones again. Even the politicians melted into the remains of the gathering. You knew right then this was pretty serious business.

The only bold souls who held fast were Big Jim and the mayor.

You could see Mayor Bixley was in a big league dilemma. He wanted as bad as anyone to leave the scene of this train wreck of a celebration. He didn't want to be anywhere near the mask and whatever lay behind it, but he knew in his heart that it was his responsibility to deal with the situation. He took an oath of office, after all, although he was darned if he could remember much of it at this critical juncture. He did recall the Storm of '61, a monster tornado that sheared off the south end of Main Street. The Blizzard of '65, which buried the town in drifts up to the second stories of the main street stores.

And now the Mask of '67, and whatever story it held in store for the town.

The Mayor took a step forward, a step back, like he was square dancing, then finally found the gumption and stepped up to the platform, Big Jim close behind, face to mask with what he hoped was still, at her heart, our Betty.

"Uh . . . welcome . . . uh . . . on behalf of the fine people of . . ." the mayor glanced back as even the slow-footed finally fled the scene. "Uh, on behalf of the mayor's office, I'd like to welcome you back to, to . . ." What was the name of that town again, Mayor?

He could see a bit of her eyes through the metal, and this bit is what he focused tight on, trying vainly to block away the rest.

"It's all right, Mr. Mayor. It's been a long trip. I'm very tired. Is the Quint Hotel still in business?" Her voice sound reasonably normal. Not metallic or automatonish at all.

"Why, yes it is!"

"Would it be possible for someone to give me a ride there?"

Here was where Big Jim stepped up.

"Betty Lynn, I would be happy to give you a ride. That is, if it's not an imposition, Mr. Mayor."

"No, no, not at all, you help yourself m'boy," said the most relieved man in the county, shoving Big Jim into his place on the platform.

"Should I have your bags sent over to the hotel then?" the mayor asked, retreating in record time back toward the station.

"Yes, thank you," the homecoming girl said placidly.

Big Jim and Betty Lynn stood all by themselves on the platform, in the station and most likely in a three-block-square perimeter.

Although there was silence now, the casual observer would not characterize it as an awkward silence. It was a normal silence for two people, former consorts, one whose face was uncovered, the other masked in a very medieval and perhaps sleek fashion.

"It's been a long time, Betty Lynn."

"Yes, Jim, it has."

Now here's a question that people have pondered ages after this all happened: how was Big Jim able to look beyond or between the mask while all the other would-be well-wishers couldn't bear to be in the same zip code?

Was it love—blind, stupid, incoherent love? Did she still burn so brightly in his heart that the mask was no more than a beauty mark to his eyes?

Or was he just desperate, his dreams of the perfect life so lost that he would grab hold of any residue, in any form it took, that brought him back to the happier times he once knew. This Betty reminded him of the lost golden youth he had left behind, and no matter what it looked like, even if he didn't know what it looked like, he was going to grab onto it and not let go. It wasn't going to get away again. Not this time. The ring would stay on her finger. That's how bad his heart was these days. That was the theory, anyway.

"I have a confession to make, Betty Lynn."

"Yes, Jim?"

"I don't have a car . . . I mean, not here. I walked . . . it's only three blocks to the hotel. Do you mind walking?"

"Not at all. It was a long trip. It would be good to stretch my legs."

So they walked, somewhat like they had walked together years earlier, although it would be a stretch to say it was just like old times.

The looks they got from the man on the street were old, too. Ancient, primordial looks. The looks on the protruding faces of Neanderthal man when the shadow of a saber tooth tiger appeared outside his cave. Not as many stares from those off the street, trembling blinds on the closed shop windows. They still didn't want to look, but couldn't look away, etc.

Except for Clem at the Fix-It Shop, who said nonjudgmentally, "What kind of metal is that then, stainless steel? Well by golly you sure won't have to worry about rust."

Which left plenty of time for some tentative reminiscing, avoiding the obvious, which had nothing to do with old times and everything to do with these strange new times.

"So Betty Lynn, does the old hometown still look like you remembered it?"

"Pretty much, I think. I suppose a lot of the old gang is gone."

"A lot of them, yeah. A lot of them are coming back for the reunion, though. To remember the times when we were young."

"But you stayed."

"I feel comfortable here. I had some bad luck, too. A rotten marriage. Some drinking implied. Staying with my ma, now. Yeah, pretty funny for a guy my age. But she needs someone now, with Dad gone then. It's just a temporary thing, until I get myself squared away, hopefully sooner rather than later."

"You don't have to explain, Jim. I think it's very gallant of you." She stopped in front of the Princess movie theater, closed down now, the torn edge of a poster still in one of the display windows. Only one word was visible, and that was THRILLS.

"That's too bad. We saw *Blue Hawaii* and *Clambake* here, remember?"

"*Clambake*," Big Jim said wistfully. "Seems like yesterday."

In short order they arrived at the Quint Hotel, which in its time hosted governors and captains of industry. Its time was gone, though, and the building had taken on a seediness that was unique in these parts. What passed for less-than-savory characters in Millville called it home. Maybe Betty Lynn would fit right in, too. Was now the time for the Quint to host not just the offbeat but the out-and-out outré?

As soon as they headed across the dim lobby to the front desk, the clerk began shaking his head with a firmness that seemed to come deep from within.

"Sorry, we're full up. No rooms available."

"The Quint hasn't been filled up since President Eisenhower came to town."

"Well maybe Ike is making a comeback, because we're all booked up."

"There's laws against this sort of thing, Chet."

The clerk grabbed Jim's sleeve and dragged him down to the end of the counter, sending the guest book, pens, and a pocket calendar from Strum Funeral Home spinning to the floor. Whispering with fear and urgency: "Now Big Jim you should have known better than to bring her in here she can't stay here she'd empty out the joint in an hour I've got some long-term residents here that's real money don't forget that . . ."

"The thugs and mugs you let hole up in here, and you're telling me that Betty Lynn can't . . ."

"I'm telling you Big Jim, *she can't stay*."

"Is there a motel in town?" Betty Lynn asked politely, her mask filling with shadows.

"We can do better than that," said Big Jim. "Come on."

He took Betty Lynn by the arm (which felt solidly flesh-like, not that he was expecting anything else) and made for the door.

"Hang on a minute," Big Jim said, going over to the pay phone. He dug through his dungarees for a dime and stuck it into the slot. Dialed that familiar number, Tuxedo-1-3094.

"Hello, Ma? It's me. I'm downtown. Yeah. Sure. You betcha. Oh yeah. In fact, she's here with me right now. Yeah, no kidding. Dinner? I'll ask."

His mother hadn't heard what took place at the train station. She hadn't heard about the gasps. Ditto for the cries. Or, it would seem, that single exclamation point of a scream.

"I'd like that very much," said Betty Lynn.

"She said yes. Well, great. We'll be home in a few minutes. Bye, Ma."

He wondered if he should have told her about the mask.

They went outside and headed up Elm Street, another gauntlet of howling dogs and anxious children wondering why Halloween was happening in the middle of summer, cocktail hour arriving early and heavy for their parents. It was only a mask, people, a metal mask, but it really was more a question of what was behind the mask. The *not knowing* in a town that built in the heart of the city park an abstract limestone monument called *Routine*.

Dinner would be fine, his mom was a swell cook, but Big Jim did admit he was beginning to wonder what would happen when Betty Lynn tried to eat.

"MOM, YOU REMEMBER Betty Lynn."

Probably not like this, but Mom didn't let on. Oh, she had met her share of deformed and unnatural folks in her lifetime. Armless farm accident victims. Burn victims from the hog butchering plant fire of '51. A few inbreeding casualties. She had experience in the art of being pleasant in the face of faces that weren't quite what they should be. She smiled big, welcomed Betty Lynn back to town, and if maybe a little tic started above one eye, well that wasn't so bad.

"We're very proud of you, dear," Mom said, ushering them to the kitchen table. "It must be so exciting living in Hollywood, making movies and all."

"It has its ups and downs," said Betty Lynn.

Mom served dinner. Meat loaf and mashed potatoes. Lime Jell-O and pear salad. A look of puzzlement passed over Mom's face, not comprehending how her guest would eat, how to smile around it if she couldn't, perhaps she should have offered her a straw, maybe it wasn't too late . . .

Betty Lynn rose. "Would it be all right if I used your phone, Mrs. McDiffie?"

"You help yourself, hon. Right in the kitchen, next to the spice rack."

With Betty Lynn out of earshot, Big Jim's mom's tic became

a two-eye phenomena, twitching in an alternating fashion. Big Jim tapped his foot in time, thinking the expression on his ma's face was saying do you think she took offense at the spice rack comment, but there was no time for regrets as they honed in on the conversation finding its way to their ears from the kitchen.

". . . Yes, I would like that. No, but I wouldn't like that. Oh yes, I would definitely like that. Say again? Oh no, I don't think I'd like that—well maybe. Yes, 332 Old Horseshoe Road."

That's our address! Mother and son both thought.

"Okay, good-bye. Good-bye."

Betty Lynn returned to the table, and addressed Mrs. McDiffie. "I don't mean to impose, but would it be okay if a *good friend* of mine joins us?"

"Why of course," said Mom, a third tic now on a smile line in the corner of her mouth. She smiled wider, hoping it would mask the tremor.

"Thank you. He'll be here shortly."

Before Big Jim could raise his fork to his mouth, heavy footsteps sounded on the front porch. He sat up straight. Mom couldn't smile any wider, sort of froze that way.

The footfalls did stop.

A heavy knock, two, square on the door.

"I'll get it," Big Jim said, pushing himself away from table, nearly tumbling over backward.

At the door. He hesitated, picturing a man in a sleek and medieval mask, then wiped the sweat from his hand, and opened the thing already.

"Hi folks, Chet at the hotel thought you were headed out here."

"Mayor Bixley . . ."

"Got your bags, Betty Lynn," the Mayor called out. "Whoa, do I smell meatloaf?" He invited himself in while Big Jim retrieved her luggage from the porch.

"Come join us, Mayor," said Mrs. McDiffie, perhaps a little too eagerly, hurrying into the living room. "I'll set a plate for you."

"Don't mean to impose on you nice folks . . ."

"It's no imposition at all, is it son?"

"No, Ma, not at all." He left her bags by the stairs. There was strength in numbers.

Going back into the dining room, Big Jim and his mother caught sight of Betty Lynn's plate, which had been cleaned while they were distracted the mayor's arrival. The mask was clean, too. Well, that was different.

So the three of them sat back down to finish the meal, while Betty Lynn did whatever people with masks did after mysteriously downing one of the three squares.

"Well, Big Jim, I suppose you're getting your salt and pepper suit all ready for the big class reunion dance then," said the Mayor, wolfing his loaf.

"I sure am, Mayor. All the old gang will be there. Freddy Smith and Larry Bother and Little Gus, too."

"What's Little Gus doing these days then?"

"Insurance, I hear."

"Steady work, for sure."

"Betty Lynn, are you going to the dance?" Mom asked.

"I thought I might."

"Maybe you could escort her, James."

"Oh, Ma, I'm old enough to handle my own social life for gosh sake. Betty Lynn just got here. Don't want her to feel rushed. And her friend is coming anyway."

"When did you say he was coming then?" Mom asked Betty.

"Oh, he'll be here," she said with confidence.

Dessert time came first, angel food cake with whipped cream out of a tub no less, Betty's plate suddenly crumb-free after everyone's attention was diverted by a truck backfiring out on the street. Betty's friend still had not shown his face. Even during coffee in the living room, waiting for the clump, clump, clump, the knock, knock, knock, the fear, fear fear, the door opens and . . .

The Mayor seemed to be getting a bit agitated, perhaps the coffee was too strong, yes, that was why he rose from the sofa which was unstrategically located directly across from the easy chair where Betty Lynn was seated.

"Sorry to run off like this, folks," edging toward the door, "but I have a planning commission meeting to attend." At the door. "Thank you so much for your hospitality, Mrs. McDiffie. The meat loaf was top notch," a can't-help-himself glance at Betty Lynn. "It's a meal I'll remember for a long time to come." And his big car went zoom!

One feels a certain security when a major public official is in your midst. It's like the whole town is present. Maybe it's the weight, the aura, of the accumulated votes that is sensed. The image of what he represents as taught in every civics class in every corner of the United States of America.

Or maybe it's just the official's own ego shining through. Or his ability to summon law enforcement in a hurry. Or that he has a direct line to the Governor. Whatever, there was a feeling of reassurance in the air when the Mayor was in the room, colder and lonelier after he left, like they were five-year-olds walking in circles in the big woods outside town.

Fortunately, Betty Lynn appeared to yawn, her head tilting to that position anyway, a soft mewing sound heard from behind her facial hardware.

That seemed to be a signal. "Ma, Betty Lynn doesn't have anywhere to stay tonight," announced Big Jim. "The hotel was full up."

"Goodness," said Mom, setting down her coffee cup in a jittery sort of way. "Why don't you stay with us, Betty Lynn? You can have Julie's old room."

"Oh, Mrs. McDiffie, I wouldn't want to impose."

"Bosh. There will be no argument. James, why don't you take Betty Lynn's bags upstairs and show her where she'll be sleeping?"

"Sure, Ma."

Big Jim fetched her bags and toted them up the creaky stairs to the second floor of the old house, their guest following. He set them down outside the door to his kid sister's room, and turned back to look at Betty Lynn.

The moonlight streaming in through the window at the end of the hall framed her, the beams warming the mask almost to the point of beauty. The rest of her had always been pretty.

Big Jim felt emotions. "I . . . it's really great that you came back to town, Betty Lynn. It makes me think of old times, we really had some fine times. Remember, remember the time when we went to the county fair, and I won that stuffed giraffe for you in the cat pitch? And the ring I bought you on the way home?"

"I remember that ring. What a funny perfect ring that was."

But she didn't say anymore, and Big Jim couldn't see her eyes, so he led her into his little sister's room, switching on the bedside horsie lamp. The room was just as she left it when she cut out for her college years.

Big Jim set her bags by the closet. He felt funny for letting his emotions escape, and hid from them by playing the bellhop. "Bathroom is by the stairs on your right. If you need anything, my room is down at the other end of the hall."

"Thank you," she said, and squeezed his hand, just for a moment.

But that moment was enough.

Big Jim couldn't sleep. He couldn't get his mind off Betty Lynn. Here she was under the same roof, the roof he grew up under, even after whatever they had between them was over. In darkness, away from mirrors and windows that told the real story, it was easy to imagine himself in high school again. His state of mind never changed as much as his waistline. But everyone else seemed to have moved on—why, when they were having so much fun? People moved away, thinking the grass was greener elsewhere when in fact it was only cut in a different pattern.

He would ask her to the dance. Not now, in the morning, when she was refreshed and his nerve was rejuvenated. The stranger on the phone, her good friend, hadn't shown up, so he felt like the door was still open.

Big Jim still chewed on his life sleeplessly, his mind work-ing like it never had before, almost as if it was making up all those years when it was hardly working at all, and then he heard the noise.

Coming from somewhere in the house.

Upstairs.

Down the hall.

A metal on metal sound. One piece of metal striking the other. Clak. Clak. Clak.

Another sound. A human sound. A sound of discomfort? Not a scream, or a cry. Just a human sound. A sound that said no, or maybe yes.

Big Jim looked at the time. Two AM.

He sat up, eying the hallway.

Maybe she was just brushing her teeth. Or trying to wash up. Or taking off her mask for the night . . .

BY THE TIME Big Jim had crept out of his room, step by careful step in his stocking feet, a little hole in the big toe, and made it into the hall, the metal-on-metal sound had stopped.

Replaced by a sound *behind* him, from outside the house. Footsteps tapping along the sidewalk. Or was that more of a tap, drag, tap, drag?

Big Jim reversed course back into his own room and found the window.

He caught just a glimpse, no not even a glimpse, a shadow, a slice of a shadow, the suggestion of a shadow, disappearing in the deeper shadows of the heavy cedars on the corner. And then the shadow and the sound were goners.

Big Jim went back into the hallway. Quiet again. No light coming from under Betty Lynn's door. You can all go home now. The show was over. Or maybe, Big Jim thought as he went back to bed, it has just begun.

SPECULATION ABOUT WHAT was behind the mask ran through town like an Avon lady on diet pills. Plastic surgery gone awry. Disfigured by fire. A python hairdo. Nothing too extreme, however. Nothing too beyond their imaginations.

"MAYBE SHE'S JUST researching a movie role," Mom said cheerily when Big Jim came down for his bowl of sugar-frosted Jets. It was almost nine. Betty Lynn hadn't made an appearance yet.

"A movie role?"

"A horror movie or something. I don't know. It certainly would explain a lot."

Mom had been thinking, too, apparently.

"I dunno. You'd think she would have mentioned some-thing."

"And that fellow who was supposed to show up last night, maybe, maybe he was the director."

Unwanted thoughts, be gone.

"Maybe he'll put us all in the movies, wouldn't that be something?"

Thoughts about last night.

"Or maybe it's one of those hidden camera shows. The joke will be on us, that's for sure."

Did she hear or see something odd, too?

"I'll cook up some blueberry pancakes and sausage links. Why don't you go upstairs and get little Miss Sleepyhead out of bed?"

"She's probably still tired from her trip."

"It wouldn't hurt to knock on her door to see if she's awake."

"All right, Ma, I'll go see."

Big Jim tried to do it quietly, didn't want to startle her if she was still in dreamland, or the country of the mask. He nudged the door, harder, until it creaked, until he could see her. He had to look, no matter what his imagination was making him see.

What he could see was Betty Lynn, at least her bare legs, the rest her covered by the white chenille blanket, like there was nothing wrong with her, and the thought came to Big Jim that maybe whatever happened last night, if she did have a visitor, then maybe he was a force of good and freed her. Maybe that was the noise he heard.

The sleeper turned onto her back, the covers slipping off her head.

Her mask hadn't gone anywhere. As it was as the moment she stepped off the train. As it was for how long before that.

She stretched then, baring her arms, the right a bare beauty, the left encased in a very sleek and medieval way.

Big Jim reeled back into the hallway, banging against the opposite wall, a framed Norman Rockwell print, *Mother's Little Angel*, the angel unable to stay aloft, crash landing to the polished wooden floor.

"What on earth ..." his mother's voice came from below.

Big Jim met her at the bottom of the stairs. "She . . . she . . . she . . ."

Before he could articulate what it was she was, Betty Lynn appeared at the top of the stairs.

"Heavens . . ."

The intricate cages of metal now hugged both her head and her left arm, from shoulder to fingertip. They joined somewhere up near her shoulder blades.

They made the best of the situation, a head and an arm really not much worse than a head itself. So she had another body part covered with a durn mask. That didn't make her a bad person.

Breakfast went okay considering Betty Lynn's fashion statement, apparently eating her pancakes when the others were momentarily distracted by the distinctive call of the pileated woodpecker.

Betty Lynn offered to help with the dishes, but Mom shooed them out of her kitchen, and they went out on the porch to sit in the midmorning sun. The metal screen on the door reminded Big Jim of her.

"I bet this is a little slower paced way of living than you're used to," Big Jim said, as they rocked in wicker chairs, the wood a real relief.

"I like it," she said. "The sky looks so clean. It's so peaceful and everything."

There was never a right time.

"Betty Lynn," Big Jim began, "I was wondering if you'd like to go with me to the . . ."

Straight ahead, coming down the sidewalk on the opposite side of the street, a trio of teenage girls, walking that optimistic gait that only teenage girls can walk, decked out in bell bottoms and white glitter T-shirts, each wearing what appeared to be tin foil versions of Betty Lynn's mask. They saw Betty Lynn on the porch and waved with animation. She waved back with metal, and they almost swooned. They weren't mocking her, they were aping her. Betty Lynn was a Hollywood trendsetter. Usually trends took months to make it to the heartland, if they made it out here at all. Now they had to hurry home and rig up something for their own tender arms. It was grand to be young.

"They remind me of when I was in high school," Betty Lynn said, with perhaps a hint of wistfulness in her voice.

"Betty Lynn, Betty Lynn, I was wondering, well, if would you want to go to the reunion dance with me?"

"We used to go to dances a lot, didn't we?"

"We sure did. Remember, remember that time we went to that dance at the Excelsior Park Ballroom and the cops raided it."

"I had forgotten all about that. I was so scared. Gosh, that was a swell time."

But she said nothing more about his proposition, and he feared rejection, and a soul-crashing rejection it would be. He ran from the subject altogether, ashamed every step of the way.

"I bet you've met a lot of interesting people out there in Hollywood," he said.

"Oh sure."

His freshly prowling mind kept returning to the shadow on the sidewalk, the sound of metal on metal.

"I bet you go to a lot of interesting places out there in Hollywood."

"I'm pretty busy, most of the time."

This wasn't good. As bad as talking about the weather. It did look like a cold front was coming through. And man, look at those cirrus clouds. No no, have to nudge the conversation back onto personal things.

The ring.

"Betty Lynn, do you still have the ring I gave you? I don't mean that in the way it sounds, I didn't expect you to be wearing it or anything, I was just . . ."

"I understand."

"Curious."

"Of course . . ."

"Okay."

The phone rang from inside. Mom came out onto the porch. "Betty Lynn, it's for you."

"Thank you." Betty Lynn rose. "I'll be right back," she said to Big Jim.

The girls went inside. Big Jim couldn't hear what was said. He didn't want to hear. It was hard enough to look, to see.

In a few moments Betty Lynn reappeared, resumed her rocking.

She looked at Big Jim, mask full frontal, and said in an abrupt yet friendly way, "Why yes Jim, I'd be happy to go to the dance with you."

⁓

THAT MEANT A new dress, but the shops they visited were coincidentally all out. Even the ones they could see packed on the racks were spoken for. Big Jim didn't know much about shopping for women's clothes, so he gave them a pass.

Anyway, given Betty Lynn's current state, the alterations bill would have been staggering.

As they attempted to shop, Big Jim kept hoping for a breakthrough with Betty Lynn, something to lift him out of his would-coulda life and open up, revive, his relationship with her.

Why did we break up? he wondered, trying to recollect. They didn't so much break up as break apart. They had something between them, and then the next thing he knew they didn't have it anymore. Like an all-conference quarterback who suddenly couldn't hit his receivers.

There were a lot of things he didn't know much about, Big Jim realized, and not for the first time. Realizing you don't know is half the battle. He wondered how she remembered their split. Was it hard on her? She left town, but that probably didn't have anything to do with him. She wanted to be a big star. Didn't she?

Was all this my fault? Big Jim wondered.

They hit their old haunts: Awsumb's Drive-In, best burgers and malts in the county, closed last year, even loiterers would have looked good now. Queen Anne Kiddieland, for its once-beautiful merry-go-round, perfect for the big kids they were, abandoned now, the horses sold off at auction, the rest of the grounds a graveyard of rust and ruin, no more likely to be revived than the childhoods of its visitors. The Jungles, the secret wooded area behind the high school, still there, but oak blight had taken its toll, and the scene of so many illicit pastimes seemed so slight and sad, unable to hide even the smallest of sins.

They smiled and laughed but inside Big Jim was feeling

something lacking. How do you feel what isn't there? The sense that something should be there but ain't. Like the phantom arm of an amputee. Maybe the spark just wasn't there anymore. Some of the life had gone out of the town, too.

But it's more than that, Big Jim thought. Betty Lynn is hiding from me. It seemed like the more of her body was hidden, the more of her heart was taken away.

Questions hung in the air like fog along the lakeshore.

Where do you live?

You wouldn't have heard of it.

What does your family think about your fame?

Florida is so far away.

Do you remember what the ring looked like?

It was a funny thing, wasn't it?

It was funny. It was so different. They had bought it from a scruffy man who set up a peach-crate stand on the edge of the county fairgrounds one day in the middle of the fair's mid-August run. They had been looking for something to symbolize their relationship, the bond they felt, nothing so extreme as an engagement ring, something original, and interesting. At first they didn't see anything in the man's purple velvet-lined case, then, tucked into the dusty corner of the display, Betty Lynn dug out the ring. It fit her perfectly. He only charged them five bucks for it. From that day forward, until the day they broke apart, Betty Lynn wore it on her finger.

That night Big Jim slept the sleep of the disturbed.

He listened for her visitor, and was not disappointed. But by the time he reached Betty Lynn's room, the stranger was gone. He was like that.

Her left leg was now masked. As her affliction evolved,

the sleekness seemed to fade, and the medievalness became dominant. There was no choice now, thought Big Jim, backing out of her doorway. He calmly headed downstairs, through the kitchen, then down to the basement, flipping on the light. He removed several items from the tool rack and returned to the upper levels.

I'm not going to lose you again, Big Jim thought, going into her room, kneeling down by the bed. He proceeded to work on her leg armor with a needle-nose pliers, trying to twist the metal, but it wouldn't budge, Betty Lynn waking up before he could get busy with the hacksaw.

"Jim . . . what are you doing!" She pulled away from him, sitting up against the headboard. "*You can't do that,*" she insisted, "*you just can't.*" She said it in an upset but not angry way, as if they didn't have permission.

⌒

BY THE TIME the big dance rolled around, the only part of Betty Lynn unmasked was her right leg. Even the teenage girls couldn't keep up with her. The nocturnal visits had continued, became almost routine, and although Big Jim lay in wait, the stranger always managed to get in and do his dark work before Big Jim could intervene. She had apparently stopped eating. Did she drink? He didn't know. Did she use the toilet? He wasn't sure. It was awkward for her to move about, but she managed. She sat on the porch, no longer rocking, just sort of leaning against the wall. The dress shortage wasn't an issue. Still she wanted to go to the dance. "It's no big deal," she said. "I'll manage. It'll be good to see old friends again."

"Who is he, Betty Lynn?"

"Who?"

"You know who I'm talking about."

"Oh, just someone I met."

"Is he your boyfriend?"

"That's a difficult question to answer."

"Why is he doing this to you?"

"Not every place is like Millville, Jim. There are so many worlds out there you don't know nothing about."

"Tell me where he stays in this world. I'll set him straight. This isn't right."

"Who can really say?"

"This is all my fault. If I hadn't made you leave, you never would have left. You'd still be one of us, part of me."

"Please, Jim."

"It's a joke, right? A Hollywood stunt. You're researching a part for your next movie. That's what my mom said. So you can stop pretending now. You know, Gibby Johnson did that to me when I was a kid. We were playing war and he was a Nazi soldier and we were done playing, I had to go in for lunch, my mom was calling me, but he wouldn't stop pretending, now matter how much I tried to act regular, no matter how much I pleaded with him, he kept it up and kept it up and he wouldn't stop. So he moved away and two years later I ran into him at a ball game and he shoved me up against a wall and screamed at me in gutteral German."

"They never stop."

"I'm losing you, Betty Lynn. I lost you once before and I'm losing you again." He know he didn't have her this time around, but the words had been bouncing around in his head so long they just spilled out, and he know that he was wrong, that she took it the wrong way, that someone else had her, and that wasn't right.

She struggled to her feet and clattered her way back into the house.

⁓

THE NIGHT OF the big dance. The dance of the doomed. No no, stay positive, Big Jim!

Mom decorated the metal woman with flowers, lilacs and daisies in particular, to soften the blow.

"Thank you, Mrs. McDiffie," said Betty Lynn. "That's very sweet of you."

"Isn't it time for you to get dressed, dear?" Mom said to Big Jim, who had a beer in one hand and a glass of wine in the other.

Big Jim moped his way upstairs and found the salt-and-pepper suit that he hadn't worn in years. It needed dry-cleaning, but there wasn't time now. No one would notice anyway, their eyes would be elsewhere, even as much as they would want to look away. He tried to picture the evening. The stares and spit-takes when they shuffled into the gym-nasium. The futile attempts at doing the Freddy. The small talk of the insane. The naming of the royalty, a big moment, and what if they won. They might. A big sympathy vote. Would there be a crown? Another appendage for her already heavy metal ensemble.

Big Jim looked at himself in the mirror, then looked away, then turned the mirror so that it faced the wall, then turned so that he faced the wall, too, then just sat down and gulped his drinks.

Eventually, the alcohol had the effect of making him think he had the nerve to go downstairs and face what his life had become. There was still hope, he told himself. He could save Betty Lynn yet, save himself. Yes, I can do it! he thought blearily. I can make a better life for myself. I can recover what I lost, the hopeful, got-the-world-by-the-tail fellow I used to be. I can do it.

It was a heavy burden being Betty Lynn, but with Big Jim's help she was able to get down the front steps and across the driveway to his car.

He opened the passenger door for her but try as she might she wasn't able to maneuver into the bucket seat. She was simply too big to fit into the vehicle. Her sleek and medieval arms were locked into place some distance from her side. No, she wasn't too wide; his car was too small. If only he had made a success out of his life, he would have been able to afford a luxury driving machine with room to spare for all the metal women in his life. Betty Lynn would have looked fine riding in the backseat of his Lincoln Town Car.

But a Gremlin, no.

So there they stood on the sidewalk, the dance a short half hour and long mile-and-three-quarters away, and no means to get there. He could see his mom in the window, and knew what she was thinking. The shame came at him like a hot summer wind.

"We should just skip it," Big Jim gallantly suggested. "Stay home and listen to music or something. I've still got all my old eight-track tapes. We'll have our own party."

"No," Betty Lynn insisted. "The dance is important to you. I can make it, see?" She began to move awkwardly, clanking down the street, threatening to topple over with every step.

Big Jim put his arm around her and tried to help, but she was so cold, and he was so drunk.

I should take her to the hospital, or to Clem's Fix-it-Up Shop, thought Big Jim. He could help.

They made it a block, two, before Betty Lynn had to stop and lean against a lamppost.

"Let's go back home, Betty Lynn," said Big Jim to the immobile object of his dreams. "It's too far to the high school. We'll never make it. It'll be getting dark soon."

"We can do it," she said. "It's not too much farther." Betty Lynn struggled onward a few feet before tipping over alongside a fire hydrant, metal striking metal, an echo that carried far in the darkness.

"The reunion isn't that important, Betty Lynn," said Big Jim, trying to embrace her through the cold buffer. "I had all sorts of ideas of what might happen there, but I don't care anymore. I don't care what you look like or anything . . ." His voice got small and he began to cry. "I just want to be with you."

Out of the darkness behind came a dark figure, making a clattering noise.

Big Jim felt his heart duck and cover, and the rest of him wanted to join in. He tried to see through the sheen of tears, wiped them from his eyes.

The mysterious figure grew distinct, and familiar.

Big Jim stood up. Took a step forward.

"Mom . . ."

She walked toward them, pulling Big Jim's ancient red Davy Crockett wagon behind her. "Time to come home, Jimmy," she said in a soft, caring voice.

Big Jim nodded, head down.

They got Betty Lynn loaded on the wagon and headed

back. Once they reached the driveway, they hoisted her to her feet and guided her back into the house.

"Let's put her back in her room," said Mom. "She'll be more comfortable there."

They maneuvered her up the stairs and down the hall. Betty Lynn didn't resist or say anything as they tucked her into bed.

"Poor dear, she needs her rest," Mom said, quietly shutting Betty Lynn's door behind them, awaiting the last leg of her cryptic journey.

THERE WERE NO answers to anything anymore, Big Jim thought, laying on the floor of his room, the bottles of beer surrounding him like a magic circle. Just more questions. Every door that was opened, every painful struggle to make a life for himself, to find a place for himself in the land outside of the cocoon of Millville High, to bridge the gap between the inside Big Jim and the outside bigger world, led like a branching creek in a score of different and probably disastrous directions. The Masking of Betty Lynn was just another divorce, pink slip, booze fit.

Lost in his thoughts, these new thoughts coming in his mother's house, the room of his childhood, beneath faded baseball pennants and dusty model airplanes still hanging from the ceiling, in the shadow of footballs from gridiron triumphs that seemed like yesterday. The past was far too alive for comfort.

Lost in thoughts. Big Jim McDiffie. Who would have believed it?

Lost in thoughts, when the clak, clak, clak sound came again from down the hall.

Big Jim felt no panic, he felt as calm as he had at any time in his life.

He climbed out of bed on the final night of the quiet siege and followed the well-worn path down the hall to Betty Lynn's room, weaving as he walked, the alcohol still having a good old time in his bloodstream.

The door was closed.

He gave it a gentle push with the palm of his hand.

The moon beamed into her room, a wave of ice cream whiteness, falling across her bed.

He tried to focus his eyes.

She wasn't in the bed.

She wasn't in the room at all.

There was an indentation in the bed, on the white sheets, matching her form. But no Betty Lynn.

Gone. She was gone.

There was something on the bed, though, Big Jim saw through his blurry angst. Something left behind.

A small trinket, about the size of a coin.

He came to the bedside.

An off-trail combination of the sleek and medieval. Intersecting loops of silver. Funny and perfect.

Big Jim looked at the window, at the empty street, not even a strange shadow to break the spell, all roads leading into darkness, forever darkness.

There are so many worlds out there you don't know nothing about.

Then Big Jim retreated to his boyhood room, that

hauntingly familiar bed, squeezing the old ring tight in the palm of his hand until he fell asleep.

David Prill is the author of the cult novels *The Unnatural, Serial Killer Days*, and *Second Coming Attractions*, and the collection *Dating Secrets of the Dead*. His short fiction has appeared in the *Magazine of Fantasy and Science Fiction*, *Subterranean*, *Cemetery Dance*, and *SCI FICTION*. He lives in a small town in the Minnesota north woods.

The Night Whiskey

❧

Jeffrey Ford

ALL SUMMER LONG, on Wednesday and Friday evenings after my job at the gas station, I practiced with old man Witzer looking over my shoulder. When I'd send a dummy toppling perfectly onto the pile of mattresses in the bed of his pickup, he'd wheeze like it was his last breath (I think he was laughing), and pat me on the back, but when they fell awkwardly or hit the metal side of the truck bed or went really awry and ended sprawled on the ground, he'd spit tobacco and say either one of two things: "That there's a cracked melon" or "Get me a wet-vac." He was a patient teacher, never rushed, never raising his voice or showing the least exasperation in the face of my errors. After we'd felled the last of the eight dummies we'd earlier placed in the lower branches of the trees on the edge of town, he'd open a little cooler he kept in the cab of his truck and fetch a beer for himself and one for me. "You did good today, boy" he'd say, no matter if I did or not, and we'd sit in the truck with the windows open, pretty much in silence, and watch the fireflies signal in the gathering dark.

As the old man had said, "There's an art to dropping drunks." The main tools of the trade were a set of three long bamboo poles—a ten-foot, a fifteen-foot, and a twenty-foot. They had rubber balls attached at one end that were wrapped in chamois cloth and tied tight with a leather lanyard. These poles were called "prods." Choosing the right prod, considering how high the branches were that the drunk had nestled upon, was crucial. Too short a one would cause you to go on tiptoes and lose accuracy, while the excess length of too long a one would get in the way and throw you off balance. The first step was always to take a few minutes and carefully assess the situation. You had to ask yourself, "How might this body fall if I were to prod the shoulders first or the back or the left leg?" The old man had taught me that generally there was a kind of physics to it but that sometimes intuition had to override logic. "Don't think of them as falling but think of them as flying," said Witzer, and only when I was actually out there under the trees and trying to hit the mark in the center of the pickup bed did I know what he meant. "You ultimately want them to fall, turn in the air, and land flat on the back," he'd told me. "That's a ten pointer." There were other important aspects of the job as well. The positioning of the truck was crucial as was the manner with which you woke them after they had safely landed. Calling them back by shouting in their ears would leave them dazed for a week, but, as the natives had done, breaking a thin twig a few inches from the ear worked like a charm—a gentle reminder that life was waiting to be lived.

When his long-time fellow harvester, Mr. Bo Elliott, passed on, the town council had left it to Witzer to find a replacement. It had been his determination to pick someone young, and so he came to the high school and carefully observed each of us fifteen students in the graduating class. It was a wonder he could see anything through the thick, scratched lenses of his glasses and those perpetually squinted eyes, but after long deliberation, which involved the rubbing of his stubbled chin and the scratching of his fallow scalp, he singled me out for the honor. An honor it was, too, as he'd told me, "You know that because you don't get paid anything for it." He assured me that I had the talent hidden inside of me, that he'd seen it like an aura of pink light, and that he'd help me develop it over the summer. To be an apprentice in the Drunk Harvest was a kind of exalted position for one as young as me, and it brought me some special credit with my friends and neighbors, because it meant that I was being initiated into an ancient tradition that went back further than the time when our ancestors settled that remote piece of country. My father beamed with pride, my mother got teary eyed, my girlfriend, Darlene, let me get to third base and part way home.

Our town was one of those places you pass but never stop in while on vacation to some National Park; out in the sticks, up in the mountains—places where the population is rendered in three figures on a board by the side of the road; the first numeral no more than a four and the last with

JEFFREY FORD

a hand-painted slash through it and replaced with one of
lesser value beneath. The people there were pretty much like
people everywhere only the remoteness of the locale had in-
sulated us against the relentless tide of change and the judg-
ment of the wider world. We had radios and televisions and
telephones, and as these things came in, what they brought
us lured a few of our number away. But for those who stayed
in Gatchfield progress moved like a tortoise dragging a ball
and chain. The old ways hung on with more tenacity than
Relletta Clome, who was 110 years old and had died and
been revived by Doctor Kvench eight times in ten years.
We had our little ways and customs that were like the exotic beasts of Tasmania, isolated in their evolution to become
completely singular. The strangest of these traditions was the
Drunk Harvest.

   The Harvest centered on an odd little berry that, as far as
I know, grows nowhere else in the world. The natives had
called it *vachimi atatsi*, but because of its shiny black hue
and the nature of its growth, the settlers had renamed it the
deathberry. It didn't grow in the meadows or swamps as do
blueberries and blackberries, no, this berry grew only out
of the partially decayed carcasses of animals left to lie where
they'd fallen. If you were out hunting in the woods and you
came across say, a dead deer, which had not been touched
by coyotes or wolves, you could be certain that that de-
ceased creature would eventually sprout a small hedge from
its rotted gut before autumn and that the long thin branches
would be thick with juicy black berries. The predators knew
somehow that these fallen beasts had the seeds of the berry
bush within them, because although it went against their

nature not to devour a fallen creature, they wouldn't go near these particular carcasses. It wasn't just wild creatures either, even livestock fallen dead in the field and left untouched could be counted on to serve as host for this parasitic plant. Instances of this weren't common but I'd seen it firsthand a couple of times in my youth—a rotting body, head maybe already turning to skull, and out of the belly like a green explosion, this wild spray of long thin branches tipped with atoms of black like tiny marbles, bobbing in the breeze. It was a frightening sight to behold for the first time, and as I overheard Lester Bildab, a man who foraged for the death-berry, tell my father once, "No matter how many times I see it, I still get a little chill in the backbone."

Lester and his son, a dim-witted boy in my class at school, Lester II, would go out at the start of each August across the fields and through the woods and swamps searching for fallen creatures hosting the hideous flora. Bildab had learned from his father about gathering the fruit, as Bildab's father had learned from his father, and so on all the way back to the settlers and the natives from whom *they'd learned*. You can't eat the berries; they'll make you violently ill. But you can ferment them and make a drink, like a thick black brandy that had come to be called *Night Whiskey* and supposedly had the sweetest taste on earth. I didn't know the process, as only a select few did, but from berry to glass I knew it took about a month. Lester and his son would gather them and usually come up with three good-size grocery sacs full. Then they'd take them over to The Blind Ghost Bar and Grill and sell them to Mr. and Mrs. Bocean, who knew the process for making the liquor and kept the recipe in a little safe with a combination lock. That recipe was given to our forefathers as a gift by the natives, who, two years after giving it, with no provocation and having gotten along peacefully with the settlers, vanished without a trace, leaving behind an empty village on an island out in the swamp . . . or so the story goes.

The celebration that involved this drink took place at The Blind Ghost on the last Saturday night in September. It was usually for adults only, and so the first chance I ever got to witness it was the year I was made an apprentice to old man Witzer. The only two younger people at the event that year were me and Lester II. Bildab's boy had been attending since he was ten, and some speculated that having witnessed the thing and been around the berries so long was what had turned him simple, but I knew young Lester in school before that and he was no ball of fire then either. Of the adults that participated, only eight actually partook of the Night Whiskey. Reed and Samantha Bocean took turns each year, one joining in the drinking while the other watched the bar, and then there were seven others, picked by lottery, who got to taste the sweetest thing on earth. Sheriff Jolle did the honors, picking the names of the winners from a hat at the event, and was barred from participating by a town ordinance that went way back. Those who didn't drink the Night Whiskey drank conventional alcohol, and there were local musicians there and dancing. From the snatches of conversation about the celebrations that adults would let slip out, I'd had an idea it was a raucous time.

This native drink, black as a crow wing and slow to pour as cough syrup, had some strange properties. A year's batch was enough to fill only half of an old quart gin bottle that

Samantha Bocean had tricked out with a handmade label showing a deer skull with berries for eyes, and so it was portioned out sparingly. Each participant got no more than about three-quarters of a shot glass of it, but that was enough. Even with just these few sips it was wildly intoxicating, so that the drinkers became immediately drunk, their inebriation growing as the night went on although they'd finish off their allotted pittance within the first hour of the celebration. "Blind drunk" was the phrase used to describe how the drinkers of it would end the night. Then came the weird part, for usually around two A.M. all eight of them, all at once, got to their feet, stumbled out the door, lurched down the front steps of the bar, and meandered off into the dark, groping and weaving like the namesakes of the establishment they had just left. It was a peculiar phenomenon of the drink that it made those who imbibed it search for a resting place in the lower branches of a tree. Even though they were pie-eyed drunk, somehow, and no one knew why, they'd manage to shimmy up a trunk and settle themselves down across a few choice branches. It was a law that if you tried to stop them or disturb them it would be cause for arrest. So when the drinkers of the Night Whiskey left the bar, no one followed. The next day, they'd be found fast asleep in midair, only a few precarious branches between them and gravity. That's where old man Witzer and I came in. At first light, we were to make our rounds in his truck with the poles bungeed on top, partaking of what was known as The Drunk Harvest.

Dangerous? You bet, but there was a reason for it. I told you about the weird part, but even though this next part gives a justification of sorts, it's even weirder. When the natives gave the berry and the recipe for the Night Whiskey to our forefathers, they considered it a gift of a most divine nature, because after the dark drink was ingested and the drinker had climbed aloft, sleep would invariably bring him or her to some realm between that of dream and the sweet hereafter. In this limbo they'd come face to face with their relatives and loved ones who'd passed on. That's right. It never failed. As best as I can remember him having told it, here's my own father's recollection of the experience from the year he won the lottery:

"I found myself out in the swamp at night with no memory of how I'd gotten there or what reason I had for being there. I tried to find a marker—a fallen tree or a certain turn in the path, to find my way back to town. The moon was bright, and as I stepped into a clearing, I saw a single figure standing there stark naked. I drew closer and said hello, even though I wanted to run. I saw it was an old fellow, and when he heard me approaching, he looked up and right there I knew it was my uncle Fic. 'What are you doing out here without your clothes,' I said to him as I approached. 'Don't you remember, Joe,' he said, smiling. 'I'm passed on.' And then it struck me and made my hair stand on end. But Uncle Fic, who'd died at the age of ninety-eight when I was only fourteen, told me not to be afraid. He told me a good many things, explained a good many things, told me not to fear death. I asked him about my ma and pa, and he said they were together as always and having a good time. I bid him to say hello to them for me, and he said he would. Then he turned and started to walk away but stepped on a twig, and that sound brought me awake, and I was lying in the back of Witzer's pickup, staring into the jowly, pitted face of Bo Elliott."

My father was no liar, and to prove to my mother and me that he was telling the truth, he told us that Uncle Fic had told him where to find a tie pin he'd been given as a commemoration of his twenty-fifth year at the feed store but had subsequently lost. He then walked right over to a teapot shaped like an orange that my mother kept on a shelf in our living room, opened it, reached in, and pulled out the pin. The only question my father was left with about the whole strange episode was, "Out of all my dead relations, why Uncle Fic?"

Stories like the one my father told my mother and me abound. Early on, back in the 1700s, they were written down by those who could write. These rotting manuscripts were kept for a long time in the Gatchfield library—an old shoe repair store with book shelves—in a glass case. Sometimes the dead who showed up in the Night Whiskey dreams offered premonitions, sometimes they told who a thief was when something had gone missing. And supposedly it was the way Jolle had solved the Latchey murder, on a tip given to Mrs. Windom by her great aunt, dead ten years. Knowing that our ancestors were keeping an eye on things and didn't mind singing out about the untoward once a year usually convinced the citizens of Gatchfield to walk the straight and narrow. We kept it to ourselves, though, and never breathed a word of it to outsiders as if their rightful skepticism would ruin the power of the ceremony. As for those who'd left town, it was never a worry that they'd tell anyone, because, seriously, who'd have believed them?

On a Wednesday evening, the second week in September, while sitting in the pickup truck, drinking a beer, old man Witzer said, "I think you got it, boy. No more practice now. Too much and we'll overdo it." I simply nodded, but in the following weeks leading up to the end of the month celebration, I was a wreck, envisioning the body of one of my friends or neighbors sprawled broken on the ground next to the bed of the truck. At night I'd have a recurring dream of prodding a body out of an oak, seeing it fall in slow motion, and then all would go black and I'd just hear this dull crack, what I assumed to be the drunk's head slamming the side of the pickup bed. I'd wake and sit up straight, shivering. Each time this happened, I tried to remember to see who it was in my dream, because it always seemed to be the same person. Two nights before the celebration, I saw a tattoo of a coiled cobra on the fellow's bicep as he fell and knew it was Henry Grass. I thought of telling Witzer, but I didn't want to seem a scared kid.

The night of the celebration came and after sundown my mother and father and I left the house and strolled down the street to The Blind Ghost. People were already starting to arrive and from inside I could hear the band tuning up fiddles and banjos. Samantha Bocean had made the place up for the event—black crepe paper draped here and there and wrapped around the support beams. Hanging from the ceiling on various lengths of fishing line were the skulls of all manner of local animals: coyote, deer, beaver, squirrel, and a giant black bear skull suspended over the center table where the lottery winners were to sit and take their drink. I was standing on the threshold, taking all this in, feeling the same kind of enchantment as when I was a kid and Mrs. Musfin would do up the three classrooms of the school house for Christmas, when my father leaned over to me and whispered, "You're on your own tonight, Ernest. You want to drink, drink. You want to dance, dance." I looked at him and he smiled, nodded, and winked. I then looked to my mother and she merely shrugged, as if to say, "That's the nature of the beast."

Old man Witzer was there at the bar, and he called me over and handed me a cold beer. Two other of the town's oldest men were with him, his chess-playing buddies, and he put his arm around my shoulders and introduced them to me. "This is a good boy," he said, patting my back. "He's doing Bo Elliott proud out there under the trees." The two friends of his nodded and smiled at me, the most notice I'd gotten from either of them my entire life. And then the band launched into a reel, and everyone turned to watch them play. Two choruses went by and I saw my mother and father and some of the other couples move out onto the small dance floor. I had another beer and looked around.

About four songs later, Sheriff Jolle appeared in the doorway to the bar and the music stopped midtune.

"OK," he said, hitching his pants up over his gut and removing his black, wide brimmed hat. "Time to get the lottery started." He moved to the center of the bar where the Night Whiskey drinkers table was set up and took a seat. "Everybody drop your lottery tickets into the hat and make it snappy." I'd guessed that this year it was Samantha Bocean who was going to drink her own concoction since Reed stayed behind the bar and she moved over and took a seat across from Jolle.

After the last of the tickets had been deposited into the hat, the sheriff pushed it away from him into the middle of the table. He then called for a whiskey neat, and Reed was there with it in a flash. In one swift gulp, he drained the glass, banged it onto the table top, and said, "I'm ready." My girlfriend Darlene's stepmom came up from behind him with a black scarf and tied it around his eyes for a blindfold. Reaching into the hat, he ran his fingers through the lottery tickets, mixing them around, and then started drawing them out one by one and stacking them in a neat pile in front of him on the table. When he had the seven, he stopped and pulled off the blindfold. He then read the names in a loud voice and everyone kept quiet till he was finished—Becca Staney, Stan Joss, Pete Hesiant, Berta Hull, Moses T. Remarque, Ronald White, and Henry Grass. The room exploded with applause and screams. The winners smiled, dazed by having won, as their friends and family gathered round them and slapped them on the back, hugged them, shoved drinks into their hands. I was overwhelmed by the moment, caught up in it and grinning, until I looked over at Witzer and saw him jotting the names down in a little notebook he'd refer to tomorrow when we made our rounds. Only then did it come to me that one of the names was none other than *Henry Grass*, and I felt my stomach tighten in a knot.

Each of the winners eventually sat down at the center table. Jolle got up and gave his seat to Reed Bocean, who brought with him from behind the bar the bottle of Night Whiskey and a tray of eight shot glasses. Like the true barman he was, he poured all eight without lifting the bottle once, all to the exact same level. One by one they were handed around the table. When each of the winners had one before him or her, the barkeep smiled and said, "Drink up." Some went for it like it was a draught from the fountain of youth, some snuck up on it with trembling hand. Berta Hull, a middle-aged mother of five with horse teeth and short red hair, took a sip and declared, "Oh my, it's so lovely." Ronald White, the brother of one of the men I worked with at the gas station, took his up and dashed it off in one shot. He wiped his mouth on his sleeve and laughed like a maniac, drunk already. Reed went back to the bar. The band started up again and the celebration came to life like a wild animal in too small a cage.

I wandered around the bar, nodding to the folks I knew, half taken by my new celebrity as a participant in the Drunk Harvest and half preoccupied watching Henry Grass. He was a young guy, only twenty-five, with a crew cut and a square jaw, dressed in the camouflage sleeveless T-shirt he wore in my recurring dream. With the way he stared at the shot glass in front of him through his little circular glasses, you'd have thought he was staring into the eyes of a king cobra. He had a reputation as a gentle, studious soul, although he was most likely the strongest man in town—the rare instance of an outsider who'd made a place for himself in Gatchfield. The books he read were all about UFOs and the Bermuda Triangle, Chariots of the Gods; stuff my father proclaimed to be "dyed in the wool hooey." He worked with the horses over at the Haber family farm, and lived in a trailer out by the old Civil War shot tower, across the meadow and through the woods. I stopped for a moment to talk to Lester II, who mumbled to me around the hard boiled eggs he was shoving into his mouth one after another, and when I looked back to Henry, he'd finished off the shot glass and left the table.

I overheard snatches of conversation, and much of it was commentary on why it was a lucky thing that so and so had won the lottery this year. Someone mentioned the fact that poor Pete Hesiant's beautiful young wife, Lonette, had passed away from leukemia just at the end of the spring, and another mentioned that Moses had always wanted a shot at the Night Whiskey but had never gotten the chance, and how he'd soon be too old to participate as his arthritis had recently given him the devil of a time. Everybody was pulling for Berta Hull, who was raising those five children on her own, and Becca was a favorite because she was the town midwife. The same such stuff was said about Ron White and Stan Joss.

In addition to the well wishes for the lottery winners, I stood for a long time next to a table where Sheriff Jolle, my father and mother, and Dr. Kvench sat and listened to the doctor, a spry little man with a gray goatee, who was by then fairly well along in his cups, as were his listeners, myself included, spout his theory as to why the drinkers took to the trees. He explained it, amidst a barrage of hiccups, as a product of evolution. His theory was that the deathberry plant had at one time grown everywhere on earth, and that early man partook of some form of the Night Whiskey at the dawn of time. Because the world was teeming with night predators then, and because early man was just recently descended from the treetops, those who became drunk automatically knew, as a means of self-preservation, to climb up into the trees and sleep so as not to become a repast for a saber-toothed tiger or some other onerous creature. Dr.

Kvench, citing Carl Jung, believed that the imperative to get off the ground after drinking the Night Whiskey had remained in the collective unconscious and was passed down through the ages. "Everybody in the world probably still has the unconscious command that would kick in if they were to drink the dark stuff, but since the berry doesn't grow anywhere but here now, we're the only ones that see this effect." The doctor nodded, hiccupped twice, and then got up to fetch a glass of water. When he left the table, Jolle looked over at my mother, and she and he and my father broke up laughing. "I'm glad he's better at pushing pills than concocting theories," said the Sheriff, drying his eyes with his thumbs.

AT ABOUT MIDNIGHT, I was reaching for yet another beer, which Reed had placed on the bar, when my grasp was interrupted by a viselike grip on my wrist. I looked up and saw that it was Witzer. He said nothing to me but simply shook his head, and I knew he was telling me to lay off so as to be fresh for the harvest in the morning. I nodded. He smiled, patted my shoulder, and turned away. Somewhere around two A.M., the lottery winners, so incredibly drunk that even in my intoxicated state it seemed impossible they could still walk, stopped dancing, drinking, whatever, and headed for the door. The music abruptly ceased. It suddenly became so silent we could hear the wind blowing out on the street. The sounds of them stumbling across the wooden porch of the bar and then the steps creaking, the screen door banging shut, filled me with a sense of awe and visions of them groping through the night. I tried to picture Berta

Hull climbing a tree, but I just couldn't get there, and the doctor's theory seemed to make some sense to me.

I left before my parents did. Witzer drove me home and before I got out of the cab, he handed me a small bottle.

"Take three good chugs," he said.

"What is it?" I asked.

"An herb mix," he said. "It'll clear your head and have you ready for the morning."

I took the first sip of it and the taste was bitter as could be. "Good God," I said, grimacing.

Witzer wheezed. "Two more," he said.

I did as I was told, got out of the truck, and bid him good night. I didn't remember undressing or getting into bed, and luckily I was too drunk to dream. It seemed as if I'd only closed my eyes when my father's voice woke me, saying, "The old man's out in the truck, waiting on you." I leaped out of bed and dressed, and when I finally knew what was going on, I was surprised I felt as well and refreshed as I did. "Do good, Ernest," said my father from the kitchen. "Wait," my mother called. A moment later she came out of their bedroom, wrapping a robe around her. She gave me a hug and a kiss, and then said, "Hurry." It was brisk outside, and the early morning light gave proof that the day would be a clear one. The truck sat at the curb, the prods strapped to the top. Witzer sat in the cab, drinking a cup of coffee from the delicatessen. When I got in beside him, he handed me a cup and an egg sandwich on a hard roll wrapped in white paper. "We're off," he said. I cleared the sleep out of my eyes as he pulled away from the curb.

Our journey took us down the main street of town and

then through the alley next to the Sheriff's office. This gave way to another small tree-lined street we turned right on. As we headed away from the center of town, we passed Darlene's house, and I wondered what she'd done the previous night while I'd been at the celebration. I had a memory of the last time we were together. She was sitting naked against the wall of the abandoned barn by the edge of the swamp. Her blonde hair and face were aglow, illuminated by a beam of light that shone through a hole in the roof. She had the longest legs and her skin was pale and smooth. Taking a drag from her cigarette, she said, "Ernest, we gotta get out this town." She'd laid out for me her plan of escape, her desire to go to some city where civilization was in full swing. I just nodded, reluctant to be too enthusiastic. She was adventurous and I was a homebody, but I did care deeply for her. She tossed her cigarette, put out her arms, and opened her legs, and then Witzer said, "Keep your eyes peeled now, boy," and her image melted away.

We were moving slowly along a dirt road, both of us looking up at the lower branches of the trees. The old man saw the first one. I didn't see her till he applied the brakes. He took a little notebook and stub of a pencil out of his shirt pocket. "Samantha Bocean," he whispered and put a check next to her name. We got out of the cab, and I helped him unlatch the prods and lay them on the ground beside the truck. She was resting across three branches in a magnolia tree, not too far from the ground. One arm and her long gray hair hung down, and she was turned so I could see her sleeping face.

"Get the ten," said Witzer, as he walked over to stand directly beneath her.

I did as I was told and then joined him.

"What d'ya say?" he asked. "Looks like this one's gonna be a peach."

"Well, I'm thinking if I get it on her left thigh and push her forward fast enough she'll flip as she falls and land perfectly."

Witzer said nothing but left me standing there and went and got in the truck. He started it up and drove it around to park so that the bed was precisely where we hoped she would land. He put it in park and left it running, and then got out and came and stood beside me. "Take a few deep breaths," he said. "And then let her fly."

I thought I'd be more nervous, but the training the old man had given me took hold and I knew exactly what to do. I aimed the prod and rested it gently on the top of her leg. Just as he'd told me, a real body was going to offer a little more resistance than one of the dummies, and I was ready for that. I took three big breaths and then shoved. She rolled slightly, and then tumbled forward, ass over head, landing with a thump on the mattresses, facing the morning sky. Witzer wheezed to beat the band, and said, "That's a solid ten." I was ecstatic.

The old man broke a twig next to Samantha's left ear and instantly her eyelids fluttered. Eventually she opened her eyes and smiled.

"How was your visit?" asked Witzer.

"I'll never get tired of that," she said. "It was wonderful."

We chatted with her for a few minutes, filling her in on how the party had gone at The Blind Ghost after she'd left. She didn't divulge to us what passed relative she'd met with, and we didn't ask. As my mentor had told me when I started, "There's a kind of etiquette to this. When in doubt, Silence is your best friend."

Samantha started walking back toward the center of town, and we loaded the prods onto the truck again. In no time, we were on our way, searching for the next sleeper. Luck was with us, for we found four in a row, fairly close by each other, Stan Joss, Moses T. Remarque, Berta Hull, and Becca Staney. All of them had chosen easy to get to perches in the lower branches of ancient oaks, and we dropped them, one, two, three, four, easy as could be. I never had to reach for anything longer than the 10, and the old man proved a genius at placing the truck just so. When each came around at the insistence of the snapping twig, they were cordial and seemed pleased with their experience. Moses even gave us a ten dollar tip for dropping him into the truck. Becca told us that she'd spoken to her mother, whom she'd missed terribly since the woman's death two years earlier. Even though they'd been blind drunk the night before, amazingly none of them appeared to be hung over, and each walked away with a perceptible spring in his or her step, even Moses, though he was still slightly bent at the waist by the arthritis.

Witzer said, "Knock on wood, of course, but this is the easiest year I can remember. The year your daddy won, we had to ride around for four solid hours before we found him out by the swamp." We found Ron White only a short piece up the road from where we'd found the cluster of four, and he was an easy job. I didn't get him to land on his back. He fell face first, not a desirable drop, but he came to none the worse for wear. After Ron, we had to ride for quite a while, heading out toward the edge of the swamp. I knew the only two left were Pete Hesiant and Henry Grass, and the thought of Henry started to get me nervous again. I was reluctant to show my fear, not wanting the old man to lose faith in me, but as we drove slowly along, I finally told Witzer about my recurring dream.

When I was done recounting what I thought was a premonition, Witzer sat in silence for a few moments and then said, "I'm glad you told me."

"I'll bet it's really nothing," I said.

"Henry's a big fellow," he said. "Why should you have all the fun? I'll drop him." And with this, the matter was settled. I realized I should have told him weeks ago when I first started having the dreams.

"Easy, boy," said Witzer with a wheeze and waved his hand as if wiping away my cares. "You've got years of this to go. You can't manage everything on the first harvest."

We searched everywhere for Pete and Henry—all along the road to the swamp, on the trails that ran through the woods, out along the meadow by the shot tower and Henry's own trailer. With the dilapidated wooden structure of the tower still in sight, we finally found Henry.

"Thar she blows," said Witzer, and he stopped the truck.

"Where?" I said, getting out of the truck, and the old man pointed straight up.

Over our heads, in a tall pine, Henry lay facedown, his arms and legs spread so that they kept him up while the rest of his body was suspended over nothing. His head hung down as if in shame or utter defeat. He looked in a way like he was crucified, and I didn't like the look of that at all.

"Get me the 20," said Witzer, "and then pull the truck up."

I undid the prods from the roof, laid the other two on the ground by the side of the path, and ran the 20 over to the old man. By the time I went back to the truck, got it going, and turned it toward the drop spot, Witzer had the long pole in two hands and was sizing up the situation. As I pulled closer, he let the pole down and then waved me forward while eyeing back and forth, Henry and then the bed. He directed me to cut the wheel this way and that, reverse two feet, and then he gave me the thumbs up. I turned off the truck and got out.

"OK," he said. "This is gonna be a tricky one." He lifted the prod up and up and rested the soft end against Henry's chest. "You're gonna have to help me here. We're gonna push straight up on his chest so that his arms flop down and clear the branches, and then as we let him down we're gonna slide the pole, catch him at the belt buckle, and give him a good nudge there to flip him as he falls."

I looked up at where Henry was, and then I just stared at Witzer.

"Wake up, boy!" he shouted.

I came to and grabbed the prod where his hands weren't.

"On three," he said. He counted off and then we pushed. Henry was heavy as ten sacks of rocks. "We got him," cried Witzer, "now slide it." I did and only then did I look up. "Push," the old man said. We gave it one more shove and Henry went into a swan dive, flipping like an Olympic athlete off the high board. When I saw him in midfall, my knees went weak and the air left me. He landed on his back with a loud thud directly in the middle of the mattresses, dust from the old cushions roiling up around him.

We woke Henry easily enough, sent him on his way to

town, and were back in the truck. For the first time that morning I breathed a sigh of relief. "Easiest harvest I've ever been part of," said Witzer. We headed farther down the path toward the swamp, scanning the branches for Pete Hesiant. Sure enough, in the same right manner with which everything else had fallen into place we found him curled up on his side in the branches of an enormous maple tree. With the first cursory glance at him, the old man determined that Pete would require no more than a 10. After we got the prods off the truck and positioned it under our last drop, Witzer insisted that I take him down. "One more to keep your skill up through the rest of the year," he said.

It was a simple job. Pete had found a nice perch with three thick branches beneath him. As I said, he was curled up on his side, and I couldn't see him all too well, so I just nudged his upper back and he rolled over like a small boulder. The drop was precise, and he hit the center of the mattresses, but the instant he was in the bed of the pickup, I knew something was wrong. He'd fallen too quickly for me to register it sooner, but as he lay there, I now noticed that there was someone else with him. Witzer literally jumped to the side of the truck bed and stared in.

"What in fuck's name," said the old man. "Is that a kid he's got with him?"

I saw the other body there, naked, in Pete's arms. There was long blond hair, that much was sure. It could have been a kid, but I thought I saw in the jumble, a full size female breast.

Witzer reached into the truck bed, grabbed Pete by the shoulder and rolled him away from the other form. Then the two of us stood there in stunned silence. The thing that lay there wasn't a woman or a child but both and neither. The body was twisted and deformed, the size of an eight-year-old but with all the characteristics of maturity, if you know what I mean. And that face . . . lumpen and distorted, brow bulging and from the left temple to the chin erupted in a range of discolored ridges.

"Is that Lonette?" I whispered, afraid the thing would awaken.

"She's dead, ain't she?" said Witzer in as low a voice, and his Adam's apple bobbed.

We both knew she was, but there she or some twisted copy of her lay. The old man took a handkerchief from his back pocket and brought it up to his mouth. He closed his eyes and leaned against the side of the truck. A bird flew by low overhead. The sun shone and leaves fell in the woods on both sides of the path.

Needless to say, when we moved again, we weren't breaking any twigs. Witzer told me to leave the prods and get in the truck. He started it up, and we drove slowly, like about fifteen miles an hour, into the center of town. We drove in complete silence. The place was quiet as a ghost town, no doubt everyone sleeping off the celebration, but we saw that Sheriff Jolle's cruiser was in front of the bunker-like concrete building that was the police station. The old man parked and went in. As he and the sheriff appeared at the door, I got out of the truck cab and joined them.

"What are you talking about?" Jolle said as they passed me and headed for the truck bed. I followed behind them.

"Shhh," said Witzer. When they finally were looking down at the sleeping couple, Pete and whatever that Lonette thing was, he added, "That's what I'm fucking talking about." He pointed his crooked old finger and his hand was obviously trembling.

Jolle's jaw dropped open after the second or two it took to sink in. "I never . . . ," said the Sheriff, and that's all he said for a long while.

Witzer whispered, "Pete brought her back with him."

"What kind of crazy shit is this?" asked Jolle and he turned quickly and looked at me as if I had an answer. Then he looked back at Witzer. "What the hell happened? Did he dig her up?"

"She's alive," said the old man. "You can see her breathing, but she got bunched up or something in the transfer from there to here."

"Bunched up," said Jolle. "There to here? What in Christ's name . . ." He shook his head and removed his shades. Then he turned to me again and said, "Boy, go get Doc Kvench."

In calling the doctor, I didn't know what to tell him, so I just said there was an emergency over at the Sheriff's office and that he was needed. I didn't stick around and wait for him, because I had to keep moving. To stop would mean I'd have to think too deeply about the return of Lonette Hesiant. By the time I got back to the truck, Henry Grass had also joined Jolle and Witzer, having walked into town to get something to eat after his dream ordeal of the night before. As I drew close to them, I heard Henry saying, "She's come from another dimension. I've read about things like this. And from what I experienced last night, talking to my dead brother, I can tell you that place seems real enough for this to happen."

Jolle looked away from Henry at me as I approached, and then his gaze shifted over my head and he must have caught sight of the doctor. "God job," said the Sheriff and put his hand on my shoulder as I leaned forward to catch my breath. "Hey, doc," he said as Kvench drew close, "you got a theory about this?"

The doctor stepped up to the truck bed and, clearing the sleep from his eyes, looked down at where the Sheriff was pointing. Doctor Kvench had seen it all in his years in Gatchfield—birth, death, blood, body rot, but the instant he laid his eyes on the new Lonette, the color drained out of him, and he grimaced like he'd just taken a big swig of Witzer's herb mix. The effect on him was dramatic, and Henry stepped up next to him and held him up with one big tattooed arm across his back. Kvench brushed Henry off and turned away from the truck. I thought for a second that he was going to puke.

We waited for his diagnosis. Finally he turned back and said, "Where did it come from?"

"It fell out of the tree with Pete this morning," said Witzer.

"I signed the death certificate for that girl five months ago," said the doctor.

"She's come from another dimension," said Henry, launching into one of his Bermuda Triangle explanations, but Jolle held a hand up to silence him. Nobody spoke then and the Sheriff started pacing back and forth, looking into the sky and then at the ground. It was obvious that he was having some kind of silent argument with himself, cause every few seconds he'd either nod or shake his head. Finally, he put his open palms to his face for a moment, rubbed his forehead, and cleared his eyes. Then he turned to us.

"Look, here's what we're gonna do. I decided. We're going to get Pete out of that truck without waking him and put him on the cot in the station. Will he stay asleep if we move him?" he asked Witzer.

The old man nodded. "As long as you don't shout his name or break a twig near his ear, he should keep sleeping till we wake him."

"OK," continued Jolle. "We get Pete out of the truck, and then we drive that thing out into the woods, we shoot it, and bury it."

Everybody looked around at everybody else. The doctor said, "I don't know if I can be part of that."

"You're gonna be part of it," said Jolle, "or right this second you're taking full responsibility for its care. And I mean full responsibility."

"It's alive, though," said Kvench.

"But it's a mistake," said the sheriff, "either of nature or God or whatever."

"Doc, I agree with Jolle," said Witzer, "I never seen anything that felt so wrong to me than what I'm looking at in the back of that truck."

"You want to nurse that thing until it dies on its own?" Jolle said to the doctor. "Think of what it'll do to Pete to have to deal with it."

Kvench looked down and shook his head. Eventually he whispered, "You're right."

"Boy?" Jolle said to me.

My mouth was dry and my head was swimming a little. I nodded.

"Good," said the Sheriff. Henry added that he was in. It

was decided that we all participate and share in the act of disposing of it. Henry and the Sheriff gently lifted Pete out of the truck and took him into the station house. When they appeared back outside, Jolle told Witzer and me to drive out to the woods in the truck and that he and Henry and Kvench would follow in his cruiser.

For the first few minutes of the drive out, Witzer said nothing. We passed Pete Hesiant's small yellow house and upon seeing it I immediately started thinking about Lonette, and how beautiful she'd been. She and Pete had only been in their early thirties, a very handsome couple. He was thin and gangly and had been a star basketball player for Gatch-field, but never tall enough to turn his skill into a college scholarship. They'd been high school sweethearts. He finally found work as a municipal handyman, and had that good natured youth-going-to-seed personality of the washed-up, once-lauded athlete.

Lonette had worked the cash register at the grocery. I re-membered her passing by our front porch on the way to work the evening shift one afternoon, and I overheard her talking to my mother about how she and Pete had decided to try to start a family. I'm sure I wasn't supposed to be privy to this conversa-tion, but whenever she passed in front of our house, I tried to make it a point of being near a window. I heard every word through the screen. The very next week, though, I learned that she had some kind of disease. That was three years ago. She slowly grew more haggard through the following seasons. Pete tried to take care of her on his own, but I don't think it had gone all too well. At her funeral, Henry had to hold him back from climbing into the grave after her.

"Is this murder?" I asked Witzer after he'd turned onto the dirt path and headed out toward the woods.

He looked over at me and said nothing for a second. "I don't know, Ernest," he said. "Can you murder someone who's already dead? Can you murder a dream? What would you have us do?" He didn't ask the last question angrily but as if he was really looking for another plan than Jolle's.

I shook my head.

"I'll never see things the same again," he said. "I keep thinking I'm gonna wake up any minute now."

We drove on for another half mile and then he pulled the truck off the path and under a cluster of oak. As we got out of the cab, the Sheriff parked next to us. Henry, the doctor, and Jolle got out of the cruiser, and all five of us gathered at the back of the pickup. It fell to Witzer and me to get her out of the truck and lay her on the ground some feet away. "Careful," whispered the old man, as he leaned over the wall of the bed and slipped his arms under her. I took the legs, and when I touched her skin a shiver went through me. Her body was heavier than I thought, and her sex was staring me right in the face, covered with short hair thick as twine. She was breathing lightly, obviously sleeping, and her pupils moved rapidly beneath her closed lids like she was dreaming. She had a powerful aroma, flowers and candy, sweet to the point of sickening.

We got her on the ground without waking her, and the instant I let go of her legs, I stepped outside the circle of men. "Stand back," said Jolle. The others moved away. He pulled his gun out of its holster with his left hand and made the sign of the cross with his right. Leaning down, he put the gun near her left temple, and then cocked the hammer back. The hammer clicked into place with the sound of a breaking twig and right then her eyes shot open. Four grown men jumped backward in unison. "Good Lord," said Witzer. "Do it," said Kvench. I looked to Jolle and he was staring down at her as if in a trance. Her eyes had no color. They were wide and shifting back and forth. She started taking deep raspy breaths and then sat straight up. A low mewing noise came from her chest, the sound of a cat or a scared child. Then she started talking backward talk, some foreign language never heard on earth before, babbling frantically and drooling.

Jolle fired. The bullet caught her in the side of the head and threw her onto her right shoulder. The side of her face, including her ear, blew off, and this black stuff, not blood, splattered all over, flecks of it staining Jolle's pants and shirt and face. The side of her head was smoking. She lay there writhing in what looked like a pool of oil, and he shot her again and again, emptying the gun into her. The sight of it brought me to my knees, and I puked. When I looked up, she'd stopped moving. Tears were streaming down Witzer's face. Kvench was shaking. Henry looked as if he'd been turned to stone. Jolle's finger kept pulling the trigger, but there were no rounds left.

After Henry tamped down the last shovel full of dirt on her grave, Jolle made us swear never to say a word to anyone about what had happened. I pledged that oath as did the others. Witzer took me home, no doubt having silently decided I shouldn't be there when they woke Pete. When I got to the house, I went straight to bed and slept for an entire day, only getting up in time to get to the gas station for work the next morning. The only dream I had was an infuriating and frustrating one of Lester II, eating hard boiled eggs and explaining it all to me but in backward talk and gibberish so I couldn't make out any of it. Carrying the memory of that Drunk Harvest miracle around with me was like constantly having a big black bubble of night afloat in the middle of my waking thoughts. As autumn came on and passed and then winter bore down on Gatchfield, the insidious strength of it never diminished. It made me quiet and moody, and my relationship with Darlene suffered.

I kept my distance from the other four conspirators. It went so far as we tried not to even recognize each others' presence when we passed on the street. Only Witzer still waved at me from his pickup when he'd drive by, and if I was the attendant when he came into the station for gas, he'd say, "How are you, boy?" I'd nod and that would be it. Around Christmas time I'd heard from my father that Pete Hesiant had lost his mind, and was unable to go to work, would break down crying at a moment's notice, couldn't sleep, and was being treated by Kvench with all manner of pills.

Things didn't get any better come spring. Pete shot the side of his head off with a pistol. Mrs. Marfish, who'd gone to bring him a pie she'd baked to cheer him up, discovered him lying dead in a pool of blood on the back porch of the little yellow house. Then Sheriff Jolle took ill and was so bad off with whatever he had, he couldn't get out of bed. He deputized Reed Bocean, the barkeep and the most sensible man in town, to look after Gatchfield in his absence. Reed did a good job as Sheriff and Samantha double timed it at The Blind Ghost—both solid citizens.

In the early days of May, I burned my hand badly at work on a hot car engine and my boss drove me over to Kvench's office to get it looked after. While I was in his treatment room with him and he was wrapping my hand in gauze, he leaned close to me and whispered, "I think I know what happened." I didn't even make a face, but stared ahead at the eye chart on the wall, not really wanting to hear anything about the incident. "Gatchfield's so isolated that change couldn't get in from the outside, so Nature sent it from within," he said. "Mutation. From the dream." I looked at him. He was nodding, but I saw that his goatee had gone squirrely, there was this overeager gleam in his eyes, and his breath smelled like medicine. I knew right then he'd been more than sampling his own pills. I couldn't get out of there fast enough.

June came, and it was a week away from the day that Witzer and I were to begin practicing for the Drunk Harvest again. I dreaded the thought of it to the point where I was having a hard time eating or sleeping. After work one evening, as I was walking home, the old man pulled up next to me in his pickup truck. He stopped and opened the window. I was going to keep walking, but he called, "Boy, get in. Take a ride with me." I made the mistake of looking over at him. "It's important," he said. I got in the cab and we drove slowly off down the street.

I blurted out that I didn't think I'd be able to manage the Harvest and how screwed up the thought of it was making me, but he held his hand up and said, "Shh, shh, I know." I quieted down and waited for him to talk. A few seconds passed and then he said, "I've been to see Jolle. You haven't seen him, have you?"

I shook my head.

"He's a gonner for sure. He's got some kind of belly rot, and, I swear to you he's got a deathberry bush growing out of his insides . . . while he's still alive, no less. Doc Kvench just keeps feeding him pills, but he'd be better off taking a hedge clipper to him."

"Are you serious?" I said.

"Boy, I'm dead serious." Before I could respond, he said, "Now look, when the time for the celebration comes around, we're all going to have to participate in it as if nothing had happened. We made our oath to the Sheriff. That's bad enough, but what happens when somebody's dead relative tells them in a Night Whiskey dream what we did, what happened with Lonette?"

I was trembling and couldn't bring myself to speak.

"Tomorrow night—are you listening to me?—tomorrow night I'm leaving my truck unlocked with the keys in the ignition. You come to my place and take it and get the fuck out of Gatchfield."

I hadn't noticed but we were now parked in front of my house. He leaned across me and opened my door. "Get as far away as you can, boy," he said. The next day, I called in sick to work, withdrew all my savings from the bank, and talked to Darlene. That night, good to his word, the keys were in the old pickup. I noticed there was a new used truck parked next to the old one on his lot to cover when the one we took went missing. I'd left my parents a letter about how Darlene and I had decided to elope, and that they weren't to worry. I'd call them.

We fled to the biggest brightest city we could find, and the rush and maddening business of the place, the distance from home, our combined struggle to survive at first and then make our way was a curative better than any pill the doctor could have prescribed. Every day there was change and progress and crazy news on the television, and these things served to shrink the black bubble in my thoughts. Still to this day, though, so many years later, there's always an evening near the end of September when I sit down to a Night Whiskey, so to speak, and Gatchfield comes back to me in my dreams like some lost relative I'm both terrified to behold and want nothing more than to put my arms around and never let go.

Jeffrey Ford has published several acclaimed novels including *The Physiognomy* (winner of the World Fantasy Award), *Memoranda* (a *New York Times* Notable Book, 1999), and The Beyond (The *Washington Post Book World's* Best Books List, 2001). His most recent novel is *The Girl in the Glass*, winner of the Edgar Allan Poe Award. Ford's short fiction has been published in a wide variety of venues, including his 2005 collection *The Empire of Ice Cream*. His stories will appear in the forthcoming anthologies *The Coyote Road: Trickster Tales*, *The Starry Rift*, and *The Year's Best Fantasy and Horror #19*.

Ford lives in New Jersey with his wife and two sons. He teaches literature and writing at Brookdale Community College.

The Lepidopterist

❧

Lucius Shepard

I FOUND THIS IN a box of microcassettes recorded almost thirty years ago; on it I had written, "J. A. McCrae—the bar at Sandy Bay, Roatan." All I recall of the night was the wind off the water tearing the thatch, the generator thudding, people walking the moonless beach, their flashlights sawing the dark, and a wicked-looking barman with stilletto sideburns. McCrae himself was short, in his sixties, as wizened and brown as an apricot seed, and he was very drunk, his voice veering between a feeble whisper and a dramatic growl:

⌣

I'M GOIN TO tell you bout a storm, cause it please me to do so. You cotch me in the tellin mood, and when John Anderson McCrae get in the tellin mood, ain't nobody on this little island better suited for the job. I been foolin with storms one way or the other since time first came to town, and this storm I goin to speak of, it ain't the biggest, it don't have the stiffest winds, but it bring a strange cargo to our shores.

Fetch me another Salvavida, Clifton . . . if the gentleman's willing. Thank you, sir. Thank you.

Now Mitch and Fifi were the worst of the hurricanes round these parts. And the worst of them come after the wind and rain. Ain't that right, Clifton? Ain't that always the case? Worst t'ing bout any storm is what come along afterwards. Mitch flattened this poor island. Must have kill four, five hundred people, and the most of them die in the weeks followin. Coxen Hole come t'rough all right, but there weren't scarcely a tree standing on this side. And Fifi . . . after Fifi there's people livin in nests, a few boards piled around them to keep out the crabs and a scrap of tin over they head. Millions of dollars in relief is just settin over in Teguz. There's warehouses full, but don't none of it get to the island. Word have it this fella work for Wal-Mart bought it off the military for ten cent on the dollar. I don't know what for sure he do with it, but I spect there be some Yankees payin for the same blankets and T-shirts and bottled water that they government givin away for free. I ain't blamin nothin on America, now. God Bless America! That's what I say. God Bless America! They gots the good intention to be sending aid in the first place. But the way t'ings look to some, these storms ain't nothin but an excuse to slip the generals a nice paycheck.

The mon don't want to hear bout your business, Clifton! Slide me down that bottle. I needs somet'ing to wash down with this beer. That's right, he payin! Don't you t'ink he can afford it? Well, then, slide me that bottle.

Many of these Yankees that go rushing in on the heels of disaster, these so-called do-gooders, they all tryin to find something cheap enough they can steal it. Land, mostly. But rarely do it bode well for them. You take this mon bought up twenty thousand acres of jungle down around Trujillo right after Mitch. He cotching animals on it. Iguana, parrots, jaguar. Snakes. Whatever he cotch, he export to Europe. My nephew Jacob work for him, and he say the mon doing real good business, but he act like he the king of creation. Yellin and cursin everybody. Jacob tell him, you keep cursin these boys, one night they get to drinkin and come see you with they machete. The mon laugh at that. He ain't worry bout no machetes. He gots a big gun. Huh! We been havin funerals for big Yankee guns in Honduras since before I were born.

This storm I'm talkin about, it were in the back time. 1925, '26. Somewhere long in there. Round the time United Fruit and Standard Fruit fight the Banana War over on the mainland. And it weren't no hurricane, it were a norther. Northers be worse than a hurricane in some ways. They can hang round a week and more, and they always starts with fog. The fog roll in like a ledge of gray smoke and sets til it almost solid. That's how you know a big norther's due. My daddy, he were what we call down here a wrecker. He out in the fury of the storm with he friends, and they be swingin they lanterns on the shore, trying to lure a ship onto the reef so they can grab the cargo. You don't want to be on the water durin a norther ceptin you got somet'ing the size of the

Queen Mary under you. Many's the gun runner or tourist boat, or a turtler headin home from the Chinchorro Bank, gets heself lost in bad weather. And when they see the lantern, they makes for it in a hurry. Cause they desperate, you know. They bout to lose their lives. A light is hope to them, and they bear straight in onto the reef.

That night, the night of the storm, were the first time my daddy took me wreckin. I had no wish to be with him, but the mon fierce. He say, John, I needs you tonight and I hops to it or he lay me out cold. Times he drinkin and he feel a rage comin, he say, John, get under the table. I gets under the table quick, cause I know and he spy me when the rage upon him, nothin good can happen. So I stays low and out of he sight. I too little to stand with him. I born in the summer and never get no bigger than what you seein now.

We took our stand round St. Ant'ony's Key. There wasn't no resort back then. No dive shop, no bungalows. Just cashew trees, sea grape, palm. It were a good spot cause the reef close in to shore, and that old motor launch we use for boarding, it ain't goin to get too far in rough water. My daddy, he keep checkin' he pistol. That were how he did when t'ings were pressin him. He check he pistol and yell at ever'body to swing they lanterns. We only have the one pistol mongst the five of us. You might t'ink we needs more to take on an entire crew, but no matter how tough that crew be, they been t'rough hell, and if they any left alive, they ain't got much left in them, they can barely stand. One pistol more than enough to do the job. If it ain't, we gots our machetes.

The night wild, mon. Lord, that night wild. The bushes lashing and the palms tearin and the waves crashin so loud, you t'ink the world must have gone to spinnin faster. And dark . . . We can't see nothin cept what the lantern shine up. A piece of a wave, a frond slashin at your face. Even t'ough I wearin a poncho, I wet to the bone. I hear my daddy cry, Hold your lantern high, Bynum! Over to the left! He hollerin at Bynum Saint John, who were a fisherman fore he take up wreckin. Bynum the tallest of us. Six foot seven if he an inch. So when he hold he lantern high, it seem to me like a star fell low in the heavens. With the wind howlin and and blood to come, I were afraid. I fix on that lantern, cause it the only steady t'ing in all that uncertainty, and it give me some comfort. Then my daddy shout again and I look to where the light shinin and that's when I see there's a yacht stuck on the reef.

Everybody's scramblin for the launch. They eager to get out to the reef fore the yacht start breakin up. But I were stricken. I don't want to see no killin and the yacht have a duppy look, way half its keel is ridin out of the water and its sails furled neat and not a soul on deck. Like it were set down on the rocks and have not come to this fate by ordinary means . . .

You t'ink you can tell this story better than me, Clifton? Then you can damn well quit interruptin! I don't care you heared Devlin Walker tell a story sound just like it. If Devlin tellin this story, he heared it from me. Devlin's daddy never were a wrecker. And even if dat de case, what a boy born with two left feet goin to do in the middle of a norther? He can't hardly get around and it dry.

Yes, sir! Two left feet. The mon born that way. Now Devlin, I admit, he good with a tale, but that due to the fact that he never done a day's work in he life. All he gots to do is set around collectin other folks' stories.

The Santa Caterina, that were the name on the yacht's bow . . . it were still sittin pretty by the time we reached it. But big waves is breakin over the stern, and it just a matter of minutes fore they get to chewin it up. I were the first over the rail, t'ough it were not of my doin. I t'ought I would stay with the launch, but my daddy lift me by the waist and I had no choice but to climb aboard. The yacht were tipped to starboard, the deck so wet, I go slidin across and fetch up against the opposite rail. I could feel the keel startin to slip. Then Bynum come over the rail, and Deaver Ebanks follow him. The sight of them steady me and I has a look around . . . and that's when I spy this white mon standing in the stern. He not swayin or nothin, and it were all I could do to keep my feet. He wearing a suit and tie, and a funny kind of hat with a round top were jammed down so low, all I could see of he face were he smile. That's right. The boat on the rocks and wreckers has boarded her, and he smilin. It were like a razor, that smile, all teeth and no good wishes. Cut the heart right out of me. The roar of the storm dwindle and I hear a ringin in my ears and it like I'm lookin at the world t'rough the wrong end of a telescope.

I'm t'inking he no a natural mon, that he have hexed me, but maybe I just scared, for Bynum run at him, waving he machete. The mon whip a pistol from he waist and shoot him dead. And he do the same for Deaver Ebanks. The shots don't hardly make a sound in all that wind. Now there's a box resting on deck beside the mon. I were lookin at it end-on, and I judged it to be a coffin. It were made of mahogany and carved up right pretty. It resemble the coffin the McNabbs send that Yankee who try to cut in on they business. What were he name, Clifton? I can't recollect. It were an Italian name.

Who the McNabbs? Hear that, Clifton? Who the McNabbs? Well sir, you stay on the island for any time and you goin to know the McNabbs. The worst of them, White Man McNabb, he in jail up in Alabama, but the ones that remain is bad enough. They own that big resort out toward the east end, Pirate Cove. But most of they money derived from smugglin. Ain't an ounce of heroin or cocaine passes t'rough Roatan don't bear they mark. They don't appreciate people messin in their business, and when that Italian Yankee . . . Antonelli. That's he name. When this Antonelli move down from New York and gets to messin, they send him that coffin and not long after, he back in New York.

So this box I'm tellin you about, I realize it ain't much bigger than a hatbox when the man pick it up, and it can't weigh much—he totin it with the one hand. He step to the port rail and fire two shots toward the launch. I can't see where they strike. He beckon to me and t'ough I'm still scared I walk to him like he got me on a string. There's only my daddy in the launch.

He gots a hand on the tiller and the other hand in the air, and he gun lyin in the bilge. Ain't no sign of Jerry Worthing—he the other man in our party. I'm guessin he gone under the water. The mon pass me the box and tell me to hold on tight with both hands. He lift me up and lower me into the launch, then scramble down after me. Then he gesture with he pistol and my daddy unhook us from the Santa

Caterina and turn the launch toward shore. It look like he can't get over bein surprised at what have happened.

My daddy were a talker. Always gots somet'ing to say about nothin. But he don't say a word till after we home. Even then, he don't say much. We had us a shotgun shack back from the water, with coco palms and bananas all around, and once de mon have settled us in the front room, he ask me if I good with knots. I say, I'm all right. So he tell me to lash my daddy to the chair. I goes to it, with him checkin the ropes now and again, and when I finish he pat me on the head. My daddy starin hateful at me, and I gots to admit I weren't all that unhappy with him being tied up. What you goin to do with us? he ask, and the mon tell him he ain't in no position to be askin nothin, considerin what he done.

The mon proceed to remove he hat and he coat, cause they wet t'rough. Shirt, shoes, and socks, too. He head shaved and he torso white as a fish belly, but he all muscle. Thick arms and chest. He take a chair, restin the pistol on his knee, and ask how old I am. I don't exactly know, I tell him, and my daddy say, He bout ten. Bout ten? the mon say. This boy's no more than eight! He actin' horrified, like he t'ink the worst t'ing a man can not know about heself is how old he is. He tell my daddy to shut up, cause he must not be no kind of father and he don't want to hear another peep out of him. I goes to fiddlin with the mon's hat. It hard, you know. Like it made of horn. The mon tell me it's a pith helmet and he would give it to me, cause I such a brave boy, but he need it to keep he head from burnin.

By the next morning, the storm have passed. Daddy's asleep in the chair when I wakes and the mon sitting at the table, eating salt pork and bananas. He offer me some and I joins him at the table. When Daddy come round, the mon don't offer him none, and that wake me to the fact that t'ings might not go good for us. See, I been t'inkin with a child's mind. The mon peared to have taken a shine to me and that somet'ing my daddy never done. So him takin a shine to me outweigh the killin he done. But the cool style he had of doing it. . . . A mon that good at killin weren't nobody to trust.

After breakfast, he carry my daddy some water, then he gag him. He pick up that box and tell me to come with him, we goin for a walk. We head off into the hills, with him draggin me along. The box, I'm noticing, ain't solid. It gots tiny holes drilled into the wood. Pinholes. Must be a thousand of them. I ask what he keepin inside it, but he don't answer. That were his custom. Times he seem like an ordinary Yankee, but other times it like he in a trance and the most you goin to get out of him is dat dead mon's smile.

Twenty minutes after we set out, we arrives at this glade. A real pretty place, roofed with banana fronds and wild hisbicus everywhere. The mon cast he eye up and around, and make a satisfied noise. Then he kneel down and open the box. Out come fluttering dozens of moths . . . least I t'ink they moths, Later, when he in a talking mood, he tells me they's butterflies. Gray butterflies. And he a butterfly scientist. What you calls a lepidopterist.

The butterflies, now, they flutterin around he head, like they fraid to leave him. He sit cross-legged on the ground and pull out from he trousers a wood flute and start tootlin on it. That were a curious sight, he shirtless and piping away, wearin that pith helmet, and the butterflies fluttering round in the green shade. It were a curious melody he were playin, too. Thin, twistin in and out, never goin nowhere. The kind of t'ing you liable to hear over in Puerto Morales, where all them Hindus livin.

That's what I sayin. Hindus. The English brung them over last century to work the sugar plantations. They's settled along the Rio Dulce, most of them. But there some in Puerto Morales, too. That's how they always do, the English. When they go from a place, they always leavin t'ings behind they got no more use for. Remember after Fifi, Clifton? They left them bulldozers so we can rebuild the airport? And the Sponnish soldiers drive them into the hills and shoot at them for sport, then leave them to rust. Yeah, mon. Them Sponnish have the right idea. Damn airport, when they finally builds it, been the ruin of this island. The money it bring in don't never sift down to the poor folks, that for sure. We still poor and now we polluted with tourists and gots people like the McNabbs runnin t'ings.

By the time the mon finish playing, the butterflies has vanished into the canopy, and I gots that same feelin I have the night previous on the deck of the Santa Caterina. My ears ringing, everyt'ing have a distant look, and the mon have to steer me some on the walk back. We strop my daddy to the bed in the back room, so he more comfortable, and the mon sit in he chair, and I foolin with a ball I find on the beach. And that's how the days pass. Mornin, noon, and night we walks out to the glade and the mon play some more on he flute. But mainly we just sittin in the front room and doin nothin. I learn he name is Arthur Jessup and that he have carried the butterflies up from Panama and were on the way to La Ceiba when the storm cotch him. He tell me he have to allow the butterflies to spin their cocoons here on the island, cause he can't reach he place in Ceiba soon enough.

I t'ought it was caterpillars turned into butterflies, I says. Not the other way round.

These be unusual butterflies, he say. I don't know what else they be. Whether they the Devil's work or one of God's miracles, I cannot tell you. But it for certain they unusual buttterflies.

My daddy didn't have no friends to speak of, now he men been shot dead, but there's this old woman, Maud Green, that look in on us now and then, cause she t'ink it the Christian t'ing to do. Daddy hate the sight of her, and he always hustle her out quick. But Mister Jessup invite her in and make over her like she a queen. He tell her he a missionary doctor and he after curin Daddy of a contagious disease. Butterfly fever, he call it, and gives me a wink. It a terrible affliction, he say. Your hair fall out, like mine, and it don't never come back. The eye grow dim, and the pain. . . . The pain excrutiatin. Maud Green cock her ear and hear Daddy strainin against the gag in the back room, moanin. He at heaven's gate, Mister Jessup say, but I believe, with the Lord's help, we can pull the mon back. He ask Maud to join him in prayin over Daddy and Maud say, I needs to carry this cashew fruit to my daughter, so I be pushing along, and we don't see no more of her after that. We has a couple of visitors the followin day who heared about the missionary doctor and wants some curin done. Mister Jessup tell them to bide they time. Won't be long, he say, fore my daddy back on he feet, and then he goin to take care of they ills. It occur to me, when these folks visitin, that I might say somet'ing bout my predicament or steal away, but I remembers Mister Jessup's skill with the pistol. It take a dead shot to pick a man off a launch when the sea bouncin her round like it were. And I fears for my daddy, too. He may not be no kind of father, but he all the parent I gots, what with my mama dying directly after I were born.

Must be the ninth, tenth day since Mister Jessup come to the island, and on that mornin, after he play he flute in the glade, he cut a long piece of bamboo and go to pokin the banana fronds overhead. He beat the fronds back and I see four cocoons hangin from the limbs of an aguacaste tree. They big, these cocoons. Each one big as a hammock. And they not white, but gray, with gray threads fraying off dem. Mister Jessup act real excited and, after we returned home, he say, Pears I'll be out of your hair in a day or two, son. I spect you be glad to see my backside goin down the road.

I don't know what to say, so I keeps quiet.

Yes sir, he say. You not goin to believe your eyes and you see what busts out of them cocoons. That subject been pressin on my mind, so I ask him what were goin to happen.

Just you wait, he say. But I tell you this much. The man ain't born can stand against what's in those cocoons. You goin to hear the name Arthur Jessup again, son. Mark my words. A few years from now, you be hearin that name mentioned in the same breath with presidents and kings.

I takes that to mean Mister Jessup believe he goin to have some power in the world. He a smart mon . . . least he do a fine job pretendin he smart. Still, I ain't too sure I hold with that. Bout half the time he act like somet'ing have power over him. Grinnin like a skull. Sittin and starin for hours, with a blink every now and then to let you know he alive. Pears to me somebody gots they hand on him. A garifuna witch, maybe. Maybe the butterfly duppy.

You want to hear duppy stories, Clifton be your man. When he a boy, he mama cotch sight of the hummingbird duppy hovering in a cashew tree, and ever after there's hummingbirds all around he house. Whether that a curse or a blessing, I leave for Clifton to say, but . . .

Oh, yeah. Everyt'ing gots a duppy. Sun gots a duppy. The moon, the wind, the coconut, the ant. Even Yankees gots they duppy. They gots a fierce duppy, a real big shot, but since they never lay eyes on it, it difficult for them to understand they ain't always in control.

Where you hail from in America, sir?

Florida? I been to Miami twice, and I here to testify that even Florida gots a duppy.

Evenin of the next day and we proceed to the glade. The cocoons, they busted open. There's gray strings spillin out of dem . . . remind me of old dried-up fish guts. But there's nothin to show what have come forth. It don't seem to bother Mister Jessup none. He sit down in the weeds and get to playin he flute. He play for a while with no result, but long about twilight, a mon with long black hair slip from the margins of the glade and stand before us. He the palest mon I ever seen, and the prettiest. Prettier than most girls. Not much bigger than a girl, neither. He staring at us with these gray eyes, and he make a whispery sound with he mouth and step toward me, but Mister Jessup hold up a hand to stay him. Then he goes to pipin on the flute again. Time he done, there three more of them standin in the glade. Two womens and one mon. All with black hair and pale skin. The mon look kind of sickly, and he skin gray in patches. They all of them has gray silky stuff clinging to their bodies, which they washes off once we back home. But you could see everyt'ing there were to see, and watchin that silky stuff slide about on the women's skin, it give me a tingle even t'ough I not old enough to be interested. And they faces. . . . You live a thousand years, you never come across no faces like them. Little pointy chins and pouty lips and eyes bout to drink you up. Delicate faces. Wise faces. And yet I has the idea they ain't faces at all, but patterns like you finds on a butterfly's wing.

Mister Jessup herds them toward the shack at a rapid pace, cause he don't want nobody else seein them. They talking this whispery talk to one another, cept for the sickly mon. The others glidin along, they have this snaky style of walkin, but it all he can do to stagger and stumble. When we reach the shack, he slump down against a wall, while the rest go to pokin around the front room, touchin and liftin pots and glasses, knifes and forks, the cow skull that prop open the window. I seen Japanese tourists do less pokin. Mister Jessup install heself in a chair and he watchin over them like a mon prideful of he children.

Few months in La Ceiba, little spit and polish, he say, and they be ready. What you t'ink, boy? Well, I don't know what to t'ink, but I allow they some right pretty girls.

Pretty? he say, and chuckle. Oh, yeah. They pretty and a piece more. They pretty like the Hope Diamond, like the Taj Mahal. They pretty all right.

I ask what he goin to do for the sick one and he say,

Nothin I can do cept hope he improve. But I doubt he goin to come t'rough.

He had the right of that. Weren't a half-hour fore the mon slump over dead and straightaway we buries him out in back. There weren't hardly nothin to him. Judgin from the way Mister Jessup toss him about, he can't weigh ten pounds, and when I dig he up a few days later, all I finds is some strands of silk.

We watches the butterfly girls and the mon a bit longer, then Mister Jessup start braggin about what a clever mon he be, but I suspect he anxious about somet'ing. An anxious mon tend to lose control of he mouth, to take comfort from the sound of he voice. He say six months under he lamps, with the nutrients he goin to provide, and won't nobody be able to tell the difference between the butterflies and real folks. He say the world ain't ready for these three. They goin to cut a swath, they are. Can you imagine, he ask, these little ladies walkin in the halls of power on the arm of a senator or the president of a company? Or the mon in a queen's bed-chamber? The secrets they'll come to know. They hands on the reigns of power. I can imagine it, boy. I know you can't. You a brave little soldier, but you ain't got the imagination God give a tick.

He run on in that vein, buildin heself a fancy future, sayin he might just take me along and show me how sweet the world be when you occupies a grand position in it. While he talkin, the women and the man keeps circulatin, movin round the shack, whispering and touchin, like they findin our world all strange and new. When they pass behind Mister Jessup, some-times they touch the back of he neck and he freeze up for a moment and that peculiar smile flicker on; but then he go right on talking as if he don't notice. And I'm t'inkin these ain't no kind of butterflies. Mister Jessup may believe they is, he may think he know all about them. And maybe they like he say, a freak of nature. I ain't disallowin that be true in part. Yet when I recall he playin that flute, playing like them Hindus in Puerto Morales does when they sits on a satin pillow and summons colors from the air, I know, whether he do or not, that he be summonin somet'ing, too. He callin spirits to be born inside them cocoons. Cause, you see, these butterfly people, they ain't no babies been alive a few hours. That not how they act. They ware of too much. They hears a dog barkin in the distance, a coconut thumpin on the sand, and they alert to it. When they put they eye on you ... I can't say how I knows this, but there somet'ing old about them, somet'ing older than the years of Mister Jessup and me and my daddy all added up together.

Eventually Mister Jessup reach a point in he fancifyin where he standin atop the world, decidin whether or not to let it spin, and that pear to satisfy him. He lead me back to where my daddy stropped down. Daddy he starin at me like he get loose, the island not goin to be big enough for me to hide in.

Don't you worry, boy, Mister Jessup say. He ain't goin to harm you none.

He slip Daddy's gag and inquire of him if the launch can make it to La Ceiba and the weather calm. Daddy reckon it can. Take most of a day, he figures.

Well, that's how we'll go, say Mister Jessup.

He puts a match to the kerosene lamp by the bed and

brings the butterfly people in. Daddy gets to strugglin when he spies them. He callin on Jesus to save him from these devils, but Jesus must be havin the night off.

The light lend the butterfly people some color and that make them look more regular. But maybe I just accustomed to seein them, cause Daddy he thrash about harder and goes to yellin fierce. Then the one woman touch a hand gainst he cheek, and that calm him of an instant. Mister Jessup push me away from the bed, so I can't see much, just the three of them gatherin round my daddy and his legs stiffening and then relaxin as they touch he face.

I goes out in the front room and sits on the stoop, not knowin what else to do. There weren't no spirit in me to run. Where I goin to run to? Stay or go, it the same story. I either winds up beggin in Coxxen Hole or gettin pounded by my daddy. The lights of Wilton James's shack shining t'rough the palms, not a hundred feet away, but Wilton a drunk and he can't cure he own troubles, so what he goin to do for mine? I sits and toes the sand, and the world come to seem an easy place. Waves sloppin on the shingle, and the moon, ridin almost full over a palm crown, look like it taken a faceful of buckshot. The wind carry a fresh smell and stir the sea grape growin beside the stoop.

Soon Mister Jessup call me in and direct me to a chair. Flanked by the butterfly people, my daddy leanin by the bedroom door. He keep passin a hand before his eyes, rubbin he brow. He don't say nothin, and that tell me they done somet'ing to him with they touches, cause a few minutes earlier he been dyin to curse me. Mister Jessup kneel beside the chair and say, We goin off to La Ceiba, boy. I know I say

I'm takin you with me, but I can't be doin that. I gots too much to deal with and I havin to worry bout you on top of it. But you showed me somet'ing, you did. Boy young as you, faced with all this, you never shed a tear. Not one. So I'm goin to give you a present.

A present sound like a fine idea, and I don't let on that my daddy have beat the weepin out of me, or that I small for my age. I can't be certain, but I pretty sure I goin on eleven, t'ough I could not have told him the day I were born. But eleven or eight, either way I too young to recognize that any present given with that kind of misunderstandin ain't likely to please.

You a brave boy, say Mister Jessup. That's not always a good t'ing, not in these parts. I fraid you gonna wind up a wrecker like your daddy ... or worse. You be gettin yourself killed fore you old enough to realize what livin is worth. So I'm goin to take away some of your courage.

He beckon to one of the women and she come forward with that glidin walk. I shrinks from her, but she smile and that smile smooth out my fear. It have an effect similar to Mister Jessup's pats-on-the-head. She swayin before me. It almost a dance she doin. And she hummin deep in she throat, the sound some of Daddy's girlfriends make after he climb atop them. Then she bendin close, bringin with her a sweet, dry scent, and she touch a finger to my cheek. The touch leave a little electric trail, like my cheek sparklin and sparkin both. Cept for that, I all over numb. She eye draw me in til that gray crystal all I seein. I so far in, pear the eye enormous and I floatin in front of it, bout the size of a mite. And what lookin back at me ain't no buttterfly. The woman she may have a pleasin shape, but behind she eye there's another shape pressin forward, peekin into the world and yearnin to bust out the way the butterfly people busted out of they cocoon. I feels a pulse that ain't the measure of a beatin heart. It registerin an unnatural rhythm. And yet for all that, I drawn in deeper. I wants her to touch me again, I wants to see the true evil shape of her, and I reckon I'm smiling like Mister Jessup, with that same mixture of terror and delight.

When I rouse myself, the shack empty. I runs down to the beach and I spies the launch passin t'rough a break in the reef. Ain't no use yellin after them. They too far off, but I yells anyway, t'hough who I yellin to, my daddy or the butterfly girl, be a matter for conjecture. And then they swallowed up in the night. I stand there a time, hopin they turn back. It thirty miles and more to La Ceiba, and crossin that much water at night in a leaky launch, that a fearsome t'ing. I falls asleep on the sand waitin for them and in the mornin Fredo Jolly wake me when he drive his cows long the shore to they pasture.

My daddy return to the island a couple weeks later, but by then I over in Coxxen Hole, doin odd jobs and beggin, and he don't have the hold on me that once he did. He beat me, but I can tell he heart ain't in it, and he take up wreckin again, but he heart ain't in that, neither. He say he can't find no decent mens to help, but Sandy Bay and Punta Palmetto full of men do that kind of work. Pretty soon, three or four years, it were, I lose track of him, and I never hear of him again, not even on the day he die.

Mister Jessup have predicted I be hearin bout him in a few years, but it weren't a week after they leave, word come that a Yankee name of Jessup been found dead in La Ceiba, the top half of he head chopped off by a machete. There ain't no news of the butterfly people, but the feelin I gots, then and now, they still in the world, and maybe that's one reason the world how it is. Could be they bust out of they shapes and acquire another, one more reflectin of they nature. There no way of knowin. But one t'ing I do know. All my days, I never show a lick of ambition. I never took no risks, always playin it safe. If there a fight in an alley or riot in a bar, I gone, I out the door. The John Anderson McCrae you sees before you is the same I been every day of my life. Doin odd jobs and beggin. And once the years fill me up sufficient, tellin stories for the tourists. So if Mister Jessup make me a present, it were like most Yankee presents and take away more than it give. But that's a story been told a thousand times and it be told a thousand more. You won't cotch me blamin he for my troubles. God Bless America is what I say. Yankees gots they own brand of troubles, and who can say which is the worse.

Yes, sir. I believe I will have another.

Naw, that ain't what makin me sad. God knows, I been livin almost seventy years. That more than a mon can expect. Ain't no good in regrettin or wishin I had a million dollars or that I been to China and Brazil. One way or another, the world whittle a mon down to he proper size. That's what it done for Mister Jessup, that's what it done for me. It just tellin that story set me to rememberin the butterfly girl. How she look in the lantern light, pale and glowin, with hair so black, where it lie across she shoulder, it like an absence in the flesh. How it feel when she touch me and what that say to a mon, even to a boy. It say I knows you, the heart of you, and soon you goin to know bout me. It say I never stray from you, and I going to show you t'ings whose shadows are the glories of this world. Now here it is, all these years later, and I still longin for that touch.

Lucius Shepard was born in Lynchburg, Virginia, grew up in Daytona Beach Florida, and lives in Vancouver, Washington. His short fiction has won the Nebula Award, the Hugo Award, The International Horror Writers Award, The National Magazine Award, the Locus Award, The Theodore Sturgeon Award, and the World Fantasy Award.

His latest publications are a nonfiction book, *Christmas in Honduras*; a short novel, *Softspoken*; and a short fiction collection, *The Iron Shore*. Forthcoming are two novels, tentatively titled *The Piercefields* and *The End of Life as We Know It*, and two novellas, *Beautiful Blood* and *Unknown Admirer*.

About the Editors

Ellen Datlow was editor of *SCI FICTION,* the multi-award-winning fiction area of SCIFI.COM, for almost six years. She was fiction editor of *OMNI* for over seventeen years and has worked with an array of writers including Susanna Clarke, Neil Gaiman, Ursula K. LeGuin, Bruce Sterling, Peter Straub, Jonathan Carroll, George R. R. Martin, William Gibson, Jeffrey Ford, Kelly Link, Joyce Carol Oates, Cory Doctorow, and others. Her most recent anthologies include *The Dark, The Green Man*, and *The Faery Reel* (the latter two with Terri Windling). She's been coediting *The Year's Best Fantasy and Horror* for twenty years. Datlow has won seven World Fantasy Awards, two Bram Stoker Awards, three Hugo Awards, three Locus Awards, and the International Horror Guild Award, for her editing. She lives in New York City. Her Web site is www.datlow.com.

Terri Windling is an editor, writer, and artist. She has won seven World Fantasy Awards, the Bram Stoker Award, the Mythopoeic Award for Novel of the Year, and was on the Tiptree Award short-list. She has edited over thirty anthologies of magical fiction, many of them in collaboration with

Ellen Datlow. She was the fantasy editor of *The Year's Best Fantasy and Horror* annual volumes for sixteen years, and continues to work as a consulting editor for the Tor Books fantasy line. As a writer, Windling has published mythic novels for adults and young adults, picture books for children, poetry, essays, and articles on fairy tale history, myth, and mythic arts. As an artist, her paintings have been exhibited at museums and galleries across the United States, the United Kingdom, and France. Windling is the director of the Endicott Studio for Mythic Arts, and coeditor, with Midori Snyder, of its quarterly webzine: The Journal of Mythic Arts (www.endicott-studio.com). She lives in Devon, England, and winters at an arts retreat in the Arizona desert.